This close, Jocelyn could see every detail, in living, sunwashed color.

The navy rim around the lighter blue of Will's eyes, the reddish tips of his thick black lashes, even the thread-thin crow's feet from all those years of squinting at a pitcher ninety feet away.

Without thinking, she reached up and brushed a few grains of sand and dirt from his cheeks, his skin warm and taut to the touch. "You get dirty at your job."

"Always liked a job like that."

She could actually feel herself falling into the blue of his eyes, like the Gulf, swirling around her, warm and inviting and gentle.

"When are we going to talk?" His voice was low, direct, unwavering as his gaze.

She swallowed, surprised by his determination and so fundamentally drawn to it. He still made her feel like her skin was on fire and her head was a little too light. Still.

But surely he didn't still feel that way, not after all these years. Because if he did, he sure as hell wouldn't be taking care of the person who tore them apart...

Barefoot in the Rain

roxanne st. claire

FOREVER

NEW YORK   BOSTON

Copyright © 2012 by Roxanne St. Claire

Excerpt from *Barefoot in the Sun* copyright © 2012 by Roxanne St. Claire

All rights reserved. In accordance with the U.S. Copyright Act of 1976, the scanning, uploading, and electronic sharing of any part of this book without the permission of the publisher is unlawful piracy and theft of the author's intellectual property. If you would like to use material from the book (other than for review purposes), prior written permission must be obtained by contacting the publisher at permissions@hbgusa.com. Thank you for your support of the author's rights.

Forever
Hachette Book Group
237 Park Avenue
New York, NY 10017
www.HachetteBookGroup.com

Printed in the United States of America

First Edition: October 2012

10 9 8 7 6 5 4 3 2 1

Forever is an imprint of Grand Central Publishing.
The Forever name and logo are trademarks of Hachette Book Group, Inc.

The Hachette Speakers Bureau provides a wide range of authors for speaking events. To find out more, go to www.hachettespeakersbureau.com or call (866) 376-6591.

The publisher is not responsible for Web sites (or their content) that are not owned by the publisher.

ATTENTION CORPORATIONS AND ORGANIZATIONS:
Most Hachette Book Group books are available at quantity discounts with bulk purchase for educational, business, or sales promotional use. For information, please call or write:

Special Markets Department, Hachette Book Group
237 Park Avenue, New York, NY 10017
Telephone: 1-800-222-6747 Fax: 1-800-477-5925

For Louisa Edwards and Kristen Painter...
My besties who hand me the umbrella (drink)
every time it rains.

Acknowledgments

~

My team is awesome! I can't thank every one of the many folks who help breathe life into my books, but a few individuals and groups must get their heartfelt shout-out:

I'm out of superlatives for my team at Grand Central/ Forever publishing! Led by a brilliant and keen-eyed editor, Amy Pierpont, and corralled by her indispensible assistant, Lauren Plude, these professionals are tops in the business, and I'm so fortunate to give them my characters and watch the magic happen.

Wonderful, delightful, and tireless agent Robin Rue and her right hand, Beth Miller, are with me at every turn in the professional road. Because of them, I never get lost.

My many romance writer friends, especially my fellow blog sisters, who love and support me even though I took the *murder* out of Murder She Writes. This is the A-Team, and I am proud to have been part of it for so long.

Beta reader Barbie Furtado, who never complains about reading revised versions of many scenes multiple times. It's quite possible she knows my characters better than I do, and has encouraged me every single day of this book's creation.

Acknowledgments

Multiple individuals, doctors, and specialists with the Alzheimer's Association, who took the time to provide me with information about the care, support, and research of all types of dementia. These people are heroes in every sense of the word.

Finally, my breathtaking, patient, loving, and completely wonderful family. I just couldn't treasure you guys more. And, of course, all my gratitude goes to the One who made everything and blessed me with the ability to tell stories.

Barefoot in the Rain

Prologue

~

August 1997

"I know why they call this a comforter." Jocelyn pulled the tattered cotton all the way up to her nose, taking a sniff right over the Los Angeles Dodgers logo.

Will didn't look up from stuffing socks into the corners of his suitcase. "Why's that, Joss?"

"Because..." She took a noisy, deep inhale. "It smells like Will Palmer."

Slowly, he lifted his head, a sweet smile pulling at his face, a lock of dark hair falling to his brow. Lucky hair. Jocelyn's fingers itched to brush it back and linger in the silky strands.

"Don't tell me," he said. "It stinks of sweat, grass, and a hint of reliability?"

"No." She sniffed again. "It smells like comfort."

He straightened, rounding the suitcase to take a few steps closer to the bed, leveling her with eyes the same color as the Dodger-blue blanket. "You're welcome to take it to Gainesville. My mom bought me a whole new set of that stuff for the apartment."

"I'm sure it would be the envy of my roommates." Girls she didn't even know, except as names on a piece of paper sent to her by a resident adviser named Lacey Armstrong. Would Zoe Tamarin and Tessa Galloway be her friends? Would they make fun of her for bringing the next-door neighbor's comforter to her dorm room next week?

"Do you want it?" he asked, the question touchingly sincere.

"No, I don't need it," she replied. "I need..." The word stuck. Why couldn't she just say it, tell him, be honest with her best friend in the whole world who was leaving for college—a *different* college—tomorrow morning? "You."

He did a double take like he wasn't sure he'd caught that one-syllable whisper. "That's a very un-Jocelyn-Bloom-like admission."

"I'm practicing to be the new me."

"I hope you don't change *too* much up there at UF. I like you just the way you are."

I like you. *I like you.*

Lately, those three words were being tossed around like his baseballs during practice. It was almost as if she and Will wanted to say more. But they couldn't. That would change everything in the delicate tightrope of friendship and attraction they'd walked for all these years.

"Anyway," she said quickly, "you're the one who's going

to change. Living off campus, traveling with the University of Miami baseball team, fending off those pro offers."

"Please, you sound like my dad now."

"I'm serious. No one will recognize the golden boy of Mimosa Key when he comes home at Thanksgiving."

"You're the one with a full academic ride and so many scholarships you're *making* money going to school, Miss Four-Point-Six Smartypants."

"You're the one who's going to be on a box of Wheaties someday, Mr. MVP of State Championships."

He rolled his eyes. "Shit, now you really sound like my dad." Shaking his hair back, he came a little closer and propped on the side of the bed, the mattress shifting under his weight. "So what about Thanksgiving?"

"What about it?"

"You coming back home, Bloomerang?"

Her heart did a little roll and dive at the nickname he'd given her years ago.

Jocelyn Bloom-erang, he called her. Because you always come back to me, he'd say after she'd been MIA for a few days. But the truth was, she had no real reason to come back to this barrier island hugging the coast of Florida. Except him, and he was headed for bigger and better things.

In answer to his question she just shrugged, not wanting to lie and really not wanting to ask a question of her own: Would he ever consider taking her with him on his journey to fame and fortune?

"You're not coming back, are you?" he asked.

"I...might." She locked her elbow and let her head fall on her shoulder, hiding behind the hair falling over her face. "You know how things are."

He stroked her cheek and smoothed that fallen hair over her shoulder. "I know how things are."

They didn't have to say more than that. Ever since the Palmers had built this addition to their house so their star-athlete son could have a gym attached to his bedroom, he'd also had a front-row, second-story seat to the drama unfolding at the Bloom house next door. The windows behind his power-lifting station let in light—and noise.

He'd heard enough to know what happened next door. That was why he left the door at the bottom of the steps open, so Jocelyn could slip up to the safety and comfort of her best friend's loft.

And she had, so many, many times.

"Your mom will miss you," he said, his voice surprisingly tight.

"My mom…" She wanted to say mom would be fine, but they both knew better. "Was born without a spine."

"Which means she'll miss you even more."

"I'm not the parent-pleaser you are, Will. Well, I can't please him, obviously, and I don't need to please her. She refuses to leave him and, you know, half the time I think she feels like she *deserves* what she gets."

He didn't respond; what could he possibly say? Jocelyn's dad was a ticking time bomb and no one ever knew when the fuse would blow. All they knew was that her mother would end up bruised. Or worse. And, honestly, it was only a matter of time until that fist made contact with Jocelyn.

"But I *do* have a spine," Jocelyn said, lifting her chin. "And next week can't come fast enough for me."

Something flickered in his eyes. Sadness? Pity? Longing? "I wish Miami didn't start a week earlier than Florida."

"You're ready," she said. "You've outgrown the shrine."

He laughed at her favorite name for his loft. Did he know that when she said that, she meant a different kind of shrine—a sanctuary? That was what it was for her. This second-story suite might be his workout room and bedroom, but it was her safe harbor; the sight of his gazillion trophies and framed newspaper articles always made her feel safe and secure from the mess next door that was her home.

Or maybe it was just the broad, strong shoulders of a boy who always let her lean on him that made her feel so safe and secure here.

She realized he was looking directly at her, his expression serious, his hand still resting against her neck.

"What?" she asked.

Without answering, he tunneled his fingers into her hair, inching her closer. "It's our last night, Jossie," he whispered. "And I'm going to miss the hell out of you."

Warmth curled through her, unholy and unfamiliar—no, it was familiar enough, especially in the last few months They'd been dancing around this all summer, both too scared to tear the safety net of their friendship and do what they were thinking about constantly.

They'd almost talked about it. Almost kissed. Frequently touched. And every time they parted, Jocelyn felt twisted and tortured and achy in places that had never ached.

His Adam's apple rose and fell as he tried to swallow. Unable to resist, she touched that masculine lump on his throat.

"When I met you, Will, you didn't have one of these."

A smile threatened. "I didn't have a lot of things I have now."

"Like this manly stubble." She brushed her hand along the line of his jaw, his soft teenage whiskers ticking her knuckles.

"Or these massive guns." He grinned and lifted his arm, flexing to show off a very impressive catcher's bicep.

Then his eyes dropped from her face to her chest. "Speaking of things someone didn't have."

She felt her color rise and, oh, Lord, her nipples puckered. There was the ache again.

"Will…" She looked down, directly at the sight of a shockingly big tent in his jeans. He hadn't had *that* when he'd moved in seven years ago.

She stared at the bulge, her throat dry, her chest tight, her hands itchy. Dear God, she wanted to touch him.

"Jossie," he whispered, trailing a finger up her throat and across her bottom lip, sending fireworks from her scalp to her toes and a whole lot of precious places in between. "I don't want to leave without…"

She looked up at him, his face so near now she could count his sinfully long black lashes. "You think it's time…" She took a slow breath. "That we…"

"It's not about *time*," he said, a hitch in his voice nearly undoing her. "You have to know how I feel about you."

"I know."

"No, you don't."

"I'm your best friend," she said quickly. "The girl next door. The only person in town who doesn't swoon at the sight of your number thirty-one on the cover of the *Mimosa Gazette*."

She thought he'd smile, but he didn't. Instead, he closed his eyes. "You're so much more than that."

Was she? God, she wanted to be. She really, really wanted to be. But if this friendship was ruined, then what?

They'd hugged a million times. They'd kissed on the cheek. They even made out a few times when they were fifteen, but then he started dating some dimwit cheerleader. Everything physical had stopped, but their friendship and his unspoken offer of an escape from the hell of her home kept on going.

But this summer, with college looming and the clock ticking and hormones raging and—

He kissed her. One soft, sweet, gentle kiss and everything in her body just melted.

"Joss," he murmured into her mouth. "I have to ask you something."

She backed away, the seriousness of the question scaring her. "What?"

"I need to know how you feel about me."

She almost laughed. "How I feel about you?" Didn't he know? Couldn't he tell? He was *everything* to her—her rock, her crutch, her soft place to fall. Her hero, her fantasy, her one and only. "Will, I...I..."

"I love you, Joss." His eyes welled up with the words, making them twenty times more sweet and perfect.

She cupped his jaw, searching eyes the color and depth of the Gulf of Mexico they'd spent so many hours swimming in over the last seven years. The words were on her lips, as warm and sweet as his kiss. But something stopped her. Something deep inside held on to those words and wouldn't let them out.

"I love you," he repeated, having no such problem.

Did he? Did he really love her? Love was so tenuous. Hadn't she heard those very words spoken to her mother and, ten minutes later, the smack of a palm against flesh?

His hand slipped out of her hair, down the column of her neck, over her breastbone. "Jocelyn, I'm dying here."

For love or...

He eased her back on the bed, covering her with his body.

Sex.

Was he dying for her to say I love you or...

He nuzzled into her neck, kissing her lightly, each touch of his lips like a little firebrand on her skin that made everything tight and hot and needy. The comforter balled up between them, lumpy but not thick enough to block out the pressure of his body.

He rocked his hips slowly first, then a little faster. Colors flashed behind her eyes at the intensity of the pleasure. Fiery ribbons of need and heat curled between her legs as she met each beat of his hips.

Grabbing the comforter, he yanked it away, throwing it to the side so he could get closer to her. All she could hear was the loud huffs of breath, both of them panting already as they found a rhythm. A rhythm of kissing, touching, rubbing, riding.

"Will..."

"Is it okay, Joss? Tell me it's okay." He nearly growled the words into her throat, kissing her as one hand—one shaking, large, masculine, beloved hand—slid over her cotton tank and settled on her breast.

She gasped at the shock of the sensation, making him lift his head. "You all right?"

"Yes. That feels good." She barely mouthed the words, her eyes damn near rolling back into her head it felt so amazing. His hand was so big he covered her whole breast, palming her until her nipple felt like it would pop.

His other hand went under her top, over her stomach, into her bra, touching, touching, *touching*.

"Oh my God," he moaned, pumping harder against her. "I can't believe how amazing you feel."

She couldn't answer, too lost in the newness, the strangeness, the complete wonder of Will's calloused, strong hand on her skin. His whole body quivered, and she knew he was as overcome as she was.

"Take it off," he pleaded, struggling with the top. "Take it off."

He pulled the T-shirt over her head, pushing up the bra without bothering to unsnap it, her breasts so small they popped right out.

He stared at her, searing her skin with the intensity of his focus. "Just like I imagined."

"You imagined?"

"Jocelyn, seriously? Do you not think I—"

"Don't." She put her hand on his mouth. "Don't tell me. Just...keep going."

"Are you sure?"

She nodded, driven by the need that burned low in her belly and deep in her chest.

This was inevitable, really.

All these hours in this room, together. She'd go home and kiss her pillow, touch herself, imagine Will's fingers and mouth and his...

She slid her hand between them, closing over the hard shaft in his jeans, making him grunt with surprise and pleasure. He kissed her chest again, moving from one breast to the other, fumbling with her shorts.

"I have a condom," he whispered between ragged breaths. "Want me to get it?"

"In a minute, yeah." She wrapped her arms around his neck. "Are you a virgin, Will?"

Still for a second, he finally admitted, "Um, not exactly."

"I am."

She heard him swallow hard. "I figured that. I won't hurt you, Jocelyn. I love you."

He *loved* her.

"Tell me," he urged, tugging at her zipper. "Tell me you love me."

"I will." When he was inside her. When they were one. Then she would tell him. "Just don't stop."

"Not a chance." He slipped his hand into her panties and she almost screamed when his finger touched her. "I love you so much, Jossie." Inside. "I love you." Deeper. "I love you. You have no idea how much…oh, damn, you feel good."

Heat coursed through her as she rolled into his palm, lost in his words, his hands, his beautiful, beautiful—

"You goddamn fucking bastard!"

The whole room vibrated with the shout as Jocelyn screamed and Will leaped off her, both turning to meet the blazing gray eyes of Guy Bloom.

"Get off her!" Guy's barrel chest heaved with fury, stretching his sheriff's uniform as he marched closer, already lifting his arm to a position she knew all too well.

"No, Dad, no!" Jocelyn screamed, jumping up, grabbing at her bra to pull it down.

But it was too late. Her father glowered at her, his face red, spittle at the corners of his mouth. "I'm going to fucking kill you."

"No!" She got the cups over her breasts just as Will stepped in front of her, arms outstretched.

"Deputy Bloom, please, I'm really sorry—"

Guy shoved him to the side to get to Jocelyn. "You whore! You cheap, trashy whore!"

"No, Dad, I'm not—" The crack of his palm snapped her head back.

"Stop it!" Will pushed him, hard enough to make the older man stumble.

He dropped his head, nostrils flaring like a bull as he stared at Will. "You touching an officer of the law, young man?"

"Don't hit her."

Guy wiped some sweat from his upper lip, his attention fully on Will now as they stared each other down. Will's fists pumped, his jaw clenched.

Oh, God. Oh, *God*. "Don't, Will, please."

He never even looked at her. "Don't you touch her." Will's voice was little more than a growl.

"You want to take me, boy?"

Will just stared.

Guy took a step closer, highlighting the fact that he was a good four inches shorter and thirty years older than his enemy. Will could kill him.

"Please, Will." She started to stand and Guy shoved her back on the bed.

It was all Will needed. He lunged at Guy, who ducked fast and whipped out his pistol.

Jocelyn screamed. "No, no!"

Thick fingers curled around the trigger of a gun she'd seen a million times on the counter. A gun even *he* never had the nerve to pull out when he lost his temper.

Will froze.

"There will be no skin off my back if I shoot the boy who attacked my daughter."

"He didn't—"

"Shut up, you little whore!" The words echoed through the loft, so wrong in this place of safety, like a curse screamed in a church.

"Or better yet, why don't I just put an end to that superstar baseball career of yours? One phone call." He snorted as if he liked the idea. "One phone call from the sheriff's office to the University of Miami and you can hang up your cleats, you little prick." Guy broke into an evil, ugly smile. "Rapists don't get scholarships. Rapists don't get drafted to the big leagues. Rapists go to jail."

Will still didn't move. Not even his eyes. Only his chest rose and fell with slow, pained breaths as he surely realized who had the real power in this room.

That was something Jocelyn had known since the first time her dad had what she and her mother called "an episode." But they learned that the only thing to do, the *only* thing, was to stay calm until it ended. And take what he dished out.

"Get out, Joss," her father ordered.

She looked down for her T-shirt and suddenly his big hand was on her arm.

"Never mind clothes, just get out." He yanked her off the bed.

"Hey!" Will stepped closer, inches from the gun still aimed at her. "Don't hurt her."

"I could say the same thing to you, Palmer." He gave Jocelyn a solid push, still looking at Will. "And believe me, nothing would give me more pleasure than to take you off the fucking pedestal this town has you on and see you rot in jail for raping my daughter."

"He didn't rape me!"

The back of Guy's hand cracked across Jocelyn's face, his wedding ring making contact with her tooth.

Jocelyn slammed her hand over her mouth to fight a sob.

"Stop it!" Will cried. "You're a goddamn animal!"

Guy shoved the gun right into Will's gut, making him double forward with a grunt, his eyes popping in horror.

"No one's gonna blame a sheriff for killing the kid who dragged his daughter into his room and forced himself on her!"

Another sob escaped Jocelyn's mouth. "Dad, please, please." She wept the words, her whole body trembling. "Don't hurt him. Please don't hurt him."

Guy's shoulders slumped a little as he angled his head to the door. "Go. I'll take care of you at home."

"Please," she cried, grabbing his arm, her near nakedness forgotten. "Don't shoot him."

"Go!" he bellowed.

Frightened, she stumbled to the door, turning to take one look at Will when she reached the top of the stairs. His eyes were red-rimmed in fear, his face white, his big, healthy, athletic body at the mercy of a gun six inches from his heart.

She'd done this to him. Her father could destroy Will's life, everything he'd worked for, all his plans, his future. She loved Will—really, truly loved him—far too much for this.

"I'm sorry..." she whispered before running down the stairs, pausing halfway to grip the railing and listen.

"If you ever, *ever* go within five feet of my daughter again, I will ruin your name, your face, and your precious fucking arm. You get that?"

Silence.

Squeezing the rail until her knuckles turned white, Jocelyn waited, bracing for a shot, a word, anything.

But there was just silence. Of course Will couldn't fight for her. Couldn't risk his life for her. No girl was worth that kind of love.

As long as Guy Bloom was alive, he had the power to ruin Will's life. The mean, miserable bastard always had the power. So there was only one thing she could do. Let Will go, forever.

She heard Guy's footsteps and she scrambled to beat him outside, wanting to run across the lawn to their house, hoping to lock herself in the—

He caught up with her at the pool.

"Get in the goddamn house."

What would he do to her? What did it matter? Nothing could hurt as much as the decision she'd just made. Nothing could hurt as much as losing Will, but she had no other choice. She loved him that much.

Chapter 1

∽

*F*ifteen *Years Later*

The situation had gone way past dire.

Will stood in the living room of his next-door neighbor's house and surveyed the mess, the low, dull throbbing that had pounded at the base of his skull since he'd stopped by at lunchtime rapidly escalating into a screaming mother humper of a headache.

Son of a bitch, it was like a pack of wild dogs lived here instead of one confused, pathetic, and forgotten old man who couldn't remember his own name.

"William!"

But he knew Will's name and used it often, in that shaky, feeble voice that threaded down the hall right now.

"William, is that you?"

"It's me, Guy." On a sigh that shuddered through his

whole body, Will stepped over a pile of magazines that had been torn into a million pieces—the new scrapbooking project, no doubt—and picked up a basket of yarn with threads and spools stuffed inside. He put it on a table next to the remnants of the sandwich Will had made Guy for lunch, then headed down the hall.

"I decided to clean out this old closet," Guy called from one of the extra bedrooms.

This couldn't be good.

Shit. Clothes were strewn everywhere: men's suit jackets, women's dresses, kids' shorts, and a small mountain of worn shoes. Where the hell did he get all this crap? His wife had been dead ten years now. Hadn't he cleaned out anything?

"Guy, what are you doing?" Will fought to keep any anger out of his tone. If he so much as raised his voice by one decibel, Guy cried like a baby, and that ripped Will's heart into pieces.

"I saw a show called *Clean House* and got this idea." Guy stood in a walk-in closet holding a pile of what looked to be old blue jeans. His glasses were crooked, his white hair tufted and messy, his blue knit pullover stained from something red. Punch or Red Zinger tea, probably.

He'd made tea? "Did you remember to turn the stove off?"

"I might have. I was really enjoying this show on that decorating channel. Big black woman gettin' all in your face about cleaning up stuff." He grinned, his lemony teeth a testament to years of stinking up the local sheriff's office with the stench of Marlboros. And yet he lived while his wife had been the one buried by cancer. And his daughter...

Will pushed that thought out of his head.

"I think she was named Nicey. Smart lady."

Will just stared at him. "Who are you talking about?

"The lady on TV," Guy said. "She says the secret to happiness is a clean house."

Will glanced around at the piles of crap. "Looks like you're a long way from happiness in this house."

"That's the thing, Will! That's the thing about the show. This crew comes in and takes your house apart, sells your stuff in a yard sale, and cleans it so everything is perfect."

"Everything *was* perfect," Will said, picking up a bright-yellow dress sized for a young girl. Had he ever even seen Jocelyn in this dress? "Why do you still have this stuff?"

Guy gave him his blankest stare, and God knew he had a shitload of different blank stares. "I don't know, son."

Son.

Will had long ago stopped trying to convince the old man that was a misnomer. "C'mon, bud. Let's make you some dinner and get you situated for the night."

But Guy didn't move, just kept looking into the closet wistfully. "Funny, I couldn't find any of your old clothes. Just girl stuff. Your mother must have thrown them out before she died."

His mother had moved to Bend, Oregon, with his dad. "Yeah, she must have," he agreed.

"Do you think they'd come here, Will?"

"Who?"

"The *Clean House* people. They say if you want to be on the show, you just have to call them and tell them you want *a clean house*." He dragged out the words, mimicking an announcer. "Would you do that for me?"

"I'll look into it," he said vaguely, reaching to guide Guy away from the mess. "How 'bout I heat up that leftover spaghetti for you?"

"Will you call them?"

"Like I said—"

"Will you?" Eyes the steel gray of a cloudy sky narrowed behind crooked glasses on a bulbous nose.

"Why is it so important?"

"Because." Guy let out a long, sad sigh. "It's like starting over, and when I look through this stuff it just... makes me feel sad."

"Some memories do that," he said.

"Oh, William, I don't have any memories. I don't know what half this stuff is." He picked up a rose-patterned sweater that Will remembered seeing Mary Jo Bloom wear many years ago. "It all just reminds me that I don't remember. I want a fresh start. A clean house."

"I understand." He managed to get Guy down the hall with a gentle nudge.

As he sat down in his favorite recliner, Guy reached for Will's hand. "You'll call those people."

"Sure, buddy."

In the fridge Will found the Tupperware container of spaghetti, but his mind went back to the yellow dress upstairs.

The thought of Jocelyn pulled at his heart, making him twist the burner knob too hard. He dumped the lump of cold noodles into a pan, splattering the Ragu on his T-shirt.

"Where's the clicker?" Guy called, panic making his voice rise. "I can't find the clicker, William! What did you do with it?"

Will pulled open the dishwasher and rolled out the top rack, spying the remote instantly. At least it wasn't at the bottom of the trash, like last week.

"I've got it." He checked the pan of noodles and took the remote out to Guy, who'd given up and turned on the TV manually, stabbing at the volume button so the strains of *Entertainment Tonight* blared through the living room.

Again with the crap TV? Alzheimer's didn't just rob him of his memories, it changed every aspect of his personality. The bastard county sheriff had turned into a little old lady obsessed with celebrities and home crafts.

Will gently set the remote on Guy's armrest, getting a grateful smile and a pat on his hand.

"You're a good son, Will." Guy thumbed up the volume and the announcer's voice shook the speaker.

"...with more on this shocking breakup of Hollywood's happiest couple."

God help him, couldn't they watch ESPN for just one lousy dinner? But the trash TV blared with an excited announcer's voice, hammering at his headache.

"*TMZ* has identified the 'other woman' in the stunning divorce of Miles Thayer and Coco Kirkman as a life coach by the name of Jocelyn Bloom."

Will froze, then spun around to see the TV, with a "What the hell?" of disbelief trapped in his throat.

"Known as a 'life coach to the stars,' Jocelyn Bloom has been working for Coco Kirkman for over a year, giving her daily access and, evidently, much more, to Coco's movie-star husband, Miles Thayer."

Will just stared, blinked, then took a step closer. The picture was grainy, taken by a powerful lens at a long distance, but not blurry enough to cast any doubt that he was looking at the woman he'd been thinking about a few seconds ago. Ebony hair pulled tight off her delicate features, giant dark eyes, narrow shoulders taut and stiff.

Jocelyn broke up a marriage?

"*TMZ* has published a series of texts sent between Jocelyn Bloom and Miles Thayer," the announcer continued, his voice full of barely restrained joy. "The most salacious texts detailed sexual acts—"

Will lurched toward the chair, grabbing the remote to thumb the Mute button.

Guy looked stunned. "That's the good part!"

Will opened his mouth to argue, but a change in the screen snagged his attention. This shot was closer and clearer and, holy shit, she looked good. Better than ever, in fact. "You know who they're talking about?" he asked Guy.

"Some movie stars. Who cares? I like that stuff."

"Some movie stars and…" *Your daughter*. "No one you recognized?"

Guy snorted. "I don't know those people's names, Will. I barely know my own. What does salacious mean, anyway?" He tried to get the remote.

"It means…" Things he didn't want to think about Jocelyn doing with anyone. "Sexy."

"I can take the dirty stuff, pal. I'm too old for it to have any effect." Guy managed to grab the remote and get the sound right back. Unable to help himself, Will turned back to the TV.

"Jocelyn Bloom has yet to talk to the media," the reporter said. "Or issue a statement to deny the accusations. Right now all we know about this woman is that she is a certified life coach and counts Coco Kirkman among a long list of wealthy and well-known clients."

Will looked hard at Guy once more, but the older man just stared at the TV without so much as a flicker of recognition.

"What the hell's a life coach, anyway?" Guy asked with a soft harrumph. "Sounds like an excuse to pick rich people's pockets and bust up their marriages." He punched up the volume.

Was that who Jocelyn Bloom had become?

"According to an attorney for Coco Kirkman, Ms. Bloom has been a close confidante for well over a year, and during that time, she has been frequently an overnight guest of the couple."

Will's stomach tightened as he forced himself to leave the room.

"Fuck!" Smoke and the smell of charred food filled the kitchen, and he lunged for the pot handle to slide the scorched spaghetti off the burner. "God damn it *all*!"

As he shook his hand more out of sheer rage than any real pain, a string of new curses fell from his lips. Pulling it together, he stirred the spaghetti and folded the bits of black into the noodles. Guy'd never notice a burned dinner. Hell, Guy would probably never notice *dinner*.

Forcing the image of a girl he once loved out of his head, Will put the food on a plate and carried it into the living room, where, thank Christ, Guy had switched to a game show.

"Where's yours?" Guy asked as he straightened his chair so he could reach the TV table. "Come and spin the wheel of fortune with me."

When Will had returned to Mimosa Key, he'd *tried* to hate the old coot, he really had. But over time, well, shit, how can you hate a guy who had no memory of what a nasty prick he'd ever been? The worst thing Guy Bloom did now was start and never finish a shit-ton of craft projects.

"Not tonight, Guy. I have some work to do."

"You worked all day." There was a tinge of sadness in his voice, enough to tweak Will's guilt. Guy was lonely, plain and simple, and Will was all he had.

"Just have to check my e-mail and pay some bills." Because who else was going to pay Guy's bills? He glanced at the TV, his mind's eye still seeing Jocelyn's beautiful features instead of an aging game-show hostess prancing across the screen.

"I'll check on you later, Guy." Meaning he'd be sure the old man got in bed and had a light on and didn't mistake his own reflection for a burglar.

Before Guy could ask him to stay, Will slipped out, crossing the patio and the small lawn that separated the houses. Inside, he dropped into a kitchen chair and stared at the pile of Guy's mail. Doctors' bills, insurance bills, pharmacy bills, and more doctors' bills. All to keep Guy relatively stable. A losing battle, on every front.

And the cost of private nursing? Astronomical.

Will knew exactly how much money Guy had; he wrote out the checks every month. The account just got smaller and smaller. Stabbing his hair, he blew out a breath, imagining just how much money Jocelyn charged as a life coach. How much she'd get for selling her story about sex with Miles Thayer to some tabloid.

Didn't matter. As far as anyone knew, Jocelyn had been home exactly three times in fifteen years after . . . that night. He'd heard she came home for her mother's funeral almost ten years ago and once, about a year ago, after the hurricane wiped out Barefoot Bay, Will had seen her at a

Mimosa Key town council meeting. But the minute she'd laid eyes on him she disappeared again. And although he wasn't there, he'd heard she'd made it to Lacey and Clay Walker's beach wedding.

Now she lived in another world, three thousand miles away, breaking up movie-star marriages. Funny, he was the one who was supposed to have become rich and famous, while she'd wanted to live in a comfy house in the country, if he recalled her childhood dreams correctly.

Fifteen years and a lot of water had passed under that burned bridge. And he couldn't exactly blame her. Or call her for help. Or even, as much as he tried, forget her.

And God knows he'd tried.

Chapter 2

⌒

Jocelyn did everything she could to get comfortable, but it just wasn't going to happen on a cross-country flight. She shifted in the plane seat, her back and bottom numb, her head on fire from the itchy wig, her hand throbbing from filling three notebooks for a grand total of...too many lists to count.

The lists gave her some measure of peace, but not much. Each had a title and a theme, a strategy with potential action items, and those all had priority ratings, a deadline, and, of course, her very favorite form of punctuation: the check mark.

So far, only one action item was checked, although it was more of a survival technique than anything strategic: *Get out of L.A. and hide.*

Nor was her destination exactly her first choice on a list of possible hiding places, but all her wealthy friends and clients—owners of multiple chalets in Aspen and getaways in Italy—had been conveniently unavailable. No surprise, really.

But Lacey had come through, of course, as the truest of true friends. When she'd suggested that Jocelyn take refuge at Casa Blanca, Lacey's partially built resort in Barefoot Bay, there'd been no hesitation. Jocelyn needed sanctuary from this personal storm, a place to avoid the media and figure out just where to take her life from here.

Funny that such a decision had to be made on the island of Mimosa Key, but beggars and homewreckers couldn't afford to be choosy.

Except that Jocelyn was neither.

Two seats away, a young woman skimmed the pages of *People* magazine, blind to the fact that the "other woman" in Miles Thayer's broken marriage was sitting a foot away, sipping water and wishing it was something stronger.

Jocelyn stole a few glances at the pages as she closed her notebooks and tucked them into her bag, narrowing her eyes at the image of Coco Kirkman on the cover of the magazine.

That defenseless shadow in her eyes had served her well in front of the camera, making her an empathetic character no matter who she played. That vulnerability had attracted Jocelyn, too, reminding her of another woman who needed a little help developing a spine. Coco was a young, talented, still-fixable version of Mary Jo Bloom, but, once again, Jocelyn had failed to make that fix.

Leaning against the glass, Jocelyn peered down at the swampy Everglades of Florida's southwest coast, the lush, tropical wetlands so different from what was now her home state. California was brown most of the year, horribly overpopulated and packed with people who *thought* they were rare birds, not *real* rare birds.

But this? This little corner on the Gulf of Mexico was home. A shitty home full of heartaches and bad memories, but it was home. And if her dear friend from college hadn't also lived on this island, she'd never, ever have come back here again.

And that might be sad, because Mimosa Key, for all its dark memories, was a pretty place. Especially Barefoot Bay. The picturesque inlet on the north end if the island was far away enough from those memories that Jocelyn could feel safe and secure. Relatively.

As the plane came to a stop and the deboarding announcements were made, the woman flipped the magazine onto the empty seat between them. "Feel free to take it," she said to Jocelyn, giving her a quick look.

For a moment, Jocelyn tensed, expecting shocked recognition. *Oh my God, you're the chick who had an affair with Miles Thayer!*

But there was only a cool smile, and Jocelyn's gaze dropped to the blaring, glaring lies across the cover.

Coco Is Crushed! Sexy Life Coach Steals an American Angel's Husband!

"No, thanks," Jocelyn replied, turning away.

At the medley of snapping seat belts and clattering overhead bins, Jocelyn tugged the long blonde wig and adjusted her sunglasses, not caring that the sun had already set here on the East Coast. If she could fit a hat over the stupid wig, she'd have worn that, too.

The regional airport was small, and she spotted Lacey and Tessa right past Security, standing close and peering over heads to find her. Lacey looked as radiant as she had the day Casa Blanca's groundbreaking ceremony had turned into her impromptu wedding to Clay Walker. Her reddish-blond curls framed her freckled face, a slight frown pulling as she scanned the crowd.

Next to her, Tessa looked relaxed if not radiant, tanned from hours in the gardens, toned from her uber-healthy lifestyle. Her deep brown eyes passed right over Jocelyn.

Only when Jocelyn dragged her carry-on in front of them and slowly raised her glasses did they gasp with recognition.

"Oh my God," Tessa said.

"Joce—"

Jocelyn put her hand over Lacey's mouth. "Shhh. Let's cut out of here, stat."

"I didn't even recognize you." Tessa reached for a strand of wig hair, but Jocelyn ducked.

"Exactly. C'mon, move it."

Lacey put her arm around Jocelyn and Tessa grabbed the rolling bag, both of them flanking her like bodyguards.

"There are no paparazzi in the airport," Lacey assured her, moving so slowly that Jocelyn wanted to scream. "And certainly none in Mimosa Key."

"Which is why I'm here," Jocelyn said. "We can skip Baggage. I've got everything here. Let's go."

"Can't." Tessa moved even more slowly, nudging them all away from the exit.

"*Must*," Jocelyn shot back. "I gotta get this wig off."

"Over here," Lacey said. "She's already landed."

"Who's already landed?" The airport wasn't that big, but it felt like she was crossing the Sahara from one gate to the next.

"You really think Zoe Tamarin could stand for the three of us to be together and *not* get in on it?" Tessa asked, her expression changing as she pointed to more people deplaning a few gates away. "There she is. Spent a fortune she doesn't have to fly direct from Phoenix and time her arrival with yours."

Instantly Jocelyn spotted Zoe, with her wild blonde waves and sunny smile, weaving through the crowd, waving madly. As much as Jocelyn feared Zoe would suddenly scream her name, the fact that the four of them were together sent a shudder of sheer joy through her. She'd pay Zoe for the plane ticket, and it would be well worth the cost.

"Woo-hoo! I made it!" Zoe practically danced through the crowds, her jade green eyes sparkling as she locked on Tessa and Lacey. Thankfully, she didn't even notice or recognize Jocelyn.

Lacey moved ahead, reaching Zoe first, hugging her and whispering in her ear. Instantly, Zoe's head popped up and she zeroed in on Jocelyn.

She stared, raised one eyebrow, then just shook her head as she approached Jocelyn and Tessa. Reaching out for a hug, she folded Jocelyn in her arms.

"That wig is so fake I can't even joke about it," she murmured in Jocelyn's ear.

"But you will." She hugged her friend. "Thanks, Zoe. I'm glad you're here."

Zoe fluffed some strands of Jocelyn's wig and rolled her eyes. "As if I'd miss this." She turned her attention to Tessa; once again there was a shower of squeals and hugs. "I'm glad you called me," Zoe said to Tessa, wrapping them all into a group hug. "We come together when there's trouble, right? That's what we did for Lace after the shit storm. Now that's what we do for you…*during* the shit storm." She leaned in and whispered, "Seriously, Miles Thayer, Joss? He's so not your type."

Jocelyn just closed her eyes. "For the love of God, can we please get in the car so I can get this thing off my head."

A man passed and took a long look at Jocelyn, making her cringe and drag the sunglasses down for coverage. "Did you see him stare at me?"

"That's how all men look at blondes," Zoe assured her, linking arms and nudging Jocelyn forward. "Especially fake ones."

Jocelyn kept the sunglasses on until they were in Lacey's car. Then she ripped off the wig and scratched her scalp, yanking at the clip that held her long hair in a tight knot. "Oh my God, that feels good."

Lacey grinned into the rearview mirror. "There's our Joss again."

"Give me this thing." Next to her, Tessa snagged the wig. "You don't need this here, okay? No reporters, no paparazzi, no one to hide from."

Well, there was at least one person to hide from. "Depends. Where did you decide I'm staying, Lace?" Last year when she'd come to help Lacey rebuild her life, she'd stayed at the Ritz Carlton in Naples and while her friends didn't exactly understand her adamant decision not to go to certain parts of Mimosa Key, they'd abided by it. She couldn't do that now; the media would be all over her in a hotel that public.

"Zoe's staying with me in the house I rent in Pleasure Pointe," Tessa said.

Too close for comfort. "I'm not staying there," Jocelyn replied quickly.

"We know," Lacey assured her. "You're staying in Barefoot Bay."

"So speaketh the former dormitory resident adviser and elder statesmen of the group," Zoe said.

"Two years. Not that elder," Lacey shot back.

"One year married to the younger man and she's a teenager again. All right, woman." Zoe turned in the passenger seat to face Jocelyn in the back. "Dish."

Where she was staying was an easy topic compared to this one. They'd want the truth, and it would be tricky. But she was ready. "There's nothing to dish."

Again, Zoe gave a signature eye roll. "Come on, Joss. Miles Thayer? He's like the hottest human on earth. I want gory details, including size, stamina, and any kinky shit."

"Zoe," the other two said.

But Jocelyn just shook her head. "All right, ladies. Listen to me. I'm going to say this once and once only. I did *not* sleep with Miles Thayer. I barely speak to Miles Thayer, and when I do, there's not the remotest molecule of affection or attraction between us. I hate Miles Thayer and, if you want to know the truth, so does Coco Kirkman."

They all just stared at her.

"Why?" Tessa asked.

"I'm not going to say," Jocelyn said, her voice taut. "And if I can't count on you three not to believe the crap in the tabloids, then turn around and take me back to the airport. I'll hide somewhere else."

Tessa put her hand on Jocelyn's arm. "You can count

on us," she said. "You can also count on Zoe being crass and thinking exclusively about sex."

"There was no sex. Sorry to disappoint you, Zoe. And none of this leaves the car, got it?"

"I'm not disappointed," Zoe assured her. "I'm proud of you for resisting his hotness. But if there was no sex, really, *why* is Coco claiming you broke up her marriage?"

Jocelyn dropped back on the seat, letting out a long, slow breath. "It's complicated," she said, the vague tone getting a quick, suspicious look from Tessa. "But Coco wants out of the marriage and this . . . is her way."

"Her way?" Lacey's voice rose with incredulity. "Why not just file for divorce? It's Hollywood, for heaven's sake. Why throw it all on you?"

Because Coco's shoulders weren't strong enough to handle the repercussions. And this was the only way.

"She needs to put the blame on someone other than herself," Jocelyn said, conjuring up her best shrink-like tone.

"Okay, but that doesn't explain why you don't publicly deny every word," Tessa demanded.

"Really publicly," Zoe added. "Like a billboard on Sunset Boulevard." She boxed her hands as if she were reading the headline. "*I Am not a Marriage-Wrecker.*"

"But I *am* a life coach," Jocelyn said. "And billboards on Sunset Boulevard are as fake and cheesy as the rest of that town. But with my job comes certain ethics about privacy. I know *stuff.*"

"So she makes you her fall guy?" Tessa asked. "I don't get it."

And they wouldn't, until they understood what "stuff" Jocelyn knew. And if they knew that, then . . .

"Look, guys, I don't want to talk about it. I just need to breathe and think and hide."

Tessa snorted. "Which, knowing you, will make you batshit crazy in two days."

Jocelyn smiled at her, not denying the truth of that. But every single client had put her on hold—or fired her last week. "Anything for me to do at Casa Blanca?"

"The resort's barely built," Lacey said. "So unless you're handy with a hammer, you're going to have to work in the food gardens with Tess."

She held up her thumb. "Totally brown. Unless your plants need life management."

"You know, Joss," Lacey said. "I've been doing all this research on high-end resorts and some of the best ones offer life coaching to their clients. Do you think you could help me figure out how I can incorporate that into my menu of services?"

"I'd love to." She leaned forward and put a hand on Lacey's shoulders. "By the way, marriage really suits you, girl. You are quite literally glowing."

She laughed. "That's because when Clay kicks me out of the construction trailer, I get to 'research' spas and their treatments. Doesn't suck."

"Don't listen to her," Tessa said. "She's madly in love and it shows."

Lacey grinned. "He's awesome, as you guys know. How can I ever thank you all enough for talking me into the hot young architect?"

"Like we had to do a lot of convincing," Zoe said with a laugh.

All the way over the causeway and up to Barefoot Bay, they chattered about Lacey's first year of happy marriage, her challenges with a teenage daughter, and the resort they'd all invested in financially and emotionally.

For the first time in over a week, Jocelyn felt certain this trip had been a very good idea. Even when they passed Center Street and she glanced to the south and memories threatened, she ignored them.

There would be absolutely no reason to see her father while she was here, none at all. So she didn't bother to bring him up and, being the friends they were, neither did the girls.

How long would that last?

Chapter 3

~~

Something was different at Casa Blanca. Will could practically smell a change in the salty air of Barefoot Bay the minute he climbed out of his truck in front of the resort's construction trailer. The Gulf of Mexico was dead calm, the water a deep cobalt blue as the sun made its first appearance over the foliage along the eastern border of the resort's property line. The construction parking lot was empty, of course, and the structures stood silent in various degrees of completion.

Still, the air pressed, heavy with change. Funny how he could sense that. Like when the wind would pick up in the outfield, a signal that the game's momentum was about to shift.

Scanning the main building, he noticed a few additions since he'd last been to the job site. Clay and Lacey Walker ran a tight schedule, determined to get Mimosa Key's first exclusive resort up and running within the year, so it was no surprise that the subs had been hard at work on Friday while he'd driven to Tampa to pick up the flooring for one of the villas.

There were definitely more roof tiles on the main structure, the creamy barrels adding to the many textures of Clay's Moroccan-inspired architecture. And the window contractor had been busy, too, having left at least a dozen giant sheets of plate glass propped along the side and front of the curved entry, ready to be installed when the roof was completed.

But the main building of Casa Blanca was of no real interest to Will. His work centered on the six private villas the resort's most well-heeled guests would rent. He'd spent the better part of the last year building those smaller structures, including all of the finishing carpentry in Rockrose, the first completed villa at the north end of the main path.

He peered through the palm fronds and elephant-ear leaves that had grown lush since a hurricane stripped the trees over a year ago. He studied the unpaved road that led to the villas. Deep, fresh wheel grooves cut through the dew-dampened dirt. Had someone driven up there on a Sunday?

Even if there had been a sub here on a Sunday—which was really unlikely—the construction crew was primarily focused on Bay Laurel, the villa closest to where he stood now and the destination of the African wood flooring he'd loaded in his truck.

Why would someone drive up the path? Lacey and Clay's new house stood at the very far north end of the property, but you couldn't drive all the way up there from here; they'd take the back road around the property.

He paused at the passenger door, pulling it open to grab the cup of coffee he'd picked up at the Super Min on his way to the site. As he unwedged the cup from the holder, a drop of hot black liquid splashed through the plastic top, dribbling onto the seat.

Well, not the seat. Onto the newspaper he'd left there. And not exactly a newspaper, either, unless the *National Enquirer* qualified.

The headline taunted him.

Coco Cries on Set: "I Was Blind to the Affair!"

Why the hell did he buy that shit, anyway? To revel in someone else's misery? To get the dirt on a woman he'd once thought was perfect?

Well, hell, people change. Who knew that better than Will?

Holding the coffee in his right hand, he used the other to lift the front page to see the blurry shot of a woman with long dark hair, big brown eyes, and features so burned in his memory that he didn't need a wide-angle lens to capture them.

She had only changed for the better, at least physically. The years had been kind, even if the media wasn't. The memory that had haunted him for almost half his life nearly swallowed him whole when he looked at her picture.

Then don't look, you idiot.

Closing the page, he nudged the door closed with his hip and finished his coffee, intrigued enough by the tire prints to follow them after he tossed the empty cup in the trash. He strode along what would eventually be the resort's scenic walkway, canopied by green and lined with exotic flowers from Africa. Each villa was named for a different bloom found on this path.

He passed the partially built villas, mentally reviewing each construction schedule, but his thoughts stopped
the instant he rounded the foliage that blocked Rockrose,
the only fully finished villa.

That's what was different.

He squinted into the sun that backlit the vanilla-
colored structure, highlighting the fact that the french
doors along the side were wide open, the sheer curtains
Lacey had installed fluttering like ghosts. There was no
breeze, so someone had to have the overhead fan on in
there.

Shit. Vandals? Squatters? Maybe Lacey's teenage
daughter or one of her friends taking advantage of the
place?

There was no other explanation. Rockrose had been
given a CO two weeks ago. But a certificate of occupancy didn't mean *actual* occupancy, and Lacey kept the
secluded villa locked tight so that none of the construction
workers traipsed through or decided to use the facilities.

He took a few steps closer, instinctively flexing his
muscles, ready to fight for the turf of a building that somehow had become "his."

He took cover behind an oleander bush, slipping
around to get a better view into the bedroom. He could
see the sheer film of netting Lacey had hung from the
bed's canopy, the decor as romantic as Morocco itself.

If anyone defiled one inch of that villa there'd be hell
to pay. He'd laid the marble in the bath, shaved the oak
wood crown molding, and hand-carved the columns on
the fireplace mantel from one solid piece of rosewood.
The whole job had given him more satisfaction than picking off a runner trying to steal second ever had.

Irritation pushed him closer to the deck, another damn thing he'd made with his own two hands. If some stupid kid had—

The filmy gauze around the bed quivered, then suddenly whisked open. Holy hell, someone was *sleeping* in that bed. He bounded closer, sucking in a breath to yell, then one long, bare, shapely leg emerged from the clouds of white.

His voice trapped in his throat and his steps slammed to a stop. The sun beamed on pale skin, spotlighting pink-tipped toes that flexed and stretched like a ballerina preparing to hit the barre.

The other leg slid into view, followed by an audible yawn and sigh that drifted over the tropical air to make the hairs on the back of his neck stand up. He took a few stealthy steps, wanting to keep the advantage of surprise but, man, he didn't want to miss what came out of that bed next.

The feet touched the floor and a woman emerged from the netting, naked from head to toe, dark hair falling over most of her face. Not that he'd have looked at her face.

No, his gaze was locked on long limbs, a narrow waist, and subtle curves that begged to be handled. Her breasts were small, budded with rose-colored nipples, her womanhood a simple sliver of ebony that matched her sexy, messy hair.

She stretched, widening her arms, yawning again, giving him a centerfold-worthy view as her breasts lifted higher. Every functioning blood cell careened south, leaving his brain a total blank and his cock well on its way to being as hard as the planks of African wood in his truck.

Son of a bitch. He backed up, ducking behind the oleander and cursing himself for being some kind of pervie Peeping Tom. He had to get back down the path and come back later—noisily, in his truck—to find out who the hell she was.

A footstep hit the wood deck and Will inched to the side, unable to stop himself from looking. At least she had on a thin white top now, and panties. With both hands, she gathered her hair up to—

His heart stopped for at least four beats, then slammed into quadruple time.

Jocelyn.

Was it possible? Was he imagining things? Was this a mirage spurred by a couple of lousy pictures in the paper and three days of fantasies and frustration?

She let go of her hair, shaking her head so that a thick, black mane tumbled over her shoulders like an inky waterfall. Then she closed her eyes and turned her face to the rising sun.

Any doubt disappeared. Along with common sense and years of rationalization and a decade and a half of telling himself he had no choice—even though he knew differently.

Everything suddenly changed at the sight of Jocelyn Mary Bloom. The sun was warmer. The air was cleaner. And his heart squeezed in a way it hadn't for fifteen years.

She turned, rubbing her arm as if a sixth sense had sent a chill over her. "Is someone there?"

Make a joke. Say something funny. Walk, smile, talk. C'mon, William Palmer, don't just stand here and gawk like you've never seen a female before.

"It's me."

She squinted into the bushes, then reared back in shock as he stepped out and revealed himself. Her lips moved, mouthing his name, but no real sound came out.

"Will," he said for her. "I thought someone was trespassing."

She just stared, jaw loose, eyes wide, every muscle frozen like she'd been carved out of ice.

He fought the urge to launch forward, take the three stairs up to the deck in one bound and...thaw her. But, whoa, he knew better with Jocelyn Bloom. One false move and *poof*. Out at the plate.

"What are you doing here?" They spoke the words in perfect unison, then both let out awkward laughs.

"Lacey brought you here?" he guessed.

She nodded, reaching up to run a hand through that mass of midnight hair, then, as if she suddenly realized how little she had on, she stepped back into the shadows of the villa, but he could still see her face.

"How about you?" she asked.

He cleared his throat. "I work here."

She looked completely baffled. "You play baseball."

"Not at the moment. I work for the builder. You?"

"I'm staying here."

Hiding here, more like. The pieces slid together like tongue in groove. She'd run away from the mess in L.A., and her best friend had cloistered her in a place that wouldn't even show up on a GPS yet, let alone at the other end of a reporter's camera.

Then another thought hit him like a fastball to the brain. "You alone?" He must have had a little accusation in his voice, because she raised an eyebrow and looked disappointed.

"Yes," she said quietly, sadness in her eyes and a softness in her posture.

Shit. He'd hurt her. He regretted the question the

instant it had popped out. She was hiding from prying eyes and personal questions and what had he done? Pried and questioned.

He held up a hand as though that could deliver his apology and took a few steps closer. "How long are you here? I'd love to…" *Talk to you. Kiss you until you can't breathe. Spend every night in your bed.* "Get caught up."

"I shouldn't be here that long."

In other words, no. "Too bad," he said, hiding the impact of disappointment. "Maybe I'll see you on the south end when you go home."

"I won't go there." The statement was firm, clear, and unequivocal. *Don't argue with me,* dripped the subtext.

She wouldn't even *see* her dad? A spark flared, pushing him closer, up the stairs. She wouldn't even do a drive-by to see if her old man was dead or alive? Because he'd bet his next paycheck she didn't know … anything.

Something hammered at him, and this time it wasn't his heart reacting to the sight of a beautiful, not entirely dressed woman. No, this was the physical jolt of a whole different kind of frustration.

"So, what exactly do you do for the builder?" she asked, apparently unaware she'd hit a hot button.

But her casual question barely registered, her astounding near nakedness practically forgotten despite God's professional lighting that gave him a perfect view of her body under those slips of white silk.

"Carpentry," he said through gritted teeth, a little surprised at how much emotion rocked him. He had to remember what she'd gone through, what her father was in her eyes, but right now all he could think about was a harmless, helpless old man who had no one to call family.

Even though he had a perfectly good daughter standing right here.

"A carpenter just like your father," she said, nodding. "I remember he was quite talented."

"Speaking of fathers." He dragged the word out, long enough to see her expression shift to blank. "I'm back in my parents' house. They moved out to Oregon to be closer to my sister and her kids."

In other words, I live next door to your father. He waited for the reaction, but she just raised her hand, halting him. "I really have to go, Will. Nice to see you again."

Seriously? She wouldn't even hear him out?

She backed into the opening of the french doors, hidden from view now. "I'm sure I'll see you around, though," she called, one hand reaching for the knob to close him out.

He grabbed the wood frame and held it as tightly as he had when he'd installed the very door she was about to slam in his face. "Jocelyn."

"Please, Will."

"Listen to me."

"I'm sure our paths will cross." But her voice contradicted that cliché. And so did history. One wrong word and Jocelyn would find another hiding place in another corner of the world.

Was he willing to risk that? If he so much as spoke the name Guy Bloom, she'd be on a plane headed back to California. But, damn it, shouldn't she *know*?

He let go of the door and she pushed it closed. He thrust his boot in the jamb to keep the door from closing.

"Will, I have to—"

"Your father has Alzheimer's." He had enough

•

strength in his foot to nudge the opening wider and see the shocked look that drained all the color from her cheeks. "I take care of him."

He slipped his boot out and the door slammed shut.

Well, he was right about the winds of change. And maybe that change was simply that after half a lifetime, he could finally get over Jocelyn Bloom.

Keep telling yourself that, buddy. Someday you might believe it.

Chapter 4

⌒

Mimosa Key curved exactly like a question mark, forming the perfect metaphor for the childhood Jocelyn Bloom had spent there. As she took the curve around Barefoot Bay in the car she'd borrowed from Lacey—with the excuse that she had to go shopping for clothes—and headed to the south end of the island, Jocelyn considered the eternal question that loomed for the seventeen and three-quarters years she'd lived on this barrier island.

What would happen next?

With Guy Bloom, no one was ever sure. When she was very young, nothing had been terribly out of the ordinary. But then, overnight it seemed to her childish perception, he'd changed. He'd go weeks, even months, on an even keel—hot tempered, but under control, before he'd snap. Dishes and books could sail across the room, vicious words in their wake. And then he had to hit someone.

More specifically, he had to hit Mary Jo Bloom, who took those beatings like she'd deserved them. Of course, with maturity, perspective, and the benefit of a psychology degree, Jocelyn now knew that *no one* deserved that. No one.

Your father has Alzheimer's.

Not for the first time that morning, she had to ask the obvious: Were his episodes some kind of early sign of the disease? When she'd been home for Mom's funeral he seemed fine. But maybe the signs were there all along and she'd missed them.

Guilt mixed with hate and anger, the whole cocktail knotting her stomach even more than it had been since she'd seen Will Palmer.

Will.

She closed her eyes, not wanting to think about him. About how good he looked. How hours on the baseball field had honed him into a tanned, muscular specimen who still had see-straight-through-you Wedgwood blue eyes, a shock of unexpected color against his suntanned skin and shaggy black hair.

God, she'd missed him all these years. All these years that she gave him up so he didn't have to be saddled with a girl who had a monster for a father and now—

She banged the heel of her hand on the steering wheel.

He *took care* of the bastard? It didn't seem possible or right or reasonable in any way she could imagine.

Like it or not, Guy was her parent. If he had to be put in a home, she'd do it. But before she could tackle this problem with a list of possible solutions, she had to figure out exactly how bad the situation was and how far gone he was with dementia.

The word settled hard on her heart. She knew a little about Alzheimer's—knew the disease could make a person cranky and mean. Wow, Guy must be a joy to take care of, considering he'd already been a ten on the cranky-and-mean scale. Why would Will volunteer for the job?

Because Will had one weakness: the softest, sweetest, most tender of hearts. And wasn't that what she'd once loved about him?

That and those shoulders.

She pressed her foot against the accelerator, glancing at the ranch houses and palm trees, the bicycles in driveways, the flowers around the mailboxes. This was a lovely residential neighborhood where normal families lived normal lives.

Right. Where dysfunctional families made a mockery of normal. Where—

Oh, Lord. Guy was on the porch.

He was sitting on the front porch swing, hunched over a newspaper, his mighty shoulders looking narrow, his giant chest hollowed as if it had been emptied of all that hot air.

Looking at him was like looking at something you remember as a child, only as an adult, that something doesn't seem nearly as big or daunting or dangerous.

Mom had bought that swing, Jocelyn recalled, with high hopes that the family would sit out there on warm evenings, counting the stars and watching the moon.

Fat chance, Mary Jo.

There were no such things as family nights in the Bloom household. And right there, in a faded plaid shirt and dusty gray trousers and a pair of bedroom slippers, was the reason why.

As Jocelyn slowed the car alongside the curb, Guy looked up, a sheet of newspaper fluttering to the ground. He looked right at her, icy fingers of awareness prickling her whole body.

She waited for his reaction, some emotional jolt of recognition by him, but there was none.

Okay, then. He wasn't going to acknowledge her. Fine. That would make the whole thing easier. It was entirely possible he didn't recognize her, if what Will said was true.

But her knowledge of Alzheimer's said he'd be able to remember things that happened long ago but not what he had for breakfast. If so, he must be wallowing in some unhappy memories.

Good. That's what he deserved.

He stood slowly, frowning now, angling his head, and even from this far she could see his gray eyes looked more like rain clouds than sharp steel, and his hands shook with age, not rage.

"Can I help you?" The question came out hoarse, as though he hadn't spoken to anyone all day.

She turned off the ignition and opened the door. "You don't recognize me?"

He shook his head. What was he? Sixty-five? Sixty-six? He looked ninety.

"What do you want?" He sounded *scared*. Was that even possible? Nothing scared the former deputy sheriff.

"It's me, Jocelyn." She stepped onto the lawn, her heels digging into the grass like little spikes into her heart.

"Whatever you're selling, I'm not buying."

"Guy, it's me." She wasn't about to call him Dad; he'd relinquished that title on a hot summer night in 1997 when he threatened to ruin the life of a young man. The same young man who now *took care* of him.

Injustice rocked her, but she kept a steady path toward him.

"Do I know you?"

"You did," she said.

"You do look familiar." He rubbed a face that hadn't seen a razor in quite some time, frowning. "Pretty, too. What's your name, young lady?"

Had he ever called her pretty? She couldn't remember. Maybe when she was little, before his violent streaks became the norm rather than the occasional nightmare.

She ran her tongue under her front teeth, a tiny chip on the right front tooth her sacred reminder of just what this man could do.

"I'm Jocelyn. I'm your daughter."

He laughed, a hearty sound, and another thing she had no memory of him doing. "I don't have a daughter. I have a son." He reached out his hand, the gesture almost costing him his balance. "I bet you're looking for him. He's out now, but never stays gone too long."

"You don't have a son."

"Don't I?" He shrugged and gave her playful smile. "I have a sister, though."

No, he didn't. He didn't have a son or a sister—or a *memory*. But suddenly his jaw dropped and his silvery eyes lit with recognition. "Oh my word, I know who you are."

"Yep, figured you would." She reached the cement walk and crossed her arms, just in case he had some notion of hugging her or shaking her hand.

"You're the lady from TV! I saw you on TV!"

His voice rose with crazy excitement, but her heart

dropped. So the Hollywood gossip machine had been making noise on Mimosa Key.

"Didn't I see you on TV?" He screwed up his face into a tapestry of wrinkles, pointing at her, digging deep for whatever thread of a memory his broken synapse was offering. "Yes, I'm certain of it! I saw you on TV."

"You probably did," she said with resignation.

"You work for Nicey!"

Nicey? She slowly shook her head. "No, I'm Jocelyn."

"Oh, you can't fool me." He slapped his thigh like a rodeo rider. "That William. He is the most remarkable young man, isn't he? How'd he get you here? Did he call? Send pictures? What'd he say that finally convinced you to come and help me?"

"He told me about your situation."

"So he did write a letter." He chuckled again, shaking his head. "That boy is something else." He reached for her arm, but she jerked away before he could touch her. "All right, all right," he said. "Let's just start with a little chat before we go in. Because, I hate to tell you, young lady, you have got a lot of work to do."

"Work?" She didn't have a clue what he was talking about.

"Well, you'd like to talk first before you, uh, get to gettin'?" He bared his teeth in a stained but self-satisfied smile. "See? I'm a fan."

A fan?

"Sit down here," he said, indicating the porch swing. "We'll have a nice talk." He inched from side to side, trying to look over her shoulder. "No hidden cameras?"

"I hope not."

He laughed again. Had he ever laughed that much

before? Could Alzheimer's make a person happier? "You never know, those camera folks can be foxy."

"Yes, I do know that," she agreed, following him to perch on the edge of the swing.

Okay, fine. They could play this little game while she assessed just how bad he was and then she'd do what she surely had to do. Put him away somewhere. He probably wouldn't like hearing that.

Face your issues and solve your problems, life coach. You have an old man who needs to go into a home. You owe him nothing but . . .

Nothing, actually. Still, she wasn't entirely heartless.

"Would you like some lemonade?" Guy asked.

"No." She tugged her crossed arms deeper into her chest.

"Will there be a yard sale?" he asked.

She blinked at him. "A yard sale?"

"To get rid of all my junk."

Maybe he *wanted* to go into assisted living and just didn't know how to ask, or how to pay for it. In that case, he wouldn't give her a hard time. Everything would be nice and easy.

"Well, I guess that's a reasonable question," she said, mentally ticking off what needed to be done while she was here. "I suppose we could have a yard sale, although it would be easier just to throw everything away."

"Everything? Aren't they sometimes allowed to keep the things they treasure most?"

They? Patients in homes? "I suppose, yes." She bit back a dry laugh at the very thought that he'd ever treasured anything. He certainly hadn't treasure his wife and daughter. "What would you like to keep, Guy?"

"Well..." He rubbed his hands over his worn pants, thinking. "I guess my needlepoint and knitting."

The deputy sheriff of Mimosa Key did needlepoint and knitting? When did that happen? After his early retirement or his wife's death? "Sure, you can hang on to that stuff."

"And my recliner?"

Oh, he had loved that throne. Although by now he probably had a new one. "I guess it depends on space."

"You'll handle everything or what? You bring in a team?"

"I'm pretty efficient," she said. "I'll need a few weeks, I imagine, to get all the paperwork together, but I'll start the preliminary work tomorrow." God, this was going to be simple. He wanted to leave. No fight.

And with Guy, that was saying a lot.

"It won't be hard because I'm all alone," he said, sounding unbelievably pathetic.

Yeah, and whose fault was that? "That's...good," she said.

"Don't have a wife," he said sadly, adding a slightly wobbly smile. "I mean, I did, but I can't remember her."

Words eluded her. He *forgot*? What he'd done? How much misery he'd inflicted? Did he forget the time he threw an encyclopedia at his wife's head or poured her favorite cologne in the toilet or—

"If you're ready to go in, I can make tea," he said, clearly on a whole different wavelength than she was.

Tea? Since when did he make tea? Oh, he could certainly fling a pot of it at someone who pissed him off.

She would *not* forget, even if he had.

He pushed up. "Come on, then, um...what'd you say your name was again?"

"Jocelyn." Did she really have to go in? No, she didn't have to put herself through that. Not yet. She'd go back to the villa, make some action lists and phone calls. That would be so much better than touring her childhood home with the man who ran her out of it.

"Actually, Guy, my work here is done."

"Done?" He laughed heartily, the strangest sound Jocelyn could ever remember hearing. A real laugh, from the gut. "I don't think so, Missy. I kind of knew you were coming, so I started cleaning everything out for you."

He knew she was coming? "Did Will call and tell you?"

"Nah, William would never ruin the surprise." He pulled open the screen door, then pushed the wooden front door, which was no longer the chipped dark green stained wood she remembered from the last time she was here. This door had been refinished and painted a glossy white.

Will?

Another ribbon of guilt twisted through her, followed instantly by a squeeze of fury. How could Will be so nice to him? After what had happened?

"Come on, come on." Guy urged, waving an age-spotted hand.

She'd have to go in sometime.

She followed him into the front entry, instantly accosted by the dark punch of miserable memories. The linoleum was the same, yellow and white blocks that covered the entry and led into the kitchen that was oddly placed in the front of the house. That weird exposed brick wall, painted white now, still stood, separating the entrance from the kitchen and living room around the corner.

Without thinking, she touched the shiny paint of the bricks, her hand slipping through one of the decorative openings. He'd thrown her mother against this wall once. She jerked her hand back and took a good look around, into the kitchen, past the dining room, down the hall to the bedrooms.

Holy, *holy* crap.

The entire house was one giant hot mess. Kitchen cabinets were open, vomiting dishes, glasses, cookware, and utensils. In the dining room, the buffet doors gaped wide to reveal empty shelves, but stacks of china and vases and a few tea sets covered the dining room table.

This was what Will called "taking care of him"?

"I know, I know," Guy said, shaking his head. "I got a little ahead of myself, but it was that marathon they ran this morning."

Jocelyn finally looked at him, trying to make sense of his words. But nothing made sense.

"Who ran a marathon?"

"On TV! I don't remember seeing you, though." He put a hand to his forehead, pressing hard as if he could somehow force his brain to cooperate. "Doesn't matter. You're here now and . . . and . . ." His features softened into a smile, raw appreciation and affection filling his expression. "Oh, Missy. I can't tell you how glad I am that you're going to help me."

"You are?" She still couldn't believe he wasn't going to give her an argument about moving, even if he didn't have a clue who she was.

"Of course I am." He reached for her again, this time snagging her hand. He squeezed it between his two fists, all the strength of those thick hands gone now, just weak, gnarled fingers that didn't seem capable of the fury they'd unleashed so many times. "I've been waiting for you ever since I saw you on TV."

She blinked, shocked. "You have?"

"Well, I think it was you." He squirreled up his face again.

"The pictures were blurry, but it was me," she admitted. "There's more to it than you see on TV, believe me."

"Oh, I bet there is." He laughed and squeezed her hand. "But just so you know, you're not making a mistake. I need this so much. It's all I've thought about since I saw you on TV."

A wave of pity washed over her, watering down a lifetime of old feelings. Well, at least this would go smoothly. Then she wouldn't have to feel guilty about locking him in some home. And maybe she could let go of some of that hate. Maybe.

"So, what happens first?" He asked brightly. "When do the camera people get here? And, when do I get to meet that big black bossy lady with the flower in her hair?"

"What are you—"

Behind her the screen door whipped open and Jocelyn turned to see Will frozen in the doorway, looking at her with almost the same degree of shock he'd had this morning outside the villa.

"William!" Guy practically lunged toward him, arms outstretched. "You are the best son in the world. How can I thank you for getting her here?"

The older man reached up and grabbed Will in a bear hug, flattening his gray-haired head against Will's chest.

Over his head, Will stared at Jocelyn, his mouth open but nothing coming out.

"You did it," Guy said, finally leaning back to beam up at Will. "You got *Clean House* here and this pretty girl is going to make my life perfect. I love you, son, you know that?"

Jocelyn put a hand on the cool brick wall to steady herself. Not because the old man misunderstood why she was there. Not because he thought she was there to make his life perfect. Not even because he thought Will Palmer was his son and she was a stranger.

He'd just never, ever said the words *I love you* unless he was weeping in apology for having hurt someone or broken something. The words had always been meaningless to him.

But not now. Guy really did love Will. And as Will patted Guy's back, comforting the old man, it was clear that Will loved Guy, too.

And the irony of that was one bitter pill on her tongue.

Chapter 5

Jocelyn looked more real, more beautiful, and even more stunned standing in the entry of her own home than she had when Will had accidentally discovered her at Casa Blanca.

With one more gentle pat on Guy's back, Will gave Jocelyn a pleading look, hoping she'd just go along with this.

"He thinks I'm from a TV show called *Clean House*?" she asked, obviously still confused by what had unfolded. "Why don't you tell him—"

"I'm so glad you're here," he said, a little forcefully as he eased Guy away from him. "Why don't we go talk privately about..." His gaze moved beyond her to the kitchen. "Holy shit, Guy, what the hell happened here?"

"Now there's no need to cuss, son. I just got a little ahead of the game. This lady, this...uh, uh...what was your name again?"

"Jocelyn," she said with barely restrained patience. "Jocelyn *Bloom*."

Guy didn't even blink at his own name. "This Jocelyn is going to straighten it all out and set things right for me. That's what she does, right? Isn't that what you do, Missy?"

Will held his breath, watching a series of emotions play over her refined features. Dismay drew her dark brows together and doubt made her lower lip quiver slightly. But she finally lifted that deceptively delicate chin and nodded.

"Yes, actually, that is what I do."

Will exhaled slowly, fighting the urge to give Jocelyn a hug of gratitude. "Why don't we go somewhere and talk about the details," he suggested. "Guy, you take a load off in the living room and I'll show Jocelyn around."

"Is this the part where they do a tour?" Guy asked. "The 'before' tour?"

"Yes," Will said, stepping closer to Jocelyn. "But you have to sit down and let me take Jocelyn on the tour."

"Why?" he asked. "I want to show her everything."

Will gave another look, practically begging for help.

"He's right. I have to see everything without you. Go sit and we'll be back after I've looked around."

Oh, man. He could kiss her. "C'mon. We'll start out in the..." He looked around at the chaos. "Garage. It's through the laundry room over—"

"I know where it is." She rounded the brick wall and made her escape through the unused—and just as messy—office that led to the laundry room.

"Will." Guy grabbed his arm. "Thank you." He reached up for another hug. "I don't deserve you, you know that? You're such a good son."

"It's okay, Guy. Let me talk to her." Will inched him aside, knowing Jocelyn was damn near liquid mercury when it came to disappearing between a man's fingers. She could well be gone when he got into the garage.

He found her standing at the door to the garage, listening to the exchange. Shit.

"Hey, thanks," he whispered, coming closer. "Let's go out there and talk."

She slipped into the garage and he followed, closing the door and gathering his wits. He'd thought of nothing, absolutely nothing, all morning but the impact of seeing Jocelyn Bloom.

He'd talked to Lacey and found out that Jocelyn was here for an "indefinite visit"—and he supposed he knew why—but after how she acted this morning, he didn't imagine she'd come to see Guy on her own. At least not this soon.

"I'd been hoping to bring you down here myself," he said, giving voice to his thoughts. "I thought I'd ease you into what to expect."

She arched a dubious brow. "Then why did you make that closing shot about you taking care of him? I mean, what was that if not a way to get me here?"

"Desperation, I guess. Look, Jocelyn, I—"

"I'm sure there's plenty of desperation in this situation. But I'll take care of it for you and you'll be free. I'll take care of the problem."

He blew out a breath, his hands aching to hold her, his heart still not settled from the unnaturally wild beat that had started when he saw Lacey's car in front of the house. "It's really not a problem," he said slowly.

"Caring for an infirm old man who—"

"He's not exactly infirm."

"—is living like a pig and—"

"That mess just happened."

"—once threatened to kill you and now thinks you're his son."

He stared at her. Of course that night would be right under the surface, waiting to bubble up, waiting to rip him apart, waiting to suffocate him in guilt because Will had been able to forgive, if not forget.

"He's changed, Jocelyn."

She gave a mirthless, dry cough. "I see that."

"No, I mean, he's really a different man."

"He has no idea who I am," she said, still cool and controlled and pretending to be unaffected by something that *had* to affect her. "But he certainly has a fondness for you."

"He's confused." He attempted a smile. "I guess that's obvious."

She folded her arms tightly against herself, defensive and still defiant. "I guess I should say thank you for what you've done."

But, whoa, she sure didn't sound like she meant it. "Look, I came back here a year and a half ago to fix up my parents' house and get it on the market and I had no intention of speaking to the man." He stuffed his hands in his pockets as if that could stop the need that still made them ache. All these years and he *still* wanted to touch her.

"So why did you?"

"Because I'm...human. And he was in sorry shape." Alone, pitiful, and, god damn it, a really nice guy. "I started just by taking his trash to the front on pickup day and then cutting his grass when it got to be a mess.

Normal, neighborly things. I fixed a few things, like his broken sink and the back screen door that didn't close and—what?"

With each word she'd grown paler, smaller, more constricted in her posture. "What? You're asking me *what*, Will? Do you know why the screen door was broken?"

He swallowed hard. "I can guess."

"Then why would you do *anything* for him?"

He took a slow breath. "Because he's sick, Jocelyn."

"Then you should have called me."

Guilt slammed him. He *should* have called her. Not just when he realized how bad Guy was, but fifteen years earlier when she disappeared from Mimosa Key without saying good-bye. He knew she was up at UF, but he didn't call. He just let time go by, and then too much time went by.

"I saw you last year for thirty seconds and you bolted."

She swallowed guiltily. "I had a . . ."

"Phone call, I remember. But how could I call you then when it was obvious how you felt?" He recognized his own rationalization and swiped a hand through his hair in frustration.

"I'll get the house cleaned up and get him squared away," she said quietly. "I hope that can be done with a minimum amount of fuss or, to be honest, interaction with him."

He tried to focus on her words, the efficient tone snapping him to attention. "You mean, you'd go along with this? You'd pretend to be on that show? Because that would be great. You know, when he doesn't get his way, he—"

"I *know* what happens when he doesn't get his way." Her voice was icy, and he could have kicked himself. Of course she thought she knew what happened when he didn't get his way, except she didn't know this Guy; she knew a different Guy. "And like I said, I do this for a living. You'd be surprised how many people are willing to pay for a life coach to do nothing more than organize closets and files. Then we'll get him situated somewhere."

He tilted his head, trying to understand. "What do you mean?" Except, deep in his heart, he knew exactly what she meant.

"In a home somewhere."

Yep. Exactly. "He's in a home. *His* home."

She raised her chin, looking remarkably strong for such a petite woman. But she'd always been strong. Even at her weakest, most broken moments, Jocelyn had a backbone of pure titanium. It was one of the things he'd once loved about her. One of many.

"He can't stay here," she said simply. "And you can't be expected to care for someone who isn't your father, no matter how much he thinks he...likes you."

Did she think he couldn't still read every nuance in her tone and delivery? They'd known each other since they were ten. "He said he loved me."

"Yes, well, I imagine he says a lot of strange things." She bit her lip and crossed her arms so tight he could see each tendon straining in her hand. Man, she was wired for sound.

"That probably hurt your feelings, since he doesn't even recognize you."

She let out a dry laugh. "You're assuming I *have* feelings where he's concerned, Will. Or did you forget what kind of man he was?"

"I didn't," he said softly. "But he did."

"And that makes everything okay?" Her voice rose with incredulity.

"I understand how you feel because I felt the same way when I first got here. But over time, shit, he kind of grows on you."

Her eyes grew wide in shocked disbelief.

"Maybe you could…" *Give him a chance.* Was that even possible? "Think about this a little more."

"I've thought about it enough." She turned as if she were looking for something—or just couldn't face him anymore.

"I just don't think he needs to be put away like some kind of criminal."

She whipped back around to flatten him with a dark glare. "He *is* a criminal and you might have gone all soft at the sight of him, but I didn't. I won't. I never will."

"Maybe there's another way," Will said. "He's old and out of it. He's sick and demented. But this is his home. It would be cruel to—"

"Cruel?" She threw the word back in his face like a ninety-five-mile-an-hour fastball. "Are you serious? He wrote the book on cruel. He hit my mother, Will. He threatened to shoot you. He…he…" She clenched her jaw and drew in a shaky breath. "He is a very bad man."

What was she about to tell him? What happened that last night? By the next day Jocelyn had left Mimosa Key; he never knew how she got away. And, shit, he'd been too scared to find out. Scared to lose his scholarship. Scared to lose everything he'd promised his own father. Scared of the recriminations of pursuing a girl he thought he—no, a girl he really *did* love.

He hadn't been willing to pay the price, and he'd had to live with that. Had to pay it now, in a different way.

"Jocelyn." He took one step closer, slowly taking his

hands out of his pockets, that need to reach for her still strong. Instead he cracked his knuckles like he had a million times in the dugout during a tense inning. "I understand your position. Maybe you could...*we* could...find someone to live with him. Or stay with him during the day."

"That's—"

"Expensive, I know. God, I know exactly what it costs and he doesn't have that much money left and neither do I, or I'd—"

She waved him quiet. "I would never expect you to pay for his care. He's my problem and I'll have a solution. That's what I do, really. This is right in my wheelhouse."

"In your *wheelhouse*?" He almost choked on a batting term he'd heard a hundred times on the field, the expression wrong right here in so many ways.

"Yes, this is what I do. I'm a life coach, Will. I put people's lives back together. I help them find solutions to the problems of life. I organize, structure, prioritize, and master their everyday lives. Usually I teach them how to do that for themselves, but in this case, I'll just skip that step."

She sounded so *clinical* "Actually," she continued, slowing down as if a thought had just occurred to her. "If it's going to make things easier for him to believe that I'm from some TV show, then fine, I can play that game, as long as we can get him away somewhere."

"Where?"

"I don't know. I'll find a facility."

A facility. "You can't just lock him up. He's a person," he said stiffly.

"He's an anim—"

"Not anymore he's not!" His exclamation echoed through the garage, making Jocelyn's eyes pop wide and her cheeks pale. Son of a bitch, that was the wrong thing to do. "The disease has changed him," he added softly.

"Alzheimer's doesn't affect your soul." She hissed the last word, then closed her eyes to turn away. "Does the car run?" She gestured toward Guy's old Toyota.

He cleared his throat and jammed one more knuckle that refused to crack. "Yeah, I start it up every week or so to make sure the battery doesn't drain."

"Good, then I won't have to rent one to go to the mainland. You don't have to worry about him anymore, Will."

He put a hand on her shoulder and slowly turned her toward him. "It's not him I'm worried about."

She held his gaze, inches away, the first glimmer of vulnerability in her eyes. Shaking him off, she slipped out of his touch. "I better get to work."

"Now?" He practically spit the word. "Today? This minute?"

"Of course. There's no reason to wait." She put her hands on her hips as she looked around the garage and up to the loft, where more boxes were piled. "Are any of those empty cartons? I'll need them. And these." She snagged a box of Hefty bags from the worktable, yanking out a sheet of thick black plastic. "I'm sure there's plenty of trash around here."

He just stared at her. Who was this woman? Where was the tender, vulnerable, soft young girl he'd been so madly in love with when he was seventeen?

She snapped the bag with a satisfying crack. "Don't you have to go back to work?"

He took a step backward. "Yeah, I do. I'll be back here later."

"Why?"

"To make him dinner."

She lifted an eyebrow. "I'll handle it."

On a soft exhale, he just nodded like he understood. But, shit, he didn't really understand anything about her anymore.

Chapter 6

⌣

The show's on!" Guy came bounding into the dining room where Jocelyn had made stacks of three different china patterns, not enough of any one to make a complete set. "You have to come and watch it with me," he insisted.

"I don't have time for TV," she said, scooping up one pile of plates to fit them in a box she'd found in the garage.

"Not the blue roses!" Guy said, slapping his hands on his cheeks in horror. "I love them."

She looked up at him, still completely unused to every word that came out of his mouth. "Since when?" she asked.

"Since..." His shoulders slumped. "I don't know, I just do. They have sentimental value."

She almost choked. Her only memory of this wretched china pattern was when a bowl had gone sailing across the table one night because Mom had made mushroom soup.

"They have no value," she said, tamping down the memory.

"But I really like flowers."

She looked up, the memory worming its way into her heart anyway, stunning her that same man who *hated fucking mushrooms* could *really like flowers*.

"I'm sure you do," she said. "But there aren't enough to sell as a set, so I'm pitching these."

He shook his head like he just didn't get that as he lifted one of the blue rose teacups off a saucer, dangling it precariously from his finger.

She tensed, squaring her shoulders, her breath caught in her throat as she stared at the delicate china hooked to a thick forefinger. Any second. Any second and...*wham!* Whatever was in his hand would get pitched in the direction of the closest wall to make the loudest crash.

But he just moved the cup left and right like a pendulum, a smile pulling at his face. "You gotta gift me." He practically sang the words, his voice lifting playfully.

For a second, she couldn't speak. Just couldn't wrap her head around this man. "Gift you?"

"You know, I give up something precious and you gift me with something in return. A sofa. New carpet." He sucked in a breath and dropped his mouth in complete joy. "One of those fancy flat TVs!"

"I'm not going to—"

Gingerly, he set the cup back on its saucer, making the tiniest ding of china against china. Then he held out his hand to her. "You need a little refresher on your own show, little miss."

"My own..." *Clean House.*

"I've seen most of them before, 'cause they keep

running the same ones over and over." He closed his hand around her arms, his thick fingers lacking in strength but not determination. "But I don't mind the repeats. Come on, let's get to gettin', as they say."

"As who say?"

He clapped his hands and let out a laugh. "Very funny."

She followed him into the living room, where the TV blared a commercial. He gestured for her to sit on the sofa and settled into his recliner, waving the remote like a magic wand.

"I'm holding on for dear life to this thing. The way you're tossing stuff away you're likely to hide it."

She sat on the edge of a heinous plaid sofa that she didn't remember, something her parents—or Guy—must have bought after she left. Would Mom pick anything this ugly?

"Relax," Guy said, using the remote to gesture toward the sofa back. "It's the fastest hour on TV. But you know that."

She didn't relax, dividing her attention between a home improvement show hosted by a soulful, insightful, no-nonsense woman named Niecy—that must be who Guy called Nicey—and the man next to her.

She really had to do more research on Alzheimer's. Didn't the disease turn its victims nasty and cranky? Or did it just change a person completely? Because this man was...

No, she refused to go there. Leopards, spots, and all that.

"Watch the show," he insisted when he caught her studying him. "This is what you're going to do for me."

Niecy Nash went about her business of taking control

of a family's mess, tossing the junk, selling what could be salvaged, then redecorating their homes, all the while helping her "clients" see what was wrong with their lives. Kind of like what Jocelyn did, only funnier.

Was *that* what she was going to do for her father?

Absolutely not. She already knew what was wrong with him—then and now. She wasn't redecorating anything, just researching assisted-living facilities and solving this problem. It gave her something to do while she was here, anyway.

"Cute show," Jocelyn said, pushing up from the sofa following the big reveal at the end.

"It's more than cute," Guy insisted. "It's all about what makes people tick. You like that, don't you?"

"Made a whole career around it," she said casually. "I better get back to the china."

"You gotta gift me for it."

"No, no." She headed back into the dining room, armed with a little more knowledge of how to play his game. "She 'gifts' for things that have huge sentimental value. Half of a chipped china set has no sentimental value. No gifting."

"How do you know what has sentimental value to me?" he demanded, right on her heels.

She stopped cold and he almost crashed into her. Very slowly she turned, just about eye to eye with a man who had once seemed larger than life, but gravity had shaved off a few inches, and surely guilt weighed on his shoulders.

"I'm willing to bet," she said without looking away, "that you can't go through this house and find a single item that means anything at all to you."

She didn't intend for the challenge to come out quite that cruel, but tears sprang from his eyes, surprisingly sudden and strong. "That's just the problem," he said, his voice cracking.

She took a step back, speechless at the sight. Not that she hadn't seen him cry; he could turn on the tears after an incident. He could throw out the apologies and promises and swear he'd never hit his wife again.

And Mom fell for it every time.

"What's the problem?" she asked, using the same gentle voice she'd use on a client who was deluding herself over something. "Why are you crying?"

He swiped his eyes, knocking his glasses even more crooked. "You don't get it, do you?"

Evidently not.

"You don't understand how some things matter," he said.

"Yes, I do," she said, as ultra-patient as one of the crew on *Clean House* dealing with a stubborn homeowner. "Why don't you answer a question for me first, Guy?"

"Anything."

"Did you really live in this house?" Or did he just make it a living hell for the people who did? "Did you love anyone here? Make anyone happy? Build anything lasting?"

"I might have."

"Did you?" she challenged, resentment and righteousness zinging right down to her toes. It was bad enough that he didn't remember the misery he'd inflicted, but to twist the past into something happy? Well, that was too much. That went beyond the symptoms of a sad, debilitating disease and right into unfair on every level.

Forget the past if that's nature's cruel punishment, but, damn it, don't *change* the past.

"I think I did," he said weakly.

"You think you did?" She swallowed her emotions, gathering up the sharp bits that stung her heart, determined not to let them hurt quite this much.

"I don't know," he finally said, defeat emanating from every cell in his body. "I just don't know. That's why I've been so scared to throw anything away. I thought it might help me remember."

A wave of pity rose up, a natural, normal reaction to the sight of a helpless old man sobbing. Pity? She stomped it down, searching wildly for a mental compartment where she could lock away any chance of *pity*.

She had no room in her heart for sympathy or compassion. Not for this man who had made her childhood miserable and stolen any hope of her having a normal life. *With Will*. With that big, strong, safe, handsome man who still made her knees weak and her heart swell.

"Well, you have to give up that hope," she said harshly, talking to herself as much as the old man in front of her. Without waiting to see his pained reaction, she turned to walk to the table, ready to finish this task, make order, and accomplish her very simple goal. She had to take charge of this situation, not let the situation take charge of her.

"Why?" he asked, right on her heels. "Why do I have to give up that hope?"

She ignored the question, scooping up the teacup and saucer.

"Why should I give up hope?" he insisted, falling into a chair. "Is this like, you know, the part of the show where they make the person look inside their soul?"

Oh, don't go there, Guy. You won't like what you see.
"This isn't a show," she said stiffly. This is real life.

"Is this like a pre-show? Where they get the people ready before the cameras come?"

She could feel the threads of patience pulling, fraying, threatening to snap. God, was she as bad as her father? She'd always feared that horrible blackness was hereditary, but years of psych classes taught her she could overcome whatever ugliness she may have inherited from Guy.

She took another calming breath and continued packing the china.

"What should I do?" he asked.

She looked up, mentally searching for a way to get through to him. "You should start to make new memories." She slid four salad plates into the carton on the table and turned back to the buffet. "This will be a good change for you. You can replace the old stuff with new and better stuff."

In a home somewhere with people just like you.

But she couldn't say the words. Behind her, he was silent, no sniffling, no breathing. Oh, God. Was she about to blow? He was too, too quiet.

Very slowly, she turned. His head rested on the table, his shoulders shuddering with silent sobs. "I want to remember," he blubbered.

Automatically, she reached for him, then jerked her hand away like she'd almost touched a hot surface. "Maybe you don't," she said simply. *Maybe nature is doing you a favor, old man.*

"I really, really do." He lifted his head, and his glasses slid down to the bottom of his teary nose, his eyes red, his lips quivering. "It's all I want in the whole world, Missy.

A single memory. One crystal-clear story of my past that doesn't flash and fade before I can hold on to it and enjoy it."

She stared at him. "I...can't help you." Only that was a lie. She had so many memories, enough to fill up this house. She could tell him a lifetime of stories. Once upon a time there was a nasty man who had no control, a weak woman who'd given up control, and a scared little girl who lived for any shred of control she could muster.

"Then make one up," he said.

"What do you mean?"

"That can be your gift, you know?" He sat up a little, an idea taking hold. "In exchange for throwing away my china, you gift me with a memory."

"But it wouldn't be...real." Or nice.

He just lifted one brow, and, for a single, crazy second, she thought he knew exactly who he was talking to. Was that possible? She swallowed hard. Could he really know her, and he'd lied all this time? "Guy?"

He nodded, excited, sniffing a little. "You have one? A memory?"

"How could I?" she asked. "If I just met you?"

"You're so smart and kind," he said. "And you've been through half my stuff. You did the whole kitchen. The drawers are very neat now, even that junky one with the batteries. Surely you know enough to gift me with one memory."

"Okay," she agreed, looking around, taking in the remnants of their lives: a teapot her mother's friend brought from England, a salt and pepper shaker set painted as Santa and Mrs. Claus, a set of yellowed lace doilies her mother had loved.

The doily.

Somewhere, in her head, a little gold lock turned on, an imaginary safety box where she'd tucked away the bad stuff, never to be pulled out and examined again.

Until she had to.

The box opened and there she saw the crystal vase perched on that very doily, stuffed with a vibrant bunch of gladiolas that Mary Jo Bloom had bought at Publix for just $3.99.

"Four bucks," she'd said with a giggle in her voice to her little girl. *"He can't get too mad about four dollars, can he?"*

Her mother had placed the vase on the kitchen table, foot-long stems popping with life and happiness.

"Everyone should have fresh flowers in their life, don't you think, Joss?"

Jocelyn opened her eyes, barely aware she'd closed them, and stared at the man across the table from her, ignoring the expectant excitement in his eyes and seeing only the anger, the disgust, the self-loathing that he transferred to his family.

"Do you remember the day you came home from work and your wife had fresh flowers on the table, Guy?"

He shook his head slowly. "I'm sorry. What did they look like?"

"They were gladiolas."

He lifted one of his hunched shoulders. "Don't know what that is, Missy."

"They're long-stemmed, bright flowers," she explained. "They come in long bunches and they spread out like flowery arms reaching up to the sky, a bunch of ruffles for petals, in the prettiest reds and oranges you've ever seen."

He gasped, eyes wide, jaw dropped. A memory tweaked?

"You came into the house and saw the flowers..."

"All red and orange? Like long sticks of flowers?" He nodded, excitement growing with each word.

"You wanted to know how much they cost."

"In a glass vase?" He hadn't heard her, she could tell, as he pushed back the chair. "I know these flowers. I remember them!"

"Do you remember what happened, Guy?"

He almost toppled the chair getting up, making Jocelyn grip the table in fear. What was he going to do? Reenact the whole scene?

"Wait here," he said, lumbering out of the room.

Did he want the memory or not? Didn't he want to know about how he'd picked up that vase, screamed about wasting money, and thrown that bad boy across the linoleum floor, scattering water and flowers and one terrified child who tore under her bed and covered her ears?

You have no right to be happy!

Those were the precise words he'd said to her mother. She could still hear his voice echoing in her head.

"I found it! I found it!"

Just like that little girl, Jocelyn slapped her hands over her ears, squeezing her eyes shut, drowning out the sound of that man hollering. *God damn you, Mary Jo, God damn you.*

Why did he hate her so much?

"Look, Missy!"

He slapped a half-finished needlepoint pattern clamped into a round embroidery ring on the table.

"Those are gladiolas," he said proudly.

The work was awful, no two stitches the same size,

loose and knotted threads, but the shape of a tangerine-
and peach-colored gladiola was clear, the wide-hole netting made for beginners bearing the design of a bouquet
in a glass vase.

"I never could finish it," he said glumly. "It made
me sad."

"That's the memory making you sad."

"It is? What happened?"

She looked at the craft, each little row of stitches so
clearly the work of someone who'd labored to pull that
silky yarn and follow the simple pattern.

"Does it really matter, Guy?" she asked.

His shoulders slumped, tears forming again. "I just
want to know why this makes me so damn sad. Every
time I look at these flowers, I want to cry." A fat drop
rolled down his cheek. "Do you know why, Missy?"

Of course she did. "No," she lied. "I don't know why
they make you sad."

" 'Sokay," he said, patting her hand with thick, liver-
spotted fingers, a fresh smile on his face. "Maybe that
Nicey lady will help me figure it out when they do the
show."

"Yeah. Maybe she will."

Chapter 7

◡

Nice work, Palmer."

Will didn't look up at the sound of a female voice, barely audible over the scream of his mitre saw. He recognized the voice, though. "Just a sec, Tessa." Cutting wood this costly required a steady hand and a completely focused brain, and, shit, he'd been fighting for both of those since he'd left Guy's house a few hours ago.

When he finished cutting the plank, he shut off the saw and shoved his safety goggles onto his head, meeting his visitor's gaze as she stood in the doorway of Casa Blanca's largest villa, Bay Laurel.

"You like?" he asked, gesturing to the one-quarter of the living-area floor he'd managed to nail down.

"I do." She raised her bright red sports water bottle in a mock toast. "This must be the astronomically expensive

African wood that Clay's been talking about for two months, right?"

He grinned. "I picked it up on Friday." Grabbing his own water and a bandanna to wipe the sweat from his forehead, he paused to admire the wood he'd laid so far. Scary thing was, he didn't remember leveling or nailing half those planks. His head was not in the game. But the wood was gorgeous, perfectly grained and beautifully stained. "Bay Laurel's going to be spectacular when it's done."

"As nice as Rockrose?" Tessa asked. "I saw it last night all finished for the first time."

"Yeah, I understand we have our first guest." He picked up the freshly cut plank, dusted off the sawed edge, and rounded his cutting table to return to the floor.

She nodded. "Small world, isn't it?"

He threw her a look as he passed, trying—and failing—to read the expression on a face he'd gotten to know pretty well in the months they'd both worked at Casa Blanca.

"Sure seems that way," he said, laying the board so he could get the blind nailer on top of it and start hammering.

Tessa stepped over the new wood, getting her footing on the underlayment that hadn't been covered yet, and settled into a corner of the room like she was ready to chat.

Not that unusual; they'd had plenty of conversations about the resort, her gardens, the other construction workers when someone irritated them. But he knew that she knew—no, he didn't know what she knew.

And that made everything awkward.

He kneed the nailer against the board and waited to let her set the direction and tone of the conversation.

"So you and Jocelyn were next-door neighbors."

So *that* would be the direction and tone.

"Moved in next door when we were both ten," he confirmed, scooping up the soft-headed dead-blow hammer to start nailing the flooring. This was a critical plank, part of a decorative band of darker wood that offset the shape of the room, an idea he'd had and really wanted to make perfect to impress Clay.

He'd have a better shot at perfection if he wasn't nailing at the same time he was having this conversation.

But Tessa sipped her water and watched, not going anywhere.

He raised his hammer just as she asked, "Were you two close?"

He swung and missed the fucker completely.

"Sorry," she said sheepishly. "I didn't know it was like batting."

"It's nothing like batting," he said, shifting his knee on the pad and looking over at her. "And, yeah, we were good friends." The next question burned, and he couldn't help himself. "She never mentioned me?"

Tessa looked at him for a beat too long, a lock of wavy brown hair falling from her bright-yellow work bandanna, her soft brown eyes narrowed on him. She never wore makeup, he'd noticed, not even for employee parties or barbecues at Lacey and Clay's place. But her eyes were always bright and clear, probably from all those vitamins and organic crap she ate.

"No," she said simply. "Not once."

He nodded and raised the hammer again. This time he hit it direct and hard, a satisfying vibration shooting up his arm. *Not once.*

Why would she mention him? He'd never even called to find out where she was, if she made it to college, how she made it to college. *Not once.* And she'd never called him, either. He'd stopped waiting sometime around the middle of his first baseball season, a mix of relief and loss dogging him like a yearlong dry spell at the plate.

"I remember when Lacey was fighting for the permits to build Casa Blanca last year, I saw Jocelyn," he said, remembering how he'd practically jumped her before she'd shot out of the town hall. "And another girl was there with you, a blonde."

"That was Zoe Tamarin. The three of us were in a triple dorm room. Lacey was the resident adviser. Zoe's here, too, by the way. She flew in last night and is staying at my house."

"Really? College reunion or something?"

She screwed up her face like he was clueless. "Jocelyn's in trouble," she said, the words sending a weird punch in his chest. "The four of us are really tight. When someone has a problem, like Lacey did last year or Jocelyn does now, we rally."

"That's...nice." So she'd found another safety net when he was out of the picture. He wasn't sure how that made him feel, but the next hammer swing was even harder.

"How close were you two?" she asked.

"Maybe you should ask her."

She snorted softly. "You don't know her very well, do you?"

"Funny, I was just thinking that. I don't really know her much at all anymore."

"Well, she's not the most, uh, forthcoming person. She's very private."

She'd always played things close to the vest, but not with him. She had been open with him. But that was so long ago. He slid the nailer along the wood plank and nestled it into place, then raised the dead-blow hammer again.

"You don't think she had an affair with that Thayer guy, do you?" she asked just as he swung.

God damn it, he missed again.

"Sorry, Will."

He closed his eyes, silently accepting the apology and delaying his response.

"Do you?" she asked again.

"I haven't thought much about it." Which was pretty much an out-and-out lie. He'd thought plenty about it when he heard it on TV and still had the damn tabloid in his truck.

"Well, she didn't," she said. "It's all lies."

"Then why doesn't she say something to shut up all these yapping reporters?"

She took a sip of water. "In true Jocelyn fashion, she won't say. But I know her and I can assure you, she's caught in the middle of something that is unfair and untrue."

"That's a shame." And he meant it. She'd had enough crap in her life. "Good that she can ride it out here in Barefoot Bay."

"Well, she does have her dad here, but..." Her voice trailed off. "Do you know him?"

That one came in like a curveball, low and slow and totally unexpected. Good thing he caught curveballs for a living once.

He hammered a few times, thinking. How much had

Jocelyn told her friends? Any other woman, he'd guess everything. Jocelyn wasn't any other woman, though. And how much did she want known? Probably nothing.

"I live in my parents' old house, right next door to him, so, yeah, I know Guy Bloom."

Tessa inched forward, interest sparking in her eyes. "What's he like?" When he didn't answer, she added, "I'm not prying or anything, it's just that she doesn't talk about him much. At all, really."

He slammed the last nail and leaned back on his haunches to survey the board before pulling out his level.

"He's old," he said, doubting that he was giving away any state secrets. "Not real healthy. I, you know, keep an eye on him now and then." Like every morning, afternoon, and night.

"Nice of you."

He shot her a look. "Decent and humane. I'd do it for anyone, any old man living next door."

"Whoa." She held up a hand and smiled. "I just said it's nice, Will."

Puffing out a breath, he let his backside fall onto the underlayment, shaking his head, words bubbling that he just had to fight.

"What is it?" she asked.

"Look, she's private, you just said so. I don't want to speak out of school."

"Will, we all want to help her," she said, leaning forward. "We love her. But last time she was here and probably this time, too, she won't go anywhere near that part of Mimosa Key. She refuses to go south of Center."

"Well, she's south of Center right this minute."

"What's she doing there? I thought she was shopping."

He cracked his knuckles and looked at his fresh-laid floor. This woman was one of Jocelyn's best friends, a replacement for him all those years ago. Maybe they could help her—and help Guy.

He wouldn't reveal old secrets, just new ones. "He has dementia," he said softly. "I think she's down there trying to figure out what to do with him."

With a soft gasp, she lifted her hand to her mouth, eyes wide. "I had no idea."

"Neither did she."

"Oh my God, poor Joss. What's she going to do?"

It was a rhetorical question, he knew, but he answered anyway. "Let's see, she's going to organize his life, catalog his stuff, research facilities, pack him up, sell his house, move him out and anything else she can put on some kind of to-do list."

"Oh." She almost smiled. "That's our girl. So she was always a control freak?"

"Not as much as she seems to be now." He dragged his hands through sweaty hair, committed to the truth now. "I don't think it's the absolute right way to go. I'd just like her to think it through. He's not..." He blew out a breath. "He's changed from when she last saw him."

She thought about that for a moment, maybe struggling with how much *she* should reveal. "I don't know... details, but my guess is a change in her father's personality can only be an improvement. That's just conjecture on my part, but I did spend four years in college with her and I picked up a little here and there."

He just nodded, carefully choosing his words. "He wasn't the nicest guy in the world. But now, well, I'd just like to see him comfortable."

"Well, one thing about Jocelyn," Tessa said. "She's fair. And she's a really good life coach with a track record for helping people find balance and joy."

Then maybe she needed to work on her own life and not Guy's. And, hell, Will could use a little balance and joy, too. "Then maybe she just needs time to figure out the best way to help him. I'm just not sure how to convince her of that."

Tessa smiled. "My advice? Whatever you want, let her think it's her idea and she's in charge. Otherwise, wham, she'll—"

"Be gone." He heard the hurt in his voice and, from her look, so did Tessa.

"She has mastered the disappearing act."

You can say that again.

Tessa pushed up, gnawing on her lower lip with worry. "I wonder if she needs help down there."

"No, no," he said quickly. "Honestly, Tess, don't. She's fine and I'm going back really soon. I don't think she'd want—"

She waved her hand. "Don't worry, Will. I've been her friend for a long time. I figured out how to deal with her secretive nature ages ago, and I won't tell her you shared this. I'll wait to see how much she tells us."

"Thanks." He grabbed his bottle to take a gulp of water, wiping his mouth, realizing how glad he was to have someone to talk to about this. "You know, I'm just still getting used to the idea that she's here."

She gave him a slow smile. "Like her, do you?"

Jeez, was it that obvious? "I've always liked her." Understatement alert. "I've always . . . really liked her."

She cocked her head, thinking. "So you must be the one."

"The one?"

She let out a little sigh, like puzzle pieces just snapped into place as she nodded at him. "Wow, I'd never have put you two together."

"We weren't, not really. Why?"

"She got drunk once." She laughed softly. "*Exactly* once, as this is Jocelyn we're talking about. Zoe took her to a frat party one night and brought her home totally toasted." She was looking at him, but remembering something else.

"And?"

"Zoe was with her when she was, uh, you know, puking her guts out. Then Zoe left—probably went back to the party if I know her—and I had the privilege of getting Jocelyn in bed."

He tried to imagine her drunk, sick, helpless like that. Tried and failed. "What happened?" he asked.

"She told me . . ." She caught herself, shaking her head. "Never mind. File it under too much information for an ex."

"I'm not an ex; we were just friends."

"But she said she—" She cut herself off, firing total frustration through him.

"C'mon, Tess. I just told you more than I should have. Can't we have a little quid pro quo here?"

She considered that, no doubt balancing her fairly new friendship with him and her much longer, deeper friendship with Jocelyn.

"She said she was in love with someone back home but . . ."

In love. "But what?"

"But it didn't work out."

Because he'd been a coward and an idiot. "We had some...obstacles."

"You didn't hear that from me," she said, stepping back over the wood to get to the door. "I gotta go talk to Lacey."

He stood, brushing sawdust off his pants, his brain whirring like his mitre saw, howling just as loud, telling him what he had to do. "When you see Lacey, tell her I had to take off early. And I might not be here tomorrow. Personal day."

She just smiled. "*Very* personal, I'd say."

Chapter 8

⌒

The front door popped open, startling Jocelyn. She and Guy turned to find Will in the entry, a red bandanna wrapped around his head, a smudge of dirt on his white T-shirt, a look of horror on his face as he stared at Guy.

"Why are you crying?" he asked. He shifted his gaze to Jocelyn and she could read the question: *Did you tell him where you're sending him?*

"Of course I'm crying, son!" Guy stood and ambled to William, arms outstretched. "You've seen the show! They don't get the ratings if they can't get the old farts to cry."

Will looked at her. "So the whole *Clean House* thing is still going well?"

"It's . . . going," Jocelyn said.

"She's gifting me with memories," Guy said.

"She is?"

"And you know what she deserves, William?"

A whisper of a smile pulled at Will's mouth, an old smile she recognized, one that always took her heart for a ride. He held up a bag. "Enchiladas from South of the Border. There's beer in my fridge, too. Can you stay, Joss?"

A strange pressure squeezed Jocelyn's chest. A longing to say yes, so real and strong and natural it nearly took her breath away. She really, really wanted to curl up and eat enchiladas with Will and Guy.

How insane and wrong was that? Wrong, on every level. "I promised Lacey I'd go over to her house tonight," she said quickly, standing up. "But thank you."

"Will you be back tomorrow?" Guy asked anxiously.

"I have some, uh, calls to make in the morning." To assisted-living facilities. "Maybe later or the day after. Don't make any messes while I'm gone, Guy."

"I promise, Missy." He broke away from Will and held out both arms. "Let me give you a hug."

She froze. "That's okay."

"Come here." He threw both arms around her and squeezed, moving his face to one side to give her a clear shot of Will, who just drank in the scene, clearly unsure what to make of it.

"Thank you," Guy whispered in her ear, still loud enough for Will to hear and react with a raised eyebrow of surprise.

"Okay," she said stiffly, backing away without returning the hug. She had her limits. "Bye, now."

She headed for the door, snagging her bag from the planter where she'd set it out of years of habit.

"Let me walk you out," Will said quickly.

"That's okay."

But he had one hand on the front door and one hand

on the knob, enclosing her in the space between. He felt warm from sunshine and work, a smell that reminded her so much of when he'd come home from practice to find her holed up in his room, seeking shelter.

Softening, she looked up at him, fighting the urge to brush aside the lock of hair that had fallen over his eye.

"I need to talk to you," he said, in barely more than a whisper and far too close to her ear.

She started to shake her head, but he was so close, so strong, so familiar. She nodded instead. "Let's talk outside."

They headed down the narrow front walk in silence as Jocelyn dug for the keys in her purse.

"Lacey's probably wondering where I've been all this time," she said. "Or did you tell her?"

Behind her, she heard him blow out a breath, making her turn as they reached the driver's door of Jocelyn's borrowed car.

"You did, didn't you?"

"I told Tessa—"

"Oh, great."

"Very little, Joss. Nothing about...history. I told her you were here and that your dad is sick and that you're figuring out what to do."

She nodded. "I'd have to tell her that much, anyway," she said.

"You keep a lot of secrets, don't you?"

"Yep, you've been talking to Tessa. She who hates secrets."

"Well, she said she's your best friend."

"One of them, but even best friends don't need to know everything."

He took a step closer, heat rolling off his big body and the car right behind her, the Florida sun baking everything under it, even in November.

"You're lucky," he said after a minute.

"How's that?"

"To have so many best friends."

She smiled. "I know. I have three great ones."

"Four."

She frowned, not following. "Are you counting Clay as the husband of a best friend?"

"I'm counting me."

The statement stole her breath for a second, leaving her without a quick reply.

"I was your best friend once."

Was. Once. *So much more.*

"What happened, Jossie?"

Again, her breath got trapped, squeezing her chest. "You know what happened. I just had to..." *Let you be free of me.* "Move on."

"What happened...after you left that night?"

"What happened?" He sure as hell really didn't want to know, did he? This man who'd made every decision in his life based on loyalty and love, including the decision to help and care for a man who had once threatened to kill him?

No, he surely didn't mean *that*. He meant why did she cut him out of her life. "College happened, Will."

He put a hand on the roof of the car behind her, trapping her completely. "We have to talk."

This close, she could see every detail, in living, sun-washed color. The navy rim around the lighter blue of his eyes, the reddish tips of his thick black lashes, even the thread-thin crow's feet from all those years of squinting at a pitcher sixty feet away.

Without thinking, she reached up and brushed a few grains of sand and dirt from his cheeks, his skin warm and taut to the touch. "You get dirty at your job."

"Always liked a job like that."

She could actually feel herself falling into the blue of his eyes, like the Gulf, swirling around her, warm and inviting and gentle. "Do you like being a carpenter, Will?"

"When are we going to talk?" His voice was low, direct, as unwavering as his gaze.

"I'll be back in the next few days," she said, purposefully vague even though it was obvious he wanted to be anything but.

"Cancel tonight. Have dinner with me."

She tried to back away, but the car was right behind her. "I can't. I promised—"

"Lacey, I know. But you've known me longer."

She swallowed, surprised by his determination and so fundamentally drawn to it. He still made her feel like her skin was on fire and her head was a little too light. Still.

But surely he didn't still feel that way, not after all these years. Because if he did, he sure as hell wouldn't be taking care of the person who had torn them apart. So his loyalty—the steadfast, unwavering loyalty that thrummed through his veins—must be directed at Guy now.

And then she knew what he wanted from her: to change her mind. "You want to talk me out of this, don't you?"

"No."

She absolutely didn't believe him. "Are you sure? Because five hours ago you were pretty dead set against putting him in a home."

He closed his eyes. "I still am, but I want to talk to you."

"There's nothing to say."

His eyes flashed. "After fifteen years? There's a lot to say. A lot to catch up on." He leaned closer, his face inches away. Too close. Too warm. Too attractive. "Please, Jocelyn. We go too far back, we shared too much to just act like casual acquaintances with a"—he gestured toward the house—"issue. We have to discuss . . . everything."

"Like what?"

"Like your life and mine, like where you've been, who you've. . . ." His voice trailed off, uncomfortable. "If you've ever thought about me."

She almost laughed. Almost told him the truth.

Just every damn night and most days, Will.

"Of course I've thought of you. I—"

"So have I." He got closer, too close. The magnetic force field between them sparked and arced and drew her to him. Instead of giving in, she put her hand on his chest, ready to push, stunned to feel his heart slam like a jackhammer. His chest was damp, hard, and so, so warm under the thin cotton T-shirt.

Before she could take her hand away from the heat, he pressed his on top of hers. "Don't shut me out." *Again*. He didn't say the final word, but she could hear it, unspoken but deafening.

"I . . . I . . ." It was like the earth was shifting under her, a terrifying tilt that made her feel like she was losing control. She tried to snap her hand away, but he pressed harder. "I won't shut you out. I'm sure I'll see you a lot while I'm here getting Guy's things in order." She slid her gaze toward the house. "We'll catch up."

Very slowly, he closed his fist over hers, slipping his hand around hers so that their fingers entwined. "I just want to know who you've become."

"Why?"

His eyes flickered in surprise. "Why? Because I cared about you. I... wondered about you."

Not enough to hunt her down, though. She swallowed the thought; leaving Will without saying good-bye and never calling him had been her decision. He just went along with it.

She took a deep, shuddering breath. "Okay, but you might not like everything I have to say."

"I'm willing to take that chance." He pulled their fisted hands up to his mouth, searing her knuckles with his warm breath. "Because... seeing you again, well..." He lowered his head, touched her cheek with his, and whispered in her ear. "Not a single day has passed where I didn't think about you."

Her heart stuttered and she closed her eyes, letting the words settle over her.

"That's understandable," she said with as much cool as she could muster. Which, under the circumstances, wasn't much. "You see my father every day."

"That's not why."

She looked up at him, almost ready to confess that she'd thought about him, too, a million times, a thousand nights, and every morning when she woke up alone.

"William! I can't find my glasses!"

He blew out a soft exhale of frustration, sending unintended chills down her overheated skin. Leaning away, he turned to the front door. "Check the dishwasher, Guy."

"I did! Found my favorite cup with the birds on—hey, are you two kissing?"

Will stepped away. "I'll be right there, Guy." He fought a smile. "I'll never hear the end of this."

But she just looked at him, baffled. Didn't he realize that the very reason they'd lost fifteen years was standing in the doorway teasing them?

So was he trying to woo her with memories or did he have an agenda where Guy was concerned? Did he think he could get her to change her mind?

She wanted to find out. "I'll talk to you, Will. Not tonight, but soon."

"I can't wait."

Damn it, neither could she.

"I'll get a bottle of wine, stat." From her front door, Lacey deadpanned her opening salvo, and made Jocelyn laugh for the first time all day.

"Is my stress that obvious?" she asked as she entered Lacey's brand-new home tucked away in the north corner of the Casa Blanca property.

"No. Tessa had a nice long talk with Will today."

"Really." Was that why he all of a sudden seemed interested in what she'd been doing for the past fifteen years? He hadn't asked about the scandal. Had Tessa told him anything?

"Really." Tessa came out from the large country-style kitchen, two goblets of something red and inviting in hand. "You don't have to look at me like I read your diary," she said, handing a glass to Jocelyn. "It's just time to talk to your friends, hon."

"One of whom is already in here drinking and waiting for you," Zoe called from the family room.

"Come on in." Lacey put a gentle arm on Jocelyn's

shoulder, already in her role as nurturer and peacemaker, as she had been since the first week they'd all met at Tolbert Hall. The worst of Jocelyn's bruises had healed by then, thanks to the most unlikely of guardian angels, and she'd managed to hide the rest.

Still raw from the day's events despite the fact that she'd stopped in her villa and showered off the memories that had rained on her all day, Jocelyn let Lacey guide her toward the high-ceilinged great room. The scent of tomato and basil wafted from the adjacent kitchen, and a batch of fudgy brownies tempted from the granite island.

Jocelyn inhaled it all, giving Lacey a hug. "You've been baking. Lucky for us."

"Brownies? Hardly taxing my baking capabilities. But you smell those herbs? Homegrown by our very own Tessa Galloway."

Tessa gave a little bow of acknowledgment. "It's only going to get better when I finally learn how to work this sandy soil. But the herbs are doing nicely, so I put them in a lovely whole-wheat vegetable lasagna for us tonight. Completely organic and healthy."

Jocelyn tapped her wineglass with Tessa's, eyeing her warily. "All that gardening, and still time to chat with the construction workers."

Tessa smiled. "Come on and sit down. We'll talk."

Jocelyn took a second to look around, since her first tour had been so quick when she'd arrived. True to his word, Clay had made building this home the first priority at Casa Blanca, and already the signs of a happy family could be seen. A framed picture of Clay, Lacey, and her daughter, Ashley, taken last Christmas, hung in a place of honor near a fireplace. A soft fleecy throw over the back of the sofa looked like it was probably getting plenty of cuddle time, and the pool outside the wide-open sliding glass doors was dotted with a beach ball and inner tube, no doubt the setting for some relaxing family hours.

"I'm not getting up," Zoe said, sprawled on some cushions on the floor with a wineglass in front of her. "I may never walk again."

"What's the matter?"

"I took her to my hot yoga class," Tessa said.

"Also known as the second level of hell," Zoe said, trying to work out her neck. "But the instructor was almost as hot as the room temperature."

"He certainly liked you."

Zoe laughed. "Who doesn't? Sit down, Joss, and buckle in for the Spanish Inquisition."

Oh boy. She fell back into the corner of an overstuffed sofa. "I've had a tough day." In other words, *Take it easy, gang.*

They didn't respond as Tessa curled up in a big chair across the table and Lacey brought in a tray of veggies and dips, setting it on the table, then taking the seat next to Jocelyn.

"Is Clay here?" Jocelyn asked when the awkward silence went on one second too long.

"He went to Ashley's soccer practice and they're going out to dinner together afterwards," Lacey said. "Stepfather and -daughter bonding time."

"They're doing well, then?" Jocelyn reached for a carrot, knowing the small talk wouldn't last long.

Lacey nodded and patted Jocelyn's arm. "C'mon, kiddo. We know you weren't shopping all afternoon."

Jocelyn put the carrot on a cocktail napkin without

eating it, choosing instead to hold up her glass to the group. "How about we start with a toast?"

"Great idea." Tessa raised her glass. "To honesty among lifelong friends."

"To knowing you are loved and safe in this room," Lacey added.

"To a rocking game of truth or dare." Zoe grinned and raised her glass. "What do you want to drink to, Joss?"

She took a deep breath, looking from one to the other. "To not talking about me behind my back."

They shared a guilty look and all drank, except Lacey, who squeezed Jocelyn's arm. "We would never say anything bad, you know that. We love you." She set her glass down without taking a sip and scooted closer. "And you don't ever have to talk about anything you don't want to talk about."

Tessa exhaled softly. "Except you know how I feel. I hate when we have secrets."

"Then tell me what Will told you today," Jocelyn challenged.

She shrugged. "Not much, but he told me you went down to see your father, which we all know is weird because you are . . ." She hesitated, looking for a word.

"Estranged," Lacey supplied.

"And he said your father is sick," Tessa continued. "That's all. Well, pretty much all."

Jocelyn gave her a hard look.

"I mean, I think he . . . kind of has the hots for you." Tessa added. "But that's just conjecture. He didn't say."

Zoe sat up, yoga pain gone. "You *so* forgot to tell us that part."

"Honestly, I already knew that," Lacey said, plucking a

zucchini disk and nibbling on it with a sly smile. "Remember the big town council meeting when I presented the Casa Blanca plans and Clay..." She made a gooey face. "You know, practically proposed?"

"We remember!" Zoe made a kissing sound. "So does the rest of this island."

"We got there late," Jocelyn said, remembering the wild ride from a hospital hours away. That day had been crazy, and she had no recollection of seeing Will that time, although she had seen him at the previous town meeting. "Was he there?" she asked.

Lacey nodded. "When I first got there with my dad, I saw Will, and the very first thing he asked about was you. And not in a casual way."

"In what kind of way?"

"An interested way."

"When were you going to tell me this?"

Lacey exhaled, searching her friend's face. "Honestly, Joss, I thought it was Will keeping you from going south of Center when you visited. That maybe you had a history. I mean, I know your relationship with your dad is—"

"I have no relationship with my dad."

"I knew that, but I just thought there must be something important between you and Will. Wasn't there?"

She sipped wine. "Define 'important.'"

On her knees, Zoe crawled closer to the table. "S-E-X."

"No, we never..." Almost. Nearly. Wanted to. Still wanted to.

That last thought shot through her, surprising her with its intensity. "We were really close when we were young, really good friends. He was a great source of..." *Fantasies.* "Comfort for me."

"What kind of comfort?"

"Why didn't you tell us about him at school?" Lacey asked.

Jocelyn ignored Zoe's question but answered Lacey's "We just went our separate ways," she said. "He went to the University of Miami and had a big baseball career. I went to UF and met..." She lifted her glass, the early effects of the wine helping to dull the edges of her nerves. "The three best friends a girl ever had."

"Aww," Zoe said, coming around the table on her knees to curl her fingers around Jocelyn's hand. "That's so sweet." She tightened her grip. "But don't deflect. Did he hit you?"

"What?" She reared back at the question, so unexpected, especially from Zoe.

"Zoe!" the other two said in unison.

But Zoe didn't take her eyes off Jocelyn. "On the first or second night at school, you were changing in the room, and I saw some bruises on you."

Her blood chilled. "Will didn't hit me, no. Will has never ever hurt me. On the contrary, he..." *Tried to defend me. Was willing to take a bullet for me.* Wasn't he? Thank God they never had to find out.

"He what?" Zoe urged.

"He was exactly what I needed at the time."

No one spoke, the only sound the soft hum from the pool motor just outside.

"Jocelyn," Lacey finally said. "We know your dad is really sick. And we know you have a rocky relationship with him. You need us, honey, and you can trust us with anything. Even things you've never told anyone else."

Perspiration tingled despite the cool evening air that

tumbled in from the patio. All three of them looked at her with concern and love.

Which just made guilt smash at her heart. If they knew that she'd told Coco—a client and, yes, a friend—and not them? Lacey would be hurt. Tessa would be furious. And Zoe would remind her every chance she got.

But she'd told Coco for a reason, and these three women didn't have any reason to know except that they were more like sisters than friends. They could be trusted, and tender. Plus, with Will doing a full-court press to keep her from putting Guy in a home, they could be her allies.

"I hate my father," she said simply.

Yes, it was kind of hard to hate that weepy old man she'd spent the afternoon with, a man who couldn't remember her name, but she still hated who he was and who he'd been.

No one spoke, giving her time to sift through her emotions to find the right words. "He…" *Beat my mother. Kicked me so hard he broke a rib. Made me the control freak I am today.* "Was physically abusive."

"Oh, baby."

"Jeez."

"Shoot the em-effer."

Jocelyn smiled at Zoe. "Don't think the thought hadn't occurred to me. But I did the next best thing. I left home and never looked back. Until today, it was my intention to never speak to him, look at him, or think about him until the day his death notice arrived in my mailbox."

That silenced all of them.

"I know I sound harsh," she said. "Especially now, when you look at the guy. He's like a little old lady, doing needlepoint and watching HGTV. But I know what he is... what he *was*." Her voice cracked and Zoe handed her the wineglass.

She half smiled, accepting it with a slight tremble in her hands, then taking a deep drink.

Tessa leaned closer, pain clouding her eyes. "Some people should not be allowed to be parents."

"No kidding." One more drink and her limbs finally felt a little heavy, while the weight on her heart felt a little lighter. "Before I left for school, I... he..." Shit. "There was a pretty bad night." Her voice cracked, which she tried to cover with a fake cough. "Will was there."

"Did he hit Will?" Tessa asked.

She shook her head. "He was more mad at me than he was at Will, but he did have a gun." When Zoe gasped, Jocelyn added, "He was the deputy county sheriff on Mimosa Key at the time, so he was, you know, law and judge and jury. And my father. So I basically decided at that moment that Will, who was on a direct trajectory to huge success, would be better off if we didn't ever see each other again."

"And he agreed?" Zoe asked.

"He must have. He never tried to track me down at UF and our friendship ended."

"And now he's taking care of the guy you hate," Tessa said.

Zoe grunted softly. "That's gotta hurt."

"But that's Will," Lacey said. "He'll always do the right thing. That's his nature."

"I don't think it's the right thing," Jocelyn said. "I know that's cold, but I don't. And he's my father, not his. Despite what Guy thinks."

"Guy thinks Will is his son?" Zoe choked on that.

"He's pretty confused." She put the glass down hard enough to splash a little wine on the napkin. "Is the intervention over yet? I'm starving."

"Not an intervention." Lacey sidled up closer and put her arm around Jocelyn. "And, really, we've all suspected it was something like this. Honestly, Joss, Will's keeping your father's condition pretty quiet. I knew he checked on him once in a while, but he's been mum on how bad Guy is or, honestly, I'd have told you so you didn't get blindsided when you arrived."

"I wasn't really blindsided. I saw Will this morning and he told me how me how sick Guy was, so I went down there today and..." Another mirthless, dry laugh. "He doesn't remember me, he doesn't remember the past, and he sure as hell doesn't remember..." *That night.* "Anything he did to his wife or daughter."

They all sighed, a collective exhale of dismay and disbelief. All except Zoe, who narrowed her eyes with a question. "Maybe Will didn't know how bad it was with your dad for you."

"He lived next door. He had a front-row seat."

Tessa leaned forward. "You know what you need, Joss? You need to work this out. You need to get past this."

Jocelyn frowned at her. "I *am* past it. Why do you think I took all those psych classes? Why do you think I'm a life coach?"

"I don't think you're past it," Tessa said. "Or you could talk about it."

"I am freaking talking about it! What do you want, Tess? Pictures? Scars? Details?"

Tessa dropped to her knees so that only the coffee

table separated them. "I'm sorry, Joss. I don't want to upset you, really. We just want to help you."

"Then change the subject. I've never talked about it this much."

"Even in therapy?" Tessa asked. "Didn't you have to go through therapy to get your degree?"

"Nothing...deep." She'd been quite adept at avoiding the topics she didn't want to discuss.

"Not even to get certified as a life coach?"

She lifted a brow. "In California? Hang a shingle, baby, and get some bigmouth clients." She waved her hand to erase any wrong impression that might leave. "I am certified by several organizations." She reached for some grapes, plucking them from the stems, hating the hot and cold sensations that rolled through her.

Lacey put her hand on Jocelyn's leg. "You know we just want to help you and support you."

She nodded, taking a bite of a giant green grape. "Then help me find an assisted-living facility for him."

Tessa leaned her elbows on the table. "You sure that's what you want to do?"

"Yes, I'm sure. I'm not taking care of him."

"*Will* is," Tessa said.

"Which is...kind."

"How did he handle it?" Tessa asked. "I mean, everything that went on with your dad when you were young? Did Will ever try to stop him? He seems like he would have."

She shot a look at Tessa, surprised by the little jolt of jealousy that Tessa—and Lacey—had gotten to know Will Palmer when he was so lost to Jocelyn.

"My dad was the law back then. No, no. He was so far

above the law it could give you a nosebleed. And Will had a big-time career to worry about."

"As if he'd put his career before something like that," Tessa said.

"He is loyal to a fault," Lacey agreed. "Definitely our best and most reliable subcontractor, who just seems to work and live with all his heart."

"He was always that way," she said, feeling an unnatural sense of propriety. After all, she'd known— and loved—Will before they did. "And still is that way because he doesn't want to put Guy in a home, or at least wants me to think about alternatives."

"Would you think about alternatives?" Tessa asked.

Before she could answer the oven beeped and Lacey stood slowly, waiting to hear Jocelyn's answer before leaving the room.

Jocelyn shrugged. "I have a lot of work to do down there first. And he..." She smiled, knowing they'd laugh. "He thinks I'm with *Clean House* and I'm going to put him on TV after I straighten things up and have a yard sale."

Zoe popped up and gave her head a shake. "So you better git to gittin', uh-huh!"

Jocelyn cracked up at the spot-on Niecy Nash impression, welcoming the levity and a chance to get up and help Lacey in the kitchen. But as she did Tessa was up, too, taking Jocelyn's hand to hold her back.

"Hey," she whispered. "You know we just want to help you."

Jocelyn nodded, not trusting her voice.

"And so does Will."

One more nod and Tessa pulled her a little closer.

"He's been hurt, too."

Jocelyn just looked at her. "I read somewhere he was married." Not that she'd Googled him on one particularly lonely night back in L.A. or anything.

"He was divorced before he got here. I always thought that was what put the little bit of, I don't know, sadness in his eyes. Or maybe being so far away from baseball and not having a coaching job offer."

More inside information that Tessa had and Jocelyn didn't. Who could she blame? She'd never called Will, had never kept in touch, and, of course, neither had he.

"But today I thought maybe…" She waited a few seconds until Jocelyn nudged her.

"Maybe what?"

"I think it's you who hurt him."

"*Me?*"

"I don't know. Maybe it was his ex-wife. Short marriage—he never talks about it. You should find out."

She intended to. When they had that "catch-up" conversation he wanted so much.

The thing was, she wanted it, too.

Chapter 9

ᴗᴗ

Will turned his truck into the Super Min, as he did every day on his way up to Barefoot Bay, to shell out a few bucks for Charity Grambling's coffee. Like the owner of the convenience store, the coffee was bitter and a little past its prime. But it was usually served with a side of opinion or gossip, which Will filed away or shared with Clay if it had anything to do with Casa Blanca.

And her gossip often did focus on the resort, since Charity, along with a few of her family members, considered herself the last word on everything related to Mimosa Key. The building of Casa Blanca, the island's first true resort, was pretty much the biggest thing happening in Charity's world.

The bell dinged as Will pushed open the door, a charming reminder of earlier days when this was just a corner store and not the Shell Gas Station and Super Mini

Mart Convenience Store. Without looking up, Charity whipped the magazine she was reading out of sight, shoving it under the counter before she leveled a beady brown gaze at her customer.

"Morning, Will."

"Charity." He nodded and headed toward the back to grab a couple Gatorades for the job, pulling open the cooler door to check out the abysmal selection. Fruit punch and the blue shit. He let out a loud exhale.

"Sorry, I can't sell enough of it to get you that original flavor, Will," Charity called back. "You'll have to go back to the big leagues for that. Gonna happen anytime soon?"

He grabbed two sixteen-ounce reds and carried them back to the counter. "You'll be the first to know if the Yankees call, Charity."

She gave him a smile that didn't reach her eyes or make her leathery old face any more attractive. Scooting around on her stool, Charity held her bloodred fingernail over the cash register. "Will that be all?"

He gave her a look. "And coffee." Like he hadn't been getting a medium black every day since they'd broken ground at the resort.

" 'Kay." She tapped the register but didn't complete the transaction. "How're things up at the white elephant?" She never failed to make a dig, still stinging over the loss of her fight to stop Lacey and Clay from building a resort that might steal some business from the dumpy motel her daughter owned.

"Moving along real well," he said. Or they would be if he could get his head around Bay Laurel's floor today.

"Taking any guests yet?" she asked pointedly.

"Nope." Not unless he counted Jocelyn. Still,

something about the way she asked gave him pause; Charity had an uncanny knowledge of what was going on anywhere and everywhere on Mimosa Key. It wouldn't surprise him if she'd somehow sniffed out the return of one of their most infamous residents.

"I heard that one of those teeny little houses is all done and Lacey spent a fortune decorating it to look like something out of a Humphrey Bogart movie."

How did she *know* this stuff?

"We're a long way from taking guests," he said.

"Even just one?"

He gave her a hard look. How could she know? From the magazines she sold? Had one of them leaked Jocelyn's flight information or something? They were capable of anything.

He turned to the rack of tabloids, ready to grab them all and clear them out if he had to. It would only help locally, of course.

The entire top rack was empty.

He peered closer, glancing at the other monthly titles below. *Maxim* and *Cosmopolitan*, some fishing rags and a stack of *USA Today* next to the *Mimosa Gazette* on the bottom. Nothing that would have word about Jocelyn. But those cheesy tabloids, like the *National Enquirer* he'd picked up the other day, were all gone.

Shit. Had the entire town sucked up the news because she was a local girl?

"What are you looking for?" Charity asked sharply.

"The magazines."

"Sold out."

"Completely?"

She shrugged. "Is that going to be all, then, Will?"

"When do the new tabloids come in, usually?" he asked.

She narrowed her eyes at him then hit the register key with an officious snap. "You taking a sudden interest in the latest on the movie stars in rehab, Will?"

"Something like that." He glanced at the empty rack again, pulling out his wallet. "It's Tuesday," he said, thinking out loud. "Will more magazines come in this week?" He'd buy every one of them if he had to, just to keep the locals from drinking that stupid Kool-Aid and somehow changing—or forming—their opinions about Jocelyn.

"Varies." She took his money and started to make change, faster than usual, he noticed.

The bell rang and they both glanced at the door, seeing Deputy Slade Garrison with two other men, one holding a small video camera.

"Charity, can I talk to you a minute?" Tough enough to be respected but still young enough to be respectful, Slade's tone was deferential toward Charity.

"What do you want, Slade?" Her gaze zeroed in on the camera, a touch of color draining from her face. "Something the matter?"

Standing near the coffee station, Will set up a cup, listening to the exchange while he poured.

"These gentlemen are from an Internet Web site and TV show known as *TMZ*."

The coffee splashed as Will missed the edge of the cup.

"What the hell is that?" Charity asked, setting Will's change on the edge of the counter with a loud slap.

TMZ? Holy shit. Will knew what it was. He knew exactly what it was—*thanks, Guy*—and why they'd be here. Son of a bitch, if Charity had given away the fact that Jocelyn was in town, he'd kill her.

"They stopped into my office," Slade said, not answering her question. "They are looking for some information on a former resident who I don't personally know, but I told them if anything is going on here in Mimosa Key, you'd know about it."

Only in a town the size of Mimosa Key would visiting reporters get an escort from the sheriff's department.

Charity stood, pushing back her stool and lifting the countertop so she could step out. When she did, a couple of Will's coins dropped but she ignored them, her unwavering focus on the men.

Of course. Charity would be in her element now. The most gossip-crazed busybody in the state of Florida with a chance to be on *TMZ*? Her head would explode.

And if she so much as uttered the name Jocelyn Bloom, Will would break their fucking camera and run them over with his truck. Right in front of Slade.

Will eyed the two men, one stepping forward and handing a card to Charity.

"Bobby Picalo," he said, flashing a fake-white smile and running a hand through hair that had spent too much time in the sun or maybe a salon. "Reporter-at-large for TMZ.com." Slimeball freelancer, in other words. "We're a news-gathering organization."

Will almost groaned out loud. *News*? They call this news? And, shit, this bastard would have Charity plastered all over TV tonight——or all over the Internet in an hour—and sixty more slimeballs just like him would be barreling over the causeway by tomorrow morning.

He had to stop her.

"What brings you to Mimosa Key?" Charity asked.

"We're tracking a big story out of Los Angeles and we

think it's possible a source we'd like to talk to is on this island. A young woman by the name of Jocelyn Bloom."

Despite the fire that shot through him, Will stayed perfectly still, not reacting, not breathing, just waiting, the coffeepot poised in the air.

Charity said absolutely nothing.

"Do you know her?" the reporter asked.

Charity glanced at Deputy Garrison, who didn't respond, then she lifted a skeletal-thin shoulder. "I've heard of her."

Maybe she wanted them to beg so she could negotiate for more airtime. That'd be just like her.

"From the papers or do you know her personally, ma'am?" Picalo asked.

"She used to live here years ago. Maybe came back now and again, but I think she's on to much bigger and better things than a little town like this."

Will gently set the coffeepot back on the burner. Was this Charity Grambling? Not attacking the opportunity to be in the middle of a national scandal? Something was not right.

"Does she still have family living here?"

Another look at the officer and then a sideways look at Will. If he didn't know Charity better, he'd have sworn she'd sent something like a warning. To him?

Because if these pricks went anywhere near Guy, he'd—

"Her mother passed 'bout a decade ago," she said. "And her father took an early retirement from the sheriff's office. Right, Slade?"

"That's right," Slade agreed. Will waited for him to mention that the retired sheriff lived a few miles south, but he stayed silent.

"No other family?" the man asked, looking from Charity to the sheriff.

"No." Charity locked her hands on her hips. "No one."

Will couldn't believe what he was witnessing. Charity missing out on the chance to gossip to a reporter? Why? Money, of course. She must want to have her palms greased thoroughly before she parted with any information.

"But if someone knew her or saw her here, how would—"

"I'd know about it, young man," she said, bouncing on her sneakers and crossing her arms with a remarkable amount of moxie considering that she was well north of sixty, at least. "I know every damn thing that happens on this island, and every person who lives here. She's not here, hasn't been for years, and won't be probably ever again. I suggest you head back to Hollywood for your story."

"Well, I—"

"You heard the lady," Slade said.

Charity flicked her fingers toward the door. "Good-bye now, gentlemen."

They backed out and Charity went with them, as if she didn't trust them to hang out in the Super Min parking lot.

No money, no airtime, no nothing.

What was *wrong* with this picture?

Holding his coffee, Will went back to the counter to grab the bills she'd left there for him, noticing the two quarters that had fallen to the floor. He set the coffee on the counter to crouch down and scoop up his change.

As he did, he happened to look at Charity's four-legged stool, and the pile of newspapers and magazines behind it.

Not just any newspapers and magazines. Tabloids.

He leaned closer, getting a better look. On top of the

stack, Jocelyn's face was as clear as it had been in his fit-
ful sleep last night.

A stack of tabloids nearly six inches high. They
weren't sold out; she'd taken them off the racks.

Why?

He'd known Charity Grambling since he was a kid,
bought gas for his first car at the Super Min, and snacks
on his way home from baseball practice. As long as he'd
known her, she'd never veered off track from what she
was: a know-it-all, greedy, meddling, opinionated trou-
blemaker who considered herself the law and last word on
Mimosa Key.

So something wasn't right. And that couldn't be good.
Not if Charity Grambling was involved.

She came back in, a sour puss deepening the lines on
her face.

"Not like you to hide from the spotlight," he said,
pocketing his change.

"That's not the spotlight," she said gruffly, heading
back to her counter. "Those idiots are just…liars." She
slipped behind the counter and closed the top, securing
herself -and her stash of tabloids—again. "What are you
looking at?" she demanded.

"I'm just wondering about those magazines, Charity."

He could have sworn she swallowed. "What magazines?"

He indicated the empty rack. "The ones that are, you
know, sold out."

"Why are you so doggone interested?"

"I'd like to buy one. When will you have some to sell?"

" 'Bout the same time I get your precious original-
flavored Gatorade," she growled, waving to the door.

"You better get to work, Will. The Eyesore on the Beach isn't going to build itself."

"Charity, I—"

"I'm not in a talking mood, Will, or didn't you notice?"

"I noticed. I noticed plenty. Like what you said to those men."

"Don't you be talking to them," she warned, pointing one of her crimson talons at him. "We don't need those busybodies sniffin' all over Mimosa Key."

"No, we don't," he agreed. "We have our own busy-bodies, thank you very much."

She had the good humor to laugh. "Hell, yeah. This town ain't big enough for more than one busybody, don't you forget it."

"Not about to, ma'am. And, uh, thank you."

She just nodded, her mouth uncharacteristically closed.

Outside, the men had driven away but Slade stood next to his sheriff's car talking to a young woman Will recognized as Gloria Vail, Charity's niece.

For a minute, Will considered enlisting the deputy's help to protect Jocelyn, but after what he'd just witnessed, he wasn't sure whom he should trust or why.

Either way, Jocelyn needed to know the enemy was on the island.

The mosquito netting around the bed wasn't really necessary on a cool November morning, but Jocelyn drew it closed anyway, cloistering herself in the white gauze while she tapped her laptop and researched her options for assisted-living facilities.

She focused her search on the neighboring mainland

towns of Naples and Fort Myers, resulting in a number of options. Just as she clicked through to the second Web site, she heard a man clear his throat.

"You decent in there?"

Will. Just the sound of his voice made a quick electrical current shoot through her.

"Define decent. I'm dressed."

She could have sworn she heard him *tsk* in disappointment. "You taking visitors?"

Outside the netting, she could see him leaning on the jamb of one of the french doors, his familiar, masculine scent suddenly so out of place among the lingering aroma of herbal incense Tessa had sworn would make her sleep better.

Tessa had been wrong.

"You can come in," she said, leaning across the bed to push the sheer curtain open. "I'm working."

He smiled and, damn, if all the sunshine outside didn't pour right into the room. His eyes looked as blue as the sky behind him, his sizeable body suddenly taking up all the space in the room. "Nice office."

"Isn't it?"

He drew the curtain back a little farther, that soapy, sunny Will scent crazy-close now. He wore a white T-shirt that wouldn't be as clean by the end of the day and ancient khaki cargo shorts, and held a work belt in one hand, a cup of coffee in the other.

"You better have two of those," she said, eyeing the coffee. "I can't get an answer at room service to save my life."

He laughed at the joke and held the cup out to her. "Lacey's in a roofing meeting, I'm afraid."

She took the coffee and sipped, raising her eyebrows. "Whoa." She swallowed and made a face. "Super Min?"

"Some things never change."

"Come on." She patted the bed in invitation. "You're going to find out what I'm doing on this computer sooner or later."

Setting his tool belt on the floor, he sat on the edge of the bed to check out the computer screen. "I hope to God you're not at the TMZ Web site."

She almost choked. "I'm not a masochist, Will. Why, have you been there today? Is there new dirt online?"

He took a slow breath as if he wanted to tell her something, then shook his head, indicating the computer. "What's that?"

She turned the screen. "The Cottages at Naples Bay." She clicked to the next site. "Summer's Landing." And the next. "Palm Court Manor." And the last. "Esther's Comfort."

He held up his hand to stop the next click.

"I like the sound of that one," she said. "But I can get into one called Autumn House later today."

"Into one today? You're moving him today?" He couldn't keep the dismay out of his voice.

"No, I meant into one for an interview. Placement is much harder and most of these homes have a waiting list." Which she'd bet some cash could shorten.

He pushed down the laptop screen and gave her a direct look. "Why are you in such a hurry?"

"Because I long ago found that if you do the most distasteful tasks the very first thing in the day, they're done. I've extended that strategy to my everyday life. The longer I sit on this—"

"The more chance you might change your mind."

She just shook her head. "I'm not going to argue with you, Will. I'm going to Autumn House today."

"Then I'm going with you."

Not a chance. "No, thank you."

"You can't go alone."

She frowned at him. "I most certainly can, but if I need company, I'll get one of my friends."

"I am one of your friends," he said. "I'll go with you."

"You have to work."

"I'll...call in sick."

And he would, too, she just knew it. Then she'd be with him all day, too close for comfort as he launched his campaign against her plan. No, that would never work. "Will, you can't go with me and that's that."

"Why not?"

"Because you'll distract me."

He lifted his eyebrows as if that amused and didn't surprise him.

"And you'll try to talk me out of my plan."

"You need me there and I'm not backing down."

Damn the little thrill that went through her. Did he want to be with her that much? Did the idea of that have to feel so good? "I do not need you there."

"Anyway, you need a bodyguard." His serious, even ominous expression erased any little thrills.

"Oh, Lord. The media found me."

He put a hand over hers. "Not yet, but they're looking."

"They've been to Guy's house?" For some reason, that terrified her more than if they'd found her.

"No, I don't think so, but we should get down there and warn him not to open the door to anyone."

"Then how do you know?"

"They came into the Super Min."

She gasped softly. "Was Charity there?"

"Yeah, and she not only didn't talk to them, she kicked them out on their asses and made sure Slade Garrison knew not to give them any information. So Charity's either overdosed on her nice meds or something is up."

Neither one. But she wasn't about to tell Will the real reason behind Charity's behavior. Some secrets would last forever.

"Not only that," he continued, "she hid the tabloids." He shook his head, baffled. "I've never known her to not exploit every possible opportunity to gossip, and this was on a national scale."

Of course he'd think that. Most people would. But most people didn't know Charity Grambling like she did. "Who was it, TMZ?"

He nodded.

"Bottom-feeders," she said, lifting the computer screen. "Let me call these places and make appointments with every one of them."

"Let's just start with one, Joss," he said. "Let's go see one. Together. Let's find out if it's the right thing to do. And I can tell Lacey I won't be gone all day, which will make her happy."

"And I can work on Guy's mess this afternoon," she agreed.

"And we can have dinner together tonight."

She drew back. "Why?"

"We still need to talk."

"We'll have all afternoon to talk."

He put his hand over hers, so warm and big and

familiar. She couldn't help looking at it, at how his fingers eclipsed hers, at how strong and capable that hand was.

"We have fifteen years to catch up on," he said. "That's going to take longer than a trip to Naples and back."

She opened her mouth to argue, to turn him down, to put up the wall she had first erected on that horrible night in his loft and promised herself she'd never, ever tear down.

But nothing came out.

And then she nodded.

"Is that a yes?" he asked, his eyes dark blue with hope.

Another nod, still not completely sure what she'd say if she opened her mouth.

"I just want you to forgive me," he said.

For a second, she wasn't sure she understood. "Forgive you?"

"For never calling, for never finding you, for never making sure fifteen years didn't pass without...us..."

His voice trailed off but it didn't matter; her pulse was thumping so loud she could hardly hear him.

"Will," she whispered, "I'm the one who made sure all that time passed. I wouldn't have returned your call and I figured...this was better."

"Better?" He gripped her hand, picking it up, bringing it to his lips and holding her gaze. "Better for who?"

"For you."

He closed his eyes and kissed her fingertips. "It wasn't better for me."

Her heart folded in half, smashed by regret and, damn, hope. Maybe an afternoon with him would squash that for good.

Or maybe it would make her hope for more. There was only one way to find out.

Chapter 10

‿‿

Why did that dang thread always get stuck on the up-loop? Guy pushed his glasses up his nose and angled the hooped plastic mesh toward the window to get a good look. Not that the artwork could look *good*. No, this was one messy piece of needlepoint.

Maybe William would show him that little movie on the computer again with the lady who explained this needling to children. That had really helped.

With a sigh he studied the whole project again, letting his eyes unfocus so he could appreciate the shape and colors of the flowers and not the bumps and lumps of his mistakes. He'd gotten half a petal done since yesterday and then he'd lost interest. Why couldn't he stay with one thing long enough to finish it?

Same thing with his memory. Stuff disappeared as quickly as it showed up, always with those flashing lights like on a Christmas tree, teasing him in color so bright and bold then fading to black and white, before they disappeared altogether into gray nothingness.

But ever since that girl landed on his front porch, a few lights were coming on. And staying on. Threads of memories wrapped around his broken brain like it was this plastic embroidery net, then the colors almost caught, and, boom, they were knotted in shadows again.

Still, when he looked at her something deep in his gut stirred.

He knew her. And not just from the TV.

That was the thought that kept getting tangled just like this silky orange yarn.

He *knew* her. Was that possible? He had carefully lined up the needle and was ready to push it through the hole when the doorbell startled him and the needle jumped out of the spot.

"Son of a gun!" No Girl Scouts sold cookies at this time of day, so he hoped it wasn't some salesperson, 'cause he wasn't buying. He had enough junk in this place.

He pushed up, setting down the whole frame and embroidery panel on his chair, then rounded the decorative brick divider to get to the front door. Standing on his tiptoes, he squinted at two men, not recognizing either of them.

"Yeah, what is it?" he called.

"Mr. Bloom? Mr. Guy Bloom? Former deputy sheriff of Mimosa Key?" He was the former sheriff, he knew that for a fact. Didn't remember a blasted thing about it, but William had told him, so it must be true.

"What can I do for you?" he asked. Wait a second! Could these be people from the show? Where was Missy?

Shouldn't she be here? Dang, she might get in trouble for showing up so late, and he didn't want that to happen. "You with the TV show?" he asked.

He saw them look at each other, one with kind of thinning hair holding something black in his hand, the other with those horn-rimmed glasses and hair that women used to call "frosted." Which looked kind of ridiculous on a man, if you asked him.

"Yes, and the Web site."

Did *Clean House* have a Web site? *Of course, you old coot.* Everybody and his cousin was on the stinkin' computer.

"Can we talk to you a minute, Mr. Bloom?"

"About the show?"

After a beat, the man said. "About Jocelyn."

That was her name, even though Guy could never remember it. He'd heard William call her "Joss." But he didn't know where she was, and what if they came in here and didn't like him as much as she did? What if they looked around and didn't see the potential or had someone with a messier house and kids? They loved kids on that show.

The only thing he could do was play dumb. A little smile lifted his lips. Like *playing dumb* would be any challenge.

"I don't know anyone named Jocelyn," he said, his hand on the dead bolt, holding it firmly in the lock position. "Sorry."

"Your daughter, Jocelyn," he said.

Something stabbed his heart, not too hard, not as sharp as that embroidery needle he'd just been holding, but he felt the jab just the same.

"I don't have a daughter. I have a son."

He lifted up on his toes to catch the two men giving each other confused looks.

"You aren't Guy Bloom, father of Jocelyn Bloom? The sheriff said you lived here."

Wait a second, he *was* the sheriff. Well, not anymore.

A thin trickle of sweat, surprisingly cold, meandered under his collar, finding its way down his back.

"You got the wrong man. My son is named William and he's not here. I don't have a daughter."

"Are you sure?" Frosty asked.

"What kind of a question is that?" he fired back even though, heck, it was a darn good question. He wasn't sure what day it was, what street he lived on, or who was the president of the United States. But he kept that mostly to himself, so he didn't wind up in some nuthouse somewhere.

"Are you positive you don't have a daughter?" the man demanded, his tone making it clear he didn't believe Guy.

"I do not have a daughter," Guy confirmed. Suddenly the mail slot opened and a little white card tumbled in.

"That's my number, Mr. Bloom. If you change your mind, I can make it worth your while to talk. Extremely worth your while." He waited a moment, then added, "Like fifty thousand dollars worth your while."

Fifty thousand dollars! Is that how the show worked? "For remodeling?" he asked, imagining just how much money they spent on all that paint and furniture and the pretty blonde girl who reorganized all the shelves and closets.

"You can use it for whatever you want if you give us access to or information about Jocelyn."

"Why do you want it?"

"No one can find her, sir. And a lot of people want to talk to your daughter."

"I don't have..." He picked up the card. *Robert Picalo, TMZ*. Shaking his head, he slipped the card into one of the open spaces between the bricks, where he used to keep his keys when he could drive.

What a funny thing to remember. For a moment he put his hand on the cool bricks, remembering his keys so distinctly it shocked him. And...a woman. The color in his head was soft and peachy, light and—

"Call me if you change your mind, Mr. Bloom."

Who was he talking to?

He turned and looked out the little window again at two men. Who were they? Before he could ask, the men headed down the walk, talking and looking around.

Oh, that's right, he remembered with relief. They're with *Clean House*. He grabbed the memory and squeezed so it wouldn't go away, just as the bald guy picked up the black thing he was holding—was that a camera?

Oh, now they're taking pictures of the place! Video pictures.

"It's gonna be fine," he said to himself, turning around when they got in a van parked on the street. "Missy'll know what to do.

Are you positive you don't have a daughter?

The words echoed in his head, making him unsure whether he'd just heard them or made them up.

Maybe he did have a daughter.

On an instinct that he didn't understand, he ambled down the hall to his bedroom and, in just that space and time, those dang Christmas lights flashed again, burst of yellow. Orange. Red. Green.

Gone.

He shook his head, standing in the bedroom. What had he come in here for?

Pressing his fingers to his temples with a low growl of frustration, he tried to push the thoughts from the outskirts into the middle of his brain, imagining those little lines and valleys opening to tell him what the hell he had come into this room to get.

"God damn it!" He punched the doorjamb.

He couldn't remember. Couldn't remember what he was doing, watching, thinking. Everything was shrouded in fog.

Frustration popping in every vein, he opened the closet door, hoping to remember. A sweater? Shoes? Something to eat?

No, no, not here.

And then he remembered the box.

In the closet, he pushed the clothes to the side, determined to find his secret box. William didn't know about this box. The pretty TV girl didn't know about the box. No one knew about the box he kept inside the safe at the back of his closet. The "safe" was really a door built into the wall, painted over, and almost impossible to see. Good thing, because if it were a real safe, he sure as hell wouldn't be able to remember the combination. But in that hole in the wall was the big pink box.

The top was curved and had an embroidered rose glued to it. On the front, a key with a ragged silver tassel rested in the lock, but the lock didn't work anymore. He lifted the lid and peered inside.

Two rings. One tarnished necklace. He lifted out the top section and found what he wanted underneath. The picture. Of a man and a girl, sitting in a rowboat.

The girl was maybe six or seven? He didn't know. But she was deep inside a shiny silver boat not much wider than a canoe, oars in her hands, long dark hair blowing in the wind as she looked at the camera and smiled, front teeth missing. A man sat behind her, grinning from ear to ear.

There was a wisp of a memory. The girl's laughter, her head turning around, a word on her lips.

Daddy.

For a long time he just stared at the girl, and something inside him broke off in little pieces.

Daddy. *Daddy.*

"Guy? Are you here?"

William! He snapped the box closed, shoved it into its hiding place, and pushed himself up, shaking like a kid who'd been caught smoking in the boys' room.

"Guy? Where are you?"

Missy was there, too! A smile shot through him as he pushed his way out of the closet. Wait till she saw how far he got on those flowers.

"I'm back here in my room, you two."

You two. They made a heck of a nice couple, didn't they?

"Oh, I'm so glad." She came in, her long hair pulled back in a ponytail. Lord, the girl was a feast for the eyes, even ones as bad as his.

"We just came to check on you," she said.

"I'm fine. Could use a little lunch, though."

"I'll make him a sandwich, Will. You talk to him."

As she headed back down the hall, William came into the room, putting one of his big hands on Guy's shoulder in that way that made Guy feel so safe. There was just no one like his William.

"You okay, Guy?"

"Fine, fine, yeah. Why?"

Will looked at him funny. "You looked flushed."

"Me?" He touched his cheek. "I was just, you know, thinking about things."

Will guided him to sit on the bed, always so gentle for a big kid. Always so kind. "God, I love you, William."

He smiled. "I know, buddy. Listen, I want to talk to you about not letting—"

"What is this?" Missy stood in the doorway, eyes wide, face pale, a little white card in her hand. "They were *here*?"

She held out the card and William took it, looking just as stunned. "Did you talk to this man, Guy?" he asked.

Did he?

"What man?"

"Oh, God." Missy put both hands to her mouth, a look of panic making her big brown eyes look like giant saucers. "Please tell me you didn't tell them I'm here."

A flash of light popped in his head and he grabbed that thought, standing up, determined to hold on before the clouds came back. "I told them I didn't know who they were talking about."

"You did?" she asked. "You're sure?"

Was he? Son of a gun, he wasn't sure about anything. "I didn't let them in, I swear."

"It's okay, Guy." William eased him back to the bed. "You didn't do anything wrong."

But the girl looked horror-stricken. "You better stay here, Will. I'm going to—"

"Not alone, you're not."

"But you have to stay with him."

A little anger boiled through Guy, firing some synapses that were mostly dead. "Stop talking about me like I'm not here!" he boomed, pretty loud, because Missy gasped again and took a quick step backwards.

Then her face kind of froze. "I'm going, Will." She turned like a soldier and marched down the hall.

Oh, no! He'd made her mad! "Missy!" he called, jumping up to follow her, a wave of remorse strangling him. "No, don't get mad! I'm so sorry. I'm sorry!" He choked on the last words, hating that he was about to cry, turning to William for help.

"Just stay here, Guy. Let me handle this, please." Will gave him a quick squeeze on the shoulders. "Just wait here and let me talk to her. Please."

"She's upset, William. I hurt her feelings. I yelled at her." A light flashed in his head again, a pale baby blue this time. A familiar color that reminded him of sadness. "Talk to her, William. Don't let her leave. I like her. I like her so much."

William gave him a tight smile, nodding. "So do I, buddy. Just trust me on this."

Alone, Guy counted to ten. Again. And again, and so many times he had to have made a hundred. Then he stood and slowly walked down the hall, where he could hear them whispering in the kitchen.

Oh, he didn't want to hear what she was saying. He could just imagine her words: *I hate him. I have to leave. I can't stay with him.*

Where had he heard that before? He squeezed his temples, hard enough to make his head ache.

But when he walked into the kitchen William was standing next to her, his hand on her shoulder, and she held a phone to her ear.

"Is she calling someone from her show?" Guy asked.

William held up one finger, signaling for him to be quiet and wait.

"Zoe?" she said. "I need you to do me a huge favor, hon. I mean, major *huge*. Can you come over to my father's house and, um, hang out with him for a while?" Babysit, was what she meant, but Guy knew better than to argue.

After a pause, she nodded. "I knew I could count on you."

William breathed a sigh of relief and, back in the recesses of Guy's brain, the blue light faded, replaced by a familiar fog.

Chapter 11

Déjà vu teased Jocelyn as Will's truck rumbled up to the causeway. She closed her eyes, giving in to the peculiar sensation of knowing this wasn't the first time all these same internal chemicals and external forces synergized into this distinct moment.

"You okay?" Will asked, reaching over the console to put his hand over hers, his fingertips brushing her thigh.

She didn't yank her hand out from under his, but she didn't turn her palm to hold his hand, either. Even though she wanted to, just for the sheer pleasure and comfort of holding Will's hand, his blunt, clean fingertips still one of her favorite things to grasp.

That was part of her déjà vu, too. A big part. After the fear and anger, there was always Will. She looked down at his fingers, the massive width and length of them, the dusting of dark hair, the power of his wrist. Will had gorgeous, masculine hands. And huge. He used to say he didn't need a catcher's mitt.

"Joss?"

"I was just thinking I've done this before."

"Ridden over the causeway?"

Yes, with a desperate determination to escape the thunderous voice and threat of violence ringing in her ears. "Run away from him, wishing I could do something to change...him."

"Nature did that for you."

She shot him a look. "The old Guy is there, Will, right under the surface. You saw how he yelled at me."

"For one little second, Joss."

She snapped her hand away. "Don't defend him. I can take anything but that."

He left his hand on her leg. "This really could have waited a day or two," he said. "I feel like we should have stayed with him instead of calling Zoe."

"You could have."

"As if I'd let you come over here alone. I just don't know why we couldn't wait a few days."

"First of all, procrastination is for losers." She could have sworn she saw him cringe ever so slightly, but she was too focused on making her many points. "Second, the media is going to find me. It's only a matter of time un—"

"No, no. That's not true. We'll talk to Slade Garrison—he's got a good crew of deputies—and set him straight. He needs to know you're in town so he can divert any reporters that try to find you. And he can put an unmarked car or two at Guy's house and you'll be completely safe at Casa Blanca."

She didn't say anything, turning to look out at the

water instead. Sun danced off the waves and a giant cabin cruiser cut under the bridge, leaving a bright-white wake. Bet it was nice on that boat, lost in the air and salt water. Away from it all. Alone.

Or maybe with Will.

"Can I ask you a question, Joss?"

"Mmmm." The answer was noncommittal, but she knew him well enough to know he'd ask anyway.

"You didn't have an affair with that guy, did you?"

Oh. She hadn't been expecting that question—although it was natural and normal and should had been expected. Deep inside, she wanted Will to know she hadn't. She didn't answer.

"I wish you'd say no," he said softly. "Real fast and vehement, too."

"I did not have any kind of relationship with Miles Thayer. But any aspect of my client relationship with Coco is confidential, and I won't talk about it."

He choked softly. "She doesn't give a shit about protecting your reputation. Why should you care about hers?"

She turned to him, a question of her own burning. "Did you think it was true?"

He hesitated long enough for her to know the answer. Damn it. Maybe she hadn't thought this through enough. She'd sacrificed so much for Coco.

"I hadn't seen you for more than fifteen seconds in fifteen years," he finally said. "I didn't know what to believe."

That was fair, she guessed. "Do you believe it now?"

"Not if you tell me it's a lie. I believe you. And honestly..." He captured her hand again, this time holding so tight she couldn't let go. "You don't like overrated skinny blond guys who can't act their way out of a paper bag."

She laughed softly. "True."

"And nobody can change that much. You wouldn't sleep with a married guy."

"No, I would not, so thanks for that vote of confidence. I wish my clients felt the same way." Since she'd lost two more that morning.

"They probably do, but Coco is the one they have to side with because she's more powerful in the industry."

She sighed. Of course Will got it; he always *got* it. "Yep."

He turned his hand and threaded their fingers. "I still don't see what it would hurt to at least make a statement."

"It would hurt her," she said simply.

"That's what's stopping you? Did you sign some kind of confidentiality agreement?" He turned as he reached a light on the mainland, his eyes flashing blue. "Because a good lawyer could—"

"No, Will, stop. Respect and professional ethics are stopping me. You need to go right at the next light, I think."

"I know how to get there."

"You've been to Autumn House?"

"I looked into a couple of places when I first got here."

For some reason, that shocked her. Why hadn't he told her that? "And?"

"Besides being crazy-ass expensive, they didn't seem that great to me."

"You've visited this place already?"

He shook his head. "Not this one, but others. I did call here, but reconsidered."

"I can afford it," she said quietly.

"Even if your business is in trouble?"

There was that. "I've saved a lot of money."

"What about new business?"

She shrugged. "I'll get it."

"Could be challenging in L.A. after all this."

"I've faced bigger challenges."

He smiled, shaking his head a little.

"What? I have."

"I know you have. But do you have to be so damn tough about everything? It's like you have a hard shell around you."

She did. "I've had that for so long I can't imagine what it's like not to have that kind of protection. I've had it for ... since ... a long time."

He closed his eyes as if she'd punched him. She leaned forward to grab her bag so she didn't have to look at him or feel his referred pain. Pulling out the address, she tried to read, but the words danced in front of her eyes.

"It's not too far," she said, forcing herself to read and think about where they were and where they were going. Literally, on this street—not emotionally, in her head.

"Jocelyn."

She ignored the tenderness in his voice, the warmth of that big hand, the comfort it always gave her. "Two more lights," she said, her voice tight.

"I know."

She cleared her throat as if that could just wipe clean the conversation about protection and hurt and shells she stayed inside of. "So why didn't you look at this place again?" she asked, grasping at small-talk straws.

"I decided he needed to be home."

The words jolted her. The caring. The concern for a person who had threatened to ruin his life or end it.

"I can see you don't like that."

"Am I supposed to, Will?"

He blew out a breath, letting go of her hand to turn the wheel. "I know he's your dad, not mine, and you resent that I take care of him."

Was that what he thought bothered her? That *he* took care of *her* father? He didn't even remember what took them apart. What had left *a hard shell around her*?

She had to remember that he didn't know everything.

"I just couldn't sit at my house and ignore the fact that he needed help," he said.

Well, they had that in common. Wasn't that the reason she was in this situation in the first place, with Coco? "You should have just picked up the phone and called me. I'd have taken care of the situation."

"Well, I didn't."

"Why not?"

He threw her a look. "Maybe because I felt like I owed you something."

Her? What could he owe her? "Me? Why?"

"Because if it weren't for me, that…night would have never happened. You wouldn't have left or you would have come home." He swallowed, his voice thick with regret and remorse. "I blame myself for what happened that night."

"You shouldn't," she said simply. "You should put the blame where it belongs."

"On you?" He sounded incredulous.

"No, Will. On Guy Bloom." She pointed to a large white stucco building set back on a lawn, a simple sign at the parking lot's edge. "We're here."

When he pulled into the lot and parked, she started to open the door, but he took her hand and pulled her closer.

"What's it going to take?" he asked.

The question and the intense look in his eyes stunned her. "To decide he shouldn't go into a home?"

"No." He reached over and grazed her jaw with his knuckles, his touch fiery and unexpected and chill inducing. "To break that shell?"

"I'm sorry, Will. It's unbreakable."

But he just leaned in and breathed his last few words, the closest thing to a kiss without actually touching. "There's no such thing."

"Doesn't your husband want to come in, too?"

Outside the director's office door, Will turned to catch Jocelyn's slightly surprised look and the color that rose to her cheeks. It was a natural assumption on the woman's part. They'd never said they weren't married during the tour, just that they were there for Jocelyn's father.

"I'll wait out here while you talk," he said, gesturing toward the lobby.

Jocelyn's dark eyes searched his, but then she nodded and stepped into the office of the admissions director. Admissions. Like it was a freaking college instead of an old folks' home with the patently ridiculous name of Autumn House.

Should be *Dead of Winter End of Days House*.

Will had seen enough of their rainbows and happy-face bullshit in the past twenty minutes of walking through the special areas where visitors could go. Nothing he wanted to know would be visible during that surface skim. And the truth wasn't going to come out behind that director's door when Jocelyn asked ask more hollow questions like "How often are they fed?"

For Christ's sake. This wasn't a kennel.

Or was it?

But he had swallowed all those comments while Bernadette Bowers, director of admissions and patient relations, spewed the party line.

A year ago he'd visited two similar facilities. Neither one had been as upscale as this place, he had to admit as he cruised through the softly lit lobby of the main house and nodded to the receptionist hidden behind a plastic palm tree. But they were the same beasts: God's waiting room. With fake plants.

Maybe this wasn't the kind of place where they let someone hang in a wheelchair for eight hours, forgotten. Maybe this wasn't where an old man could rot in bed, forgotten. Maybe this wasn't a place where someone with virtually no training but a good heart forgot some meds and the results were dire. He got the feeling that Autumn House was better than most of these homes.

But it wasn't Guy's *home*.

He pushed open the front door and stepped out to the patio, scanning the manicured grounds, the perfectly placed hibiscus trees, the carefully situated tables and chairs.

All empty.

Okay, maybe it was too hot for old folks to come outside. Or maybe no one took them. Or maybe they were short-staffed.

The door opened behind him, and he turned, expecting Jocelyn, but another woman came out, fifty-ish, mouth drawn in sadness, eyes damp.

" 'Scuse me," she mumbled, passing him.

"Can I ask you a question?" The request was out before he gave himself time to think about it and change his mind. But wasn't part of the "tour" talking to the customers?

The woman hesitated, inching back a bit. "Yes?"

"Do you have a…" He almost said "loved one," but corrected himself. "A relative living here?"

She nodded, absently dabbing an eye and biting her lip.

"How is it?" he asked. "We're considering this for my…we're looking at the facility."

She didn't answer right away, clearly choosing her words and wrestling with her emotions. "It's expensive, but one of the better facilities."

"How's the care?"

She shrugged. "You know."

No, he didn't. "Doctors?"

After a second, she let out a breath. "Some are better than others."

"Staff?"

"Good, but no place is perfect." She tried to sound upbeat, but he could read between the lines, especially the two drawn deep in her forehead.

"Would you make the same decision again?" he asked her, knowing he'd way overstepped the boundaries of two strangers sharing a casual conversation.

"I really had no choice," she said. "My mother's not able to be at home."

He nodded, understanding.

"If she was or if I could be with her twenty-four-seven, of course that's what I'd do. But you have to be realistic. You have to compromise." She tilted her head and gave a smile. "Your parent?"

"No, my friend." He wasn't exactly sure when Guy Bloom had become his friend, but he had. And the word felt right on his lips.

Just then, the door opened and Jocelyn stepped into the

sunshine, looking cool and crisp and not nearly as defeated as the sallow-skinned woman he'd been talking to.

"We're all set," she said quietly.

"You *enrolled* him?" He couldn't think of a better word, not when a flash of white hot anger burst behind his eyes.

"Not yet. Of course I have to see another place or two, but, overall, I'm quite satisfied."

With what? The chilly cafeteria? The dreary halls? The single room for a man who was used to living in an entire house?

Jocelyn glanced at the other woman and gave her a quick smile, not warm enough to invite conversation.

"Listen," the lady said, turning to Will, keeping that tenuous connection they'd somehow found in a moment's time. "I don't know your situation, but if you have any option at all for home care, any possible way to keep from taking this step, do it."

Jocelyn stepped forward, her back ramrod straight. "You're right."

Hope danced in him.

"You *don't* know our situation," Jocelyn said. "But thank you for the advice. Let's go, Will."

He stood stone still as she walked by and headed toward the parking lot.

"Thank you," he said softly to the woman. "Good luck."

Jocelyn was almost to his truck by the time he caught up with her.

"Don't reprimand me for being a bitch to her," she said as he reached for her door. "This isn't your decision to make."

"You weren't a bitch," he replied. "It's a tense situation." And, damn it, she was right, it wasn't his decision. But that didn't stop him from caring about the outcome.

She climbed into the truck and yanked her seat belt. "Yes, it is tense. Were you talking to her?"

"Briefly." He closed the door and started around the back of the truck.

"Wait, sir. Wait!" The woman from the porch was jogging toward him, a hand outstretched. "I just want to tell you one thing."

Jocelyn stayed in the car, but he knew she was watching in her side-view mirror, possibly hearing the conversation even though her door was closed.

"What's that?"

The woman put a hand on his arm, her fingers covered with veins and age spots, making him revise his age estimate. "They're fine with the new ones. The ones that haven't gone too far... away. But the really bad ones?" She shook her head, eyes welling. "They are lost and forgotten."

Forgotten. Exactly as he suspected. He patted her hand. "Your mother's not forgotten. She has you."

She smiled and stepped away.

He waited for a minute, then climbed behind the wheel of the truck. He shot Jocelyn a glance, his mind whirring through his options. Her father was her responsibility, that was true. He couldn't demand that she change her mind about this, but maybe he could get her to think a little more about it.

"Hungry?" he asked.

"Not in the least."

Damn. " 'Cause we're not that far from Kaplan's."

Her eyes widened and she smiled. "Oh my God, those Reubens."

It wouldn't be their first trip down to Marco Island; they'd gone often after baseball games when he'd be plagued with late-night teenage boy starvation and she just wanted to get out. Especially that last summer, they'd probably driven down to the deli near the marina a dozen times.

"With extra Thousand Island and no ketchup on the fries," he said, smiling. "The lady does not like wet fries."

"Aww, you remember that."

He remembered so much more than that it wasn't funny. "So, yes?"

She considered it for a minute, then nodded. "But I have to wear this hat." She reached into her bag for the baseball cap she'd brought. "I don't want anyone to recognize me."

"They won't recognize you."

"Don't be so sure," she said, tugging the cap on.

He pulled the brim a little. "I hardly recognize you, Joss."

She paused, looking up at him, her eyes so brown and soulful it damn near cut him in half. "What's that supposed to mean?"

"You've changed, is all."

"So have you," she shot back.

"True." He shrugged. "I've been through a lot."

"Why don't you tell me everything over Reubens?"

"Everything?"

"Everything."

That wasn't why he wanted to go to Kaplan's. He wanted to talk her out of rash decisions, but instead he made one himself. " 'Kay."

Chapter 12

⌒

The closer they got to Kaplan's, the more Jocelyn felt her mood improve. Maybe she was hungry, after all. Or maybe she felt relaxed for the first time since they'd left Mimosa Key, on a familiar road that reminded her of late nights and long talks and a wonderful boy she once loved.

She slid a sideways glance at him, her gaze lingering on his shoulders, which were even broader than they'd been back then. In fact, everything about Will was stronger now. His profile, his muscles, his personality. He still had a heart as big as his hands, but he moved like a man in complete control.

And, damn, she liked watching him. He took her breath away when he smiled, something he'd done more and more on the short ride to Kaplan's down the beach road.

"Place has changed a lot, don't you think?" he asked,

indicating the behemoth skyscraper condos that now entirely blocked the view of the water.

"Exactly what they're trying to avoid on Mimosa Key."

"We *are* avoiding it," he said. "Clay's architecture is the polar opposite of this heinous-looking stuff. Casa Blanca is going to be one in a million."

She heard the pride in his voice. "You love working there." It was a statement, not a question, and filled with a little wonder when she realized how true it was.

"I like it," he admitted. "Way more than I thought I would. It's amazing to be part of something like that from the ground up." He angled his head toward her. "You know, you're an investor."

"I am, which is why I'm surprised Lacey never mentioned you were working there."

"Did you ask?"

Honestly, no. "I had no idea you were a permanent resident of Mimosa Key. When I saw you last year at that town meeting, I figured you were there on behalf of your parents or something."

He sighed. "Or something."

"What does that mean?"

"I never planned to stay this long," he admitted, pulling into the strip center. They were long enough past the lunch crowd to get a space close to the deli. "Let's go in. I'll tell you about it inside."

She kept her hat pulled low and sunglasses on, but she shouldn't have worried. The waitress who greeted them and walked them to a booth by the front window never even noticed her. She only had eyes for Will.

He put a hand on Jocelyn's back to guide her, staying close until she slid into the booth, and then he sat across from her, taking the menus and ordering iced tea for both of them.

After a minute, feeling more ridiculous than disguised, she took off the sunglasses and glanced around to see what had changed in fifteen years. Not much, but Will leveled his eyes directly at her. The power of his stare warmed every corner of her body.

"Does it look different?" he asked.

She met his gaze, grabbed for a moment by the deep blue of his eyes. She'd never gotten used to how unexpectedly blue they were against his sun-burnished skin. "The kid across from me does."

His lips curved in that slow, sweet, soul-melting smile that used to take her from heartache to happy in ten seconds. "He's not a kid anymore."

"I noticed."

He lifted a brow, silently asking for more.

"You have a couple of crow's-feet."

He squinted, exaggerating the crinkles at the sides of his eyes. "What else?"

She didn't answer right away, loving the excuse to examine every inch of his face, and the little roller-coaster ride her insides took as she and Will focused on nothing but each other.

"You let your hair grow out longer."

"No annoying coach insisting on a trim."

"And that's what's most different of all," she said, leaning back as the waitress delivered two iced teas. When she left, Jocelyn finished the thought. "You don't play baseball."

He touched his stomach and feigned hurt. "You think I'm getting soft?"

Hardly. "I've never known you not to be on your way to a game, coming from a game, talking about the game, pissed off 'cause you lost a game, or whistling 'We Are the Champions' because you kicked the holy hell out of the Collier High Blue Devils."

She thought he'd grin because she'd remembered the rival high mascot, but he just looked down at the tea, turning the glass and revolving the paper napkin with it.

"My career is . . . on hold." He snorted softly and added, "He said optimistically."

She just waited, knowing Will well enough to expect more. But he picked up his tea and took a long drink. She watched his eyes shutter closed and his throat rise and fall with each gulp.

Then he thunked the glass on the table and exhaled softly. "Speaking of baseball, we should get you a Marlins hat instead of that designer thing."

"Speaking of putting walls and shells around yourself, you should tell me what the heck is going on with your career."

A smile teased. "Good comeback, Jossie. Lose the hat and I will."

"Why?"

He reached over and tapped at the brim, pulling it off and making her hair fall around her shoulders when the strands slipped through the hole in the back. "Because I like your hair and I can't see your pretty face when you have that thing on."

"That's the idea," she said, cutting a glance toward the empty booth across from them.

He lifted the hat and looked inside at the stitching. "Dolce and Gabbana? What the hell is that?"

"Expensive. Why are you being optimistic when you say your career is on hold?"

"Because, my friend who buys expensive hats..." He twirled the red-and-blue cap on his finger, a cocky move that belied the thick emotion in his voice. "Will Palmer, number thirty-one, holder of a few obscure and meaningless winning stats in the annals of minor league baseball, is finished playing."

He tried the hat on and, of course, it barely covered the top of his head.

"Finished forever?" she asked.

Setting the cap on the table, he avoided her eyes. "Unless I can score a coaching job and, man, they are hard to come by in the majors or minors. My agent's looking, and I'm trying to remain hopeful."

"You don't think you'll get a coaching job?"

"I don't know," he said honestly. "Every day the hope thread gets a little more frayed."

"What about carpentry? Do you like what you're doing? I mean you're so good at it."

"You know, I do like it, but it's so..." He shook his head as if what he was about to say amazed him. "Meaningless?"

The use of a question surprised her. "Building resorts and jaw-droppingly beautiful villas that will bring hours of pleasure to the guests and mountains of money to the owners? What's meaningless about that?"

He laughed softly. "Touché, life coach."

"You always loved to work with your dad. I remember when he built the shrine—er, the addition."

He grinned. "It remains a shrine since I've moved into the master."

She tried not to think about the room and all the memories wrapped up in that loft. "So you don't...use it?"

"Just to work out."

"Is it weird, sleeping in your parents' old room?"

"I redid the whole thing, knocked down a wall, built out the closet, remodeled the bath. The whole house is practically new. The place is way more ready to sell this way."

"But you haven't put it on the market yet."

He shrugged. "I'm...waiting."

"For what?"

Before he answered, the waitress stepped up to the booth, blinded him with a smile, and asked for their order.

"Two Reubens with fries." He closed his menu and handed them both to her but winked at Jocelyn. "Hold the ketchup on the the lady's order."

She smiled, the memory of the time he'd accidentally put ketchup on her fries during the midnight meal they'd shared still vividly clear. They'd fought and laughed and felt so damn comfortable.

That was just a month or so before—

She snapped her napkin on her lap and straightened the silverware until they were alone again.

"So why haven't you sold their house? What are you waiting for?" she asked, grabbing at the conversation before he could read her expression. He'd been so good at that.

"Well, a coaching job, obviously. That's the next natural step in my career."

"And if that doesn't materialize?"

He leaned all the way back, hooking his arms behind his head, a move that emphasized the biceps she was trying so hard not to stare at. "Guess I'll have to figure out what I want to do with my life."

"Better get on that, Will. You're thirty-four."

"Yep. Know any good life coaches who can help me?"

She grinned. "I sure do, but she's expensive."

"Of course she is." Relaxing, he picked up the hat and popped it up, landing it perfectly on the sugar carousel. "Not cheap to buy Something-and-Cabana hats."

She automatically righted the hat and neatly piled the Splenda packets back in order. "She has been known to work for a discount if she really likes you."

"Do you really like me, Joss?"

She tapped the sugar into place, then restraightened the whole pile. Her heart slipped around in her chest a little, the feeling so intense and sweet it almost took her breath away.

"I've always liked you, Will," she said carefully, searching for a way to keep this light. "And that means you may have the special-friend discount."

"Which is?"

"My services for only a Reuben and fries. Buy lunch and we'll fix up your life."

"If only it were that easy." His voice had a surprising sadness to it that pulled at her.

"Is it that bad?"

"Let's see, I'm not on the run from the *National Enquirer*, wrongly accused of adultery, and being forced to play *Clean House*, so I guess it could be worse."

She had to laugh. "All right, let's start coaching."

"Right now?"

"I loathe procrastination. You want life coaching, let's go. What are you prepared to die for?"

He just stared at her. Blinked, then frowned. "What did you say?"

"What are you prepared to die for? That's the first question I ask in the initial interview," she explained. "I have to know what's the most important thing to a client, and then we take it from there in bite-size pieces."

"Do you know what *you're* prepared to die for?" he asked.

"This is not my interview."

He took another sip of tea, definitely a delay tactic. "It's a stupid trick question," he finally said after he swallowed. "The answer's the same for everyone. Love, family, friendship, truth, honor, justice, and a grand slam in the World Series." He paused, then grinned. "Okay, that might not be on your list."

"None of those things are on my list, Will." Not a single one.

He looked stunned, enough that she was a little embarrassed.

"Well, I might die for one of my friends, if I had to, but I don't really have a family, and I can't honestly say I'd die for honor or justice, though I value it, and I doubt I'll ever go to a World Series."

"You skipped the first one."

Love. She'd skipped it on purpose. Still she frowned, as if she couldn't remember the first thing on his list of things to die for.

"Love," he reminded her.

"Oh, so I did," she said. "Well, I've never..." Oh, yes she had. "I haven't been married, but you have." Thank God for that question-flip technique she'd learned in training. "Why don't you tell me about her?"

"Does my marriage and divorce have to be part of the life-coaching interview?"

"Understanding your marriage might help us get a better picture of your…" *Heart.* "Problems."

"Then my problems would be blonde, crazy, insecure, and camera-happy." He angled his head and looked a little puzzled. "And that's kind of interesting, isn't it?"

That his wife was blonde, crazy, insecure, and camera-happy? Zoe would eat that gossip with a spoon. "How so?"

"That my ex was everything you're not."

His ex had a name. Nina Martinez. And she might have been blonde and crazy, but she was also drop-dead gorgeous. "See?" she said with false brightness. "A breakthrough already. Life coaching works."

The waitress sidled up to the table with steaming platters, the delectable smoky tang of corned beef wafting along with her. As the woman set Jocelyn's plate down, she glanced at her. And then did a double take.

Instantly, Jocelyn cast down her eyes, staring at the plate, but the grill marks on the sandwich swam in front of her eyes. Shit. *Shit.*

"Do I know you?" the waitress asked, forcing Jocelyn to look up and meet an unrelenting frown, the face of a woman digging through recent memory and about to come up with celebrity gossip.

"We used to be regulars here," Will said quickly. "And that's all we need, thanks."

"Ohhh." She drew out the word and looked from one to the other, but settled her attention on Jocelyn. "Well, I just started here, so, that's not it."

"Thank you." Jocelyn said sharply, picking up her fork

and knife despite the fact that she wouldn't use either one on this meal.

The waitress got the message and left.

"Eesh," Jocelyn said on a sigh. "How long will I have to hide like this?"

"Until you tell the truth."

Which would be never. "You don't understand."

"I understand you're protecting a person who has no compunction about throwing you under a bus."

She set the silverware back down, lining it up perfectly, gathering a lot of possible responses and discarding most. "We all do what we feel is right regardless of what other people think."

"More life-coach bullshit," he said, picking up his sandwich and making it look petite in his giant hands.

"Is it?" she fired back. "I'm doing what I feel is right even though you don't agree with it just like you're doing what you think is right with my father even though I don't agree with it. How are the two things so different?"

He just shook his head and took a bite. After he swallowed, he said, "There was one other thing about my ex-wife that's different from you."

Jealousy made a quick sting at her heart. "What's that?"

"She'd have never let the issue of another woman drop. Don't you want to know more about my marriage?"

She knew enough, actually. "Of course. How did you meet? How long were you married? Why did it end?"

He looked up just before taking his next bite. "Not 'Was she pretty'? That's what most girls want to know."

Except this girl already knew his wife was on the

cover of *Fitness* magazine once. "Last I looked, I was a woman, not a girl."

"Sorry." He looked at her and smiled, slow and bad and good all at the same time. The kind of smile that made Jocelyn's whole insides rise and flutter and sigh. "You are a woman. A beautiful one."

And flutter again.

She picked up a fry and nibbled the end. "We were talking about your wife."

"Ex."

"Semantics."

"Incredibly important semantics." He took a slow, careful bite, wiping his mouth with a napkin, drawing out the silence for a few seconds. "Well, let's see. We met at the baseball field, we were married for three seasons, and it ended when it became painfully clear I wasn't headed to the majors or a career in any kind of limelight, which was all that mattered to her."

She smiled. "Most people count their anniversaries in years, not seasons."

"She was my manager's niece," he said with a shrug, searching out his own fry. "It was definitely a baseball-centric marriage."

"She was Latina, right?"

He whipped his head up at the question. "How do you know that?"

Damn it *all*. Why had she revealed that? "I saw something in the paper."

"In Los Angeles?" Obviously, he didn't believe her. "Sorry, but I didn't make any papers outside of Florida." He pointed a ketchupy fry at her, unable to hid the happiness that had just hit him. "You Googled me."

She felt her cheeks warm, ate instead of answering.

But he laughed, a satisfied, bone-deep laugh. "You did. When? Recently? Yesterday? After you saw me last year?"

"A couple of years ago. And, really, this is supposed to be *your* life-coaching session, not mine."

"Why?"

"Because you don't know what you want to be when you grow up and I do."

"I meant why did you Google me?"

She blinked, hovering between the truth and a lie. She slid in between. "I was curious how you'd been."

He nodded slowly, searching her face. "Never thought about calling, though, did you? Or an e-mail?"

She shook her head just as the waitress walked by again, slowly, looking at Jocelyn, who lowered her head and let her hair cover her cheek. "I think I've been busted."

"I'll say. Who knew you'd Google me?"

"I meant by the waitress, Will."

He nodded. "I know." She turned toward the wall as Will gave the woman a sharp look and she scooted away. He reached over the table and put his hand over Jocelyn's.

"It's okay, Jossie."

Déjà vu rolled over her again, much stronger this time, a whole-body memory that didn't just hint of the past but lifted her from today and dropped her right back into every feeling she ever had for Will.

Respect. Appreciation. Admiration. And something so much more, so much deeper. "But if you want to leave, we can," he said.

"No, let's work on your career. What exactly are you doing in order to get that coaching job?"

"Waiting to hear from my agent."

"Then you mustn't want it very much."

He shook his head vehemently. "That's where you're wrong. I want it very much."

"Then the first word you use for your 'action' wouldn't be 'waiting,'" she shot back. "You'd be calling, meeting, searching, networking, applying, fighting, clawing, interview—"

He held up his hand. "I get the picture."

"Do you?" She propped her elbows on the table and rested her chin on her knuckles. "Prove it."

"What's to prove? When you finish in the minors, you get a coaching job in the minors."

"Are you passionate about coaching?"

"I'm passionate about..." When he hesitated, her whole body tightened in anticipation. What was Will passionate about? She wanted it to be—

"Baseball."

"Of course."

"Surely you didn't forget that about me."

"I didn't forget anything about you." Lord, why had she told him that? Because he had that gift: He made her so comfortable she forgot to maintain control.

The admission made him smile, not cockily like when he found out she'd Googled him, just—well, she couldn't quite read those dozen different emotions flickering in his dark blue eyes. "Then we're even. And you know that from the time I was five, I've lived, breathed, and slept the game. You know I love baseball. It's all I know, all I've ever known."

"You know," she said, "I have a choice right now."

Lifting his eyebrows in question, he waited for more

explanation. "You do? I thought this was about my choices."

"It is. But I have to make a choice." She sipped her drink and chose her words carefully. "When I am coaching a client and I believe they are self-delusional, I have two choices. I can either let them off easy because they don't really want to face the truth and they'd rather write a check and believe they found their answers, or..."

He didn't respond, scratching his neck a little, as if he wasn't quite sure where she was going with this. And might not like it when he was.

"I can challenge them to face the truth head-on and deal with what that means."

"You think I'm self-delusional?"

"I think you're not that passionate about baseball."

"Are you nuts? If I'm not, what the hell have I been doing for the last, Jesus, thirty years since my dad bought the first tee and put a bat in my hand?"

She just stared at him. "Precisely."

"Precisely *what*?"

"Will, baseball has always been your father's passion. Good God, I can remember him talking about you playing for his beloved L.A. Dodgers since the day you guys moved in."

"He always hated that I couldn't get into that franchise," Will admitted. "But we shared the passion, Joss. You can't get as far as I did without it."

She wasn't sure about that. "With your natural talent, you could get very, very far. And you did. But—"

"But what?" He damn near growled the demand. "But if I had been more devoted, I *could* have gotten into the majors? I *could* have played for the fucking Dodgers?"

She flinched and his hand shot across the table to take hers. "Sorry, I didn't mean to get mad like that."

"No problem," she lied. "That's exactly why I let some clients take easy street. It's easier for me, too." She slipped her hand out from under his. "And I'm not saying if you were more devoted your career would have gone differently because, frankly, the past doesn't matter anymore, unless it helps you see your own patterns."

He nodded, but she could tell agreeing with anything she was saying wasn't easy.

"I'm suggesting," she said, "and quite seriously, that if you were truly, madly, and deeply passionate and in love with the idea of doing something with your baseball career, you would be doing it and not 'waiting for someone to call.'" She air-quoted the phrase.

Picking up a fry, he swiped it through his ketchup and shook off the extra. "My name's out there," he said, working to keep the defensiveness out of his tone, and failing. "My agent has me in with every minor league team in the sport, and the first bullpen or base-coaching job available, I'll be considered."

"Is that the kind of coaching job you want?"

"That's where you start."

She pushed a little harder. "I don't know, it seems to me that you could manage a whole team if you wanted to. You've always been the captain, always the leader."

He took in a slow breath, obviously uncomfortable with the subject.

"Hey, you volunteered to be my client," she said. "It's not always easy. But when you dig deep and force yourself to think about what puts a bounce in your step and joy in your soul, then you might adjust your career goals."

He didn't answer right away, then said, "I know this is going to sound crazy, but my parents lived their entire lives and gave everything they have for my success. I still feel like I can't let them down, you know?" He hesitated a minute, the wheels turning as he worked it out. "Maybe I don't want to be a minor league coach, but that would somehow be a slap in the face to my dad, who did everything so that my career—my *whole* career—would go the right way. And, shit, my *liking* to be carpenter? That's like my ignoring everything he ever told me. A carpenter was a failure to him, somehow. Blue-collar and...*ordinary.*"

She nodded, truly understanding and recognizing his predicament. "But you can't make lifelong decisions because of sacrifices your parents made when you were a kid, Will."

"I know that." He smiled. "That's why I'm waiting. And you want to know something else? I think your standard life-coach question is meaningless, completely rhetorical, and tells you nothing about the person."

"About what you're prepared to die for?"

"A stupid question, if you ask me."

She leaned forward, more interested than insulted. "But the answer tells me everything about a person. It tells me what matters to them."

"Nope, it tells you what they think should matter to them, not what really does. I'm more interested in what someone has sacrificed for in the past."

"What do you mean?"

"Like for me, I sacrificed my life for baseball. College was a joke. I never went to a party, didn't join a fraternity or a club or anything. I just practiced, played, traveled, and studied. I sacrificed everything for baseball, so I think you're whole theory is bogus."

She shrugged but couldn't help smiling. "I still think you had a breakthrough."

"You just want me to pay for lunch." He grinned and put a hand on the check the waitress had left on her last trip by, one of at least five in the last ten minutes. "So what about you, Joss? What have you sacrificed?"

She looked him right in the eye, so drawn to him, so certain of him, it slammed her right back into the past.

"Ah, speaking of a breakthrough," he said. "I can see it on your face." He leaned so close she could see every lash now, every fleck of navy in his eyes, every hint of whisker stubble, even the tiniest bit of ketchup in the corner of his mouth.

Her whole being ached to kiss it off. And she hated ketchup.

"No breakthrough," she said. "This was your life-coaching session."

"Answer my question. What have you sacrificed to achieve your passion?"

She swallowed, but even that couldn't keep down the truth. "I sacrificed everything for love."

His jaw loosened as the waitress zoomed over and scooped up the check and money. "Keep the change," he said without taking his eyes from Jocelyn. "You did?"

"Everything," she assured him. Everything that mattered, given up one summer evening in a stairwell outside his bedroom.

"I gotta tell you, Joss, whoever he is—or was—I hate his fucking guts."

He wouldn't if he knew the truth. "Why?"

"Because I'm jealous of someone you loved," he said simply. "It should have been me."

The food thunked to the bottom of her stomach and she actually felt a little sick.

It was you.

"If you felt that way, why didn't you call me when we went to college?" she asked.

He closed his eyes. "I was waiting for you."

She tried to smile, but her mouth trembled a little. "I think I see a pattern here, Will Palmer."

He laughed, tipping her chin with his knuckle. "Damn, life coach, you're good."

"Only if you break your pattern, Will."

"Yeah. Well, I intend to." The low, sweet promise in his voice reached right into her chest and squeezed her heart.

Chapter 13

~

Guy slapped the jack of spades on the table and gave Zoe the dearest look she'd seen in—well, since she'd left her great-aunt in Flagstaff, Arizona.

"You old coot," she said, dropping her remaining card on the pile and shaking her head. "You beat the pants off me in Egyptian Rat Screws. That is not easy to do."

"I'm really good at cards," he said, fighting a smug smile.

She leaned on one elbow and pointed at him. "You like older women?"

"I might be dumb but I'm not blind, Blondie. You're not older than me."

"Not me." She laughed, waving her hand. "My great-aunt. She's pretty hot for eighty...ish. How old are you?"

He angled his head, thinking. "I don't have a clue."

She didn't know whether to laugh or cry, he was so

damn sweet. "Well, you're not her age, I can assure you of that. I'll go with sixty-five. Still, you'd like Pasha."

"Who's Pasha?"

"My hot great-aunt who is, I might add, almost as good as you at the game I just taught you an hour ago." She marveled at that; for a man suffering from Alzheimer's, there were still a few sharp cells at work up there.

The doorbell rang and his eyes widened. "Who's that?"

She pushed up. "No way to know until I answer it. But I hope to hell it's a reporter."

"Why?"

She grinned. "So I can channel my inner Meryl Streep." She peeked through the window in the door and smiled. "They're back," she called out. "Stay in the kitchen, Pops. I'll handle this. Oh!" She turned to him. "What's your real name? Is Guy short for something?"

"Alexander." Then he gasped. "Where the heck did that come from?"

She laughed. "Your memory, smarty-pants. Now stay there." She shook her hair and arms, took a deep breath, and opened the door. "Yes?"

The little bald eagle stepped forward. "We're looking for Mr. Bloom. For his daughter, actually."

"Daughter-in-law," she said. "You found her."

He frowned. "His daughter, Jocelyn Bloom."

She let out a full-body put-upon sigh, leaning on the doorjamb and shaking her head. "When are you nitwits going to get it through your head? This is not the man you want, no Jocelyn Bloom lives here, and anything you're reading in the paper is not true."

None of that was, technically, a lie.

Baldie wasn't buying. "We have proof that this is the childhood home of Jocelyn Bloom who lived here with her parents, Guy and Mary Jo." He lifted up an official-looking paper, and Zoe curled her lip.

"They did live here, like, eons ago. This is the home of Mr. Alexander."

Again, not a lie. But distrusting eyes narrowed at her; he was no doubt familiar with the runaround. "Where's Jocelyn?"

"Beats me, but you guys are barking up the wrong address."

"She used to live here."

Zoe leaned forward and flicked a finger at the paper he held. "Your info is wrong. Buzz off and don't come back or you'll be facing the sheriff himself. We're sick of you all."

"There've been other reporters?" A note of worry cracked his voice.

"A few. They're gone, and so are you."

She closed the door and instantly another white card slipped through the mailbox hole. Zoe ripped it into tiny pieces and shoved it right back out.

"That ought to keep the creeps at bay for a while," she said, brushing her hands like she was good and finished and heading back to the living room, where Guy was shuffling the deck for the next game.

"What's she look like?" he asked.

"Oh, it was a he. Bald and ugly."

He grinned. "I meant your aunt."

"Great-aunt. And, trust me, she is—great, I mean." Zoe dropped onto the sofa across from Guy, giving him raised eyebrows. "So you do like older women?"

"I figure if she's anything like you, yeah."

"Aw, you sweet thing." She started collecting her cards as he dealt slowly and with great precision. "She's funka-licious for an octogenarian."

He laughed. "I don't know what that means, but I think I like it."

"It means she spikes her gray hair, has too many ear-rings, and has a weakness for beer."

"At eighty?"

She shrugged. "Youth is wasted on the young, you know."

"I'd like to meet her." He scooped up his cards and tapped the half-deck carefully. "What happens when you put down an ace, again?"

"The other person has four tries to beat it."

His shoulders sagged a little, a gesture she recognized as one Pasha made when she was just a little overwhelmed at the moment. "Let's take a break," she suggested, set-ting down her cards. "I think I'd rather just talk for a little while. You want more of that delicious tea?"

"Nope, makes me have to pee."

She laughed again. "I love that you say what you're thinking. It's always been a problem for me."

"It bothers my son."

His son. "Will?"

He nodded.

"Did it always bother him? You know, like when he was little?"

He considered that, chewing on his bottom lip. "I'd like to work on my needlepoint now."

Either he couldn't remember or didn't want to say. Or didn't want to lie. Because a thought kept niggling at her: Was it possible Guy really *did* remember the past?

"Sure," she said, getting up to gather the cross-stitching he'd shown her earlier.

Maybe he did remember who Jocelyn was and maybe he did know Will wasn't his son. Because what better way to wipe your personal slate clean—especially if it was messy—than to conveniently forget everything you ever did? It was that or just run away when people got suspicious; God knows she knew that trick well enough.

He didn't strike her as that cunning, but who knew?

She handed him the frame with the thick "training mesh" that a kid would use to learn needlepoint, along with some pearl cotton thread and a needle. "How'd you learn this?" she asked, wondering just how hard it would be to trap him.

"Will taught me."

"Really? How'd he learn?"

"Computer videos. That tube thing."

"YouTube." She watched his hand shake ever so slightly as he pulled the thread through to execute the most basic half cross-stitch. "Will's good to you," she said, carefully watching his reaction.

He looked up, his gray eyes suddenly clear. "I love that boy more'n life itself."

More than his own daughter? "What was he like as a kid? A baseball player, I understand."

Guy's eyes clouded up again and he cast his gaze downward. "I don't recall."

"You don't recall or you didn't really know him that well?"

He refused to look up. "You know, my mind."

"No, actually, I don't know your mind. Surely you have a picture of him? His trophies? Where are they?"

"In his house, next door." He stabbed the needle. "I don't go over there."

"Why not?"

He shrugged. "I just don't."

"Why not?"

The needle stuck in a hole and he tried to force it, pulling some of the thread and making an unsightly lump. "Let's go back to talking about your beer-drinking old aunt."

She leaned forward. "Why don't you ever go to your son's house?"

He looked up. "I did once."

"And?"

"It made me cry." His voice cracked and his eyes filled and Zoe felt like a heel.

"I'm sorry," she said, taking the frame from his hands so she could try to undo the tangled stitch. "I shouldn't have made you talk about it."

He just shook his head, swallowing hard. "I can't remember," he said, wiping at his eyes under his glasses. "But…"

She got the thread through, saving him from that one little mistake on the needlepoint anyway. "But what?" she prompted, handing it back to him.

"But you wouldn't be the first person to try to prove I'm lying."

"I'm…" Her voice trailed off as he lifted his eyebrow. Then she just started to laugh. "Shit."

He grinned. "Shit what?"

"Shit, you and my aunt would really hit it off."

Smiling, he leaned back and worked on his flowers in silence.

• • •

"There's a marina around the corner, remember?" Will asked as they stepped outside the deli. "Want to go down there? It's too pretty to—" *Go look at more old-age homes.* "Do anything indoors."

"Sure." She slipped the sunglasses on again and tugged at the brim of her red cap. "And we can finish your life-coaching session. You want to?"

"I want..." He reached under the cap and pulled the shades down her nose. "You to take off these stupid things. I can't see your eyes, Jossie."

A smile threatened but she shook it off. "I have to."

"No." He slid the glasses off and slipped them into his pocket, reaching to put his arm over her shoulders. "I'll protect you from the roving paparazzi."

She laughed. "You like playing bodyguard."

"Who's playing?" He squinted into the parking lot, then pressed an imaginary earpiece. "The coast is clear. Let's get Bloomerang to her yacht."

She smiled up at him, the prettiest, widest, sweetest smile he'd seen from her yet. "You used to call me that."

"Because you always came back to me," he reminded her with a squeeze.

She held his gaze for the longest time, the magic that used to connect them so real at that moment he could feel the physical presence of it. "I liked it," she admitted. "I liked being your Bloomerang."

"I liked it, too." His voice was gruff, even to his ears, and he covered the emotion by pulling her into him. She slid her arm around his waist, the most natural, and wonderful, move in the world. She felt small and compact next to him, and he could have sworn she actually relaxed a little.

He led her along the walkway of the strip mall, past a consignment store and a frame shop, his eye on the entrance to the marina at the other end.

"You always were good at protecting me," she said softly.

The words slowed his step—imperceptibly, he hoped. "Not good enough," he murmured.

She looked up at him. "Maybe 'protect' is the wrong word. You always gave me...security. Safety. Sanctuary."

He tucked her tighter against his torso. God, he'd tried.

"Safety and sanctuary," she said, "were what I said I'd be prepared to die for when I was first asked that question in my therapy."

He wanted to respond to that, to mull it over, but another question popped out instead. "You were in therapy?"

"It's part of getting a psych degree. Oh, Will, look." At the marina's grand arched entrance, she stopped. "It's like a different place."

The quaint little neighborhood dock, with its hand-painted sign, weathered bait-and-tackle stand, and rotten boathouse, was completely gone. In its place was an expanse of four individual mooring peninsulas, each chock full of million-dollar yachts, cabin cruisers, and high-tech fishing boats. Along one side, a bustling yacht club blocked the view with giant columns and bright orange Spanish tile. A sleek marble marker announced they'd reached *Marco Harbor*.

"Kind of sad to see the little neighborhood marina turned into this," Jocelyn said as she slipped out of Will's arm and walked along an asphalt drive that led to the boats.

They headed down the first maze of docks between

boats so big they cast a shadow over them. As Will took Jocelyn's hand, the squawk of a heron and the rhythmic splash of water against hulls were the only sounds. Some rigging hit a mast, the clang like a musical bell over the quiet harbor, and, in the distance, the steady thump of—

They both looked at each other as the sound of running feet registered at the same instant.

"There she is! Right there!"

They whipped around at the woman's voice, seeing their waitress jogging toward them holding up a cell phone, a man next to her with a more professional camera.

"That's Miles Thayer's lover!"

Jocelyn froze in shock, but Will instantly nudged her forward. "Run."

They did, taking off down the next hundred-yard mooring, ducking behind a massive trawler, then scooting around a corner to hide.

"Damn it," she whispered, her breath already tight.

"They went this way!" the woman yelled.

Will turned one way, then the other. They could run out into the open toward the storage unit, jump in the water, or climb onto an empty boat.

He nudged her toward the back of the trawler. "Climb up!"

Without arguing, she grabbed the railing and scrambled up to the deck, and he followed, leading her around the cabin to the opposite side, away from the dock.

"Get down." He pushed her to the fiberglass deck, flattening her and covering her so they could both fit in the narrow space of the portside walkway. Under him, she struggled for quiet breaths, every muscle taut.

"Oh, God, this is a nightmare," she whispered.

"Shhh." He kissed her hair and put a finger over her lips. "We're completely out of sight. They'd have to get in every single boat to find us. Just stay still and quiet."

They heard footsteps and voices on the next dock and Jocelyn turned to him, her face inches from his, their eyes locked on each other. They both held their breath, and he clutched her a little tighter, his legs wrapped around her, her backside tucked into his stomach.

The footsteps on their dock were like thunder, loud enough to feel right through the fiberglass.

"They found us," she mouthed, her eyes wide.

He just shook his head a little and put his finger over her lips.

God, she was pretty. Her curves fit right into him, her hair tickling his face, her lips, curving in a secret smile, warm on his fingertip.

He wanted his mouth there, not his fingertip. Wanted their lips to touch so badly it made his mouth ache, and his muscles hurt from fighting the urge to close that one whisper of an inch that separated them from a kiss.

"They must be on one of the boats." The woman's voice carried over the water, as clear as if she were five feet away. They heard a splash as someone climbed onboard a boat nearby.

"Well, find them, damn it," the man said. "Do you have any idea how much a picture of her is worth to the tabloids? Jesus, Helen, we could retire."

"I'll find them," she said, determined. "I'll climb in every boat in this marina and I will find you, you fucking homewrecker!"

Jocelyn cringed at the last three words, hollered into the wind.

"You could tell her," he whispered. "You could tell her the truth."

She shook her head and somehow inched even deeper under him, sparking every powerful, protective need. And, man, he had many needs where Jocelyn was concerned, but protecting her was always at the top of his list.

"Excuse me? Can I help you?" A new voice called out, one of male authority. "That's not your boat, ma'am."

"I'm looking for someone," the woman said. "They're..." Her voice trailed off and the other man spoke to her, too far away for Will to make out the words.

"You cannot get onboard a boat you don't own. Sorry." More footsteps. "You're going to have to leave, ma'am."

Under him, he felt Jocelyn relax ever so slightly.

"But there's a woman hiding on one of these boats! She's wanted by the...people."

"Why don't you two just come with me, please?"

Their footsteps retreated, the voices faded, and after a minute it was silent but for the lapping waves and the soft chime of sail rigging in the breeze.

"Should we try to get out of here?" Jocelyn asked.

He closed his eyes, picturing the layout of the harbor they'd just run through. If they could slip off this boat and travel over one row, they could get behind the storage unit. But more likely, marina management would be all over them and their pursuers would be ready to pounce outside the marina.

"Let's just wait," he said.

"Like this?"

He smiled. "You got a better idea?"

She shifted a little and squished up her face. "My hip bones are smashed."

He lifted up an inch, hating the loss of warmth. "Scooch around. But don't rock the boat. Literally."

She carefully slipped out from under him, rolling to press her back against the side of the cabin. He turned on his side, making them body-to-body and face-to-face. And damn near mouth-to-mouth.

She slid her hand between their chests, reaching up to touch his face tenderly. "Thank you, Will. Thank you for cooperating. I know you don't agree with or understand what I'm doing, but I really appreciate this."

" 'Sokay," he assured her. "Are you comfortable?"

"I'm always comfortable with you, Will. You *are* comfort to me."

The compliment touched him. "You say that now. Wait until your right arm, backside, and both feet fall asleep." He leaned his face closer to hers, so close he lost focus. So close their noses touched. So close he could feel her warm breath on his lips. "Unless, of course, you keep the blood flowing."

"I suppose you have an idea for how to do that."

"Plenty of them." He added just a hint of pressure, and instantly everything came rushing back, all those old achy needs.

He always, always wanted her.

"Guess what I'm about to do?" he asked.

"Rock the boat?"

"For once, I'm not going to...*wait*." He closed the space and easily, softly, barely let their lips brush, the contact sparking tiny explosions of white lights behind his eyes.

How could she still do this to him? Fifteen years, three thousand miles, and their whole adulthood they'd been separated and just this much of a kiss and every feeling came thundering home.

But he held back. Their mouths weren't completely opened, and their tongues stayed poised for that first encounter, hands still but already heavy with the desire to touch.

And way down low, he started to grow hard.

Her mouth was sweet and supple, and pliable as she finally relaxed and offered her tongue. He took it, curling it with his own, tasting mint tea and sweet memories and—her.

A tiny whimper made him need to touch her throat, just for the pure pleasure of feeling that tender skin pulse under his fingertip. He closed one hand around the narrow column of her neck and, with the other on her shoulder, inched her closer.

She didn't stiffen or fight him, but leaned into the kiss and pressed her palm on his chest. Right over his thumping heart.

They broke the kiss but stayed a hair apart, opening their eyes at the same time.

"What are we doing, Will?"

"Hiding from the cameras." He kissed her again, and she added some pressure of her own, so he slid his hand down her throat, over the slightly damp, completely soft skin just under the dip of her collarbones.

Her hips rocked slightly, enough to fire more blood to his already overcharged erection, his breath tight as he worked his mouth over her jaw and back to her ear.

She moaned softly.

It was all he needed to hear to kiss her again, to delve his tongue deeper and slip his hand into her silky hair.

She smelled like the sun, tasted like magic, and felt like—

Like nothing he'd felt for fifteen years.

Dragging his hand through her hair, he took his palm lower, over her shoulder, over her breastbone, just to the rise of her body where he could count the heartbeats, as rapid as his. One more kiss, one more breath, and he slowly caressed her breast.

Her whole body shuddered instantly.

"Did I find your weak spot?" he murmured into her mouth.

She sighed. "It appears you *are* my weak spot."

Something about the way she said it, the catch in her voice, slammed into his chest. "I'm lucky that way."

Their lips brushed again, a soft groan of satisfaction rumbling in Will's chest as he intensified the kiss, melting their mouths together and sliding his leg up enough to tuck her deeper into him.

"I can't just kiss you," he admitted, fondling her breast, already itching to touch her bare skin. "I want it all."

She froze for a second, leaning back.

"Not here, obviously," he added at the look of panic on her face.

"Then we better slow down," she said, her voice husky.

"Is that what you want?"

She closed her eyes. "I don't know what I want, Will."

"Then let me give you options. We could just kiss..." He took her mouth again, finishing the suggestion with a long, wet, completely well-received kiss. "And I could touch you." He thumbed over her nipple, loving the way it responded. "And we could, you know..." He rocked his erection into hers.

So far, she just kept her eyes closed, saying nothing.

"Or we could..." He slid his other hand over her shorts, dipping between her legs, and her eyes snapped open. "Don't worry, honey. Nothing you don't want."

"I don't want...to do this...out here."

"Think we could break into the cabin?"

She laughed a little. "No. Just..." She was already having a hard time breathing evenly; her pupils were dilated, her heart hammering. "Just kiss me some more. That's safe."

Safety and security were so important to her. He had to remember that. Had to.

"Why don't we just talk?" he suggested.

She gave him a smile. "Sure. What do you want to talk about?"

"You."

"What about me?"

"Back in the restaurant you said you sacrificed everything for love. Who was this clown who hurt you?"

The strangest look darkened her eyes. "He didn't hurt me. It was my choice."

"What happened?"

She shook her head. "I don't want to talk about it."

"I do. Were you in love with him?"

She just smiled, and, damn, that kicked him. Of course Jocelyn would meet other men, fall in love, but he didn't have to like it.

"But you've never been married, right?"

"Not even close."

"Then who was he? How'd you meet him? How long were you together? You said you sacrificed for love. What did you sacrifice?"

"Why does it matter to you?"

"I told you, I hate the guy. He hurt you."

"He didn't do anything to me," she assured him.

"He's the reason for your shell, isn't he?" The shell he was going to crack if it was the last thing he ever did. "You don't trust men because some joker broke your heart."

She caressed his face again, the look in her eyes unreadable. "He didn't hurt me and he's not the reason I protect myself. You know the reason, Will."

Guilt kicked him harder than ten tons of lust, and it hurt. Guy was the reason.

"And that's why it's killing me that you've forgiven him."

It was worse than forgiveness. He loved Guy Bloom when, really, he should hate him. But he couldn't. Would that cost him any chance he might have with Jocelyn?

"Will." She touched his face with soft, gentle hands. "I think we can try to make a run for it now."

"I think we should wait."

She lifted one brow. "The only thing worse than a procrastinator is a paralyzed procrastinator."

Shit. That was his whole life in a nutshell: the paralyzed procrastinator trapped in a holding pattern.

But he was holding a woman who wanted a man of action. And he didn't ever want to let go of her again.

"All right, then, Bloomerang. Let's go."

Chapter 14

⌒

An hour after Will had easily hustled them through the marina and safely around the back of the strip mall, Jocelyn finally felt back in control.

Barely.

Her body still hummed from his touch, and the certainty that she could look up and see a camera lens at any minute had her just as on edge. She took deep breaths and studied the intersection where they were stopped, known as "the Fourway" for as long as she could remember.

It was right on this very spot that she'd been picked up and taken away, bruised, battered, and broken. If Will knew that...

"Did Lacey tell you Clay's promised Charity a free front-elevation re-do for the Super Min when Casa Blanca is finished?" he asked, the question eerily mirroring her deepest thoughts.

"No." She studied the old wooden sign and tried to imagine something more modern. And failed. "It's been that way forever. Is it some kind of peace offering?"

"More or less. There's still a lot of bad feelings, but Clay's a charmer, you know."

She laughed. "I watched him charm Lacey."

"He's determined to win over every businessperson in Mimosa Key, because he thinks they'll be important for sending new business. Plus, the Super Min's an eyesore and it's one of the first things you see when you come over the causeway. This island has to attract big bucks, not shrimp fisherman."

"That's exactly what Charity and her sister, Patti, didn't want."

"They'll come around," Will said confidently. "I've seen Charity back down in the face of Clay's devilish smile."

Jocelyn eyed the convenience store. "Then maybe I should go in there and at least say hello." At his surprised look, she added. "To help the cause and my investment in Casa Blanca."

"If you want. Like I told you, she did surprise me by not selling you out and hiding those magazines."

It didn't surprise Jocelyn, not one bit. Mimosa Key might think Charity Grambling was a sixty-year-old Mean Girl, but Jocelyn knew better.

"Hey, look, there's Slade Garrison." Will veered into the next lane to pull into the parking lot of the Fourway Motel, across the street. "We should talk to him."

A uniformed deputy Jocelyn didn't recognized stood by the car, talking to a woman with dark hair, who looked up and laughed at something he said.

But she did recognized the woman. "That's Charity's

niece, Gloria." She'd changed a lot in fifteen years, but Glo still had a pretty smile and a youthful, fit figure. Unlike her cousin, Grace, Charity's daughter, Gloria never seemed to have a self-serving agenda. She didn't work at the Super Min or the Fourway Motel, but styled hair at Beachside Beauty a few blocks away.

"Is she still single?" Jocelyn asked, and just as she did, the young officer put a hand on her shoulder, the gesture both intimate and familiar.

"Slade's been after her a while but something's keeping them apart." Will smiled. "Not that I follow too much of the Mimosa Key gossip."

She laughed. "Can't really live here and not know it."

Will pulled into a parking spot right between the Super Min and the Fourway. "I'm going to talk to Slade when he's alone," he said.

Just then, the deputy sheriff leaned closer to Gloria and she glanced left and right as if to see if anyone was watching. Then she stood on her tiptoes and kissed Slade lightly on the mouth.

"They make a nice couple," she mused. "Is he a good guy?"

"Yeah." He cut a glance at her. "Were you friends with Gloria?"

"Not really." She hadn't been close friends with anyone, except Will. It was too risky to bring any friends home, in case Guy had an episode. But Gloria had been in the car that night. "But I know her well enough."

Gloria and Slade separated and Will put his hand on the door handle. "You want to wait here?"

"I want to . . ." Did she really want to do this? *Yes.* Last year when she'd been here Charity and Lacey had been so wrapped up in legal maneuverings that she'd stayed away from the Super Min. "I want to go in and see what's up with Charity."

"Really? You want to tell the town crier that you're here? That might be pushing it, Joss."

"You go talk to Slade." She put her hand on his arm. "I'll handle the other voice of authority on this island."

As she started to pull away, he took her hand, keeping her in the truck. "You okay?" he asked.

"I'm fine."

"Not freaked out about what just happened?"

Did he mean making out on the boat or running from the cameras? Because both of them freaked her out more than she'd like to admit. "No," she lied. "Not freaked out."

"Good." He tightened his grip and leaned toward her. "Because I'm not done, Jocelyn. I want…" He closed his eyes and blew out a breath, giving her the impression he'd been thinking a lot about this while they'd driven over here. "I want a chance with you."

"A chance?"

"A chance. For us. Again."

She just looked at him, then nodded. "I'll be here a while," she said. "We can talk while I figure things out with Guy."

He smiled. "I might not want to wait for *everything*, you know."

She wasn't quite sure how to interpret that, but a slow burn low in her belly told her exactly how her body interpreted his words.

And, honestly, could she spend that much time with Will and not think about sex? Not want it?

She should put a stop to that right away, shouldn't she?

But instead she stroked his hand and slipped out of the truck without answering, trying to think about Charity but in her mind hearing Will's words instead.

I might not want to wait for everything, you know.

But she had. And what would he think of that?

She looked over her shoulder in time to catch him crossing the parking lot, moving economically and smoothly, like the strong athlete he'd always been. A whole new wave of longing swept over her, almost as powerful as it had been on that boat. All she could think about was how that body felt pressed against her, his mouth against her throat, his hands—almost everywhere.

Talk about losing control. Just giving up everything she held on to with two tight fists—if she let herself feel or fall—it could hurt so much more to have to walk away from him this time.

Pushing back the emotions, she pulled open the door of the Super Min and when the little bell dinged she smiled at the woman behind the counter. "Hello, Charity."

Sharp brown eyes squinted into the sunlight of the doorway, and then Charity's normally sour expression softened, a network of wrinkles breaking into a tentative smile.

"I hoped you might have the nerve to come and see me this time."

Jocelyn took a few steps closer, glancing around the store. Two men with work belts and hard hats were in the back, probably construction crew from Casa Blanca. The rest of the convenience store was empty.

And so were, she noticed as she walked closer, the tabloid racks.

"I wasn't here very long last year," Jocelyn said as she reached the counter and paused. "But I heard what you did with those reporters and I wanted to come in and thank you."

Charity lifted a bony shoulder as if an act of kindness on her part was an everyday occurrence instead of the rarity they both knew it was. "We don't need that kind of crap on this island."

"They might come back."

"And my position hasn't changed. They're not welcome and I haven't seen you."

Jocelyn put her hands on the counter. "Not the first time you've covered for me, is it?"

Another shrug. "Heard he's sick," she said.

She nodded. "He is."

"Good. I worked too damn hard to get him out of a sheriff's uniform to ever let him get back in one."

Jocelyn shook her head. "He's not capable of doing the job anymore."

"He wasn't back then, neither." Charity reached across the counter and patted Jocelyn's hand. "You got nothing to worry about, honey. No stinkin' reporters'll get to you if they have to get through me."

"Thanks, Charity. For everything."

She rolled her eyes. "Honey, you thanked me enough with that loan when Patti got so sick and needed that heart valve replacement."

"It didn't have to be a loan," Jocelyn said quietly. "I wanted it to be a gift."

"Twenty thousand dollars? You gotta be kidding."

"I owe you that and more, Charity."

She waved. "Keep that to yourself or you'll ruin my reputation as the Wicked Witch. You think I don't know what people call me? I live for that shit."

The back door popped open and Gloria stepped out of the ladies' room on the other side of the candy rack, her eyes so bright she might have been crying, except she looked absolutely radiantly happy. At the sight of Jocelyn, her jaw dropped.

Charity held up her hand. "Don't say her name, Glo. She's our little secret."

Gloria smiled. "You're back." Then she inched back, giving Jocelyn the once-over. "Truth or lies?"

Jocelyn sighed. She had a special bond with these two women. She trusted them. "It's not true."

"Oh, too bad. My cousin Grace has the hots so bad for Miles Thayer. She'd want every detail."

"My daughter Grace has the hots for everyone, that's her problem."

"No," Gloria shot back. "That's her husband, Ron's, problem." She winked at Jocelyn. "See? Some things never change on this island. I'd love to talk, Jocelyn, but Slade's off work and we're going out."

"Did you tell your mother you're going to be out tonight?" Charity asked, referring, of course, to her sister, Patience Vail, Gloria's mother and the recipient of Jocelyn's secret loan a few years ago.

Gloria bit her lip. "Aunt Charity, I'm in my thirties."

"Not too old to tell my poor sister when you'll be home."

"Later," she said, slipping past Jocelyn, giving her a smile. "Nice to see you again, Jocelyn."

As the bell rang with Gloria's exit, the two construction workers came up with armloads of soda and chips.

"I better go," Jocelyn said.

"Just you wait," Charity ordered, ringing up the men first. "I have to tell you something."

Jocelyn turned, not wanting to make eye contact with the strangers, picking up a copy of the *Mimosa Gazette*, her gaze on the headline. *New Roads to Be Approved for Barefoot Bay.*

So Lacey was making headlines in the *Mimosa Gazette*, she thought with a smile. Good for her. When the men left, Charity pointed at the paper.

"I was going to fight that resort, you know."

"Of course you were."

"But that damn Clay Walker came up for a way for that road to have another Shell station that we can get the franchise rights to. We'd have two gas stations in north Mimosa Key and I'd own them both." She grinned. "How could I fight that?"

"You're going to be very glad when Casa Blanca is finished," Jocelyn told her.

Charity looked skyward, like she hated to admit it. Then she crooked a finger to get Jocelyn closer, lowering her voice even though the convenience store was empty.

"How sick is he?" she asked.

"Pretty bad. I'm going to put him...somewhere. Not sure where, though."

"Check hell. I heard there's plenty of vacancies."

Jocelyn smiled.

"He meets the criteria," Charity insisted. "And if the devil needs a referral"—she leaned even closer to whisper—"I still got them pictures."

"You do?"

" 'Course. They're in a safe-deposit box down at the credit union. They're yours if you want them. I'm keeping them just in case, you know."

"Just in case of what?" The thought of those pictures still being around made Jocelyn a little nauseous.

"You know, if he ever tries anything again."

She shook her head. "He won't. He's freakishly changed. Nice, even."

"I heard a rumor to that effect. And you can bet those pretty diamond earrings you're wearing that I didn't repeat that rumor, 'cause I spread the truth."

"It's true he's sick and—nice."

She snorted noisily. "You know what they say about a rat-bastard wifebeater and his spots."

"Shhh." Jocelyn closed her eyes.

"Well, it's a fact. And I don't regret for one minute what I did, young lady. Call it blackmail if you want, but that man was a disgrace to the uniform and a terror to his family."

There was no way to argue that.

"But the pictures are yours if you want 'em."

Did she? She could destroy them. Or use them to remind her of why she couldn't get all soft inside where Guy was concerned. "Yes, I do," she said. "I want them."

Charity nodded. "Fine. I'll get them for you. And in the meantime, I haven't seen you, and I doubt you'd ever come back here. Oh, and I stopped carrying the tabloids."

"Bet that's hitting your bottom line."

Charity huffed out a breath and waved her bright-red nails like a flea was in front of her. "I don't give a hoot what's hitting my bottom line, long as no man is hitting me." She reached her hand out for a formal shake, the gesture striking Jocelyn as odd, but she took the older woman's weathered hand. "We stick togeth—"

The bell rang and Will caught them shaking hands. Jocelyn knew from his expression there'd be some explaining to do. Just as she knew that she'd never give him the full explanation.

"Bye, Charity." Jocelyn let go of the other woman's hand and stepped away.

"You ready?" Will asked, holding the door open.

With a nod to Charity, she followed Will back into the warm sunshine.

"What the hell was that all about, Joss? I had no idea you were such good buddies with her."

She just shrugged. "Not everybody hates Charity Grambling."

"Well, she might be acting really nice to you now, but, believe me, she lives and breathes on gossip, so I'd be careful how much you tell her."

The irony of that statement made Jocelyn smile. If it weren't for Charity Grambling, she'd never have been able to escape Mimosa Key. If she'd stayed, Will would have seen the evidence of Guy's fury that night.

His career would have been spent in jail because he wouldn't have let Guy Bloom live.

Yeah, plenty of irony there. Irony she didn't want to share.

"I briefed Slade," he said. "He'll keep an eye out for more reporters and send a cruiser around my neighborhood."

She nodded, grateful for the assist but tired from the whole ordeal. "You know, Will, I'm going to pass on dinner tonight. I'm wiped out. I think I should just go up to Barefoot Bay."

He glanced over his shoulder at the Super Min, as if he blamed Charity for Jocelyn's change of heart. " 'Kay." As he opened the truck door, he leaned in, "But I'm still not done with you."

Chapter 15

⌒

Will hadn't slept more than two hours, maybe three, hot and hard and miserable for most of the night. By five, he'd abandoned his sweaty bed and headed upstairs to his old workout room to pump iron and punch out the frustrations.

Which hadn't helped a bit since all he'd done was stare at his old bed and remember all the hours he and Jocelyn had spent there. On the bed, not in it. Either way, it was some one hundred and eighty fucking months later, and he was still imagining what he wanted to do to her on *or* in that bed.

After an icy shower, he packed up what he needed for the day and made his usual trek across the backyard to the Bloom house, tapping on the back kitchen door before using his key to go inside.

Most mornings he found Guy in front of the TV or working on some craft. Sometimes the old boy was still asleep and Will made sure he was up and knew more or less what day it was.

And some days, like today, Guy was busy in the kitchen, making his own breakfast, whistling a tune and acting like nothing—absolutely nothing—was wrong with him.

These days baffled Will, of course, but right now it just infuriated him because Jocelyn wasn't here, seeing just how *normal* Guy was.

Sometimes.

"Good morning, William!" He looked up from the small center island, where he was measuring milk for his oatmeal. "Can I interest you in a heart-healthy breakfast? That Doctor Oz is always yapping about the power of the oat."

"I'm good, buddy. Just stopping by to see how you're doing."

Guy beamed at him. "You are the best son in the world."

Was he "normal" enough this morning to handle the truth? "I'm not your son," Will said quietly. "And you know that."

He braced for waterworks, but Guy's smile never wavered. "Does the blood matter that much? You're as much a son as I could dream of having."

Oh, yeah, he was in good shape today. "Thanks." Will jutted his chin toward the oatmeal. "And, you know what? I'll have a bowl of that if you're pouring."

The days like this were so rare, and Will didn't really feel like rushing out of here, leaving Guy alone.

"I was just wondering," Guy said as he reached for another cereal bowl. "You think that *Clean House* gal's comin' back here today?"

"Jocelyn?" Will took a seat at the kitchen table, eyeing the other man. When he was this lucid, Will had to wonder. Didn't he recognize his own daughter? Didn't Guy remember Will and the night he'd threatened to end his career or his life?

Didn't he remember anything?

"Yeah. Do you think, William? I really like her."

"Me, too," he admitted.

Guy turned from the microwave before he punched the numbers to warm his oatmeal. "I can tell."

"That obvious, huh?"

"She's a looker."

Will blew out a breath and stabbed his fingers in his hair, the thoughts that kept him awake all night plaguing him. Of course he was still attracted to her. Still lost in pools of brown eyes tinged with vulnerability and a fight for control. Still wanted to take away that control with his mouth, open her up with his hands, get inside her with his—

"Well, would you?"

Will shook his head clear. "Sorry. Would I what?"

Guy chuckled. "Oh, she's got you good. You don't even know what day or time it is."

Will skewered him with a look. "You should talk."

That made Guy laugh more, smiling as he went about the business of serving them both oatmeal, smug with his ability to be the one to handle the chores today.

After he had his first taste, Will put his spoon down and looked at Guy. "C'mon. What did you just ask me before?"

Guy gave him a look of sheer incredulity. "You expect me to remember that?" His shoulders shook with more laughter. "I'm funny today."

"Were you always funny?" Will asked, knowing the

answer but wondering what the hell this old man thought he used to be. He didn't know his own daughter, he didn't know his own neighbor; did he know himself?

"Can't say." Guy slurped his oatmeal. "But what the hell difference does it make? I'm funny now."

Really, what the hell difference *did* it make? Why couldn't he get Jocelyn to see that? Not just because she might change her mind about putting the old guy away but because she could forgive him.

And if she forgave him, if she could take that monumental, impossible, unbelievably hard step and forgive this man who didn't even remember who he'd been, then she could let go.

Because right now she couldn't let go of a penny if her fingers were greased, let alone a lifelong hate match she was determined to win.

Until she let go, she couldn't do anything that he had been thinking about doing all night.

"You look mighty serious, William."

"I'm just thinking."

" 'Bout Missy?"

He smiled. "Yeah."

"You got it bad, boy. Oh, I know what I was going to ask you!" His whole face brightened.

"What?"

"Why aren't you married?"

He flinched a little at the question, thrown like an unexpected knuckleball that bounced off the plate and into the dirt. "I was," he said. "I'm divorced."

Guy nodded, scraping his spoon around a nearly empty bowl. "I was married."

Will stayed very still. "I know."

"Her name was Mary...Beth."

"Jo," he corrected, and Guy looked up with a shocked expression. "Mary Jo," Will added. "Not Mary Beth."

"Really? Are you sure?"

"Yes." Will stood slowly, picking up his bowl, watching for signs that Guy was about to lose it. Some conversations just sent him over the edge of frustration because he wanted to remember and couldn't.

"Bet she was pretty," he said softly. "That Mary Jo."

"She was." He rinsed the bowl and opened the dishwasher. "Do you want to know something about her?"

When he didn't answer, Will turned to see Guy very slowly shredding his paper napkin into long strips, concentrating with everything he had, his thick fingers shaking a little.

"Do you, Guy?"

He looked over the napkin at Will. "I saw a show about *papier mâché*. Did you know that's a French word?"

"I guess." But how did Guy know that and not his own wife's name?

"I think I'm going to try that."

"Do you want to know about Mary Jo?" Will insisted, a burn of frustration stinging his gut.

"Don't know any Mary Jo," he said, then he balled up the napkin pieces and squeezed so hard his knuckles turned white. "And I don't want to."

And, just like that, Guy's moment of clarity was over.

"I gotta go, buddy," Will said, crossing the kitchen to take Guy's bowl. "I've got to run a few errands in town before I head to work. You going to be okay?"

"Who, me? I'm fine, William. Just fine. I'll see you at lunchtime."

"There might be a sheriff's cruiser in the neighborhood," Will warned.

He pushed up. "Yeah, yeah, I know. I'm a celebrity now because of that television show." He chuckled. "Hope that Missy comes by later to see me."

He shuffled away, his bedroom slippers tapping against the linoleum, a sound as heartbreaking as anything Will had ever heard.

Serenity hung over Barefoot Bay like the lone pelican that hovered over the still Gulf waters looking for breakfast. Morning on this beach was beyond divine, silent but for the soft breaking of the surf and the occasional cry of a gull, perfect for an hour of yoga before a day of—whatever the day would hold.

Jocelyn dug her toes into the morning-cool sand and tried to conjure up a mental to-do list. There was little she hated as much as an open day.

Okay, she could visit more homes. Or she could pack more of Guy's boxes. She could always help Tessa garden or go find Zoe for some shopping or—an unwanted chill danced over her. She could find Will.

Which was all she really wanted to do.

A bolt of frustration pushed her across the beach, closer to the hard-packed sand where she could begin her stretching exercises. Find the source of frustration and eliminate it, the inner life coach demanded.

Will, of course. He made her frustrated and needy and out of control. A few stolen kisses and Jocelyn's much-ignored libido had kicked into overdrive, torturing her with thoughts of his hands and his body and his—hands.

But it wasn't just Will. She felt lost, somehow.

Disconnected from a business that had occupied her brain every waking minute, distant from a city she mostly loathed but had managed to call home.

It was no wonder she felt out of sorts and lost.

As she approached the water's edge, two sets of footprints pulled her attention. Fresh, deep, one large, one much smaller.

The footprints of a couple walking side by side down the beach.

Jocelyn placed her bare foot in the smaller set and followed the steps, headed south, with the lapping waves on her right. The footprints continued for about a hundred feet, then turned toward the water.

This couple had gone for a morning swim together.

For a moment she stood and stared at the horizon, imagining what it would be like to be that free, that much in love. The smell of salt and sea hanging heavy in the morning air, in the arms of a trusted man, giving yourself so completely.

The ache that took hold of her engulfed her full body, and it was not just sexual.

Jocelyn ached for love.

She let the next wave wash that thought away, following the footsteps when they continued about forty feet away, knowing exactly whose footsteps she was walking in. Of course they took her right to the construction trailer.

She stepped up to the door of the trailer and tapped lightly. "Any owners in here?" She pushed the door just enough to get a peek of Lacey and Clay, kissing at the coffee machine in the front reception area. They turned, both sporting soaking wet hair and satisfied smiles.

And Jocelyn ached some more.

"Joss!" Lacey said, a flush on her cheeks. "You're up early."

"Not as early as some of our resident swimmers."

They laughed and shared a look. "We take a dip every morning on the way to work," Clay told her. "Probably won't be able to do that soon, so we're taking advantage of it."

"You know, when the guests come it'll be awkward," Lacey said quickly.

"You don't wear suits?" Jocelyn asked, fighting a smile.

"They're optional." Clay winked at her. "Want some coffee?"

"I was going to do a little yoga on the beach, but I could stand a cup. Black, please."

Clay grabbed a mug from the makeshift shelves by the coffee station. "Lacey was just saying the other day that we should have morning yoga on the beach," he said. "Our guests would love that."

"Or suit-optional swimming," Jocelyn teased, taking her coffee and giving a mock toast to Clay. "They'd love that, too."

"Here's what they're going to love," Lacey said, waving Jocelyn to the wobbly card table where she unfurled a set of blueprints. "Wait until you see these, Joss."

A few minutes later, Jocelyn was still studying the plans and still speechless with admiration.

"Isn't my husband talented?" Lacey asked, the question directed to Jocelyn but her smile beaming to Clay.

"It's a team effort," he said humbly.

But it was a fact. He may be attentive and sweet and

attractive, but the man was a stunningly gifted architect, and the plans Jocelyn had just perused proved that.

"This spa and treatment center is unbelievable," Jocelyn agreed. "Mimosa Key has never even dreamed of anything this glorious. I love how high-end it is but how natural and even simple it feels."

"That's the whole goal of Casa Blanca," Lacey said. "Simple luxury in the arms of mother nature."

"Hey." Jocelyn snapped her fingers. "Nice tagline."

Clay ambled over to glance at the plans, still sipping coffee. "We have buildings to finish, roads to lay, and a whole hell of a lot of details before we can get to the fun stuff like taglines and holistic spa centers."

"You'll get it done," Lacey said, pride and certainty in her voice.

Jocelyn looked up from the blueprints. "Oh, the confidence of true love."

"I know, right?" Clay laughed, rounding the desk where he worked. "It worries me, though. The higher they go, the harder they fall."

"You're not going to fall," Lacey said before turning to Jocelyn. "He's got the financing figured out and he's found these amazing deals on everything we need. The subs love him."

Clay lifted his booted feet and dropped them on his desk, grinning at Jocelyn. "My wife forgot the walking-on-water part," he said with a self-deprecating eye roll. "And speaking of the subs, I missed my villa carpenter yesterday. Is he going to be back or are you two off gallivanting around Naples again today?"

"They weren't *gallivanting*," Lacey corrected. "Were you?"

"We looked at an assisted-living facility for my father."
And then there was a wee bit of gallivanting. "I can go on
my own if you need him. I really don't want to be the one
to slow down progress on this." She gestured toward the
plans, but Lacey moved the blueprints away.

"If you need him, take him," she said. "We'll be fine."

Clay made a face that said they wouldn't be fine at all.
"You're really getting soft, Lace," he said with a smile.

Lacey smiled back. Jocelyn had the distinct feeling
that there was a serious silent conversation going on and
she definitely did not speak the secret language.

"I'll do some more work down at my father's house
today," Jocelyn said. "I can go visit some of the other
places tomorrow. It's just that Will wants to go. He's
so..." She shook her head. "Invested."

"He cares about your dad," Clay said. "I've picked that
up in things he's said."

Jocelyn cast her eyes toward the plans, not wanting to
respond to that statement. She didn't have to look up to
know Lacey and Clay were silently communicating again.

Let them. They didn't understand; they didn't know
the whole story. Nobody did.

Well, a few people did. Unlikely people. Charity
Grambling. Coco Kirkman.

"The thing I like about Will," Clay said slowly, taking his feet off the desk so he could lean forward to make
his point, or maybe just to get Jocelyn to meet his pierc-
ing blue gaze. "Besides the fact that he is one of the most
meticulous and talented carpenters I've ever met, is that
he's, you know, full of heart."

The words, for some reason, stabbed at Jocelyn's own
heart. That was just so true—and so scary. Jocelyn wasn't

full of heart. Her heart was closed, firm and tight, and Will's was wide open and giving.

He deserved someone who could love him the way he loved, and that would never, ever be her.

"Was he always that way?" Lacey asked Jocelyn. "I mean, when I knew him as a teenager, he was just that superstar baseball player who was going to be the next Derek Jeter."

Jocelyn smiled. "I guess he's always been an emotional guy. Played baseball with heart and now he builds villas with heart." And kisses with heart.

"And now," Clay added as he stood. "He does adult day care with heart."

But that was wrong. That adult hadn't *earned* Will's heart.

"You headed out?" Lacey asked, looking up at Clay with warmth in her golden brown eyes.

"The DOT guys are coming at seven-thirty to do the embankment inspections. When the Department of Transportation shows, I'm there." He came around the back of the table, placing his hands on Lacey's shoulders to lean over and look at the plans. "So, Jocelyn, you like this high-end superorganic over-the-top-expensive spa and wellness center?"

Jocelyn laughed at the hint of sarcasm in his tone. "I think it's amazing and, as an investor, I think it's going to be quite profitable."

"It could be," he agreed. "But expensive as hell to build."

"The spa isn't important to Clay," Lacey explained. "He's all about the structures and design."

He bent over and kissed her head. "Take it easy today, okay?" he whispered.

She shot him a look and nodded. "Easy as I can considering..." Her voice trailed off and they shared one more look. "Considering what we're building here," she finished.

"Just don't get stressed out." One more kiss and he straightened, giving Jocelyn a wink. "She's the one who's going to need a spa treatment."

Lacey flicked away the idea with a disdainful fingertip. "I've had enough while I did research. I just want to get this thing done, fast. Go get the roads approved, Clay, so we can pour the asphalt and start building the privacy wall."

He gave her shoulder a squeeze but looked at Jocelyn. "She's a slave driver."

"*She's* in a hurry," Lacey corrected. "And *we* want to stay on schedule."

He saluted her. "Got it, boss. See ya, ladies."

He poured another cup of coffee and left them alone in the trailer.

"You're so happy," Jocelyn observed.

Lacey's eyes moistened a little. "You have no idea."

"No, I don't," she said on a sigh.

Lacey reached over the plans and gave Jocelyn's hand a squeeze. "You okay?"

"I'm fine. Rough night."

"Were you with Will?" she asked.

"No, of course not. Why would I be with Will?"

Lacey shrugged. "Just wondering. You didn't come over for dinner last night and Tessa and Zoe said you didn't go out for Mexican with them. So we thought—"

"Don't think. I spent the evening alone."

"You do like your solitude," Lacey said. "Zoe says being alone is like air to you."

"Zoe's smarter than she acts. I made a sandwich with all that lovely food you stocked in my fridge. I was really tired."

"Tell me about it," Lacey said. "I crashed around nine, so it's fine." She searched Jocelyn's face again. "You sure you don't want to talk about Will?"

"Yes, I'm sure." She tapped the plans. "So how are you going to fit a life coach into all of this and what do you need from me?"

Lacey took the cue, shifting her attention to the plans. "Well, I'll have to hire, of course. People to run the spa and treatment centers, obviously, and a fitness expert, and a few trainers. I'll need an aesthetician and beauty specialists, and a masseuse. " Lacey sighed slowly. "It's going to be a lot."

"You haven't taken on more than you can handle, have you?" Because she sounded utterly overwhelmed by the work.

"Yeah, but if I knew I had a really great spa manager, someone with incredible organization and people skills…" She leaned forward. "Maybe with a little life-coaching experience and knowledge of this community…"

The implication couldn't be ignored. "Me? I'm…" For one flash of a second, Jocelyn imagined herself running a state-of-the-art spa, surrounded by beauty, peace, and people trying to improve themselves. It would be crisp, clean, pure—and safe. "I'm not your girl."

"Why not?"

She tried to laugh it off. "Um, because I have a business and a life in Los Angeles."

Lacey just lifted a brow. "You don't love living in L.A."

She didn't argue that.

"And that business is in the tank at the moment."

Deep.

"And if Zoe were here, she'd probably ask, 'What life?'"

Jocelyn laughed. "So true. But you need someone trained in spa management and hospitality."

"I'm trained in hospitality, remember? I almost have a degree in it."

"Well, then because you need someone who…" She couldn't think of another reason, damn it. "Who lives here. Or close by."

Lacey dropped her elbows on the table. "I got Tessa here, didn't I?"

"Are you serious about this?"

"Why not?"

"Aren't *you* going to run the spa?" Jocelyn asked.

"I'm going to run the resort, or at least hire the right management, and I'm going to run…" She leaned back and shook her head a little, a hint of sleeplessness suddenly evident under her eyes. "Owning this place is a huge job. Clay wants to be an architect, not a resort manager. I'm looking to farm out whatever I can and I want those people to be trusted friends. I want to surround myself with people I love and who'll love my kids and husband, so I'm starting early recruitment. Would you even think—"

"Did you say kids? Plural?"

Lacey's jaw dropped and she slapped a hand over her mouth. "Shit," she muttered. "I did."

For a second, they just stared at each other as a slow smile curved Lacey's lips. "I suck at secrets."

Jocelyn jumped up and let out a little scream. "Oh my God, Lacey!"

They hugged awkwardly over the table, nearly knocking it over, and then, laughing, they both scooted around for a proper embrace.

"Can you believe it?" Lacey squeaked, her eyes good and teary now.

"How far?"

"Six weeks."

Jocelyn leaned back, still holding her shoulders, looking at Lacey with new eyes. *That's* what was radiating off her. Not just love, but motherhood. And a damn understandable reason for exhaustion. "You want this." It wasn't a question.

"So bad."

"Does Ashley know she's going to be a sister?"

"We haven't told a soul," she said. "Not my parents, not Ashley, not Tessa." She made a face. "Which is not going to be fun."

"Why? She'll be thrilled."

"Doubtful. You know how badly she wanted a baby. All those years trying with Billy, and his new girlfriend gets pregnant before the ink was dry on the divorce settlement."

Jocelyn waved that off. "Tessa loves you and she's going to be the proudest aunt of all. Why are you waiting?"

"Just keeping it to ourselves, making sure everything's okay. But I'm getting so used to the idea, and, God, how do you keep secrets so well?"

"It's an art," she said drily. "So you don't have to worry about me. I won't tell anyone until you're ready."

Lacey dropped back in her seat, still looking worried. "I guess I'm ready, once we tell Ashley. But I am starting to stress out big time about running this place and having a baby."

"You're going to be fine," Jocelyn assured her. "You'll do it the same way every working mother does. With lists and help and sleep-deprivation and wine. Wine! You had wine the other night."

"I fake-drank." She grinned. "My plants are pretty looped, though."

Jocelyn laughed. "You are a sneak!"

But Lacey leaned in again, reaching a hand to Jocelyn. "My offer is legit and now you know just how much I need someone like you. Maybe not immediately, but after this baby is born, we'll be close to opening and I want this place to run so smoothly. But I also want to be a good mom." She touched her belly, rubbing. "So, think about it, okay? Come and run my spa for me. You'll have plenty of time to close up your business."

She rolled her eyes. "My business is closing for me."

"It would be so wonderful, Joss—"

The door popped open with a resounding bang followed by an equally loud, "I'm pissed!"

Tessa bounded inside, her boots hitting the floorboards so hard the whole trailer shook.

"What's wrong?" Jocelyn and Lacey asked in perfect unison.

Tessa waved her cell phone. "The son of a bitch did it again!" She marched across the small space and slammed the phone between them, nearly collapsing the card table. "His girlfriend is pregnant again! And he had the audacity to text me. Their first kid isn't even a year old, they still haven't gotten married, and now he has another one on the way."

Jocelyn and Lacey were stone silent, both blinking like they'd been caught in headlights, but Tessa was too worked up to notice. She grabbed a folding chair and practically threw it next to the table, plopping down with a soft curse.

"How can he text me like I'm supposed to be happy for him? Who does that, anyway—texts their ex-wife when their new girlfriend is pregnant? What the hell does he think I'm made of?"

They still couldn't quite talk. Lacey swallowed hard and Jocelyn dug for the right thing to say, coming up with nothing.

Tessa looked from one to the other, then down at the plans. "What are you two discussing, anyway?"

"M-my..." Lacey stuttered, obviously unable to come up with anything.

"Job offer," Jocelyn supplied. "She wants me to work here."

Tessa gasped and grinned and gave a solid clap. "A capital idea!"

And just like that, they managed to steer the conversation away from babies and onto business.

Chapter 16

⌒

Will climbed out of his truck at the Mimosa Community Credit Union a few minutes after the bank opened, the last of the stops he had to make that morning. Just as he reached for the handle of the charcoal-tinted glass door, it popped open, pushed by someone inside.

" 'Scuse me," he murmured, stepping to the side and nearly getting run over by Charity Grambling, who had her head down, her nose in the open end of a manila envelope.

With a soft gasp, she looked up, jerking the envelope away. Then she shot him a vile look, her features arranged in a way that screamed anger. Brows drawn, lips down, nothing but fury carved into the deep lines on her face.

Man, she'd been poorly named.

"Everything okay, Charity?"

Her dark eyes tapered as the wind lifted her frizzy carmel-colored hair, revealing a band of gray roots underneath. "No, Will. Some things are just not okay."

He hesitated, stepping farther to the side but still holding the door for her. "Sorry to hear that," he said, expecting her to fire a retort and stomp away.

But she just sucked in a breath so deep it made her narrow nostrils quiver.

Oh, boy. Charity was in a mood to gossip. "Hope your day gets better," he said quickly, trying to zip by her into the air-conditioned lobby of the credit union.

But she stood stone still, five feet two inches of granite and grit. "Where's Jocelyn?"

The question threw him enough to make him stop. Charity may be playing the good cop this week, but he'd known this woman too long to trust her. "Is someone looking for her?" he asked, purposely not answering.

"Yes, for cryin' out loud. I am. Where is she?"

He just shook his head.

"I need to see her. I have something for her. I promised it to her."

She had? Curiosity tweaked, but he tamped it down. "I can give her whatever you have, Charity."

"No way. This is eyes only. Her eyes only."

"I won't look at it."

She practically hooted with disbelief. "Like I'd believe a man."

"You can believe me."

She shook her head. "Where is she?"

"I'm sorry, Charity. I'm sworn to secrecy and my word is good. Whatever you have, give it to me. Does it have to do with her situation?"

"I'll say it does." She tapped the manila envelope against her hands.

"I know everything," he said earnestly. "I know the truth and she trusts me. Is that what you want to give her?"

She clutched the envelope tighter, scrutinizing his face like she could eyeball whether or not he was a liar.

"You can trust me." He held out his hand.

"Have her call me and come to the store."

"She might not," he said. "She's keeping a very low profile. But suit yourself. I'll tell her I saw you." He tried to slip by her, but she inched to the side.

"I can trust you for sure?"

"You have my word."

She shoved the envelope into his hands. "Give this to her. And if you even think about opening it, God'll strike you down dead. And if He doesn't, I will."

What the hell could it be? He didn't make the mistake of looking remotely curious, but took the envelope with a solemn nod and tucked it under his arm. "You want her to call you or anything?"

"Just..." She drew in another breath. "Be there if she falls."

Coming from anyone else, it would have been a cliché. Coming from Charity, who hadn't spoken five kind words in her life, the expression damn near blew him away.

And piqued his curiosity, but he kept the envelope under his arm the whole time he made his transaction at the teller window and returned to his truck. Feeling a little like he had contraband, he set the envelope on the passenger seat with his bandanna, Gatorades, and a box of protein bars that kept him going all day. After glancing around for wayward reporters who might jump or follow him, he headed up to Barefoot Bay.

How did Charity fit into the whole Miles Thayer–Coco Kirkman scandal? What could she have? Copies of those texts he'd heard about on TV? An affidavit? The confidentiality agreement? News stories? Why the hell would Charity Grambling have anything like that?

Why would she tell him to be there if Jocelyn falls?

As if he needed someone to suggest that. But maybe there was more news about to break and—

As he came around the bend near the bay, he slammed on the brakes, screeching to a stop a few feet from a road-block of bright-orange drums and two DOT trucks.

Everything on the passenger seat went sailing forward, the Gatorades thumping, the protein bars flying, and Charity's envelope shooting to the floor.

Shit, he'd totally forgotten the transportation inspection was today.

Clay and another man stepped out from behind the truck and waved.

"Hang on, Will," Clay called. "We'll get you through in a second."

Will waved back, holding the brake with his left foot and reaching down to the floor to retrieve the lost bars and juice.

And the contents of the envelope, which had slipped out and lay on the floor.

Pictures.

Will froze halfway to the floor, absolutely unable to keep his gaze from going where he'd given his word it wouldn't go. But his gaze had a will of its own and he glanced at pictures of—

He blinked, his head buzzing at the image that scarred his brain.

Pictures of Jocelyn.

Nothing on earth—no promise, no word of honor, no guarantee that he wouldn't look—could stop him from staring at the sight. His breath stopped, his heart leaped into overdrive, and he picked up a photograph with a shaky hand.

He stared at it, only half aware that his throat had closed up and out of his mouth came an inhuman whimper of pain.

He jumped when Clay pounded on the hood of the truck. "Hey, wake up, Palmer. You can go through now."

Trying to swallow, trying to breath, he just stared at Clay, not sure if he could drive or even keep himself from opening the door and puking his guts out.

Clay banged again and made a grand gesture for Will to drive.

Somehow, he did, still holding a picture that changed *everything*.

Damn it all, she couldn't even concentrate on a simple garland pose. Jocelyn's heels sank into the wet sand the same way the conversation she'd just had with Lacey pressed into her heart.

Lacey was pregnant; that was, quite honestly, not a surprise. From the moment Lacey and Clay had stopped fighting the battle and given in to their feelings, Lacey had wanted to beat the biological clock and squeeze in another child. Even with a fifteen-year-old from her long-ago college love affair, Lacey had always wanted a second child.

But that wasn't what made Jocelyn's slow rise to a chair pose so unsteady.

The equilibrium problems came from deep inside her gut, the origin of all balance. Because way in her innermost core, Jocelyn was actually considering Lacey's offer. Lacey needed her and she needed—

"Hey!"

The single word, shot like a bullet across the beach, knocked her right on her ass. Landing in the sand, she turned to see Will marching across the beach, the first flutter of happiness instantly erased by the sense that something was very, very wrong.

He carried a paper or card of some kind in one hand, his arms swinging as though he could propel himself forward faster. His face was dark with a scowl, his muscles bunched, his jaw set.

Was Guy hurt?

She pushed up, brushing sand from her yoga pants, not sure why Guy would be her first thought or why that thought would tighten her stomach with worry.

Something was wrong.

At a distance of about twenty feet, she could practically see Will's nostrils flare.

"What's the matter?" she asked, her words carrying over the breeze but eliciting no response as he marched off the remaining space and stopped right in front of her.

"Will?" She tried and failed to read his expression.

He took a slow breath, his chest rising and falling as he stared at her, the silence so unnerving she bit her lip and took a step backwards.

"Why didn't you tell me?" The question was low and husky, almost drowned out by the squawk of a gull.

"Tell you…" Her gaze fell to the large envelope he was holding. And her heart stopped.

"I ran into Charity at the credit union," he said.

Oh, no. *No.*

"She gave me something for you."

Finally, she dragged her gaze from the envelope to his face, simply unable to put words to the tornado of emotions twisting through her. "And you looked at it."

"Not intentionally. But I saw—" He closed his eyes, a shudder rolling through him. "Why didn't I know this? Why didn't you come to me? Why?"

She took another step back, the impact of the words—and him knowing the truth—too much for her to handle.

"He gave you a black eye."

Agony stretched across her chest, pressing so hard she couldn't breathe.

"He beat you." His voice cracked and he swallowed, his Adam's apple quivering "He left marks all... over... you."

She shivered, running he hands over goose-bump-covered arms, blood rushing so noisily through her head she couldn't hear her own thoughts.

"And you never told me." The last sentence was spoken on a sigh, all the anger gone, only sadness there.

She finally exhaled. "You'd have gotten yourself killed or ended up in jail. It would have cost you everything."

"Who cares? He *beat* you because of me."

No, he beat her because he was a heartless animal. "You shouldn't have looked at those."

"Kind of a moot point now, Jocelyn. You should have told me. You should have come to *me*, not Charity Grambling."

"I didn't go to Charity. She picked me up on the street."

He grunted like she'd punched him. "You left that night and didn't walk fifty feet to *me*?"

"So you could do what? Ruin your life and your dreams and your career?"

"Jocelyn." He could barely say her name. "He deserved to die."

Stepping closer, she reached for the envelope. "But he wouldn't have. And you might have. Give it to me."

He just gripped it tighter. "He could have killed you."

"He almost did." She snagged the envelope from his hands, the paper still warm from his touch. "Now you know why I never contacted you."

He tunneled his fingers in his hair, dragging them through like he could yank out the facts. "God, I hate him."

"Welcome to my world."

He opened his mouth to say something, then closed it. Jocelyn looked down at the envelope, part of her almost wanting to open it, but she couldn't stand to see those images again. She wasn't even sure why she'd asked Charity to give them to her, except for the joy of burning them.

And now they were burned into Will's brain. Where she'd never, ever wanted them.

"This can't come as a surprise to you," she said softly, tucking the pictures under her arm.

"I didn't think he'd actually hit you. Fuck, why didn't he hit me? I was the one on top of you when he found us."

"Because he's a *wife*beater, Will," she spat the word. "That kind of sick human doesn't go after other men who are bigger and stronger. They go after weak females who are dependent on them."

She started up the beach, but he was right next to her.

"What are you going to do?" he asked.

She froze and let out a dry laugh. "Do? I'm not filing charges, if that's what you mean. I did what I needed to do, Will, fifteen years ago. I left. I gave up the only thing in the whole world that mattered to me and I ran away, put myself through college, and started a life three thousand miles away. It's too late to do anything else now."

She kicked some sand as she took off toward her villa, absolutely unable to stand the way he was looking at her. She could never look at Will Palmer again without knowing he was seeing those pictures, her pummeled, helpless body.

Pictures that Charity insisted on taking and using to get Guy to resign from the sheriff's department and hole up in his house for fear of having those images on the cover of the *Mimosa Gazette*.

Will was next to her in three steps. "What did you give up?" he asked.

She slowed again, kind of unable to believe he didn't know. "What do you think?"

He frowned and then everything just fell. His shoulders, his mouth, his heart.

"I gave up you," she said, confirming what he'd obviously just figured out.

"It was me." He almost choked on the realization. She could see the moment it dawned and all the pieces of the puzzle fit. "I was the person you sacrificed for love."

She didn't have to confirm or deny; the sucker punch contorted his expression.

"You walked away from me, to protect me, when I should have protected..." He closed his eyes, unable even to voice the last word. "Oh, God, Jocelyn."

This was exactly what she didn't want. His hate and guilt, his regret and anger, his inability to look at her without feeling inadequate.

"This is why I didn't tell you."

"But I never went after you. I was...*waiting*." His lip curled in self-loathing as he said the word.

"I didn't expect you to," she replied quickly, aching to take that look off his face. "In fact, I was relieved you didn't. I didn't want you saddled with Guy Bloom any more than you..." Her voice faded away as she realized what she'd just said. "I guess I failed and you're saddled with him after all."

"Like hell I am."

She drew back, surprised by his vehemence.

"If we can't get that son of a bitch in jail, then the old-age home is the next best thing."

"*Now* you want to put him in a home?"

"Now I want to put him in a grave."

"Well, I'd prefer you didn't, since I gave up an awful lot a long time ago to make sure you didn't commit murder." She kept on walking, her eye on the villa in the distance. If she could get there, she could survive this. She could get through this moment of hell.

"Where are you going?" he demanded.

"Away." She finally turned and looked at him. "I'm going away."

"Damn it, why? Why do you always do that? You run and you hide and you disappear. You can't do that again, Jocelyn."

Oh yes, she could. "That's how I survived the first eighteen years of my life, Will. I'm not about to change. Even for you."

His face registered the hit, and while he stood stone still, she made her escape.

And, just like the last time, he let her go.

Chapter 17

ᴄ

Will Palmer, man of fucking inaction. Protected by the very woman he was supposed to protect. Hatred—for himself, for Guy, for the messy cards they'd been dealt—constricted his chest so hard he could barely breathe through the pain.

He could have gone his whole damn life and not have known that because of him, the only woman he'd ever really loved got the crap kicked out of her.

Because of him.

Shoving his hand in his pocket, he pulled out his bandanna and wiped the sweat from his face, starting the trek across the beach to the path.

This time he was not waiting for an invitation. He was not waiting for a goddamn thing ever again. Not this woman, not permission, not a decision, not the truth. Thrumming with focus and raw with emotion, he approached the villa quietly, noticing that the side french doors were closed tight. His heart finally slowing to a steady, if miserable, thump, he walked up to the door, turned the handle, and pushed it open.

"Joss?"

From the back, he heard the soft hiss of water. The shower.

"Joss?" he called, a little louder so he didn't scare her when he went back there.

She didn't answer, so he rounded the galley kitchen and poked his head into the bedroom. The bed was made like housekeeping had just left, pillows propped, the mosquito netting neatly pulled back.

Except there was no housekeeping at Casa Blanca yet.

In fact, everything in the room was pristine, like it was when Lacey decorated it to shoot pictures for her first brochures. If he hadn't heard the shower in the bathroom, he'd swear no one was staying here.

He walked to the bathroom door and put his hand on the brass lever and pushed, half expecting it to be locked but relieved when it opened a few inches.

In spite of the hiss of the shower, he heard her sniff.

She was crying, of course. The thought ripped him.

I bet she cried that night Guy beat her.

On the floor, he saw paper. Pages of it, strewn around like someone had opened a package of loose leaf and used it as confetti. Pushing the door open, he looked toward the curved glass doors that had been such a bitch to install. The water was pouring, but the stall was empty.

"Are you in here, Joss?"

This time, the sniff was accompanied by a shudder, and the sound of paper tearing.

He stepped inside and found her sitting against the wall next to the shower, wearing a bra and panties, the floor littered with handwritten pages, some with just a word or two, some with more.

She didn't look up from the notebook in front of her.

"What are you doing, Bloomerang?" he asked with every drop of gentleness he could muster.

"I was about to take a shower, but decided to make some lists."

At any other time, that would have made him smile. But nothing about her pain-ravaged face was amusing. He went in a little farther. "What's on them?"

She finally looked up, her eyes red-rimmed. "Things to do."

"What things?"

She stared at him for a second, then, without looking down, she stripped a sheet of paper off the spiral, the tearing sound echoing through the bathroom. "Goals, plans, strategies, tactics, time lines, action items."

"Of what?"

She just let out a little puff of air. "That's just the problem. I can't come up with the right theme, the right word."

He closed the space and got right next to her, slowly dropping to a catcher's crouch until they were nearly eye level. "Maybe I can help."

In response she smoothed her hand over the white page, silent.

His bad knee throbbed, so he relaxed onto the floor next to her, bracing himself on the marble countertop on his way down. He remembered the day he'd set that counter. Never dreamed he'd be in here with Jocelyn nearly naked, making lists while the shower ran.

"How do you come up with this theme?" he asked.

She clutched a pen so tightly her fingers were turning white. "It usually just comes to me. A word or phrase will resonate and then I know what's troubling me and what I need to fix."

"With a list?"

"Don't knock what you haven't tried."

He glanced at the pages on the floor, most containing a few crossed-out words. "Maybe you're trying too hard," he suggested, reaching to relieve her of the pen before she snapped it in two. "When I was in a slump at the plate or made a bunch of errors, it was always because I was trying too hard not to."

She relaxed enough to let him take the pen. "What did you do?" she asked, her voice a reedy whisper.

"Tried to psych myself into thinking nothing was wrong. Would walk up to the plate and pretend I was batting .450 instead of, you know, .110. Or I'd get behind the plate and just pretend it was practice instead of a play-off game. Stuff like that."

"Lot of pretending," she said. "Did you notice that's what you did both times? Pretend."

"Worked."

"It's stupid to pretend."

"Not if it gets you out of a slump. Try it on your list: pretend."

"Okay, let's see," she said, loading up for a shot of sarcasm. "I could *pretend* you never saw those pictures."

But he had.

"I could *pretend* you didn't know that happened."

But he did.

"I could *pretend* my childhood was completely normal."

But it wasn't.

"I could *pretend* I don't care about what you think."

"Stop right there," he said, reaching for her. "What I think doesn't make a damn bit of difference."

She took a slow, ragged breath, searching his eyes, her brows drawing closer and closer together as she fought a sob. "That's where you're wrong, Will."

She lost the battle and choked on a lump in her throat, cringing in embarrassment. "I don't want you to... know...about that."

He gripped her, careful not to squeeze, not to break. "It doesn't change anything."

"It changes everything!" Her eyes flashed and filled. "I can't stand to even look at you now."

"No, no. Don't ever say that. Never."

"I can't." A tear escaped and rolled down her cheek. "It was better before," she said, giving in to the sob and letting him pull her closer. "It was better with you not knowing."

"Maybe it was," he agreed, stroking her hair. "But it wasn't right. You and me separating because of Guy was never right. We were just getting started." He eased her away so he could look into her eyes when he said the rest. "We were just falling in love."

A soft whimper caught in her throat. "Were we?"

He traced her wet cheek, wiping the tear. "You know we were."

"I was."

"Me, too."

She leaned against his forehead. "He stole that."

"We let him," he said, his voice as rough as the nine-inch nail that felt like it was sliding through his breastbone and into his heart. "Jocelyn." He cupped her chin and held her face steady. "I'm so sorry he hurt you. It was my fault."

"No, it—"

"Yes, it was."

"You can't blame yourself for his violence."

"I should have taken him that night." Memories flashed in his mind: the gun, the look on Guy's face, the gut-deep certainty that he was about to die. And even after Guy left, all he could do was stand there like a complete idiot and stare at his shrine, paralyzed with fear.

While Jocelyn was taking what was meant for him. "I was chickenshit," he admitted. "Not going after you was chickenshit."

"He had a gun, so chickenshit was a smart call."

"Even...after. When I went to school. I knew why you didn't call me and I...was too scared of...losing everything." His throat was thick with disgust and regret, the emotions choking him. "And I did lose everything. I lost you."

She shuddered softly, as if the words electrified her.

He held her face, spreading his hands and then burying his fingers in her hair. "Everything," he whispered. "You were everything and I didn't even know it."

Closing her eyes, she exhaled slow and long, as if she'd held that breath for years.

"But, it's too late, Will."

"Is it?" He tried to pull her closer, but she froze and inched back, away from him. "Is it?" he asked again, somehow feeling her slip away emotionally as well as physically.

"Of course it is," she said brusquely. "But thank you."

"Thank—for what?"

She gave him a gentle nudge, pushing him completely away, driving him crazy. "That's exactly what I needed."

"What is?"

"The word for my list. I just couldn't figure out what I was looking to organize and now I know." She grabbed the notebook, took back the pen, and scratched the word *everything* on the top of the page as she stood up.

"Everything? What kind of list theme is that?"

"Everything I have to do to get out of here." She wrote *Guy*. "Get him moved." *Stuff.* "Pack his trash." *House.* "Sell his house." *Business.* "Get new clients." She took a few more steps, entirely focused on her list. "Oh and I have to help Lacey find a spa manager, and . . ." Her voice faded as she walked out the bathroom door.

"Where am I on that list of everything?" he called.

"You're not."

Why the fuck not?

"That's not acceptable." Will's hands landed on Jocelyn's shoulders, his grip far less tender than it had been in the bathroom. He turned her from the closet before she had a chance to grab a sundress so she could sit outside and breathe fresh air.

She didn't bother to ask what wasn't acceptable; it was clear by the look on his face, the fire in his eyes, and set of his strong jaw.

"I want to be on that list."

No, that would never work. Not now that he knew the truth. And she knew Will; he'd make room in his big old heart for Guy. And that history would always be there, haunting them. Or, worse, he'd forgive Guy and expect her to do the same. *No.* "There's no room for you on my list." *Or in my orderly, controlled, emotionally safe life.*

"Make room."

"There's no time for you."

"Make time."

"There's no..." She shook her head. "Please, Will. The same thing that's always been between us is still between us."

"Guy? I thought we had a..." He gestured toward the notebook on the bed. "A strategy for him."

"We?" She almost smiled.

"Everything's changed, now, Joss. We're in this together. Everything's changed."

"Yes, it has. You know and I...I can't stand that you know."

"I can't stand that I did nothing to stop it. That you ran away so that I could have a life and gave up everything—"

"I didn't give up everything, Will." She turned back to the closet, trying to think, digging wildly for control of the chaos in her heart. And failing.

"How did you...how did it all unfold?"

Did he really have to know this? She pushed some hangers, hard, like they were the memories she didn't want. "Charity and Gloria found me on the street. Charity took me in and respected that I didn't want to file charges."

"Why the hell not?"

She closed her eyes and exhaled.

"Because of me," he assumed, correctly.

"I didn't want you dragged in as some kind of witness the week you were off to college and your baseball career."

Behind her, he swore softly. "Then what?"

"Then Charity fixed me up, got all my stuff, got me to college. And she made damn sure my father knew she had proof of what he'd done, and forced him to resign from his job. She used to come by and check on my mother periodically, too, and let me know that everything was okay."

"So I was replaced by Charity Grambling."

"Will!" She whirled around, patience gone. "This isn't about you."

He held up both hands to stave off her anger. "I know, Joss, I know. But I can't fucking stand that I let you down like that." His hands relaxed and came down on her bare shoulders. "I want to make it up to you."

She lifted her eyes to meet his, knowing the pain and regret she saw there mirrored her own. "You have. You took care of Guy."

He grunted softly. "If I'd have known…"

"You'd have killed him."

"Then everything worked out like it was supposed to, because he's alive and I'm…and you're…and we're… together."

She lifted a brow. "Not exactly."

"I want to be. I want to be with you. I want to—"

He pulled her into him and met her mouth with his, hard and fast and unexpected. His arms tightened and he pressed hard, with no finesse but so, so much emotion.

"Give me a chance, Joss." He ground the words into her mouth. "Give me a goddamn chance to show you that."

Her fingers closed on his arms, the power in them emanating through her whole body. Everything in her responded, head to toe, heart to soul. She fought for a moment, her hands fisted, pushing and then pulling.

But she had to stop. *Had* to.

Couldn't.

Instead, she opened her mouth and let him in, bowing her back and pressing her body into his, dizzy with the thrill just that much contact gave her. He dragged his hands over her bare back, letting them slide on to her backside, adding pressure and pleasure and pain all at the same time.

She burrowed her fingers into his hair, holding his head, taking, taking, taking the kiss.

But she had to stop. Otherwise, they'd—

With superhuman effort, she finally pulled herself away, the separation actually making her ache.

"Will." She exhaled. "You are completely controlled by emotions."

And she shouldn't be. Couldn't afford to lose control and trust a man. Even Will. *Especially* Will.

His lips curved up in a half smile. "Yeah, I am."

"You can't live that way." At least she couldn't. It was too scary and made her much too vulnerable.

"That's what you don't understand, Joss. You can't live any other way; you can only exist."

She shuttered her eyes and leaned into him, shaking uncontrollably. Whole-body terror gripped her. "I don't want to lose control," she whispered.

"I noticed." He kissed her cheek, her neck, along the line of her shoulder. She could feel his erection growing, his heart pounding. "But I'm going to do whatever it takes to get on your damn list."

She dropped her head on his shoulder, the sheer bliss of it weakening her knees. "You don't want to be on my list, Will."

"That's where you're wrong. We're in this together now. Fifteen years to make up for, and I'm going to do that. I am." He tilted her chin up, stealing the strength of his shoulder but replacing it with the power of his eyes. "I am."

Deep down inside her, everything boiled and brewed and bubbled up, threatening...everything. Her legs nearly buckled under her and, sensing that, he backed her right into the bed and eased her down.

Oh, God. Was this it?

Every kiss was so hot his mouth burned her skin, one hand on her bra, the other sliding over her belly to touch her.

She let out a soft cry, pushing him with her arms while she pulled him with her legs.

What the hell was wrong with her? "Stop, Will, stop."

He did, instantly. Lifting his head to look into her eyes, his hand frozen on top of her breast. "You don't want to?"

Oh, yes, she did. She wanted to with every white-hot nerve in her body. But she—how could she tell him the truth?

Hadn't he had enough life-changing revelations? "Tell me what you're thinking, Joss. Just tell me. We're starting over, square one, new game, first inning. Tell me what you're thinking."

How could she? "I'm really, really scared." Of what was inevitable: sex. Every time, those old fears bubbled up, memories of that night when they'd been so close to losing control. And what it had cost her. "I'm scared of that feeling of not being in control."

"Tell me something I don't know."

Maybe she should. Maybe she should just tell him that because of that night—

From her dresser, the soft ring of her cell phone saved her from any confessions. She nudged him off her, getting a moan of frustration when she left his arms to get the phone.

"Hey, Zoe, what's up?" she asked after glancing at the caller ID.

"I'm at your dad's house." It wasn't the words but the utter lack of humor in Zoe's voice that made Jocelyn straighten and listen, placing her hand on the dresser for a little support.

"You are?"

"Tessa had to go to work and I was, you know, just thinking about the old dude after all the fun I had babysitting yesterday, so I thought I'd check on him."

"That was thoughtful." Which seemed to be what Guy elicited from *everyone* these days. "And?"

"You need to get down here, Joss."

She tried to swallow, but it wasn't easy. "Why?"

"Just get here. Fast."

"Okay. I'll be there soon." She tapped the screen and turned to Will, a thousand possible ways to go with this at war in her brain.

Something was wrong with Guy. How would Will react to that? The way he reacted to everything: emotionally. She couldn't deal with that now. She couldn't *control* that now. Or ever.

"What's wrong?" he asked.

"That was Zoe." She slipped by him to grab something to wear from the closet. "She ... needs me."

"Is she okay?" He blocked her, reaching to her face. "You look so pale."

"Yeah, fine. She's just Zoe. Everything's a crisis. It's

nothing. She's a drama queen, but I'm going down to, um, to Tessa's to see her. So . . ."

"So I should get lost."

She smiled. "Not in so many words."

"Then use real words and tell me what you want."

All she ever wanted: space, solitude, and security. Except—she glanced to the messy bedspread, imagining what had almost happened there.

Space, solitude, security—and, now, *sex*.

She wanted that so much she didn't trust herself to be alone with Will. "I just need some time and space," she said vaguely.

"I'll give you a little," he agreed, reaching for her waist to pull her into him. "And I'll give you a warning."

Her eyes widened at the tone in his voice.

"We're just getting started, Jocelyn Bloom. I screwed up, bad. But I have fifteen years to make up for and I'm going to. No matter what it takes, I'm going to make it up to you and I'm going to *be* your goddamn action item at the top of your goddamn list. And you know what the theme is going to be?"

Sex? Healing? Love? "What?"

"Everything." He pulled her into him and ground out the word. "I want it all."

She just blinked at him. "I've never given anyone . . . my all."

"There's a first time for everything." He trailed his finger down her throat until he landed on the soft swell of breast over her heart. "I'm going to crack that shell, Joss. I am. I'm the one."

She could have fainted the words hit her so hard.

"Will, I'm afraid."

"Of what?"

Of everything. "You crack the shell, you break my heart."

"I won't," he swore, his voice strained with the power of his promise. "I won't."

She just dropped her head to his chest, wanting to believe him so much it hurt. But that would mean letting go of all her control, and she just wasn't sure she could survive that.

Chapter 18

Jocelyn's heart stopped when she turned onto Sea Breeze, the sight before her so completely surreal she had to brake and blink to accept what she was seeing.

Guy was halfway across the street, dragging their old aluminum rowboat behind him. And Zoe was *helping*.

"What are you doing?" Jocelyn asked as she climbed out of the car.

"Oh, shit," Guy said, dropping the rope. "Now we're busted."

Jocelyn slammed the car door and marched closer, dividing her attention between Guy, who looked a bit sheepish, and Zoe, who hooked a hand on her hip and flattened him with an I-told-you-so look.

"Where are you going with that thing?" Jocelyn demanded, not even sure how they'd gotten it down from the garage loft.

"We're hiding it," Guy said.

"Where? Why?"

He looked at Zoe for help, but she just waved an innocent hand at him. "It's your gig, hot stuff. You do the 'fessing up."

"We're hiding it in the river," Guy finally said, shuffling on old sneakers. It was the first time Jocelyn had seen him out of bedroom slippers. "You probably don't know this, but there's one behind those houses," he added.

It wasn't exactly a river, but a series of crisscrossing canals that cut into the western border of Pleasure Pointe. The waterways were dotted with tiny mangrove hammocks generously referred to as "islands" even though they were little more than mounds of muck and home to gators and snakes. Locals kayaked and fished in there, just as Guy had many years ago.

In *that* boat.

"I know what's back there," she said, shifting her attention to the boat just as a sudden and unexpected memory surged up. A snapshot, really, of a moment in that rowboat, holding a paddle, smiling up at Mom, who held a camera, laughing, calling out *Say Happy Birthday, Jossie.*

She put her hand to her mouth as the impact washed over her senses, so crisp and clear she could practically smell the brackish water and feel the warm wood of a paddle in her hand.

"Why are you doing this?" She directed the question to Zoe, who really should know better.

"So you don't sell it in the yard sale," Zoe said, obviously parroting Guy.

When Jocelyn opened her mouth to respond, her father held up his hand. "Don't try to gift me, girlie, there's is nothing you can buy me that will equal what this boat means to me."

"It *means* something to you?" How was that possible? He had no memory of, let alone attachment to, this boat.

"Darn right it does."

"What?" Jocelyn got close enough to see two bright spots of color on his cheeks, along with a light sheen of perspiration from the exertion. "What does it mean to you, Guy?"

He took a deep breath, his eyes darting back and forth the way they did when he was trying to mine for a memory and came up with nothing. He finally gave a look of sheer desperation to Zoe. "Help me out, Blondie. You know I'm not good with details."

Zoe wiped a stray curl from her face, her skin also pink, either from sun or strain or mischievousness. "He was pretty dead set on the idea." She pushed up her sunglasses to add a look. "I guess stubbornness is hereditary," she said, a little too softly for Guy to catch.

"Well stupid isn't, and this is just—" Frustration zinged at the mere sight of the damn boat, little more than a tin canoe with boards and oars. But still, it had been their *boat*. "But you can't just take this to the canal and leave it there."

"Why not?" They asked in perfect unison and, worse, perfect harmony.

"It'll get stolen," Jocelyn said.

Zoe snorted. "Have you looked closely at this vessel?"

In the sunlight, the thirty-year-old aluminum looked more like aged pewter, all the shine it ever had long gone. The three wooden "pews" across the middle were faded and chipped, and the old marine numbers along one side were illegible now.

"No one'll take it, Missy." Guy reached down to pick up the rope and hoist it again, the aluminum hull making a scraping sound on the asphalt.

"You're supposed to carry it," Jocelyn said, automatically reaching toward the boat to stem the damage and stop the painful screech.

"It weighs ninety-seven pounds!" he said.

How did he remember that and not his own daughter? "I'll help you." She grabbed the side. "It's supposed to be carried upside down, overhead. Three of us can do it. Let's get it back in the garage."

"No!" he barked, making Jocelyn jump.

"Guy—"

"Missy," he whined. "Let's just take it for a ride on the river. Please?" He sounded more like six than sixty-four. "I want to show my new friend the islands and all the wildlife."

Jocelyn looked at Zoe for some backup.

"Well," Zoe said, "we do have it all the way out here and it's a really pretty day."

Not *that* kind of backup. "No, we're taking it back—"

"Jocelyn!"

"Missy!"

Again with the unison and harmony. Whatever had made her think putting these two together was a good idea?

"Really, Joss," Zoe added. "Why not?"

"Because..." She stepped in front of Zoe, her back to Guy, lowering her voice to make her point through gritted teeth. "You said there was some kind of emergency."

"There was, but I solved it."

"By dragging a canoe across the street?"

"It calmed him down. When I got there, he was in his

closet crying like a baby and blubbering about a canoe. The only way I could talk him off the ledge was if he showed it to me. Once we saw it ..." She shrugged. "Well, shoot, I like boat rides. I thought it would be fun."

"What about this is fun?"

"Holy hell, Joss, lighten up. He's got nothing. He's lonely and bored. Let's take him out on the water. What can it hurt?"

"It could hurt ..." *Me*. "Without sunscreen."

Zoe tilted her head. "Say *what*?"

How could she tell Zoe that a trip down those canals in this rowboat could hurt Jocelyn's heart, and her head, and force her to unlock boxes of lovely memories and perfect afternoons that should never, ever be set loose?

It was bad enough that the only version of Guy that Zoe knew was a sweet old man who loved needlepoint and reruns of home-improvement shows. If she knew there was actually a time when he was—

Daddy.

"I'm melting," Zoe singsonged.

"It's nice and cool in the canals," Guy said. "Shady, too."

"I ..." Jocelyn looked from one to the other, then down at the ancient boat.

She really ought to be able to go out there, take a nice little relaxing row, and move the hell on. Wasn't that what she'd tell a client? *Physician, heal thyself*.

"Okay," she said softly, bending down to get a grip on the boat. "Go get the paddles, Zoe. Can't exactly go up a creek without one, right?"

Zoe threw an arm around Jocelyn's neck while Guy shouted, "Hooray!"

"Good girl," Zoe whispered in Jocelyn's ear.

Jocelyn pulled away and gave her a withering look. "This was so not on my to-do list today."

"Ah, spontaneity." Zoe looked up at the sky. "My work here is done."

"Like hell it is," Jocelyn said. "You're paddling."

The subcontractor meeting was coming to an end and Will had no idea what they'd discussed for the last hour. Clay had run the weekly meeting, as always, and since most of the time-line discussions were about the main building, Will had zoned out.

Because all he could think about were those pictures. And the way Jocelyn had felt in his arms, how much she still got to him, all these years later. He was torn, confused, hurt, and, most of all, so full of anger and hate that he wanted to punch a wall instead of build one.

"Are you, Will?"

He did a double take at Clay's question, clueless how to answer.

"The marble inlay for Bay Laurel's master bath. Are you laying it next week?"

Was he? Who the fuck knew what he was doing next week? Of if there'd be any laying involved. "I'll let you know," he said.

Clay gave a dry laugh. "That'd be good, Will, since I'm running the show."

"Sorry," Will said, turning to leave the trailer. "Lot on my mind."

"No kidding. Come on." Clay gave him a nudge. "I'll walk over to Bay Laurel and check out your progress."

"I'm almost done," he said. "No need to check."

Clay smiled. "I think we need to talk."

Okay. Either he was getting shit-canned from this job or Clay had something on his mind. Some*one* on his mind.

They walked in silence around the other workers, taking the path to Bay Laurel, the largest villa on the property.

"So how's it going with Jocelyn here?"

That hadn't taken long. "Fine."

"You two go way back, I understand."

Will threw him a sideways look. "Yep."

"And now she's planning to put her father in a home."

Which would be too good for him. "That's the word on the street, which, obviously, you're getting."

Clay laughed. "Lacey tells me everything."

A surprising little twinge of jealousy pinched his chest. "Must be nice," he said, giving voice to it.

"We went way past nice a long time ago." At the villa, Will went inside first, while Clay lingered on the front porch to look up at the second-story soffits that had been hung by the roof sub last week.

"I'm down to the baseboards," Will said, grateful he'd taken out all his frustrations on the dead blows that morning. "A few finishing boards, some putty on the nails, and we're done."

Clay let out a low, appreciative whistle as he stepped over the threshold, a grin growing as he looked around. "Damn. That's nice wood. Worth every penny."

The dark grains gleamed in the afternoon light, even with the slight dusting of wood shavings. "Might be the nicest floor I've ever seen," Will agreed.

Clay crouched down to examine a seam and the

invisible nailing while Will waited for the verdict. "Might be the nicest floor *job* I've ever seen."

Will nodded his thanks. "So I'm not fired."

Laughing, Clay pushed up. "Why the hell would I fire you?"

Will scratched his head and looked at the floor. "Because I don't have a clue what went on in that meeting," he admitted. "And my head's not in the game."

Clay crossed his arms and walked along the side of the room, appearing to study the floor, but Will knew he was thinking. "First of all, do you have any idea what I'd have to go through to find someone of your caliber to come out to this island and work?"

"Thanks, man."

"I mean it. I wake up in a cold sweat worrying about you getting a call from some baseball team, and then where would I be?"

Will shrugged, not sure how to answer that one.

"But I have noticed you've got a lot going on the past few days. Our schedule's good, if you need some time off."

"I'm okay," he said. "I'll let you know if I need it."

Clay gave him a long look. "What happened in the car this morning?"

Shit. Clay had seen him the very minute he had found the pictures. "Nothing."

"Nothing? You looked like you saw a ghost and damn near ran over the DOT inspector's boots."

"Did I?" He made a face. "Hope we passed anyway."

Clay laughed softly, propping on a stool Will used when he sawed. "You really weren't paying attention in that meeting. Yeah, we passed, and I chalked your driving up to morning fog. But do you know how many times you spoke in our sub meeting?"

"I'm more worried about what I said."

"No need. Because you didn't say a word, but that's the thing about you, Will. You don't have to."

Will met Clay's sharp blue gaze, quite used to the younger man's longer hair, earring, and tattoo. Clay might not look like a hard-core professional, but he was one. And wise beyond his barely thirty-one years.

"What are you saying?" Will asked.

"Not saying anything, just offering an ear. I know you've got some things going on with Jocelyn and her dad. Thought maybe you'd want to talk."

Did he? Did he want to tell Clay about Jocelyn being beaten? Hell, no. About her keeping it from him and him wearing blinders to protect himself? Not particularly.

But feelings bubbled up, and the words that had tormented him all day were right at the surface. "I just found out that the one time in my life I should have done something even if it cost me everything, I did nothing." He cleared his throat, looking away. "Now I have to do something and it might be too late." He paused, the echo of his vague confession hanging in the air. "Did that make sense?"

Clay laughed. "Enough. I know what it's like to feel like you should have done something years ago and didn't. I don't want to pry, so I won't ask specifics, but I'll tell you this. Jocelyn and Lacey have been friends for a long time, so I suspect they're made of the same basic stuff. Which includes the ability to forgive someone who's acted like a moron, or an asshole, or a stubborn bonehead."

Will laughed. "Why do I think that's the voice of experience?"

"It sure as shit is. But the thing is, Lacey made it all worthwhile."

"So you fucked up and groveled back to her good graces?"

"More than once," he said with mock pride. "You have to know how important she is to you."

Will just nodded, unwilling to admit that even the thought of Jocelyn made him soft in the gut and hard in other places. He'd worn his heart on his sleeve enough for one day.

"So take the time you need." Clay pushed off the chair. "But get that marble inlay done soon."

"Will do, boss." Will grabbed his hammer. "I'll be done here before the end of the day and then I'll start the bathroom marble job."

As Clay walked out of the villa, he stopped in the doorway. "What happens if you get that call?"

Will frowned, not following.

"From a baseball team. You *are* still waiting for a coaching job, right?"

"Oh, yeah. But don't worry, Clay. The pickings are slim and that call isn't coming soon. Even if it did, I wouldn't leave you in the lurch. I'd help you find carpenters to replace me."

"I meant what happens to you and Jocelyn?"

Inside, his chest squeezed. "There is no me and Jocelyn." Yet.

This time Clay frowned, confused. "Oh, then I misunderstood. I could have sworn Lacey said that was one of the reasons Jocelyn is thinking about moving here to manage the spa. Geographic desirability and all, so I just thought..." His voice faded, probably due to the look of disbelief and hope and utter shock on Will's face. "Never mind. I'll check in with you later."

Clay turned and left before Will could ask any questions. Jocelyn was thinking about staying here?

Hope nearly strangled him. And then everything was crystal clear: He'd do anything and everything to get her to stay. What was that whole life-coaching business about, anyway? Finding your passion. The thing that gives you joy.

Well, he'd found his passion. And he'd do anything to make her stay.

Chapter 19

⌒

Is that what I think it is?" Tucked into the pew at the helm, Zoe gripped the sides of the boat and stared at the charcoal-colored gator sunning along the side of a grassy hammock, not ten feet away.

Jocelyn just smiled. "Stay in the boat, Zoe. You can't wrestle him."

"I just want a picture," Zoe said, patting her pockets.

From her perch in the center seat, controlling the oars despite her threats to Zoe, Jocelyn threw a glance at Guy, who sat on the aft bench, his face tilted toward the sunshine like a prisoner who'd just gotten an hour of freedom.

She tried to squash the guilt that image brought on, and the mess of memories churned up like the muck under the oars. Back in the earliest days of her childhood, long before his first "episode" ever turned Guy Bloom into a monster, Jocelyn and her father had spent entire days together on these canals, fishing, talking, spotting gators just like the one they'd just passed.

"I don't have my phone," Zoe said, reaching toward Jocelyn. "Give me yours, quick. I have to get a picture for Aunt Pasha! She's never seen a gator, I don't think."

"Zoe, you went to the University of Florida. That's our mascot and they were all over the lakes up there."

"But my great-aunt hasn't seen one. She may never get the chance. Phone, please."

Jocelyn fished the phone from her pocket and handed it over, using the paddle to slow them down and turn so Zoe could get a good shot.

"You know you have your phone on silent?" Zoe asked as she looked at the screen to figure out the camera.

Because she didn't want Will to call and find out where she was, and come after them. For all she knew he'd throw Guy to the gators. "Too peaceful out here for phone calls."

"You missed a text."

"Henry! Look, it's Henry!" Guy called excitedly, leaning far enough to rock the boat slightly. "Henry the Heron!"

Jocelyn sucked in a gasp and Zoe laughed, automatically counterbalancing the weight by tilting to the port side to straighten them out. "Don't worry, Joss. We're not going to capsize."

The boat wasn't, but her heart had just tipped over and sunk.

Very slowly, as if she were afraid of what she'd see, she turned to look over her shoulder at Guy.

"Henry?" she asked, her voice thick with emotion. "You...remember him?"

He grinned, crinkling up his whole face, his eyes dancing behind his glasses. "Isn't that a miracle?" He slapped his hands on his thighs and then tapped his temples. "Every once in a while, the old popcorn popper comes through with a kernel of goodness."

"See?" Zoe said, wildly snapping pictures. "Fresh air and wildlife is good for him."

"Darn right it is! Look at that big blue fellow. I've always loved him."

Jocelyn stabbed both paddles into the water, digging deep.

How could he remember a blue heron they'd adopted on a fishing excursion—and this was probably the great-great-grandson of that heron—and not remember *his own daughter*?

Or what he'd done to her?

She stole another look at him. Maybe he did remember. Maybe this was all an act, so she'd forgive him. Oh, she hated that thought, but every once in a while it sneaked into her head.

"C'mere, Henry," Guy called, making clicking noises that would no doubt spook the bird, who balanced on one long, skinny leg, his bright-orange beak aimed skyward in a regal pose. "Wish we had some bread crumbs. He loves those."

And he remembered *that*? Pain squeezed her throat, making it almost impossible to breathe. Why did this disease work so randomly? Why did he conveniently remember the nickname of a bird, yet not remember his wife or child?

Because he never *beat* the bird.

"Hey," Zoe said softly, balancing herself on two knees right in front of Jocelyn. "You okay, hon?"

She managed to nod. "I'm fine. It's hot out here."

"You want me to row for a little while? I think I could handle it."

She shook her head. "Who was the text from?" *Will. Say Will. Please, please say Will.*

Zoe tapped the screen and read. "La Vista d'Or."

An assisted-living facility in Naples. "What does it say?"

"Unexpected opening." She spoke in a whisper, even though Jocelyn's position in the middle of the boat blocked the conversation from Guy. "An unexpected opening is never good at those places."

Someone had died, and made room for Guy. Guy and his superselective memory. Guy who really did deserve to go to jail and not some high-end home. Guy who—

"Good-bye, Henry!" he called out. "Next time we'll bring bread, won't we, uh . . . Missy?"

Guy who couldn't remember her name.

Zoe leaned closer and read. "They want you to come for a tour today. You're next on the waiting list, but if they don't see you today, they give it to someone else." She looked expectantly at Jocelyn. "Want me to text back that you can't?"

She closed her eyes, trying to imagine what she wanted. Will. She'd always had Will when she needed to escape from her father. But it was fifteen years later, and she had to fix this problem herself. Now. This text was a sign, and she should follow it.

"No," she said. "I'll go this afternoon."

"You will?"

But she couldn't do it alone. And she couldn't call Will. "Can you come with me?" she asked.

For a second she thought Zoe would say no because it looked as though everything in her expression was gearing up for an argument.

"Guy'll be fine," Jocelyn assured her. "We'll tell him not to answer the door."

"All right," Zoe agreed, reluctant. "But I promised him we'd have a barbecue at his house tonight."

Jocelyn gave a look of total disbelief. "You did what?"

"C'mon, Joss..." She peeked over Jocelyn's shoulder, but Jocelyn didn't turn to look at Guy. "Have a heart."

That was just the problem. She did, and it was all torn up instead of nicely encased in its usual protective covering.

"Let's go," Jocelyn said loudly, digging the paddle in. "Party's over. I have work to do this afternoon."

"Me, too," Guy said from the back.

"What are you going to do?" Zoe asked brightly, leaning around Jocelyn to smile at Guy.

"I'm going to clean out this boat and give 'er a paint job."

"You are?" Zoe asked.

"I want to bring my boy William fishing like we did when he was little."

Jocelyn felt her jaw drop, but Zoe grabbed her knee and shook her head. "Let it go," she whispered. "Just let it go."

The problem was Jocelyn had never let anything go in her whole life. Except the one thing she should have held on to.

An hour later, with Guy happily ensconced in front of a *House Hunters International* marathon, Jocelyn and Zoe climbed into the hefty Jeep Rubicon Zoe had rented.

Zoe tapped the steering wheel with love. "I am so glad Hertz had my baby available. Remember how much fun we had in this thing when we were here last year?"

"Fun?" Jocelyn choked "I don't remember any fun."

"That's 'cause you don't know how to have it. God, I really need to work on you."

"I had fun today," she admitted, the words tasting like sand in her mouth. "Until Henry came along."

"You know what you need, Joss?"

Oh, boy. "Ah, Dr. Zoe Tamarin doles out advice. I know this prescription. Sex, travel, and a cocktail."

"God, I hate when I'm predictable. So just to throw you off, I'll tell you I was going to say you need a life coach."

"Very funny."

Zoe wove her way through the light traffic and crossed over to the causeway, hitting the accelerator so more wind whipped through the open top.

"You do."

"Stop it." Jocelyn tugged her baseball cap and shades, holding them in place. "I'm fine."

"Really? Let's review, shall we?"

"No."

Zoe settled deeper into the driver's seat, one hand on the wheel, one tangled in her mess of hair that flew like a curly platinum flag behind her. "First, you have been falsely accused of single-handedly breaking up one of the most famous marriages in the world, and yet you refuse to clear your name."

Jocelyn shifted in her seat. "I have my reasons."

"So you are forced into hiding or wearing a disguise. That's totally normal."

"Extenuating circumstances."

"Second, you hate your father—"

"For good reason."

"And yet, you care enough to find him the right place to live, make sure he's not alone for too long while you do so, and you kissed him good-bye when we left."

Ugh. She'd hoped Zoe hadn't noticed. "He kissed me. He does that now. Trust me, it's a result of his disease."

"His disease that makes him kind and affectionate, despite the fact that Alzheimer's famously makes people nastier, not nicer."

Damn it, she hated when Zoe got deep. Couldn't she just stick to sex and booze jokes? "His case is unusual, I suppose. But I still hate how he treated my mother." *And me. And Will.* "It was ... bad."

"But he's forgotten it."

"Has he? I don't know. I certainly haven't."

"You think he's faking it?" She stole a glance at Jocelyn. " 'Cause I have to tell you, the thought occurred to me, too."

"Would be convenient, don't you think?"

Zoe puffed out a breath of disgust. "It would be so fucked up there are no words. But kind of brilliant, too."

Jocelyn squeezed her hat brim against the wind. "I don't know how sick you'd have to be to forget you took your wife's favorite perfume and dumped it down the toilet because she forgot to call the plumber."

"What kind of perfume?"

Jocelyn choked. "Chanel Number Five."

"Ouch. The good stuff. But, seriously, you think the old guy is faking this?"

Jocelyn pulled the seat belt away from her chest; the

pressure on her heart was making it hard to breathe. "I wouldn't put anything past him. How could he remember Henry the Heron and not his own daughter?"

"I read somewhere that Alzheimer's patients remember the most random things, like what shoes they wore in 1940 but not what underwear they put on that morning."

"When were you reading about Alzheimer's?"

"I read a lot of stuff about old people, Joss. The woman who raised me is damn near eighty. Maybe older, maybe younger, she won't say."

"Pasha is healthy as a horse."

Zoe just looked out over the deep blue water of the Intracoastal. "So, what if this is all an act and he finds out his shenanigans are landing him in an old-age home? That would blow."

"It'd blow his cover, is what it would blow."

Zoe tapped on the brakes as the car in front of them slowed, using the chance to give Jocelyn a hard look. "Do you really think he's faking it?"

"I don't know. Maybe at times he is, maybe not. It wouldn't change my decision either way."

"But if he can take care of himself, why don't you just let him be?"

"Because he can't take care of himself," she said, ire and frustration rising. "Will has to take care of him and that's wrong. Will's not his son, regardless of what Guy thinks. So he's going, whether he wants it, knows it, or has an opinion about it."

"That's right," Zoe said. "Plus you love shit like this. Organizing, managing, shoving bad people into their proper boxes."

Jocelyn just closed her eyes and let the powerful gusts

partially drown out the words she didn't want to hear. Was she shoving Guy in a box? Well, what the hell, why not? He shoved her mother into a closet once.

"So where were we?" Zoe asked.

"On our way to Vista d'Or."

"I mean where were we on the Jocelyn Bloom Life Management Track."

"We came to the end." She folded her arms and turned away, hoping that would end the conversation.

"Without taking a trip down Will Palmer Road?" Zoe asked.

"Dead end. Take a left at the next light."

Zoe took the turn down a wide boulevard in the middle of Naples, taking in the designer stores and upscale restaurants as they passed. "Are we in the medical district?" she asked.

"I think the hospital is nearby."

"Always is near those assisted-living facilities, isn't it? And then the graveyard."

"Nice, Zoe."

"Don't tell me you wouldn't be good and happy if Guy dropped dead and made this simple for you."

Jocelyn closed her mouth, unwilling to lie. Instead she squinted at the GPS on her phone. "Just keep going a few more blocks."

"Okay, back to Will-I-Am. Did he pop your cherry?"

Oh, God. Jocelyn tsked. " Remind me again why I'm friends with you."

"Easy." Zoe grinned. "I held your head when you got drunk and threw up after the Alabama game. Remember?"

Actually, she remembered next to nothing, but Zoe

loved to remind her of that night their freshman year at Florida. "First, last, and only time I've ever been that drunk. And yet you will lord it over me forever."

"That's what friends are for. And for sharing secrets. Tell me about Will. I want to know if—" Zoe slammed on the brakes so hard Jocelyn smashed into her seat belt. Jocelyn scanned the road; no car or pedestrian or errant dog in sight.

"What the heck, Zoe?"

Zoe stared to her left, her jaw open.

Leaning forward, Jocelyn tried to see who or what had caused Zoe to nearly kill them. Dream shoes? A hot guy? No, a simple Spanish-style office building next to a frozen yogurt shop.

Following Zoe's stunned gaze, Jocelyn read the elegant gold lettering on the undertstated building.

Dr. Oliver Bradbury
Oncology

For a long, silent moment, Jocelyn just stared at the words.

"He doesn't need an oncologist," Jocelyn said. "And, whether you want to believe it or not, I'm grateful for that."

Very slowly, Jocelyn looked straight ahead, all color drained from her cheeks. "He must live here," she whispered.

"Who?" Jocelyn looked at the name again and instantly a memory flashed. "That's the same guy we saw in front of the Ritz in Naples last year, isn't it? The one who freaked you out."

"I didn't freak out," she said. Behind them, a car honked impatiently. Jocelyn expected a typical Zoe response, which could be anything from a friendly wave to the finger, but she just gently put her foot on the accelerator and drove about five miles an hour.

"You freaked out," Jocelyn said. "You dove onto the floor of this very car—or one a lot like it from the same rental company—and..." Jocelyn snapped her fingers, the whole thing coming back now. "It was an oncology conference at the Ritz. And that guy, Oliver, was there with his wi—" She let the word fall away.

Zoe was biting a damn hole in the bottom of her lip.

"You okay?" Jocelyn asked gently.

"Fine," she croaked. "Where's my next turn?"

"Zoe, who is this guy? What happened?" Other than the obvious. Only, God, she hoped Zoe wasn't stupid enough to get involved with a married man.

"Nothing. Ancient history."

It was so tempting to tease, if for no other reason than to make Zoe laugh. But something about this Oliver wasn't funny. Not to Zoe.

"Straight ahead, just a few more blocks," Jocelyn said instead, and they drove in silence until they reached a two-story stucco building with meager landscaping and, oh Lord, bars on the windows.

"I thought you said this place was in high demand."

"I got that impression from the marketing materials," Jocelyn said. "Maybe it's nicer in the back. Plus, the octogenarians probably don't notice."

"He's in his sixties, Joss," Zoe said as she threw open her door. "Not eighty, which, correct me if I'm wrong, is what an octogenarian is."

Jocelyn didn't answer, but came around the car and headed to the front door. As they got closer she saw chipped paint, a flowerless trellis, and rust on the giant doorknob.

Inside, the reception area was dim, just two beige sofas and a plastic panel hiding the top of a woman's head. Jocelyn approached her and waited. The woman didn't look up.

"Excuse me," Jocelyn said.

"Hang on." The woman continued to write something. Finally, cold gray eyes met Jocelyn's. "Yes?"

"I was contacted about an opening and came for the tour."

"Patient's name?"

"Um... well, I just really wanted to look around first."

"Insurance?"

"Some, but I really don't—"

"Hang on." She pressed an earpiece Jocelyn hadn't noticed earlier. "What is it, Mrs. Golgrath?" She closed her eyes and let out an impatient sigh. "Well, that's the only channel you pay for, so you have to watch *Singing in the Rain* one more time, dear." She paused, biting off the last word. "No, an aide cannot get to your room for at least two hours. So watch the movie. I'm sure it'll seem like brand-new every time. Good-bye, now... What?" She shook her head, still focused on the voice in her ear, impatience rolling off her like body odor. "Mrs. Golgrath, you will get your lunch when you get your lunch. Have we ever forgotten? Ever since you've been here?" She waited a second, then looked back up to address Jocelyn. "We can have someone walk you around after lunch. Maybe three o'clock. We're seriously shorthanded today."

Jocelyn swallowed. "No, that's all right."

"We have a video you can watch in the waiting room."

Jocelyn backed away, bumping into Zoe, who was right behind her. "I don't..." *Want to put even my worst enemy in this hellhole.* "... have the time."

The woman shrugged and returned to her work.

"Let's get out of here," she whispered to Zoe, practically dragging her back outside. "It looked a lot better on the Internet."

"Most things do," Zoe said drily.

They couldn't get outside fast enough, both of them sucking in the fresh air after all that stale, miserable sadness.

"I'll cross that one off the list," Jocelyn said as they reached the parking lot.

She waited for a Zoe quip, but none came. Zoe just adjusted her sunglasses and Jocelyn could have sworn she reached behind one lens to wipe her eye.

"Maybe this is a bad idea," Jocelyn said. "I should have come alone."

"No, no. It's just..."

"You're thinking about your Aunt Pasha?" Or... Oliver Bradbury.

"No, that poor Mrs. Golgrath." Her voice cracked. "I hate that stupid movie."

Jocelyn sighed and nodded. "The first place I saw was better."

"Really?"

"I swear it was."

Zoe stopped in the middle of the parking lot and took off her sunglasses, looking right at Jocelyn, not hiding the moisture in her eyes. "Do you remember that night you got drunk?"

Seriously? "Jeez, how often are we going to relive it?"

"Do you remember it?" she insisted.

"Well, since I was pretty much pickled on Southern Comfort and orange juice, I'm going to say no, I don't remember the details, just the fact that I never wanted to be that drunk again. And I haven't been."

"Then you probably don't remember what you said to me. You told me that the only thing in the world that mattered was seeing your father go to hell."

Jocelyn swallowed. "Did I?"

Zoe gave her a squeeze. "Guess some dreams die hard, don't they?"

Chapter 20

～

Will didn't trust himself to stop at Guy's house when he got home from work. No, he'd be too tempted to give the old bastard a taste of what a fist in the face felt like.

For the first time in months, probably in well over a year, Will bypassed 543 Sea Breeze Drive and pulled into his own garage next door. He didn't bother with the mail, threw his tools on the kitchen table, and didn't waste his time opening up his laptop looking for an e-mail from his agent that wouldn't be there anyway.

Restless, tense, and itching for a fight, he stripped off his work clothes, yanked on a threadbare pair of jeans, and took the stairs up to his old room two at a time.

Halfway there, he paused, closing his eyes.

He'd been in this room a thousand times since that dark evening fifteen years ago. Somewhere along the way, it had stopped reminding him of Jocelyn and even of Guy.

But now he'd have to remember. Remember how the early-evening light had cast Jocelyn in shades of gold as she curled up on his bed and sniffed his comforter. He'd have to remember the way they'd kissed and touched, the sheer breathlessness of knowing it was finally going to happen. He'd have to remember how far they'd gone: He'd had his fingers inside her and she was begging for more, rolling against him and—

"Hey."

He spun around so fast he nearly lost his balance, grabbing the handrail and barking out, "What are you doing here?" at the sight of Guy standing at the bottom of the stairs. "You never come over here."

"Thought I'd change that." Guy drew back, out of the shadows of the landing, into the fading light. "Something wrong, son?"

"I'm not your son." He spoke through clenched teeth, squeezing the handrail like it was a bat—and he wanted to use it on Guy's head. "What do you want?"

The words felt foreign and ugly on his tongue. Will didn't speak like that to Guy; he hadn't said a harsh word, except for the occasional reprimand when Guy didn't follow instructions or tossed the remote in the trash.

Guy was too helpless, too old, too lost to be spoken to like that.

Will closed his eyes and let his brain see the purple bruises on Jocelyn's thin teenage arms and the eggplant-colored shiner that had closed her eye to a slit.

"What do you mean, what do I want?" Guy came up the first few stairs, reaching for the railing.

"Don't come up here," Will said.

The older man frowned, then adjusted his crooked glasses. "I just wanted to know if you like what I'm wearing."

What? What the hell was he wearing, anyway? Bright-yellow pants and an orange sweater.

"You look like a Creamsicle."

Guy tried to laugh, but it came out more of a cough. "That good or bad?"

"Why are you dressed up?" he asked, wishing he didn't care or even want to know.

"For the party!"

"What?"

"They're having a party at my house tonight," he said, his voice implying that everyone who was anyone would know this. "The whole *Clean House* crew will be there, is what Blondie told me."

"Blondie?" Zoe, of course.

"And you know who will be there." He wiggled his finger and sang the sentence like a second-grade tease.

He knew who.

"C'mon, William." Guy took a few more steps, each one an effort, but he was clearly driven by happiness. That was what really irked.

He looked like a great big orange-and-yellow splash of happiness.

Wonder how happy he'd be when he found out what the *"Clean House"* crew was really planning? How happy he'd be to take a good long look at those pictures of "Missy" and be told flat-out that it was his hands that had battered her?

How happy would the old fucker be then?

Will waited for the words to form, the accusations to

fly, but he stood stone silent, his whole body itching and sweating.

"You do like her, don't you?" Guy asked. "I mean I might be old and have more holes in my brain than a sponge, but I can see what I can see, and you two like each other."

"It's none of your business," Will said brusquely.

That earned him a flicker of surprise as Guy held up his hands and then wobbled as he lost his balance.

"Jesus," Will muttered, lunging to make sure the old man didn't fall.

"Oh, oh! I'm okay." Guy stabbed in the air, finally finding the railing and righting himself. "Not the first time I nearly went down today."

"It's not? You fell today?" Why, oh Good Christ, *why* did he care?

"Capsized, I mean." He grinned, his teeth nearly the color of his pants. "In the boat, William. My old rowboat! We took it out today!"

"Who did?"

"The girls and me." He shrugged both shoulders in a fake giggle. "I bet we're not supposed to call 'em girls anymore, but that's what they'll always be to—"

"What girls?" Surely Jocelyn hadn't gone out in a boat with him today? Surely she hadn't left Will—kissing her and holding her and making all kinds of emotional breakthroughs—to take Guy out on a boat ride? After—

"Blondie and Missy, of course." He clapped his hands. "And we saw Henry the Heron, William! Oh, I'm going to have a surprise for you soon. Not yet, but soon. I'm starting a new project."

Exhaustion pressed and forced him up the stairs

backwards, still facing Guy so he could be sure the old man didn't follow.

"I can't come to your party," he said gruffly. "I have too much work to do."

"Work?" Guy whined. "You worked all day, son. You have to learn to have a little fun. To..." He made fists and a pathetic attempt at some kind of dance. "Let loose once in a while."

Will inhaled slowly, and then shook his head. "Can't, sorry." Why was he apologizing?

"What work?" Guy challenged.

"Your bills, for one thing," he shot back. "Your insurance forms and Medicare. Your mortgage and your utilities. You're a full-time job, Guy!"

Guy's happy face fell like whipped cream thrown against a wall. "Oh," he said. "I see."

No he didn't, but Will didn't feel a damn bit better after that outburst. He felt like shit on the bottom of a heel, which he was.

The pictures. The bruises. The pain.

"Just let me get a workout and a run in, Guy," he said quickly. "I'll check on you later."

"Zoe actually doesn't know how to throw a bad party." Tessa sidled up next to Jocelyn on the cracked vinyl cushion, setting the swing in motion and looking up at almost threatening skies. "Even if it rains, she'll figure out a way to take this thing inside, bring out the games, and have your father playing Truth or Dare before nine o'clock."

Jocelyn smiled as she watched Guy claw his way through a game of Egyptian Rat Screws with Lacey's teenage daughter, Ashley. "I can't believe she still loves to play that game and keeps teaching it to people. It's like she's spreading a sickness."

"I refuse to play it with her," Tessa said. "And let me tell you, when I lived out there in Flagstaff with Zoe and her great-aunt, they'd play four-hour Rat Screws marathons."

"I have a feeling this card game is Guy's favorite new pastime."

Tessa looked around. "Then Will ought to learn the game. Where is he, anyway?"

"I have no idea," Jocelyn said, but of course she knew exactly why Will wasn't here. He was too angry with Guy to come to the impromptu party. But that wouldn't last. He'd forgive and forget, too warmhearted to hang on to hate.

But she could, and would. Even if that meant she never had a chance to explore her feelings for Will or wallow in the sweetness of the confessions he'd made this morning.

He'd been her everything.

She stared at her father, the thief of her happiness.

Across the patio, Clay and Lacey stood arm in arm by the barbecue, laughing as they flipped burgers, punctuating almost every sentence with a kiss, a touch, a shared look of affection. No one had stolen their happiness, she thought glumly.

"You want to go try and find Will?" Tessa asked. "You'd think the aroma of cooking meat alone would get a bachelor out of his house and onto the lawn."

Jocelyn attempted a careless shrug.

"Hey." Tessa put her hand on Jocelyn's arm. "Go find him. You're staring at his house."

She looked away. "I am not."

Puffing out a breath, Tessa popped off the swing and nearly knocked Jocelyn on her butt.

"Excuse me," Tessa said, walking over to the table. "Guy, have you seen Will?"

Jocelyn watched her father, expecting his usual blank stare, his big bear shrug. But, instead, emotion flashed in his eyes, so fast probably no one else saw it. Only a person who'd spent every minute of her childhood watching that face for a clue to when it would happen would see it.

They'd talked. Jocelyn knew it instantly. What had Will said to him? And was that why he was conspicuously absent?

"He was in his house last time I saw him," Guy said.

"When was that?" Tessa asked.

Now he went blank and lifted a shoulder.

"In the last hour or so?" Tessa prodded.

"I saw him out jogging," Ashley said, her next card poised over the playing table. "He was running up toward the high school when we got here. Okay, you ready? Slap!"

Ashley threw down a card and Guy was right there with her, the conversation forgotten as Tessa came back to the swing.

"It's going to rain in the next half hour," Tessa said. "Probably when we're eating, so I better see about setting a table inside."

Jocelyn stood. "I'll help you."

"No, you won't."

"I don't want to just sit here, Tess."

Tessa gave her a look. "Go find him. Tell him whatever it is that has you sighing and staring upstairs at what I can only assume was once his bedroom."

"I—"

"I'll cover for you. Go, quick before it rains." She held out her hand to help Jocelyn up, adding a knowing smile. "I saw you two arguing on the beach this morning," she added softly. "He's probably waiting for you to invite him to our little party."

Jocelyn just laughed softly. "Secrets are so overrated around here."

"They are with me." She bent over to the cooler of drinks that Clay and Lacey had brought, snagging a beer. "Take him this as a peace offering."

"We're not at war."

Tessa just lifted her brow and gestured for Jocelyn to go.

A few minutes later, Jocelyn had escaped out the front, unnoticed. Tucking the beer in the pocket of her white cargo pants, she traced her old familiar route toward the high school.

If she knew Will—and she did—she knew exactly where he was.

Twilight hung over the Mimosa High baseball field, and the clouds that had rolled in from the east made it even darker.

But Jocelyn didn't need the field lights. She just followed the familiar ping of a baseball knocking against a metal bat. Rhythmic, steady, a whoosh of wind, a ding of noise, and the soft plop of a ball hitting the outfield.

Was he batting alone?

She walked behind the home dugout, pausing as she always did at the numbers painted on the back wall, each circled with a baseball and a year. The Mimosa Scorpions' most valuable players.

And there was none more valuable than the superstar of 1997, number thirty-one, team captain William Palmer.

Whoosh, *ping*—that was a long ball—*thud*.

She trailed her fingers over the red paint of his name, then walked around the dugout, staying far enough from the chain-link fence to see him but not be in his field of vision.

Speaking of visions.

He wore nothing but hundred-year-old jeans, hanging so low she could practically see his hipbones and the dusting of dark hair from his naval down to his—

She forced her eyes up, only to stop on his chest, bare, damp with sweat, every muscle cut and corded as he took his swings.

Low, deep, and inside her belly, desire fisted and pulled.

He held the bat on his right shoulder and tossed a ball up—she spied a white plastic bucket full of baseballs next to him—then, in one smooth move, he'd grip the bat and take a swing, sending the ball high in the air or straight down the middle. There was a name for this practice. Fun something? She couldn't remember, but the sight of him swinging took her back in time, when the same sensations of need and want had rocked her young body.

She'd nearly given in to them. What would have happened if Guy hadn't walked in on them that night? How different would their lives be? Would they have made it in the long haul? Or would she still be living in L.A. and so, so alone?

Foolish even to think about it, she chided herself. The past couldn't be changed.

Still, it could be remembered. For at least ten swings

of the bat, she just stood next to the dugout and drank in the sight of Will at the plate, his swing a little different now, a little slower, a little less confident than when he'd been a cocky high school superstar. So much was different about Will now.

His hair had curled at the ends from sweat despite the black bandanna he'd wrapped around his head. His body had lost that sinewy look of youth, but had grown into broader planes, more mature muscles, even better shoulders to lean on.

Without thinking, she took a step forward, closed her fingers over the cool metal of the chain-links, and—

Instantly got his attention.

For about as long as it took a fly ball to reach the fence, they stared at each other.

"I brought you a peace offering," she finally said, holding up the beer bottle.

He leaned over and picked up another ball, tossed it left-handed, then took a powerful swing. "That'll go down nice after hitting infield fungoes."

Fungoes. That was the word. "Haven't heard that term for fifteen years."

He smiled and slammed another, far and long, the ball bouncing along the ground until it came to a stop deep in center field.

That was no *infield* fungo. "Hitting 'em a little hard tonight, aren't you?"

"There's a glove in the dugout if you want to field," he said.

A smile pulled. "You think I can catch those fungoes?"

"I'll hit puff balls for you, Bloomerang." He grinned and used the bat to gesture to the dugout.

Bloomerang. *The girl who always comes back.*

She stepped down into the dugout, set the beer on the bench, and grabbed the brown baseball glove. "They just leave this stuff out here?" she asked.

"My key still works the equipment room."

That made her laugh. "Seriously? They haven't changed the locks in fifteen years?"

"They haven't changed a lot in fifteen years."

As she stepped out onto the field, she slipped the mitt on her left hand. "But you have, Will."

"We all have, Jossie."

She trotted out to center field, her thin, flat sandals all wrong for baseball. "Hang on," she said, kicking them off. "Okay, batter."

She got into position behind second base, hands on knees, butt stuck out. "Bring it."

He popped her a slow and easy grounder, rolling the ball so gently she had to walk forward to get it before it stopped. "You can do better than that, Palmer."

"Let's see your arm."

Grabbing the ball, she straightened, held it up, and threw it straight into the dirt.

"Ah, the perfection of the female throw."

"Screw you."

From forty feet away, she could see him grin.

"Is this what you'll do as a coach?" she asked.

"At fielding practice." He hit another one, a little harder down the middle, and she managed to stop it.

"Ugly," he said. "But you got the job done."

She threw it back. "What about all those balls all over the outfield?"

"I'll clean up when I'm done."

"When are you going to be done?"

He slammed a fly ball. "Go back, go back," he called, and she did, wanting to be that woman who just turned the mitt and caught it and not the one who cowered behind the glove hoping it didn't bop her in the head.

She stuck out the glove and missed the catch.

"Oh, man," he said, disgusted. "Run the bases, scrub."

"What?"

"You heard me. Run the bases. Complain and you do it twice."

She put her hands on her hips and opened her mouth to—

"Three times around."

"Hit the ball, Palmer."

"Catch the next three and I'll let you go."

She laughed, spreading her feet for balance, the grass soft and cool on her toes, so utterly grateful for this moment of pure pleasure. The air was thick with the rain that would surely come and the unspoken truce that they were just here to play.

"Fun job you have," she said just as he was ready to toss a ball and hit it.

"Throwing balls in the air?"

"Playing. Just relaxing."

"Well, I don't actually have it at the moment." He tapped another softie right to her. "That's one," he said.

She threw it in the general vicinity of home base and he jumped to the side and snagged the ball before it hit the dirt.

"Still a great catcher," she said.

"Passable and my knees are screaming at me. Ready?"

He hit this one a little harder, but she dove for it and went sailing on the grass and caught it, holding up the ball with far more drama than the situation called for.

"Uh, you have to throw a grounder to a base or you didn't make an out."

She waved the mitt. "Details."

He had the next ball, but instead of tossing and hitting it, he stood very still, looking at the field. It was so dark she couldn't quite read his expression, but she knew Will's body language.

"You're not mad anymore," she observed.

"That's not what I was thinking."

"What are you thinking?" she asked, a funny, unholy tendril of anticipation curling up through her chest at the intimacy in his tone.

"I was thinking that..." He hooked the bat on his shoulder and held out the ball. "You're even prettier than you were when you were a teenager."

Her heart hitched.

"And you were really pretty then."

She smiled, knowing he couldn't see her in the dark but giving him thanks for the compliment anyway. "You're prettier now, too," she said.

Laughing, he threw the ball in the air, flipped the bat down, and whacked that ball long and high and all the way to the fence.

She didn't even try to get it. Instead, she just turned and watched it bounce off the centerfield fence.

"First one there gets the beer!" he said, throwing the bat and starting to run.

The instant she realized it was a race, she took off, but he caught up to her in seconds, slowing down so they reached the ball at the same time, both of them diving for it, both of them hitting the grass.

And because it took no thought to do the most natural thing in the world, Jocelyn reached for Will and he pulled her close and kissed her with the same power he'd used to hit that ball.

Chapter 21

Oh, man. The only thing better than the tangy, fresh smell of outfield grass was the bone-deep pleasure of rolling in it with Jocelyn Bloom.

The instant their mouths connected, Will tried to ease her down and get above her, over her, on her. The need was swift and desperate and so pent-up he let out a groan.

She pushed him on his back and leaned over him instead. "My white pants are going to get grass stains," she murmured into the kiss.

"You're right," he said with mock concern. "Better take them off."

She laughed, still kissing him but maintaining all the control, on top, hands on his face, her every muscle taut. "One of us half undressed is enough."

No it wasn't. He flipped her firmly on the grass,

looming over her, liking it so much better up here. "Every once in a while, you've got to let go of control."

"Who said?"

"I said. What are you doing here, anyway?"

Her lips curved up as she placed one finger in the dead center of his bare chest. "Came to see you half undressed."

"You can do that anytime," he said. "Just ask."

She walked her fingers up his chest, up his throat, settling on his Adam's apple, one of her favorite spots in the world.

Déjà vu sparkled behind his eyes for a second, then was gone as quickly as it had come. Trailing her finger higher, she traced the line of his jaw, then his mouth, finally looking into his eyes.

"We never finished," she said softly.

"This morning?"

"That night. This morning. This whole life. Everything with you is like...unfinished business." She managed a shaky smile. "You know that kind of thing drives me almost as crazy as the permanent grass stains I'm getting on my favorite cargo pants right now."

"It's good for you," he said. "You need to be driven crazy, Joss. Let go and let me..."

She didn't move, the only sound their evenly matched, and slightly intensified, breathing. "Let you what?"

"Drive you crazy."

She barely nodded and he lowered his face to hers, starting soft and sweet, which lasted about four seconds, then everything intensified to—more. Her breath caught in her throat, and her leg curled around his, her bare foot grazing his thigh and sending a heat flare straight to his balls.

Instantly, he was hard for her.

The second she felt his erection she put both hands on his shoulders and started to push him away, but he kept kissing, kept torturing her tongue and nibbling on her lips and grazing her front teeth until her fingers relaxed. For a long, long kiss, he felt her suspended between surrender and second thoughts.

"Will," she whispered. "I'm not sure I can do this."

"We're just here for practice, Jossie," he assured her. "Nobody's going to hit a home run, I promise."

"Promise?"

He nodded. "We're just hitting fungoes." He kissed a path from her lips to the opening of her collar, easing the material back to expose more skin. "Emphasis on fun."

She laughed softly, arching her back just enough for all her pressure points to hit his, sending a surge of blood from his brain right down to the most pressure-filled point of all.

As hard as the bat he'd just tossed to the clay, he rocked slightly, his erection right over her pelvic bone, making her suck in a quick, sweet breath.

"See?" he said. "Just make a little contact."

"Is this entire makeout session going to be baseball puns?"

He chuckled into the next kiss. "Yeah, it might be. First base is this, right?" He opened his mouth and gave her his tongue, which she sucked and licked and shared with a sweet moan of pleasure.

"You like first base?"

She sighed, angling her head to offer her throat. "It's safe. I can handle first base."

They kissed some more, but he couldn't control his

hand. Couldn't resist sliding around her ribs and stealing a touch. Her only response was a sharp intake of breath, so he flipped the first button and then the next.

"We appear to have a runner headed to second," she teased, making him laugh.

"The catcher's busy. This guy's got the base."

She moaned her yes and he finished the next two buttons, delighted to find a front-clasp bra that he could unsnap before her next breath. At the same time, she kissed him some more, wrapping one hand around his neck and doing a little caressing of her own on his pecs.

"Not fair," he whispered. "I don't have a shirt on."

"I noticed." She kissed him again. "And noticed." Another kiss. "And noticed some more."

He chuckled at the compliments, then began a slow rock of his hips against hers.

God, they fit. Her fingers tightened their grip on his hair, angling his head, deepening the kiss, giving him all kinds of silent permission. He pushed the shirt over her shoulders, taking the bra with it, and finally pressing their bare chests against each other.

"Will, we're outside."

He laughed. "We're on my home field, honey. I know what I'm doing."

She gasped when his hand touched her breast, the nipple budding against his palm. Blood slammed harder into his erection and he let out another groan.

She tensed enough that he could feel all her muscles clench. Was she that scared of him?

No, her dark eyes told him to go on. Shuttered, lost, falling into a place he'd never seen her go. He took a moment to drink in the shape of her breasts, the feminine slope, the deep pink nipples. Only a minute. He had to taste.

Still holding his head, she guided him there, both of their hips moving in perfect rhythm. Engorged now, his hard-on found the sweet spot between her legs, thread-bare denim and thin white cotton all that separated their bodies.

Murmuring his name, her head fell from side to side as he suckled one breast and thumbed the other.

"Oh my God, Will."

Noisily, he let go of her and headed back up to kiss her. Only then did he realize her face was wet.

The sight hit him like someone had slammed a fastball into his gut. "Are you crying? No." He wiped her face. "Don't—"

"It's rain, Will. Don't you feel it?"

The second she said it, a drop splattered on his back. "Oh, thank God. I thought I made you cry. Jocelyn, I never want to make you cry. Ever."

She bit her lip. "I'm not going to cry, but..."

"What? What is it?"

Closing her eyes, she let out a soft groan of helplessness, moving her hips against him, riding his erection. "This feels so good....I never..." Each breath was work as she rocked harder. "I never...felt anything...like this. Oh, God, Will, I can't stop."

She rammed against him, her eyes shuttered in ecstasy as an orgasm washed over her. "I can't stop," she murmured over and over again, holding him with everything she had, battering his poor, engorged cock, damn near making him come, too.

But he held on as the rain picked up, splattering over

them, so cool he was surprised it didn't sizzle when it touched their heated bodies.

"I don't believe that just happened," she managed to say, still shaking. "I just...you know...on the Mimosa High baseball field."

He grinned. "Which just became my best memory on this grass in a lifetime of many."

She finally opened her eyes, unfocused and lost. "I can't believe I lost—"

"Believe it." He quieted her with a kiss. "In the pouring rain, too."

She wrapped her arms around him, biting back a smile. "I liked it."

"No shit."

Still smiling, her eyes sparking with arousal, her cheeks flushed with a climax and wet from the rain, she wrapped her legs all the way around him. "What *is* your best memory of this field?" she asked.

"Prior to the last five minutes? Um, let me think."

"The championship game against Collier?" she asked. "No, I bet it was that grand slam junior year."

He didn't respond, but a slow chill of disbelief walked over his bare skin.

"Or maybe it was the night you got MVP as a freshman. That was big."

Holy, holy hell. "You remember all that?"

"Of course. You were..." She swallowed and gave him the rueful smile of a shared joke. "You were everything to me." Her words echoed his of that morning, as sweet as a fastball snapping into his catcher's mitt.

Except for the past tense. He wanted to be everything to her *now*.

Cupping her breast, her heart pulsing into his palm as if her blood were pumping right into him, he looked into her eyes. Around them, the world lay silent except for the gentle tap of raindrops on the grass and his back.

"Jocelyn, what's it going to take?"

"To get me in bed?"

He smiled. "I think we're on our way to that. To get you to say those words you never got a chance to tell me that night?"

For at least five, six, maybe seven beats of the heart he could feel under his palm, she just looked at him.

"You want me to say . . ."

"I lo—"

"No." She put her hand over his mouth. "Not yet. Not here. Not half naked in the grass."

"I can't think of a better time or place."

She shook her head. "No."

Disappointment thudded in his stomach, but he just nodded.

"Hey," she whispered, lifting her hips. "We gonna leave a runner on second?"

"Not if I'm calling the plays." He kissed her again, dragging his hand over her bare body, loving every curve, every moan, every sensory overload. The rain intensified, no drizzle now, but a pounding, pouring wash over everything. He slipped his hand between her legs, massaging gently, then flipping the snap and pulling the zipper of what were surely some grass-stained white pants.

"Jossie?"

"Mmmm."

"I think I'm getting to third."

He eased his hand over her lower abdomen, into her

satiny panties, onto her sweet mound. She arched up to meet his touch, giving him entrance to her slippery womanhood.

There. There. There was the everything he wanted. White lights exploded behind his eyes, blinding and—

"Shit!" They both jumped at the same time, the near simultaneous thunder warning just how close that lightning had struck.

"Off the field!" He scooped up her fallen clothes, grabbed her hands to yank her up, and tore across the field just as another jagged white line split the blackened sky and a rumble rolled over the stadium.

Her hand slipped out of his, and he whipped around to see her standing in the rain, naked from the waist up, barefoot, bedraggled, and so fucking beautiful it ripped his heart right out of his chest.

"Joss, come on," he urged. "This storm is close."

She didn't move, her expression stricken with shock and fear.

He grabbed for her hand, knowing the next strike was seconds away. He'd seen lightning hit the right field pole; he knew how dangerous this was. "Come *on*."

She relented, letting him pull her, sliding when they hit the muddy clay so he had to put his arm around her to help her keep her footing. Just as the next bolt flashed, he threw them both into the dugout, which still wasn't safe enough.

"Holy shit, that storm came fast." He stood in front of her, protecting her, giving her the wet shirt, which she bunched in front of her bare breasts.

On the bench, she looked up at him, sopping strands of hair falling in her face, the whisper of makeup smudged under her eyes.

Breathless, she nodded.

"Why did you freeze?" he asked. "Panic?"

She nodded again, sliding her lower lip under her front teeth.

"Don't worry," he said, reaching into his pocket. "We can squeeze into the equipment closet." He pulled out a set of keys and grinned. "And finish."

But she looked every bit as panicked by that as she had been by the lightning.

Chapter 22

Panic? Let him think that. It beat the truth.

Jocelyn followed Will around the dugout to the clubhouse, staying close to the concrete of the structure, one wary eye on the sky, the other on the man who led the way.

It was one thing to treasure her childhood feelings and teenage crush. It was one thing to let go of her initial anger that he was caring for Guy and see Will for the remarkable, attractive man he'd grown to be.

But the feelings that had just rocked her down to her bare toes?

No. Those were something altogether different, and those feelings *had* to stop. Now. Because those feelings belonged to a person who had no control. Or at least they belonged to a deluded dreamer who thought love was something good and grand and lasting.

Not Jocelyn Bloom. She wasn't deluded and she sure as hell didn't harbor those dreams.

"Wish we could get into the clubhouse." Will jiggled the rusted knob of the small baseball clubhouse on the other side of the dugout. "But they changed those locks." A few feet to the left, he stabbed the key into the metal door of a stand-alone structure she'd seen a hundred times but never imagined she'd walk into.

As he opened the door and guided her in, he ran his hand along the jamb. "Good. Rubber stripping. At least we won't fry if we get hit by lightning. Just..." He smiled as he pulled the door closed and trapped them in darkness. "Fry another way."

"How long do you think we have to wait it out in here?" How long would she be locked in a dark closet with Will, her new, raw, frightening feelings so close to the surface they could bubble up at the first clap of thunder—or with the first heated kiss?

"As long as you want to."

"They're going to get worried about me," Jocelyn said, blinking to get her night vision, but it was still nearly pitch black.

And then it wasn't, as Will hit the switch and the little room was washed in yellow light, revealing a five-foot-square mess of bats, buckets of balls, lost gloves, batting helmets, and giant catcher's vests hanging like dead men from hooks along the wall.

He stared at her, intense and direct. She tightened her grip on the shirt bundled against her chest and met his gaze. Could he read the vulnerability that coursed through her?

"Nothing is going to happen in here if you don't want it to, Joss. Lights can stay on."

But all the light did was highlight the set of his jaw, the burn in his eyes, and the rise and fall of his stunning chest. Against her will, her gaze dropped over that sight, down to his jeans, and—

She looked back up. "Too bright. Turn them off."

Immediately they were back in black, surrounded by the echo of thunder and the rain on the roof. The dizzying smell of leather and clay, familiar scents that transported her back a decade and a half to a time when the mere scrape of metal cleats on concrete made her knees go weak.

"What's the matter?" he asked, reading her, of course.

"Nothing, I..."

"Something's the matter."

"I..." *Think, Joss.* "I don't want the first time to be in a closet," she whispered, only a little surprised by the actual truth of that admission.

"Well, that's some good news."

It was? "What is?"

"That there's going to be a first time for us." His seductive tone, like the evaporating rain, left a fine chill on her skin. And yet she let her hands fall to her sides, the shirt still hooked to her fingertips, her bare breasts completely exposed to him.

He stood about six inches away, making no move.

"Jocelyn?"

"Mmmm?"

"Are you over that moment of panic?"

Not even close. "I am." God, she wanted to touch him. Just make this about fulfilling her need and taking that crazy ride of complete abandon again. Why did he have to mention *love* out there on the field?

She was just getting used to the idea of sex and he'd brought up the only thing scarier, the only thing that stole any shred of control.

He took one step forward and they touched. His bare chest to her bare chest. His legs against her legs. His—

Oh *God*. He was so hard.

He pressed a huge, daunting, mighty erection against her stomach and all she could do was drop her shirt with a soft *whoompf.*

"So, what happened out there?" he asked. "Are you scared of lightning?"

"I'm scared of . . ." *Love.* "This."

"Of being with me?"

Define *being*. "Maybe."

He tipped her chin with his thumb, then cupped her jaw, forcing her to look up at him. The air vent above the door let in a whisper of ambient light, enough to see how serious he was. "Are you scared of sex?"

"It always reminds me of . . . that night," she admitted. "And what happened."

"Oh," he angled his head, sympathy all over his expression, agony in the single syllable. "Then all the more reason for us to try to make new memories."

She closed her eyes. "You always know the right thing to say."

"And do." He pressed against her, making her nipples pucker against his warm, wet chest. Between her legs, the twisting coil of need tightened again. Her fingers grew heavy and numb. Her head buzzed.

This was like being drunk. Like being helpless. God, she hated helplessness. More than anything.

"It's also scary to lose control." Maybe it was both.

Loss of control, loss of sanity, equaled pain and misery. Was that the equation that added up in her head every time she felt like this?

Not that anyone other than Will had ever made her feel *quite* like this.

"I can give you control," he said softly, kissing her first on the forehead. "You want to call the shots?"

She nodded, slack-jawed at how much need coursed through her.

"What do you want to do?"

"I want to . . . not lose control."

"Then you take charge," he said, gently sliding his hands over her bare arms. "You call the game, Coach."

She wet her lips, but it didn't help her parched mouth. She put her hands on his shoulders. God, she loved those shoulders. Big, strong, reliable, sexy shoulders.

She splayed her hands over the muscles, dragging her fingers down, closer to what she wanted. Over his abs, closing her eyes so that every sense was focused on the masculine ripples of each perfectly formed muscle.

She could do this. She could do this and not hear the accusations and feel the punches, not relive the night when letting loose had caused her so much pain.

Forcing the memory away, she continued down to her knees, unbuttoning his jeans on the way, scraping the zipper.

He was naked under there, erect and pulsing and as big as she'd always imagined.

And, oh, Lord almighty, she had imagined.

"Joss." His fingers tangled in her hair. His skin smelled like salt and something sexy she couldn't identify. Not sweat. Just man.

A stone stabbed her knee and sweat stung her skin. Through the slotted vent above the door, lightning flashed, one second of near-illumination that let her see his swollen, wet, smooth tip as she freed him.

He pushed the jeans down and guided her mouth to him, murmuring, "Please."

She had control. Complete, utter, blissful control. And she took it, sucking gently at first, then using her hand to fondle and stroke him.

His knees buckled and he swore and begged and plunged in and out of her mouth, over and over again, slow then fast, deep then shallow, long strokes then quick ones. Her hands moved, her tongue licked, and her mouth took him all the way until he lost all the control she held so tightly. With a low, long, helpless growl of release, he spurted into her mouth, grasping her head with two hands and almost crying with each squeeze of pure relief.

Her head thrummed with the thrill of it. The sheer blissful wonder of making Will come with just her hands and mouth. Finally, she released his shaft and looked up at him.

His face was still wet from the—

No, that wasn't rain. Very slowly she stood, not at all sure her legs could do their job.

"Will?"

He just closed his eyes and shook his head, unable to speak.

"Oh, Will." She put her hands on his face. "Don't."

"I'm so sorry, Jocelyn." He barely whispered the words. "For not being there when you needed me."

Suddenly she was cold. In this tiny, airless room that was probably ninety degrees and a hundred percent humidity, she was cold. The chill came from inside, from her chest—from her heart. Icy, empty coldness. "Will, if you can't forget what you saw in those pictures, then I can't be with you."

He nodded, as if he understood. "I will." He pulled her into a hug, holding her close, his body still quivering from his orgasm. "I promise I will."

But could he?

When she shivered, Will bent down and grabbed her blouse, shaking it out and handing it to her. She slipped her arms into the sleeves, but it was wet and made her even colder.

"The storm's moving away. Let's go home, babe," he whispered. "I want you in bed with me tonight."

Now. She had to explain. Had to tell him the truth.

"You know that moment when... you realize that..." She fought for a breath and the right words. "You want something you can never have?"

"Yeah." He puffed out a soft laugh. "I know that moment."

"Well, that's why I froze."

"What do you want that you can never have?"

Love. Trust. Sex. A complete and total loss of control. "Um, Will, there are things about me you don't know. Things you might not believe even if I told you."

"Oh." It was no more than a soft moan. "Honey." Like he'd lost a battle, he reached for her, pulling her into him, pressing them together, squeezing so hard she almost couldn't breathe. "I don't care about your past. I don't even care if... if..."

She stilled, waiting for him to finish. "If what?" she prompted when he didn't.

"Whatever happened in California, I don't care."

It was more like what *didn't* happen, but if he wanted to go there, it was easier for her.

"Well, I'm not ready to . . . spend the night with you," she admitted.

With a soft sigh, he buttoned her blouse, all the way to the very top. "I can wait. I'm pretty good at that, as you know." Holding her hand, he led her back out into the soft evening rain.

Chapter 23

⌒

Guy looked around at the strangers in his living room, all piled in there after the rainstorm started.

Who *were* these people? A thread of fear wrapped around his chest as he glanced from one to another, trying—and failing—to put names with the faces. There was the lady with wavy copper hair holding hands with the young man who made her laugh a lot.

A teenager who never shut the heck up and couldn't say a sentence without the word "like" in it, but she'd been very kind to him when they'd played cards and he kept forgetting how many you had to put down for all the royal cards and aces.

Then there was Blondie, who blew in and out of the room like a breath of fresh air, kind of pretending she owned the place, the way she doled out drinks and jokes.

But *where was William*?

Good Lord in heaven, that's who was missing. He hadn't lost William again, had he? Not his son. Not like the other time.

An old dull ache he'd long ago learned to ignore pressed on his heart, like a mallet on the inside, throbbing and reminding him of things he wanted to forget.

His son.

"Where's William?" he called out, silencing the soft buzz of conversation as everyone turned to him at once. He felt a flush of shame for yelling and adjusted his glasses and cleared his throat. "I haven't seen him," he added sheepishly.

A woman he'd barely talked to came out of the kitchen. "Jocelyn went to find him, and then it started raining. I assume they ran into a restaurant or something."

"You assume?" Guy didn't mean to boom the question or make the teenager across from him flinch in surprise. "What if something happened to him?"

Where the heck would that leave Guy? William was *everything*.

"I'm sure they're fine," the woman said, tucking dishwater-brown hair behind her ear and giving him a quick smile that didn't quite meet her eyes.

She was lying.

"How can you be sure?" He pushed up from the recliner so fast he wobbled the table next to him and the lamp on top of it started to fall.

Blondie dove in and grabbed the tumbling shade just in time. "Easy there, big guy. He'll be home. I'll text Jocelyn now and find out where they are."

"Who the hell is Jocelyn?" He didn't care that he was yelling. These were a bunch of damn strangers. Strangers scared him. "And who the hell are all of you? I never saw any of you on that show!" He threw the remote on the floor so hard the batteries popped out and skittered everywhere.

And that very moment, William walked in the front door. Missy, looking like a drowned rat, was right beside him, eyes wide, hand over her mouth.

"What going on?" William demanded, marching toward Guy, his eyes fierce and furious.

That just made Guy madder, damn it. "You tell me, son! You disappear and leave me with a house full of strangers."

"Guy." The blonde stepped closer and he waved her off, his hand flying too close, making her duck.

"Stop it!" William lunged at him, way past furious now. His tone turned Guy's innards into water and his legs into Jell-O.

"What the hell are you going to do, Guy? Hit her?"

Guy cringed and cowered back, stunned by this William he didn't even know.

"It's okay," Blondie said, coming closer. "It was—"

"No!" William shouted. "It's not okay. It's not okay to take a swing at a woman or at anyone, for that matter, Guy. Do you know that? Do you *know* that?"

"Will." Missy slipped into the room, curling her arm around Will's, her jaw quivering. "Don't."

"Don't?" He spun on her. "I *didn't* last time, Joss, and look how great that turned out for us."

What was he talking about? Tears welled in Guy's eyes and he tried to wipe them, but that just sent his glasses tumbling to the floor. Missy immediately bent to pick them up for him.

"Here." She straightened the arms and gave them

back, and then she turned to William. "This isn't the time or place for this conversation. And it's too late, anyway."

"What are you two talking about?" Guy demanded, his mix of anger and sadness and fear all balling up in his belly. "William, you left me with all these people, and I...I was scared." He looked at the blonde, her name suddenly popping into his head like a gift from the memory gods. "Zoe was very nice and taught me how to play cards and...and..." He waved toward the couple with the teenager. "And they were nice, too, but...William."

Shoot, he was crying and there was no way in heaven or hell he could stop. "You left me and I thought... I thought..." He blubbered and Missy grabbed a tissue from a box on the table. Taking it, he blew his nose, realizing that the entire room was dead silent.

They were all looking at him. The strangers, expectantly. The girl from *Clean House*, pitifully. And William. How had it happened that William would look at him with such hatred? "Are you mad at me, William?" He could barely say the words.

William just swallowed and took one of those long breaths that he always took when Guy had left the stove on or misplaced his needlework or come out of his room hollering that there was a stranger in the mirror.

There was *always* a stranger in the mirror, and, right this minute, he couldn't stand that anymore.

"Don't hate me, William!" he cried. "That would be like losing a child all over again. I...can't."

Missy's eyes widened, but William stepped closer. "Stop crying, Guy," he said, but not in his normal voice. Not the kind voice that always made Guy feel like he really could stop crying.

"I can't stop crying," he said.

"Yes, you can." Missy came next to him. Closer, in fact, than she'd ever come on her own since he'd met her. She was a cool one, always keeping an invisible fence around her, scrunching up her face when he tried to touch her, giving him icy looks like she knew something he didn't. But right now she wasn't so chilly. She was as kind as William used to be. "Just sit down, Guy."

But he didn't move. Instead he stared at William, who stared right back. What was going on in that young man's head?

"Son, I don't want to lose you again."

William's eyes closed, but he didn't answer.

"Because when you came back to me after all those years…" Damn, Guy's voice cracked and they were all staring at him. Even the teenager. He hated to be on display like this, but if this was what it took for William to know the truth, then he'd do it. "I thought I'd lost you forever and ever. They told me you were gone."

Confusion pulled at William's brow. "I don't know what you're talking about."

"You do, though, William," Guy insisted. "You know what I'm talking about."

"Actually, I don't." He stooped over and picked up the clicker and batteries, avoiding Guy's eyes as he put the thing back together again. "But just calm down—"

"I don't want to calm down!" Guy yelled.

Missy jumped back with a soft gasp.

"Sorry," he said quickly, reaching for her, but she stepped away from him, holding up a hand.

"Don't." William was between them in a second, as if he were guarding her or something.

"I'm not...going to..." One of his loose threads tugged at his brain. An old, frayed bit he rarely thought about, but he could just imagine what was happening in his head as that thread curled into one of the many holes in his brain and tried to tie something together.

William...and this girl.

William...and...someone.

But no matter how hard he tugged, he couldn't pull the memory. "Please don't be mad at me," he said instead, to both of them. "And, William, understand how scared I get when you're gone. I lost you once, I really thought I'd never ever see you again, and all I had was my daugh—" The thread plucked and, suddenly, he could remember.

Both of them stared at him, jaws open. Oh dear, what had he done now?

"Your what?" Missy asked.

He closed his eyes. "I had a daughter."

Nobody in the room said a word; not a single person so much as breathed.

"But she died when she was really, really young." Guy reached toward William. "That's why you're everything to me, son. Everything."

" 'Kay, Guy. Let's call it a night then, buddy."

"Oh, thank you." Guy felt the waterworks, but he didn't care as he reached out to hug Will. "I love you, son. I love you so much."

Will didn't hug him back, but that was okay. He was here. His son was here.

Jocelyn managed to snag a ride back to Barefoot Bay with Lacey and Clay, even if Will wasn't happy about that. He walked her to the car and promised to talk to her tomorrow, but she'd had enough revelations, enough emotion, enough Guy, enough close calls, enough of everything.

Solitude screamed for her.

She rode in the back cab of Clay's truck with Ashley, who, while texting, sent wayward glances at Jocelyn.

"Yes, Ash, the thing with my father is a tough situation," Jocelyn finally said. "You can ask me about it, honey."

Lacey looked over her shoulder to give Jocelyn a grateful smile.

"I was really wondering why you came home all wet."

"We got caught in the rain."

She leaned close and whispered, "Aunt Zoe said you totally don't have your bra on."

Jocelyn's jaw dropped but, damn it, Clay heard and laughed.

"Listen to your iPod until we get home," Lacey said sternly, fighting a smile. "But if you want to talk about your dad, Joss, I'll come up to your villa and Clay can take Ashley home."

"Thanks," Jocelyn said. Solitude might be calling, but she really needed to talk to Lacey, too. For a minute. "I'd like that."

Ashley gave her another sideways look and Jocelyn gave her thigh a friendly punch.

"Hey, what's that for?" Ashley asked.

"For Zoe. Give it to her next time you see her."

When Jocelyn and Lacey stepped into the dimly lit villa, Lacey was the one to drop onto the sofa with a huge sigh. "Well, you missed all the drama."

"I got enough, thank you very much." She turned on the softest light in the living area and looked down at her shirt. "Why does Zoe have to notice everything?"

"Where is it?" Lacey asked, curling a long stawberry-blonde strand and giving a sheepish, teasing smile.

"Somewhere in right field."

"At Mimosa High?" She practically choked.

"Don't be scandalized. I'm sure it's not the first bra to be left at that field. Hell, there's probably an entire Victoria's Secret catalog buried under the bleachers." Jocelyn headed to the back. "I'm going to change. Help yourself to some water or . . . milk."

After she changed into sleep pants and a tank top, brushed the rain out of her hair, and clipped it up, Jocelyn returned to the living room to find Lacey flat out on the couch, sound asleep.

"Whoa, mama. Somebody's tired."

Lacey blinked, sighed, and rolled over, grabbing a pillow with a soft moan. "Oh, I'm so glad I went for the expensive fabric on these pillows."

"So your drool won't stain?"

She smiled, eyes closed. "This babymaking job is tiring."

" 'Specially when you're building a resort in your spare time, raising a teenager, and attending family drama performances."

She opened her eyes. "He's really messed up, isn't he?"

"Confused, I believe, is the proper term." Jocelyn opened a water bottle. "I kinda wish this were wine."

"There's some in there," Lacey said. "I stocked your fridge."

"No wonder you're exhausted."

"So . . ." Lacey dragged herself up. "You want to tell me what happened with Will or would you like to hear how Tessa took the news?"

Jocelyn slammed the bottle on the table hard enough to spill a little water. "You told her?"

"We told everyone. Well, we told Ashley at home first. Then we told the gang tonight."

Guilt squeezed. "Damn, what was I doing? I should have been there for Tessa."

"Zoe was there. You were leaving underwear on the baseball field. Did you do it?"

"No." She rolled her eyes. "Nothing is sacred, is it?"

"Is it?" Lacey sat up a little higher. "Is sex with Will Palmer sacred?"

What a damn good question. "It's not . . . meaningless, let's put it that way." The need to share her fears rose up a little, but she tamped it down. She shared judiciously. And so, so rarely. And this subject? Totally off limits. "How did Tessa take the news?"

"She was fine. I think she already knew."

"Really?" Wouldn't she have said something to Jocelyn? They'd talked so much about infertility in the past eight or ten years. "God, I hate how we're always keeping things from each other."

"From the Queen Secret Keeper."

Jocelyn shrugged. "My secrets are out," she said. "My dad's mean and badly . . ."

"Confused."

"Yes. And I came home from a walk with my old next-door neighbor missing some clothes. I have no secrets left." Just one.

"Coco Kirkman."

Okay, two. "No word from those reporters?" she asked.

"Clay talked to Slade Garrison and he said some are sniffing around asking questions. Don't take this personally, but most of the people on this island barely remember you. Of course Slade knows who your dad is, since he was the former sheriff, but he retired so early, even before your mom died. But since then, Guy's been off the radar, and really, those reporters are getting nowhere. Charity is your only real danger."

Charity was no danger. "I need to go see her tomorrow."

"You're safe up here," Lacey said.

"I know." A rush of affection rolled through her, making Jocelyn reach over and give Lacey's ankles a squeeze. "Thank you for this sanctuary. You have no idea how much this means to me."

Lacey smiled. "You can pay me back."

"Anything. Name it."

"Take the job."

Jocelyn laughed softly. "I walked right into that one."

"I'm serious."

"Lacey . . . I don't know."

Lacey sat up completely, awake and alert. And, oh God, on a mission. "You could be close to Will."

"What makes you think that's a plus?"

"The bra in the outfield."

She'd never live that down. "A little trip around the bases does not a relationship make."

Lacey looked skyward. "You are so into him, why are you lying to yourself? And he's like . . . wow. He adores you. It's all over his face. He couldn't even string a noun and a verb together to make a sentence in the sub meeting yesterday."

"That's not because of me." That was because of what Guy did.

"Bull."

"It's not, but listen, taking your job offer is not about Will. Or any man. Not that there really is any other man to consider, but—"

"Of course there is."

"No." She gave Lacey a serious look. "I'm not seeing anyone in L.A. Not even clients," she added with a rueful laugh.

"That's not the man I meant. I meant your father."

"Oh. Him. I'm putting him in a home." Wasn't she?

Lacey's look was sheer compassion and possibly a little mind reading. "Are you certain about that?"

Maybe she should go get the pictures hidden in her bureau and put the whole conversation to bed. "Relatively certain."

"Because Zoe said..."

"What?"

She shrugged, sliding her feet to the floor and slipping them into flip-flops. "Nothing. She was mistaken."

"What did Zoe say, Lace?"

"She thought you might be changing your mind, is all. I think she's developing a soft spot for the old guy." Lacey stood, smoothed her wrinkled top, and pulled out her phone to glance at a text. "Clay's going to meet me and walk home with me," she said.

"Okay." Jocelyn stood to hug her friend, holding her tighter and longer than she held most people. "I'm honored that you think I have this job in me."

"Are you kidding? The place would be run like a German U-boat. But it's more than that," she said, reaching up to cup Jocelyn's face. "You need to take risks, Joss. You need to take chances. If you don't, you're always going to be protected."

"And you think this new job is the risk I need to take?"

"This new job and..." Lacey pulled her closer to give her a kiss on the cheek. "Will Palmer."

"I'll think about it," she promised. Then, after a second, she smiled. "I'll make some lists."

Lacey laughed. "Excellent sign." Her phone vibrated. "There's my man. See you tomorrow."

Jocelyn let her out the front door and waved to Clay, who walked down the path with a tiny flashlight beam bouncing with each step. She watched them greet each other with a kiss, then waved good night.

When she closed the door, she stood for a long time leaning against it, her hands pressed on the gleaming wood, imagining the hands that had made that wood.

On her.

Yes, if she took the job, she'd be near Will. *And* Guy.

She'd certainly never expected this when she came here for refuge. She might have been safer staying in L.A. and dodging the media.

Still hungry for air, she opened the front door again, frowning when she saw that little light moving down toward the beach. She stepped outside and peered toward the moving light, seeing Clay and Lacey's silhouettes in the cloud-covered moonlight, strolling the beach, stopping to kiss.

That was love and yet there was no fear, no impending doom, no sense that love was a lie. Couldn't Jocelyn look to her best friend as an example instead of her own parents?

Longing squeezed her, stinging her eyes, burning her stomach. Envy, flat out and so real, grabbed hold and took complete ownership.

What would it be like to trust a man like that? What would it be like to believe in that kind of love? What would it be like... with Will?

Good God, she never wanted anything so much in her life. What was stopping her, except Guy?

On every level, it was her father who had stolen that kind of happiness from her. Would putting him away in one of those places free her? Would taking him out of the picture open her heart to possibilities?

No. She'd have to forgive and forget. One she couldn't and the other she wouldn't.

The soft ring of Lacey's laughter floated over the sand, like music in the moonlight, a reminder of what Jocelyn could never, ever have but wanted more than she'd ever realized.

Chapter 24

Jocelyn had risen at 4:00 a.m. and launched into the mother of all lists, feeling a little less burdened by the time the sun came up. Sitting on the front patio watching the water and sky change from the deep violet of night to shades of morning peach, she smoothed her hands over the pages, satisfied with every action item, priority rating, deadline, and the lovely little boxes reserved for check marks.

She had a plan. Several of them, as a matter of fact, with various strategies dependent on the rollout of different tactics for every one of her pending issues.

She closed her eyes, dropped her head against the cushion, and smiled.

In other words, anything could happen, but she would be ready for whatever it was. Maybe the first thing that should happen was some sleep. Or at least coffee.

"Hey. Wake up."

She popped up with a soft gasp, the sight of Tessa holding two large paper cups as welcome as just about anything she could have imagined.

"My supreme sacrifice for you," Tessa said, climbing the two steps to join Jocelyn and hand her a cup. "I'm drinking nonorganic Lipton from the Super Min instead of my usual Nepalese black tea brewed exclusively in the Himalayas. You, however, get Charity Grambling's finest."

"You could be carrying motor oil and I'd drink it right now," Jocelyn said, scooting over to make room on the patio seat. "Bless you, child. There's a coffeemaker in there, but I think I need to grind beans." She sipped, closing her eyes in pleasure. "Call me crazy, but I like Charity's coffee. This is early even for you organic farmers, isn't it?"

"Mmm. I didn't sleep well."

"That makes two of us," Jocelyn said, but added a gentle pat on Tessa's leg, so tanned and toned under her work shorts. "I make lists when I can't sleep." She angled her head toward the stack of paper she'd placed on the end table.

"I know that," Tessa said. "I was your roommate in college, remember?"

"What do you do when you can't sleep?" Jocelyn frowned. "Not that I remember you ever having a problem with that."

Tessa shrugged. "I go dig in the dirt, of course, which is where I am headed. Want to come and help me plant the next cycle of bok choy and kale or just take a walk on the beach?"

Jocelyn heard the subtext: *I need to talk to a friend.*
"I'll walk the beach with you."

Taking their cups, they crossed the path and maneuvered through the sea oats. The tide was low, leaving a huge expanse of untouched cool, cream-colored sand peppered with a colorful array of shells.

"Good day for collecting shells," Tessa mused.

"Perfect." The coral reef and sandbar hidden under the calm waters of Barefoot Bay offered up plentiful and exquisite shells with each high tide, and when the waters receded, collectors could score.

"I bet every single person who stays here takes home a few as souvenirs."

"Can't blame them." The thought left a little impression on Jocelyn's heart, the slightest longing to be here when those guests discovered all the secrets of Barefoot Bay.

"I'm so grateful Lacey got to keep all this land and do the right thing with it," Tessa mused. "I mean, I know development was inevitable after that hurricane, but at least Casa Blanca is going to be natural and built to respect the environment, not destroy it."

"It's going to be a great place," Jocelyn agreed. "One of a kind."

Tessa gave her a sideways look. "Great enough to lure you here?"

Jocelyn laughed softly. "It seems Lacey's suggestion has turned into the talk of the town."

"Don't worry. I didn't tell Charity or it would be. Are you even tempted to consider it, Joss?"

Why lie? "A little." A lot. "It's complicated."

"Moving from L.A., leaving your business, and

starting a whole new job?" Tessa asked. "Complicated would be an understatement. But I'm so happy to hear you're considering it."

"I wouldn't go as far as 'considering,' but, well, let's put it this way, it merited a few lines on my morning lists."

"Cool." Tess waited a few beats, then gave Jocelyn a sideways look. "Who's going to bring this up first?"

"About Lacey?"

Tessa nodded. "I'm only a little mad that she told you first."

Jocelyn sipped her coffee with one hand and put her free arm around Tessa. "She didn't tell me. It kind of slipped out."

Tessa didn't answer, looking down as though she were interested in the shells and letting her hair cover her face. Jocelyn dipped a little so she could get a good look at her friend. "Is that all you're mad about?"

Tessa paused, sipping her tea and making a face when the offensive taste hit her tongue. "God, I'm not mad. I'm just, you know . . ."

"I do know," Jocelyn assured her. "You feel like crap and, worse, you feel guilty about it. You know you should be all kinds of happy for Lacey—and you are—but you hear the clock ticking and you're not quite ready to accept the fact that you may never have your own baby."

Tessa slid her a look. "Do you have to be so raw and honest?"

"Am I right?"

No answer.

"You want euphemisms and platitudes?" Jocelyn asked. "You want me to dance around the truth? Or do you want to solve your problems?"

"Just my luck to pick the hard-ass control-freak life coach to talk to in my time of need."

"It's not like this is the first time we've talked about it, Tess. And I'm not a hard ass."

"You're tough."

Was she? "I don't feel so tough right now, but I am a life coach, so making someone look at the truth is usually my default mode. And a list," she added with a smile.

"What would be on my list?"

"Your problems."

Tessa shook her head, a soft breeze lifting one of her golden-oak colored waves. "I don't have any problems, Joss. I love my new job, I love living here on Mimosa Key."

"Your ex-husband is a baby-making machine and you want one more than you want your next breath and your closest friend and co-worker just announced she's pregnant at thirty-six."

"Seven. Which should give me hope; Lacey's a few years older than we are."

"You don't need hope, honey—you need an action plan."

"I need a new uterus."

Jocelyn puffed out some air, not quite sure how to respond to that, because Tessa was so dead set on having her own baby, not someone else's.

"And I could use a husband."

"So traditional for an organic tea-drinking hippie like you."

"I'm not a hippie!" Tessa leaned her shoulder into Jocelyn to nudge her hard. "My parents were, but I'm just..."

Jocelyn waited, knowing the next word would be the closest thing to the truth.

"Desperate," Tessa admitted on a sigh.

"Aw, Tess." Desperation was the worst. "You know you have options."

"I don't want to do it alone, and honestly, I had a husband, remember? I can't get pregnant for love or money. We tried both."

"Seriously, Tess, why won't you consider adoption?"

She shook her head. "It's not what I want." She stopped, looking down at a grouping of shells, then she bent over to pick one up. "Look at this. Pure perfection."

"Throw it away," Jocelyn said.

"Why?"

"Just toss it as far as you can."

"I like it. I want to keep it." She stuffed her hand into her pocket. "Since I moved here, I've been collecting them. I met a local artist who's kind of a shell expert, and he makes—"

"He? Interesting."

"Shut up. He makes these amazing pieces and I thought I might try my hand—"

"Throw it away," Jocelyn ordered.

Tessa stared at her, their gazes locked. "Fine." Yanking it back out of her pocket, she whipped the shell over her shoulder and angled her head. "And your point is?"

"That could be your baby."

"Oh, please."

"I'm serious. Some perfect baby is being…let go today. Somewhere, someone is having a baby that needs a good mother. That child is out there, like one of these shells, waiting for you."

Tessa started to argue, then closed her mouth, shaking her head. "I've heard the argument and I'm not going to change my mind. If you think that makes me some kind of selfish monster, then—"

"Of course it doesn't. It makes you a liar. You don't want *a* baby. You want *your* baby. Your body won't cooperate. So let go of the dream or adopt a baby."

"You should talk about being a liar."

Jocelyn almost spewed her sip of coffee. "Excuse me?"

"Telling your father you're with *Clean House*."

"I tried to tell him who I was and it didn't sink in. Don't try to make that whole charade my fault. I'm just going along with what Will wants. For now, anyway."

"Will wants you."

"Oh, Tess. Will knows too much about me."

"And that's a problem?" She choked, incredulous. "Look at it another way. He knows everything you've been through and he still cares about you. Maybe more because of it. That's a gift, Joss. That's a rare and wonderful—Oh my God, look. A fighting conch."

Tessa loped away, scooping a shell from the ground.

"What is it?" Jocelyn asked.

"A rare beauty." She flipped the shell on its back, still studying it. "This type of shell is found almost exclusively in the southern U.S. Barefoot Bay has some of the most exquisite conchs in the country."

"I didn't know that."

She held it up to the sun. "That orange iridescence means the animal that lived in this shell was hearty and maybe got into a few scrapes down at the bottom of the sea."

"Whoa. Sounds like someone's been spending an awful lot of time with the local shell expert."

"Who's about fifty-five. Can it."

Jocelyn smiled and reached for the shell. "Let me see. This is a keeper, huh?"

Tessa pulled away. "Not a chance I'm going to give you this so you can toss it and make some life-coaching point."

Laughing, Jocelyn reached for it. "I just want to see it. I swear."

"You do?" Tessa's soft brown eyes glinted. "Fine. Open your hand."

She was up to something. Still, Jocelyn obliged, palm up, and Tessa set the shell right in the middle of her hand.

"This, my friend, is a keeper." Tessa was so serious and quiet that her voice made the fine hairs on the back of Jocelyn's neck rise. "Maybe a little flawed, but still great looking." Tessa traced the soft rim of the shell. "The edges are just worn enough to know this one's been in the sea for a long time, but it's still beautiful and will last for several thousand more days before time and sand and wind break it down."

Jocelyn looked at her, sensing exactly where this was going. "Will?"

Tessa lifted one shoulder. "You can throw it back in the sea, if you like. But it is being offered to you to keep."

Jocelyn rolled her eyes. "You've gone from coaching to melodrama."

"I'm making a point using a seashell, just like you did."

"Are you giving this to me?" Jocelyn asked.

"Yeah. I am."

She leaned in and gave Tessa a kiss on the cheek. "Then I won't throw it away. And, Tess? For a gardener, you're not a bad life coach."

She laughed. "Speaking of gardens, you want to walk up there with me?"

Jocelyn shook her head. "I think I'll stay down here until the sun rises and then get to my list."

" 'Kay. Thanks for the advice."

"Same here."

They gave a quick hug and Tessa took off, but Jocelyn stood for a long time looking at the Gulf, holding her shell and thinking.

She wanted Will. She wanted him in every imaginable way.

What was stopping her? Looking down at her hand, she studied the shell. Damn it, she was so sick of shells. Especially the one around her heart.

Chapter 25

⌒

The garage was done and the sun was up.

Amazing.

Will stepped out into the morning light of the driveway, surveying his work, satisfied with the results of six hours of hard labor. The attic was cleaned out. The garage was empty except for some boxes and a half dozen bags of trash. And Guy hadn't even gotten up yet.

At the sound of an engine slowing he turned, surprised to see the Lee County sheriff's car pulling into Guy's driveway with Deputy Slade Garrison at the wheel.

"Morning, Will," Slade said as he rolled down the window.

"Slade. What's up?"

"Just checking in, making sure you haven't had any problem with the media."

"Why? Have they been around again?" Not that he

needed any more reason to accelerate his plan, but those guys would certainly give him one.

"Charity said they stopped in again, and I heard a couple of guys were in the Toasted Pelican last night asking about Jocelyn."

"Shit," he mumbled, putting a hand on the car roof to block the sun from Slade's face. "Anyone say anything?"

"Very few people know she's here."

"Charity does." And that would normally be like putting it on the front page of the *Mimosa Gazette*.

"Well, she's keeping this secret," Slade said. "For whatever reason."

Will knew the reason. Charity had been the one to pick up the pieces when Will had let them all fall apart. Guilt kicked him, as sure and strong as it had all night while he'd packed up Guy's house.

"How is the old guy?" Slade asked, his gaze following Will's to the garage.

"Moving into assisted living very soon."

Slade nodded. "Guess it's true, then, what I heard."

Will gave him a questioning look.

"So many rumors why 'Big Guy' left the force so young, even before his pension kicked in," Slade explained, air-quoting the former sheriff's nickname.

Will didn't react; now he knew why "Big Guy" had left the force: Charity's blackmail pictures. "Some of the older guys said he had trouble and started mentally slipping on the job," Slade continued.

"Must have," Will said, not interested in sharing the truth with the young man. "I really appreciate you keeping an eye out on things, Slade."

"Not a problem. Plus, it seems to make Charity happy and I'm trying to get in good with that whole family."

"Looks to me like you're in good with her niece."

Slade grinned. "Workin' on it, buddy. How about you and Jocelyn?"

Was it that obvious? "Workin' on it, buddy."

"Even though she had an affair with that movie star?"

Irritation rocked him. "She didn't. It's all a lie."

Slade's brows lifted. "Sure going to a lot of trouble to hide from the media if that actress is lying. And the guy? Miles? He's kind of letting on that it's true."

His fists balled like he was going to give a good punch to his catcher's mitt. "He is?"

"Don't you read these rags you're so busy hiding from?" Slade turned to the passenger seat and grabbed a paper, shoving it at Will. "You ought to."

"Thought Charity wasn't selling these."

"Gloria gave it to me."

Will took the tabloid but didn't look at it. "I'll use this to wrap Guy's dishes," he said. " 'Cause I don't have a dog who could shit on it."

Laughing, Slade put the car in Reverse. "Do whatever you want with it, Will. But you should know things are only getting worse for her. I'll watch this street as long as I can, but those guys..." He nodded toward the paper. "They're going to be relentless until she makes some kind of statement. Maybe you could convince her to do that."

Maybe he'd be playing in the World Series next year, too. "I'll try," he said, backing away just as another car came down Sea Breeze.

Slade used his side-view mirror to check the car. "There she is now. Perfect timing."

He pulled out and Jocelyn drove into the empty driveway, her window down, her hair blown, her expression oddly happy.

Will rolled the tabloid and ignored a jolt of pleasure as he opened her door. "Good morning, gorgeous."

She smiled, stepping out, then tilted her head to get a good look at him. "I wish I could say the same thing."

"Ouch."

"Tough night, Will?"

He dragged his hand through his hair and rubbed his unshaven cheeks. Yeah, he probably looked like hell. "I will show you exactly how tough. Brace yourself, Ms. Bloom. I have a surprise."

With the hand that held the paper, he put his arm around her and walked her toward the garage. "Never let it be said that I'm not a man of action, or one who can't make a decision."

Inside the garage, he waved a hand to the boxes and bags, everything but the very top of the loft empty. "I emptied the attic, too. And you did the kitchen and dining room. All that's left is a few closets in the house. Oh, and I signed up for two more tours at assisted-living places, so I figure we can have him settled somewhere by next week."

She stilled, turning toward him. "This is quite a one-eighty you've done. You're a life coach's dream." She took a step closer, tentatively reaching for his face. If she touched him it'd all be over. Her fingers barely grazed his unshaven cheek.

"I'd like to be a life coach's dream," he said. "If you're the life coach."

Her eyes widened, and her whole body kind of stilled. "Will, I…"

"Listen, Joss." He stopped her by taking her shoulders and holding tight. "Last night at the baseball field was..." *Life-changing.* "Really nice with you. And when we came home and found Guy throwing that little temper tantrum, I knew I couldn't drag my heels on this anymore."

She searched his face, taking in each word. "This change of heart isn't just because of—of the pictures? Of what happened that night?"

"Partially," he admitted. "I'm pissed beyond words and I kind of feel duped by him."

"He can't help that he doesn't remember."

He inched back, trying to process that statement. "Look who's had a change of heart."

"No, no." She shook her head. "I really don't have a choice where he's concerned, but I agree." She slipped out of his grasp and walked toward the garage storage loft, pointing to the boxes up there. "So that stuff is all that's left out here?"

Behind her, he tossed the newspaper on top of an open carton, unwilling to change the direction of this encounter by talking about the media and Miles Thayer. The sooner they got Guy moved out, the sooner they could get past him and on to the next problem.

Action felt good, he realized, watching her grab the ladder rails and hoist herself up, looking over her shoulder as she climbed.

"Why are you smiling?" she asked.

"Nice view," he said, nodding toward her backside.

She made a face and climbed and he followed, both of them crouching over so they didn't hit the ceiling as they made their way to the two cartons he'd left in the back corner.

"I have no idea what those are," he said. "I tried to lift them and they weigh a ton, so I figured I'd go through them and throw stuff away or sort."

Jocelyn made her way over, then settled next to the boxes, swiping at some cobwebs and brushing off a few that must have hit her face. "These came out of my mother's closet after she died."

"Oh." He sat next to her. "I didn't know."

She put a hand on top of one of the boxes but made no move to open it. "When I came home for her funeral, these boxes were all packed. I don't know if Guy did it or what, but I never looked through them."

"You want to now?" He put a hand on her back, sensing her hesitation. "We don't have to."

"I do have to," she said. "It's all I have of her."

"No it's not, Joss. You have your memories."

She sighed as if those didn't satisfy much. "All right. I'm ready. Open 'er up." She put her hand on his arm. "But be warned, I might need...comfort."

He leaned over and kissed her on the cheek. "You got it."

The soft scent of a spicy perfume mixed with the musky smell of old clothes when Will stripped the duct tape off the carton and opened the flap. He pulled out a stack of sweaters and gave her a questioning look.

"I doubt we can sell these," she said, taking the pastel-colored pile. "They're kind of dated."

"Oh," Will said, reaching deeper into the box. "This is what weighed so much."

Jocelyn got up on her knees, sneezing softly. "What is it?"

"Furniture. A small wooden cabinet." He reached in

and wedged his hands on either side of a large box. "Weird. Why put this in a carton? Have you seen it before?"

"I don't think so. Here. I'll hold the box, you pull it out."

With a little effort, they maneuvered out a stunning rosewood cabinet a couple of feet wide with two drawers.

"Wow, this is nice," Will said, grazing the polished wood. "Handmade by a pro. You've never seen this before?"

She shook her head

Will tugged on the brass knob. "It's like an old fashioned..." He pulled the drawer out. "Baby's dresser."

Full of baby clothes. Tiny, newborn, brand-new *blue* baby clothes.

Jocelyn's fingers shook as she reached for the wee navy blue sleeper with a baseball bat on the front. "Are these yours, by some chance?" she asked.

"No clue. Why would they be in your garage?"

"I don't know," she said, taking out one precious piece after another. "Weird. The tags are still on them."

They'd been folded with love, neatly lined up and separated by tissue paper. The top drawer was all onesies and tiny sleepers with feet.

The bottom drawer had little-boy T-shirts with trucks and trains, tiny shorts no bigger than her hand, socks, and three little pairs of booties.

"I should give these to Lacey," Jocelyn said. "But I don't know whose they are."

"Are you sure this box was left when your mother died?"

She nodded. "I distinctly remember seeing it come out of my parents' bedroom, all taped up by my father." She lifted the last layer of clothes to find a blue satin baby book. "Oh. Maybe this'll tell us something."

The spine cracked when she opened it as if it had never been used. But there was handwriting on the first page. Her mother's distinctive sideways scrawl. The words tore a gasp from Jocelyn's throat.

Alexander Michael Bloom, Jr.

Laid to Rest January 19, 1986

She'd had a brother? The words swam in her vision. How was this possible? She tore her gaze from the book to Will's eyes, his expression as shocked and confused as hers must have been.

"You were, what, seven years old?" he asked.

She couldn't speak, just nodded.

"And they had a baby you didn't know about?"

That wasn't possible. Her throat felt like someone had a hand around her neck and wouldn't stop squeezing. Very slowly, she turned the pages of a book created with the express purpose of memorializing a baby's life.

Baby's Earliest Days! A grainy, faded sonogram print-out on yellowed paper, far blurrier than the kind they used nowadays, was taped to the page. In the corner the letters had almost disappeared with time, but Jocelyn could make out the words.

Bloom baby boy. December 9, 1985

"Oh my God, Will." The words came out like a rasp of pain as she turned the page.

Mommy's Growing Too! A list of months from August to January with a number and a pound sign had been inserted in her mother's writing. Chills blossomed over her whole body despite the heat of the garage. Will turned the next page for her, but every single line was empty.

Baby Arrives! But that page was empty. No date, no pictures, no words.

Baby's First Bath! Blank. *Baby's Sits Up!* Blank. *Baby Can Crawl!* Blank.

Page after page of the saddest story never told. Never told *to Jocelyn*. The thought slammed her. "He must have been stillborn. Why didn't they tell me? I never even knew she was pregnant."

"You were only seven, Joss. You couldn't handle it."

"But later? When I got older." She spread her hand on the blank page reserved for *Baby's Growth Chart*, digging back into her memory banks and coming up as blank as the page. "Why wouldn't my mother have told me she was carrying—and lost—a baby boy?"

"I don't know," he said, turning a page. "Too painful, I guess."

And then a memory teased. "She went to the hospital when I was in second grade," she said, staring ahead, digging for truth. "They told me she had appendicitis. She must have been"—she flipped back to the sonogram and squinted at the old computerized numbers, quickly doing math—"about five months pregnant and lost the baby. I vaguely recall my grandparents came down from up north and stayed for a few days until she came home."

"Do you remember how she handled it?"

"No, but that's when Guy's episodes started." She blinked away the tears, clarity and understanding dawning.

This was what had made him snap. This was why he'd grown violent and moody. And why—oh, God. Realization dawned. "This is why he thinks you are his son who he was told was gone forever."

He just closed his eyes at the direct hit.

She flipped to the last page, tucked in a pocket for

keepsakes marked *Baby's First Hair*, a piece of paper was folded in half.

With a glance at Will, she drew it out, her hands trembling as the meaning of this settled on her heart. As she opened the paper, she swallowed hard at the sight of her father's distinctive handwriting.

"He wrote this," she said, her voice as wobbly as the rest of her.

Will put his arm all the way around her, holding her tight. "Let's read it together."

To my son...

She closed her eyes and let out a soft whimper.

"It's a poem," Will said, tucking her closer and letting her rest against him.

After a minute, she opened her eyes and read.

> *Today we said goodbye to you*
> *A little man I never knew.*
> *I wanted you to be my friend*
> *But now those plans will have to end.*

Jocelyn covered her mouth to hold back the sob. Will stroked her arm until she could bear to read the rest.

> *Even though you were never here*
> *I love you, son, my little dear.*
> *There are no words for all this pain*
> *No way to stop the grief and rain.*
> *Goodbye. Goodbye. Good...*

That was it.

"Who knew he wrote bad poetry?" Will asked wistfully.

She almost smiled. "The man who loves needlepoint and decorating shows? He was always in there. Always." But then that man had changed. He became a wifebeater. "He must have blamed my mother," Jocelyn said as pieces fell into place. "He must have cracked and taken out all this agony on her." She choked back the tears, turning to Will. "I shouldn't have hated him so much."

"It's no excuse," Will said quietly. "Do you want to go talk to him?"

"What good would that do? He doesn't remember. He doesn't remember anything. Not this unborn child, not me, not my mother, not what he did. He sure as hell won't remember these clothes or this cabinet." Her voice rose with each word, squeezing her, choking her.

She pushed up, desperate for air. Without a word, she scrambled to the side of the loft.

"Where are you going?" he asked.

"I need to breathe. I need to think." *I need to reevaluate everything I thought was true.* "I just need..." Her words trailing off, she got to the bottom of the ladder and took off, aching to get out of the garage.

A stillborn baby boy. That could change a man and a marriage. It could transform a family from a happy one that went fishing in a rowboat to one that fought over fresh flowers.

Will was right. It was no excuse for what he'd done, but it was an explanation. And for some reason she didn't quite understand, she wanted to cling to it.

She hit the grass of the side yard, walking without thinking, picking up speed, not entirely sure where she was going until she found herself standing at the back door of the Palmers' house, the one that led up to Will's room.

He was next to her in seconds, wrapping his arms around her, cradling her with comfort, just like always.

She looked up at him. "I need to go back up there."

"In the garage?" he asked.

"Up there." She pointed to the room. "I need you to hold me."

Without a word, he opened the door and guided her up the narrow stairs where she'd long ago let him go and led her right to the comfort of his old Dodgers blanket.

Chapter 26

⤳

Judging by the sun pouring into the bedroom window, Jocelyn and Will had slept for at least a few hours. Her legs were wrapped around his, her face pressed against his shoulder. She woke with a funny feeling in her heart, a mix of bone-deep exhaustion and something like freedom.

Was she free now?

It sure felt like it. Her whole being felt lighter, despite the news that twenty-seven years ago she'd lost a baby brother. Guy must have cracked; maybe her mother had inadvertently caused the miscarriage and Guy just couldn't forgive her.

No, it wasn't an excuse, she realized that. Nothing got him a pass for what he'd inflicted on both of them, but somehow, some way, Jocelyn felt like a chain had been unlocked from around her chest and she could breathe again.

When they'd come up here, she'd babbled and sniffled

and sobbed like a fool, and Will did what Will did best: he'd held her. And then they fell asleep, in spite of the fact that they'd spent the night apart, restless and longing for each other. Or maybe because of it.

She sighed and nestled a little deeper into his side, her arm draped over his chest, her hair spilling over her cheeks. She couldn't see his face from this angle but didn't want to risk moving and waking him.

So instead of looking at him, she just let the musky, masculine scent of Will fill her head.

Stinks like sweat, grass, and a hint of reliability?

No. It smells like comfort.

The words were as clear as if the exchange that took place in this very room had been last night, not fifteen years ago. She'd loved him then and she—

What exactly did she feel now?

Come on, Joss. *You love him. You've* always *loved him.* Curling her fingers around the comforter, she pulled it higher, loving the softness of the old blue blanket, the symbol of his ultimate dream team.

Which was funny; he'd hate L.A. Just like she did.

She blinked at the thought. She'd always acknowledged her issues with the crowded, glitzy mess that was Los Angeles, but did she actually hate living there? Maybe she hadn't realized that until she came here, which was, for better or worse, her home.

So why go back? Why not just settle right here, in these arms, with this man, in a new job, with a new life, and even a new father?

Now that she knew the truth, could she possibly forgive Guy? Maybe not, but she could tiptoe past her pain and maybe get to a better place with him. Couldn't she?

Yes. Because she could do absolutely anything for Will. Even forgive Guy.

At the thought, an unfamiliar joy warmed her from the very deepest place. It felt radiant, real, and so unshakable.

Was this love? This sense of certainty? That desire to do anything for someone else? This feeling that life couldn't get any better, combined with the awareness that it would?

Yes. This was most definitely love.

The realization made her shift in Will's arms, stretching along his hard side, sliding her leg over his, positioning herself to watch this gorgeous man wake up and grow erect at the same time. Talk about watching the sun rise.

Under her thigh, his manhood twitched and throbbed. A low groan pulled at his chest and he turned to meet her gaze.

"Why is this woman smiling?"

She just rubbed her thigh over his erection, a zing of anticipation and nervousness fighting her own twitches of arousal. "Because she's happy."

He frowned a little. "You went to sleep crying."

She chafed his hard-on again. "You went to sleep flaccid."

He made a face. "That's an ugly word."

"There's nothing ugly about..." She lowered her hand and rubbed over his tented shorts. "This."

His features shifted from sleepy to sexy as he hissed in a breath. Her gaze drifted over his face, settling on his mouth, stirring everything in her low and deep. Her thighs tightened and her breasts seemed to swell and ache.

"I'm ready," she whispered.

He had no idea exactly what those words meant. And

right now, that was fine. Someday she'd tell him; maybe soon. But if she made a big announcement now, he'd get all weird.

She didn't want weird. She wanted him.

He shifted a little to accommodate the erection and when he did, she started to untangle their legs, but Will squeezed his together, pinning her calf between his.

"You're ready?"

"The long wait is over." So, so over. She couldn't help smiling. She'd made the right decision. There'd been plenty of near misses, plenty of pissed-off almost-boyfriends, plenty of nights when she wanted to lose control but couldn't or wouldn't or chickened out.

But she was finally ready.

"Oh, Jossie." He stroked her face, brushing her hair back. "My beautiful, sweet, strong, sexy Bloomerang. I knew you'd come back to me."

Time and space hung suspended like a curtain about to fall. Her heart slammed. Her breath caught. Her whole body tensed in anticipation.

No more waiting.

He kissed her so hard their teeth tapped, both of them sucking in the breath they'd been holding. Open-mouthed, their tongues touched and explored as they moved into the most natural position, body to body, almost instantly starting to rock in a heavenly rhythm.

"I can't wait anymore, Joss," he admitted with a rasp, already letting his hands begin to roam her body. "I can't wait."

"Don't." She kissed his neck and slid her hands over his chest, as desperate as he was. "Don't wait. Don't stop. Do whatever you want. Do . . . everything."

He rolled her onto her back, shifting on top of her so he could press his whole body into the kiss. He didn't bother getting under her shirt, but stripped it off in one satisfying move that she almost instantly mirrored with his T-shirt.

His hand quivered as he took off her bra and closed his palm over her breast, letting out a helpless groan as he lowered his head to take her nipple in his mouth.

Why had she waited for this?

Because it had to be Will. It *had* to be.

He licked her nipple until she budded under his tongue, then went back to her mouth, her cheeks, her throat, her ears. All the while they pumped against each other in an age-old beat of need and desire.

Desire that usually took her to a dark place. But this time all she felt was awe and relief and more desire. With a soft moan of joy, she let him roll her over again so she was on top, and her hair tumbled toward his face.

Sitting up, she straddled his hard-on and unzipped her shorts, staring at him, taking a million mental snapshots, wanting this extraordinary, perfect moment to last. Wanting so much to make up for the big black hole of longing and waiting that had consumed her for the last fifteen years.

She slid off him to slip out of her shorts, and he ripped off his, and then, for a span of about ten seconds, they lay naked, but not touching.

She smiled, touching his lips with her finger. "The wait is over, Will Palmer. Make love to me."

He kissed her finger and closed his eyes. "That's like...confetti at the World Series parade. Nothing could feel better than those words."

Laughing, she drew her finger in and out of his lips. "Something could."

"You're right." Very slowly, as tenderly as he could, he laid her back down, taking a moment to caress her breasts and slide his hand over her body and down one thigh.

She moaned with pleasure, lifting her hips to invite his touch.

"My Jocelyn," he whispered as he trailed his finger from her belly button down to her very center.

His Jocelyn.

"I am," she whispered, looking up at him, fighting not to completely lose control and buck wildly like she wanted to.

"My best friend." He touched the most tender part of her, making her suck in a breath, but still she maintained control. "My girl next door." He lowered his head and kissed her stomach while his finger slipped inside her a little deeper. "My lover."

"Finally." The word turned into a half-gasp when his tongue flicked over her.

"I love your body," he murmured, kissing and sucking gently.

Answering with another moan, she dug her fingers into his hair and held his head where she wanted it. Pleasure exploded through her, so different from the quick release she'd had last night. This was intense, alive, deep. Hot flames licked all over her skin and every cell sparked.

"I love..." Her stomach tightened in anticipation, knowing he would say it now. He'd said it all those years ago. Will had no problem professing his love.

But instead of saying anything more, he opened his mouth over her, slipped his tongue inside, and nearly detonated her with one stroke. Arousal punched so hard her head buzzed with the loss of blood. Control evaporated, leaving only shreds of awareness, everything so insanely focused *there*. With a long, desperate cry of pure pleasure, she bucked against him, coming mercilessly against his mouth.

Still clawing through each breath, she pulled him back up, letting him kiss every inch he could find until their lips met.

She tried to talk, but another little aftershock stole her voice, so she looked up at him, barely able to get the next strangled breath. "What are the chances, Will?"

Really, what were the chances that she could have waited all these years and they would finally find their way back to this room to make love for the first time? It was as if, in the back of her mind, she knew. She *knew*. For as many times as she had questioned her own sanity, made a hundred excuses, and even lied about her sex life, she *knew*.

It had to be Will.

"You mean what are the chances that there's a condom handy?"

No, she didn't mean that at all, but she wasn't ready to tell him yet. Knowing Will, it would completely throw the game, and she wanted him now. All of him, inside her.

He reached over to the side of the bed to lift his shorts from the floor. He shook them and his phone fell with a clunk, followed by his wallet. "After last night? My wallet is stocked."

He put on the condom, then got on top of her, holding her gaze as he slipped the tip against her still electrified womanhood.

And she knew: She should tell him. It was *wrong* not to tell him. He'd be happy. What guy wouldn't want to be the first?

She took a breath and said, "I have to tell you something."

A hint of frustration darkened his eyes as he throbbed against her. "*Now*?"

"Yes. Before I...we...before you're inside me, you have to know something." She reached up and touched his face. How would he take this?

"Joss, I'm showing more control and restraint than I even knew I had. Just say it, sweetheart. Say it. Tell me you love me."

She bit her lip and lifted her hips, the move so natural. Because this was the way it was supposed to be. She loved him. She *loved* him. And really, at this moment, this close to the brink, that was *all* he needed to know. "I love you, Will Palmer."

A slow, beautiful, completely heartfelt smile curled his lips. "Yeah?"

"Always have, always will."

"Now that was worth waiting for."

So was this.

Will gritted his teeth to keep from plowing forward, inch after mind-blowing inch of tightness wrapping around him, making him want to scream. She was so damn tight.

But he held back, watching her face, taking his cues, seeing her bite her lip to make him wonder if she felt more pain than pleasure at their coupling. Still, blind with need, braced on the bed, he went deeper until he was all the way inside her.

"Are you okay?" he asked.

She bit her lip again, nodding, working for each breath. He wanted to stop, or at least slow down, but each stroke was more incredible than the last, each plunge taking him closer to release.

"Will." She pulled at him, her legs wrapped around him as their bodies moved and met perfectly. "Come closer. Come closer."

His face nuzzled in her hair, her lips next to his ear. "Listen to me," she whispered, her voice as insanely sexy as the body he was lost inside.

He barely nodded, blood pumping and pulsing, his breathing so fast and hard he could hardly hear her.

"Will." She squeezed him harder, her movements slower and more controlled. "Listen to me," she said again. "I want to tell you something. I have to."

Let her talk. Say what she wanted. All he wanted was this insane pleasure that was about to—

"I've never..."

He shook his head, unable to hear her through the rushing blood. No words got through as sweet and silky morphed into fast and frenetic, the sounds of their breath and their bodies like a deafening whoosh that pulsed and screamed and finally spun out of control.

Completely lost in raw, relentless release, he spilled into her, stroke after stroke, pump after pump, a rush so intense he had to damn near howl.

He fell on her, exhausted, depleted, and so fucking happy he could cry. She loved him.

"What did you say, Joss?" he rasped.

"I said...I've never..." She closed her eyes. "Felt anything like that before."

"Me neither. God, you're like, oh..." Somewhere on the floor his phone vibrated. He couldn't move. He couldn't think about anything except how amazing that was. And that she loved him.

She *loved* him.

The phone vibrated again.

"You going to get that?" she asked.

He managed to move his eyes to look at her. "No."

One more time the phone vibrated, then the call moved to voice mail.

"Go ahead," she urged. "I understand."

"Nothing is more important than you." Than what she'd just given him.

"It might be Guy. Does he have any idea where you are?"

Somehow he found the strength to drop his arm to the floor, feel around, and find the phone, dragging it back to the bed to read the caller ID.

Scott Meyers, Sports Management of America.

His agent?

"Is it important?" she asked.

"It's not Guy." But it might have been important. He pressed the number for voice mail, turning to look at her while he put the phone to his ear. Listening to it ring, he traced her jaw with his finger, then her lips.

Lips that had just said she loved him.

Under his touch, she smiled. "I made a decision, Will."

"Hey, bud, where the hell are you? I have news."

Will blinked at her, the buzz saw of his hyperactive agent's voice feeling completely wrong while he was looking at Jocelyn.

"What is it?" He asked her the question, but Scott's message kept rolling.

"Oh, what the hell. I'll tell you. You got an offer, dude."

"I don't want to go back to L.A., Will. I'm taking Lacey's job offer."

"I . . . you don't?"

"The Los Angeles Dodgers, dude! Fuckin' Rancho Cucamonga needs a bull-pen coach. Interview is tomorrow in the AM. Get your ass on the next plane to southern California, Palmer. We did it, man!"

"I want to stay here in Mimosa Key, with you."

There . . . here . . . *what*? His head almost exploded with the conflicting announcements.

"So call me ASAP. They're desperate and we can swing a sweet deal. Congrats, buddy. This is the one you've been waiting for, right?"

Right.

"Will?" Jocelyn perched up on her elbow, searching his face. "Is something wrong?"

Yeah. Something was really wrong. He'd waited too long.

Chapter 27

‿

Not so fast with those rash decisions, Joss."

Something in Will's voice unraveled everything inside her, his face falling fast as she told him her plans and he listened to someone's message. All her words, promises, pledges, and heartfelt announcements about love just fizzled in the face of a man who just didn't look like he wanted to hear them.

Of course he didn't. What the hell had she been thinking?

Suddenly aware of how naked and open she was, she gathered up the old comforter, her fingers closing around the frayed edge. With the material almost to her nose she felt covered, but the old scent of Will's room made her dizzy, intensified by the unfamiliar, tangy scent of sex and the look of sheer bewilderment on his face.

She cleared her throat, not trusting her voice, but he spoke first. "That was my agent."

"Oh."

He deliberately set the phone on the pillow between them, straightening it like he was buying time.

"Looks like..." His lips twisted in a smile that was more bitter than bright. "The wait is over."

The wait. "For a new job?"

He nodded, slowly, his gaze moving over her face, looking for something, and maybe hiding something, too.

"Wow," she said on a whisper. "That's..." Incredibly bad timing. "Amazing. What is it?"

"Bull-pen coach, minor leagues."

"What you wanted, right?" Except, sometime in the last hour or day or maybe week, she'd decided she wanted him. "You know, everything I just said—"

"Joss." He touched her face again, cupping her jaw, inching his warm body next to hers. "The job's in L.A."

For a moment she wasn't sure she'd heard him right.

"Los Angeles," he confirmed.

"With the Dodgers?" Her fingers clutched the comforter, the Dodger blue comforter. The physical-embodiment-of-a-childhood-dream comforter.

"The Rancho Cucamonga minor league team."

Holy hell. "That's half an hour drive from my house in Pasadena."

"So, about that decision to stay in Mimosa Key..." He stroked her cheek, curling hair around his finger.

"Yeah, you just complicated it."

"Complicated it? Decision's made." He eliminated whatever space was between them, wrapping a leg over her thigh to cuddle her closer. "We'll go together. We'll *be* together. We'll—"

She put a hand on his lips. "What about Guy?"

"What about him? Our plan is perfect. We'll have him in a ho—"

"It's *our* plan now? Up until Charity Grambling handed you some pictures you were doing your damnedest to convince me that it was a very bad idea, that Guy needed to be at home, with help, and—"

"Everything changed, Jocelyn." He sat up, too. "Everything changed in the last two days. I know what happened—"

"So do I." She backed away, still holding the blanket to cover her. "At least I have a pretty good idea. He snapped when that baby died. In fact, it makes perfect sense. Maybe he blamed my mother, maybe she had an accident, maybe—"

"No," he said sharply. "No. You can't just forgive him that quickly."

She drew back. "You've been asking me to do just that since I arrived. And it's not that quick. He's been different, he's so changed and—"

"No." He took a deep breath like he needed to gather strength to make his point. "This is too perfect. This is meant to be. A job in Los Angeles. With"—he gestured toward the blanket—"my dream team. And you live there. Jocelyn, this is perfect."

"But my father—"

"Kicked the holy crap out of you when you were young and defenseless," he shot back, pushing himself out of the bed now and grabbing a pair of shorts. "And then he threatened to kill me or at least ruin my career, so you made the decision to never speak to me again."

She started to respond, but he waved his hand to stop her. "And, I know, I went along with that, so I'm to blame, too, but, Jesus, Jocelyn. Fate and the Los Angeles Dodgers baseball franchise may have just handed me everything I ever wanted professionally." He stepped into the shorts, eyes blazing on her. "And five minutes before that, you handed me everything I ever wanted personally. And, damn it, I want both."

"What about what I want?" *One time in bed and he got all the control*? Anger and resentment fired through her sex-sated cells. No, it wasn't going to work that way.

He stared at her, as if the question made no sense. "You said you loved me."

And he'd never said it back. "I was in the middle of a climax."

He frowned. "Not exactly."

"Close enough." A lie, a complete lie. But he hadn't said it back, so...

"And you said you made a decision not to leave." He stabbed his hand in his hair, inching back, thinking. "But you haven't told Lacey, have you? So, we'll just go to L.A."

"Will we?" She shot out the words much harder than she'd intended.

"Jocelyn, listen to me."

"No." She shook her head. "You can't call the shots in my life. I don't want to go back there with all that crap hanging over my head. You can't..." *Not go to the Dodgers*. It was unthinkable.

She let out a long breath as the realization of what she was doing dawned. Once again she held the keys to his career. Last time she'd let him go have it. But this time? If she asked him to stay he would, once he gave it some thought. He was that noble, that loyal, that completely rock solid and reliable.

And, once again, she knew that the right thing to do was going to hurt like hell.

"When are you going?"

"Right away," he said, reaching for the phone. "The interview is tomorrow morning. I have to call Scott now."

"And I have to . . ." *Figure out what the hell to do with my life—and with my father.* "Go see my dad."

His eyes flashed at that. "Since when do you call him anything but Guy?"

"Since I found out that he had a great tragedy."

"A miscarriage isn't exactly like he lost *you*."

"But he did lose me."

Will almost choked. "Because he damn near killed you! And he threatened to kill me."

"But before you knew that, you forgave him, Will. You took care of him. You worried about him. You valued him. You . . ." Did she dare say it? Yes. "You *loved* him."

He just sighed. "But now I know differently."

"So you actually stopped loving him?"

"It made me . . ." He held his head like it was going to explode. "Yeah, I did. Look, we'll figure it out. We'll put him somewhere. We'll make this work, Jocelyn. I don't want to wa—"

"So you can stop loving someone that easily?" The reality of that made her breathless. "Just because they did one thing you think is wrong? You just walk away?"

"No, I—"

"What if you found out I really *did* have an affair with Miles Thayer?"

His eyes widened almost imperceptibly, but she saw the impact of the question. She didn't care. She had to know. She had to know what he was made of. Because if he wasn't who she hoped he was, then he wasn't worthy of the risk.

When he didn't answer, she pushed harder. "Would you stop caring about me because I did something that was repugnant to you?"

He swallowed. "I don't know why you don't tell the truth."

She had. To him. Wasn't that enough? "You know what your problem is, Will?"

"Guess I'm about to, right?"

"It's all or nothing with you. What did you say you wanted with me? What was the word you used? The word I heard you whisper in the bushes the morning you saw me climbing out of bed in the villa?"

This time his reaction wasn't imperceptible at all. He drew back, frowning. "What did I say?"

"*Everything.* You whispered 'everything,' just like you did in bed half an hour ago. Just like you told me in my villa. You want everything because you are an all-or-nothing kind of guy. There's no gray area."

He crossed his arms and bobbed his head a little, no argument at all. "What the hell's wrong with that?"

"It scares me," she admitted.

"Why?"

"Because if you're willing to walk away from a man you've spent a year and a half nurturing because you found out something he did fifteen years ago, then..." Wasn't it obvious? Did she have to spell it out for him? She looked at him, her bottom lip trapped under her front teeth as she bit down to keep the emotion at bay. "An all-or-nothing man is the worst possible kind for a woman who was raised in a house built on fear."

"Jocelyn." He came closer, holding out his hands. "I would never hurt you."

She just stared at him. "But what if I did something to hurt you? Could you stop loving me that easily?" Like somehow managed not to mention that he'd just taken her virginity?

His expression changed as the wheels turned. "Did you? Is that what you were trying to tell me before?"

Her fingers dug a little deeper into the old comforter, words trapped in her chest.

"Did you sleep with Miles Thayer?" he asked, a hitch in his voice. "Did you have an affair with your client's husband?"

The words cracked with the same impact as her father's ring against her tooth, making her run her tongue along the old familiar chip. "Is that what you think I mean?" she asked.

"Well, did you?" he demanded. "Is that why you don't just get out there and deny it, hiding behind some code of professional ethics instead of defending yourself?"

Oh. She couldn't take this. Looking down, she blinked at the watery Dodgers logo that now mocked her with *comfort*.

"Will. I need to get dressed. Why don't you go downstairs and call your agent and…" *Go follow your Dodger dreams.* "I'll say good-bye before you leave."

"Jocelyn." He reached for her, but she backed away, too hurt to let him touch her. On a frustrated exhale, he dropped his hand.

"Just go, Will."

All the color drained from his face as he stared at her, processing what he assumed was the truth. Let him. It didn't matter that it wasn't the truth.

What mattered was that he thought it was true and, well, with an all-or-nothing kind of guy, that left her with nothing.

Nothing except a father who really needed her.

Jocelyn washed up in Will's bathroom, collected herself, and made a very short mental to-do list. On it was one thing: forgive. Maybe the joy of doing that would ease the ache of Will's obvious doubts about her and hers about him.

She didn't stop downstairs on the way out, but slipped out the back door and crossed their yards. But before she went in to see Guy, she walked around the front—and froze midstep when something flashed in the distance. Like glass catching the sunlight.

Like a camera lens.

She dodged behind the protection of the house, crouching down behind a hedge to see a car drive slowly down Sea Breeze, the back window partially open, a telephoto lens sticking out of the back.

When the car was out of sight, she ran into the garage and slammed the button to close the door. Damn it. They'd found her. She had to get Guy out of here and up to Barefoot Bay, where they'd be safe. Clay wouldn't let anyone on Casa Blanca property and they could wait this out up there.

But for how long? How long until she was yesterday's news? How long until people forgot? Will certainly hadn't forgotten.

The thought plagued her as she pulled herself back up to the loft and bent over to creep back to the box they'd opened.

She scooped up as many of the clothes as she could

hold, and the baby book with Guy's poem tucked inside. Maybe she'd very carefully get him to look at this; maybe it would jog a memory.

On her way back down, she scanned the garage for an empty box. Just inside the garage door she saw the perfect-sized carton with newspaper lying on top. That'd work, she thought, carrying the clothes to it.

And, once again, she stopped cold.

This time it wasn't the camera, but the headlines that sucker-punched. Headlines that Will had been reading while he packed.

Miles Misses His Life... Coach!

She blinked at the words, a little dizzy at the mental image of Will holding this paper, reading these words and letting the seeds of those ugly lies take root in his heart.

It made her dizzier still to think that the next thing he'd done was sleep with her and not say he loved her when she'd confessed those feelings.

Thank God she hadn't confessed everything.

But would he have even believed her? Maybe if she'd told him he was her first, she'd never have had to see that shadow of doubt in his eyes.

Because that shadow *hurt.*

Leaning closer, she tortured herself even more by reading the first line of the story.

Refusing to reveal the whereabouts of his mistress, Miles Thayer...

She closed her eyes, and a few of the baby clothes fluttered to the garage floor. A part of her newly forgiving heart wanted to run back across the grass, risk the reporters, and scream the truth to Will.

But she shouldn't have to, she thought as she stooped

over to gather up the tiny sleeper and bootie. He should believe her. If he wanted *everything*, didn't that include trust?

Ignoring the carton, she clutched the clothes, fumbled with the knob, and let herself inside. "Guy?"

When he didn't answer, she headed straight down the hall to the bedrooms.

"Guy, are you back here?"

She heard something thud in the closet, the sudden scrape of hangers over the bar, then the door popped open and he stepped out.

"Have you been crying?" she asked, dropping the whole armload of stuff on the bed to reach for him. "What's wrong?"

"Missy." He came right into her arms and embraced her, sending a strange set of chills all over her body. "There you are."

"What were you doing in there, Guy?" Her heart sort of rolled around and swelled up all at the same time.

"I was missing someone." He leaned back. "I forget her name."

She patted his shoulder, the gesture awkward but somehow natural. She'd have to get used to that feeling now. "It's okay. I'm here now and guess what we're going to do?"

"Pack and start pricing things for the yard sale?" His gray eyes lit up and his brows rose high into his crinkly forehead.

"Better. We're going on a trip."

His smile wavered. "Where you putting me, Missy?"

Oh, Lord. She almost *had* put him somewhere. She still could. Her gaze drifted to the baby clothes. No, she couldn't.

"I'm just taking you to a very nice villa for a little bit," she said. "It's a safe little house and I'll be right up the road at my friend's house."

"Oh, I know what this is!" He clapped like a little kid. "This is the part when you send the people away to a fancy hotel so they can swim and make a plan for how they're going to change their life and live in a *Clean House*!" He shouted the last two words like an ad for the TV show.

"Kind of, yeah." That was actually a perfect way to get him out of here. And with that car circling outside, they had to move quickly.

"But we're not finished yet," he said. "Don't I get to be here for the yard sale to see how much money it made and how you're going to match it?"

God, was there no aspect of that show he didn't have memorized? "We'll come back for that," she assured him. "But let's pack up some clothes for a few days away."

He looked at the pile of blue-and-white baby clothes. "What's all that stuff?"

Now wasn't the time to walk through his shrouded memories. "Just some things I found that I want to give to my friend who's having a baby. I'll go put all of that in some bags and you find a suitcase." She gestured toward the closet. "You want me to help you?"

"No!" he said quickly, moving to block her from the closet. "You go." He flicked his hand. "Find your bag and I'll take care of mine."

"Okay. But hurry."

"What's the rush?" he asked.

"Um, the cameras are going to be here soon. You're not ready for—"

"The big reveal!" He beamed at her again. "I know this game, Missy."

"You certainly do." She lifted her arms, almost reaching for him, and then she froze. It would be a long time before hugging him came naturally.

But it did for him. He stepped into her arms and patted her back softly. "You're a funny one, Missy."

Wasn't she, though?

"What was your real name again?"

She swallowed. "Jocelyn." With a deep, steadying breath, she added: "Bloom. Jocelyn Bloom."

She could have sworn he stiffened a little, then relaxed. "You're a good girl, Jocelyn."

"And you're a good man...Guy."

In the distance she heard a car door slam, making her jump away. "Hurry up, now. Pack. I'll be right back."

Hustling down the hall, she went right to the front door, carefully peering out to the driveway.

No strange cars, just hers and—

Will was standing next to her car, on the passenger side, looking at something. She couldn't see from this angle, so she walked around to the dining-room window and carefully separated the blinds, giving her a perfect shot of him in the driveway.

He was looking at her phone; she'd left it in the console when she'd gotten out to say hello to him.

What was he doing? Searching for texts from Miles Thayer?

The thought was like a sharp spike across her heart.

Carrying the phone, he rounded the car and headed toward the front door. On the way, he slowed his step and turned as a car came down the street. The same car, with the same telephoto lens.

The driver's window rolled down. "Hey, is Jocelyn Bloom in there?"

Will ignored them, marching to the front door and unlocking it before letting himself inside. She was waiting when he walked in.

He searched her face for a moment, then said, "They've been out there for a while."

"I know," she said. "I'm taking Guy up to Barefoot Bay."

He held out her phone. "You left this in your car." His eyes were wary, cold even. She took it from him, careful not to touch his hands and suffer the electrical shock. "I thought I'd get it so those assholes circling the house didn't try to steal it from you."

"Thanks."

"William!" Guy came bounding out of the hallway. "Look what Missy found! All your old baby clothes."

Will shot her a dark look, but she interceded instantly. "Those are for my friend Lacey, Guy." She reached to take the bundle from him. "They don't belong to Will."

"But they did." Guy managed to hold on to one little sleeper, waving it up like a baby-blue flag. "Can't believe you were ever this small, son."

"They're not mine, Guy."

"Then whose are they?" Guy asked, looking from one to the other, bewildered.

Neither said a word.

"They belong to a baby who's no longer around," Jocelyn said gently, taking the sleeper from him and putting a hand on his back. "Come on, Guy. You have to focus. We need to leave quickly."

He turned to look at Will. "This is the part where I

go to the fancy hotel. You know, William? In the show? They always send the people off to a nice place. Will you be there?"

"He's going to California," Jocelyn said, hating the ice in her voice but making no effort to warm it.

Guy froze, his eyes wide with horror. "What?"

"Just for a day," Will said quickly. "You'll be with Jocelyn."

That calmed him and he let her lead him back down the hall. "When are you leaving?" Guy called out.

"Well," he said. "I was going to leave now, but..."

Jocelyn turned to look at him. "But what?"

"I don't want to go with..." He pointed toward the street.

She gave Guy a nudge ahead then returned to the dining room. "I have this covered. We'll be at Casa Blanca and Clay won't let anyone on that property."

"I'll follow you to Barefoot Bay and make sure—"

"No!" She hadn't meant for it to come out like a bark. "Just do me a huge favor and go."

"I am," he said with sharp simplicity. "I am going to California, Jocelyn, and I'll tell you why."

"I know why."

"No, you don't." He leaned a little closer, smelling fresh, like he'd just taken a shower. And washed off her and her admissions of love. "You think you know everything. You think you can control everything. You think—"

"I get the idea." She waved him to the door. "I don't know anything, Will. I was certainly wrong about you."

He looked hard at her, brows drawn over pained eyes. "And I was wrong about you."

Ouch. She swallowed, closing her eyes to keep from reacting. "Do me a favor, Will. On your way out, pull my car into the garage, and then tell those reporters that you're going to pick me up at the airport. Let them follow you there as a decoy."

"You think they'll fall for that?"

"Yes, if you're convincing. Will you do that for me?"

"Actually, I'll do a lot more than that for you."

"Don't," she said quickly. "That'll be all I need. That'll be enough."

"All right," he agreed. "Do this your way. But I just want you to know one thing." He took her chin in his hand, holding too tight for her to wrench away, forcing her eyes onto him. "I know what I did wrong all those years ago. I know what I should have done and didn't do. And now I know the consequences of that decision and"—he worked hard to keep his voice from cracking, the effort appearing more painful than if he'd actually cried—"I'm going to make that up to you."

By demanding she go back to California? By believing gossip rags and not her? "You don't have to," she managed to say.

"But I'm going to. I'm going to do what I should have done back then."

He should have gone to California to chase his father's dreams of wearing Dodger blue? But she didn't have the heart to say that to him because, deep inside, she still loved Will Palmer. She always had and she always would.

But love wasn't enough. There had to be trust, too.

"Good luck to you, then, Will. Hope you find what you're looking for in California."

He rubbed his cheek, still unshaven, nodding to her. "I will. And I won't come back until I do."

Then I'll miss you. "Good-bye."

He went through the garage and pulled in the Toyota, closing the door. Then she saw him head out to the street to talk to the driver of the car with the photographer. After a few minutes, Will pulled out of his driveway and the media followed his truck.

Jocelyn just leaned against the window and, like she had so many times in this house, she cried because she only wanted one man to love her, and he didn't.

Chapter 28

Just as Jocelyn pulled out to the empty street, Guy grabbed her arm with a sudden whimper.

"I forgot something!"

"What?"

"I . . ." He pressed his hands to his temples so hard he made dents. "I can't remember, darn it."

She looked up and down the street, expecting more reporters to jump out of the bushes at any time. "Whatever you forgot, I can come back and get it." Or someone could. "You need to stop worrying and relax."

He looked like he didn't know the meaning of "relax," leaning forward like he was about to jump out and run. "William is gone," he said. "That's what I forgot."

"William is on a quick business trip," she assured him, forcing lightness into her voice when the statement made her feel anything but. "He'll be back before you know it."

"Before the yard sale?"

"Yes," she lied. "Before the yard sale. Now put your seat belt on and let's get to this amazing hotel. You're going to love it."

She didn't see another car except for the UPS truck until they got closer to town. No one honked, cut her off, or sidled up next to her when she hit the Fourway and stopped at the intersection of Center and Harbor.

There, she spotted a sheriff's car in the parking lot of the Super Min. God willing, that was Deputy Slade Garrison and she could tell him what was going on.

As she pulled in, Guy grabbed her arm again. "I won't go in there."

"I just want to…" Did he remember Charity? "Why not?"

He shook his head hard. "No, I won't go in there."

Charity had made it her mission to force him to resign from his position as the local deputy sheriff and had essentially threatened to ruin him for what he'd done to Jocelyn. How would she react if Jocelyn said she'd forgiven her father?

Didn't matter. Now wasn't the time to worry about that; she had to talk to Slade and not sit here, out in the open.

"Stay in the car," she said, pulling into a spot along the side of the convenience store. "I'll only be a minute."

He gave her a dubious look, his mouth drawn, his shoulders slumped.

"Everything's going to be fine, Guy," she promised him.

But his eyes filled. "I miss William already."

"So do I," she admitted. "Give me one second, okay?"

As she started to climb out she heard him mumble, "Christ, I hate that woman," under his breath.

She froze, then turned back to Guy. "You *remember* Charity?"

"No," he said quickly. "I just remember I hate her."

Everything pressed on her as hard and hot as the Florida sun. "Wait here, Guy," she said, climbing out to rush into the Super Min.

Slade was leaning on the counter, talking to Gloria Vail behind the cash register.

"I have to talk to you, Deputy Garrison," she said quickly. "Privately." The deputy and Gloria shared a look that told Jocelyn Gloria knew everything that was going on. "Or not," Jocelyn added with a nod. "Just let me tell you both."

The back door popped open and Charity stepped out. "Are you okay?" she asked.

Absolutely nothing got by that woman. She was probably watching the store on closed circuit TVs in her office.

"I'm fine, but the media has definitely found me. They're at my old house, so I'm taking my father up to Barefoot Bay with me."

"You're taking him?" Charity's drawn-on brows shot up. "Why?"

She swallowed. "So he's protected."

The older woman choked, but Slade stepped into the conversation. "That's smart, Jocelyn. Did you happen to see what kind of car they're driving?"

She described it to the best of her ability and answered a few more questions, painfully aware of Charity's dark scowl of disapproval. When Slade stepped to the side to call another deputy, Charity came around the counter and took Jocelyn by the elbow.

"Come with me," she said harshly.

"I can't, Charity. I left him in the car."

"Let him rot!"

Jocelyn freed herself from the other woman's grip. "Please."

"Really, Aunt Charity," Gloria said. "Slade has this covered."

Charity flattened her niece with a glare and took Jocelyn's arm again. "This'll take one minute. Get back here. Might change your life."

"My life is changed," she said softly. "I want to forgive him, Charity."

"Oh, hell. C'mere." She gave Jocelyn a nudge to the back door and, fueled by curiosity more than anything, Jocelyn followed.

The office was tiny, cluttered, and smelled like the cardboard boxes of snack items stacked in the corner, but Charity seemed to know exactly what she wanted, going right to a filing cabinet to whip a drawer open.

"You want to forgive him, huh?"

"I want to move on." She hated the cliché, but it worked for the moment. What did Charity have in that drawer?

A thin manila file, it turned out, that Charity used to fan herself. "I've been keeping an eye on your old man."

"I know you have. At least until my mother died."

"And after." Charity slammed her hands on her bony hips. "Someone had to watch the old prick."

Someone had: Will. But she stayed very still, waiting for Charity to explain.

"After she died, he started to go downhill pretty fast," Charity said.

"I know."

She held out the file. "Or did he?" When Jocelyn didn't move to take it, Charity snapped the folder like a whip. "Don't you want to know?"

Maybe she didn't. "Whatever you have doesn't matter, Charity, because so much time—"

"It matters!" She shook the folder viciously. "You can't let someone get away with abuse!"

"The abuse is history." She had to hold on to that belief. It had taken so long to get to this point and it had cost her so much. She wasn't about to let this old busybody steal her forgiveness. Even if this old busybody nearly saved her life once. "Guy is suffering from dementia and doesn't even remember what he did."

Charity threw the file on an already overcrowded desk with a dramatic sigh. "Of course he wants you to think that, Jocelyn! What if you press charges?"

"I decided long ago I wouldn't."

"Even after your mother died?" The question was loaded with implications.

"Of brain cancer, Charity. He didn't kill her." Made her life a living hell, but didn't end it.

"Are you certain of that?"

"Absolutely. I spoke to the doctors."

"It was sudden, though, wasn't it?"

Jocelyn's gaze shifted to the file. She had no doubt her mother had died of natural causes—and possibly a broken heart. But Guy hadn't killed her.

"Just look at it, for crying out loud."

Very slowly, she reached for the file and opened it to

see a single piece of paper with *The Lee County Library System Serving Southwest Florida* scrolled across the top.

"That came courtesy of Marian Winstead."

"Marian the Librarian," Jocelyn said softly, the locals' nickname for Mimosa Key's keen-eyed librarian popping into her head.

"She doesn't like to be called that," Charity said. "As you may know, she's my lifelong dear friend and quite trustworthy."

Jocelyn read a list of books, authors, and Dewey Decimal numbers.

Elder Law: Financial and Legal Considerations for the Alzheimer's Patient

Alzheimer's and the Law

The Defense Rests: One Man's Acquittal and Dementia

"You'll notice that all of those books were checked out in a five-month period by Alexander Bloom."

Alexander. Like the baby boy. She shook her head, wishing she could throw away all of these thoughts and just start over. "What are you saying?"

"I'm not saying anything. I think that list says it all. Now, I'm not accusing him of anything that he's not already guilty of." She took a few steps farther. "It just makes a person wonder, doesn't it? Just how convenient it is for him to 'have Alzheimer's.'" She air-quoted and lowered her voice to a new level of sarcastic.

Jocelyn put down the file and met Charity's gaze. "If you're implying he's faking the dementia to cover up for anything he did or *didn't* do, you're wrong."

"You're letting him off the hook." Charity's nostrils flared at the thought. "Maybe you should take another look at those pictures I gave to Will Palmer. Count the bruises. Remember the pain. I was the one who put ice on you, you know. I was the one—"

"I know!" She shot her hands up in apology the minute the shout came out of her mouth. "I know," she repeated, softening her tone. "I just don't want to live with all this hate anymore. He's sick."

"Is he really? Are you absolutely certain of that, Jocelyn?"

She closed her eyes, picturing Guy and all he didn't know and couldn't remember.

I hate that woman.

She could still hear the echo of Guy's sly comment. "It's a very hard disease to understand."

Charity leaned so close Jocelyn could count her over-sized pores. "So's abuse. I know. I had my own broken ribs to help me *understand* it. And I got the hell out of there, and took my Gracie with me. Which is more than I can say for your poor, pathetic dead mother."

She couldn't take this. No matter what Charity had done for her, she couldn't stand here and listen to her accuse Guy of being a fake or a murderer or whatever. He was what he was—and Jocelyn had decided to get past that regardless of what Charity wanted her to do. "I've made up my mind, Charity. Thank you for the information."

As she turned to the door, Charity's hand landed on her arm. "Be a shame for that file to land in the hands of the wrong person."

Jocelyn froze and looked at her. "Yes, it would."

"You know, like the *National Enquirer.*"

Jocelyn opened the door and stepped into the store

without answering, nodding to Gloria and Slade. "Thanks again," she said softly. "If you need me, I'll be up at Lacey and Clay Walker's house."

Outside, the sun smacked her, blinding after the dreary, miserable back office of the Super Min. But it couldn't wash away the accusations and doubt. Maybe Guy had known he was forgetting things and needed to check up on his rights or insurance. Without Mom to help, and in the aftermath of her death, that would be a reasonable worry.

Maybe he was scared all the stuff he had done would come to the surface.

Maybe he—

Was gone.

Jocelyn stopped dead on the curb and stared at the empty front seat of the car and the wide-open passenger door.

"Guy!" She ran around the car, turning in a full circle, sweat already dribbling down her back. "Guy!"

She ran into the lot, looked up and down the intersection, over to the motel parking lot, everywhere, *everywhere*.

Guy was gone.

When Will landed in L.A., it was still light and fairly early, a blessing for a person who wanted to make a cross-country round trip in as little time as possible. If all went according to plan, he could be on a red-eye tonight, mission accomplished. If not, then his plan just sucked.

But he had to do something. He had to help Jocelyn— this time. And it couldn't be too little, too late. It *had* to work.

Scott hadn't been happy, of course, when Will had called him back to turn down the offer. But telling Jocelyn that he wasn't taking the job wouldn't have convinced her of anything; he had to show her he loved her. Plus, she'd have wallowed in guilt, assuming it was her decision to stay that had made his decision.

Not true at all. She loved him, and he was never going to lose her again. But until he made up for the wrongs he'd been carrying around for fifteen years, he hadn't earned her.

Well, he was about to. He hoped. Unless this stunt was an exercise in futility.

After he got situated in a rental car and figured out which freeway to take, he checked his phone, just in case. Jocelyn had called once, when he'd arrived at the airport, and, man, had she sounded miserable. A little terrified and a lot stressed out.

She'd asked him three times if he was certain the reporter followed him and he'd confirmed he had. But there must be more of them for her to be that tense. The damn reporters were probably crawling all over that island now, which made his mission even more imperative. Maybe she wasn't physically beaten this time, but she was being emotionally, professionally, and personally battered and he sure as hell wasn't going to sit back— again—and watch that happen.

Fueled by his focus, he navigated the mean, and sickeningly slow, streets of Los Angeles, threading his way through the Hollywood Hills and onto a canyon road off Sunset Boulevard. He found the address and drove up to an eight-foot-high gated entrance, then picked up his cell phone and called the number he'd taken from Jocelyn's phone. He knew he had the right number because it had worked that morning when he'd first texted and put his plan in motion.

"Bringing Jocelyn Bloom in," he said when the phone was answered. Just please don't ask to talk to her.

She didn't. In a moment, the gates slowly parted like opening arms, leading Will down a half mile of creamy white bricks to a sizable Tudor-styled house tucked into a wooded lot.

The front door opened and a woman stood in the entry, so small he thought for a moment it might be a teenage girl, not the superstar actress who thought Jocelyn was coming to see her. When he climbed out of the car, he could see her face and made a mental note never to fall for on-screen beauty again.

Coco Kirkman looked nothing like she did on TV.

"Hello." He nodded to her as he approached.

An oversized sweatshirt hung halfway down her legs, the sleeves so long they hid her hands. As he got closer, she hugged herself as if she were cold, despite the hoodie and the black scarf knotted around her neck. A few honey-colored strands of hair slipped out of a sloppy ponytail, and she brushed them away to train famously sky-blue eyes on him.

"Where's Jocelyn?" she demanded, leaning over to peek into the car as if he'd hidden her in there.

Time to come clean. "She's not here."

"Excuse me?" Her eyes flashed in horror. "Her text said she and a bodyguard would be here to talk to me. You have my private number?"

"She gave it to me." More or less.

She made no gesture to invite him in, but blocked the

door as much as her waif-like body could block anything, so he stopped at the bottom stone step, making them essentially eye to eye.

Behind her, a crystal chandelier lit an oversized entry and a sweeping marble staircase that he certainly wouldn't build in a Tudor house, but probably cost more than he ever made in a year.

"So…" She shifted from one bare foot to the other, shooting a quick glance behind her as if she expected someone to pop up any minute. "Why did she send you here?"

"She didn't," he said. "I sent you the text that you thought was from Jocelyn."

"Oh, fuck." She snorted the curse. "I can't believe I fell for that. Of course, no one in the world has that phone number but Jocelyn, so it's not like I'm a complete idiot. What do you want?"

"What do you think I want? To ask you to please, please reconsider what you're doing and tell the world it's a lie."

She lifted on eyebrow. "You think it's a lie?"

"I know it is. Jocelyn wouldn't break up a marriage any sooner than she'd jump off the Empire State Building. And she won't say why she's letting you do this, before you jump all over her for breaching life-coach ethics."

She smiled a little, a sad smile that barely reached her eyes. She leaned against the doorjamb, her arms still firmly wrapped around her middle. "You're that guy."

"What guy?"

"The baseball player."

He nodded, ignoring the little punch of happiness because Jocelyn had actually talked about him.

"So everything she said about you was true."

"Guess that depends," he said vaguely. "On what she told you."

"She told me you were ... kind."

Was he? Or did she have that mixed up with *passive*? "I have my moments."

"And reliable."

"Enough."

"And ..." She gave an approving nod. "Hot."

"I didn't come here to talk about me." He took one step closer, glancing into the house in a silent request for an invitation.

She shook her head, her eyes widening just a little. "Look, the only reason I said yes to the text is because I thought Jocelyn wanted to see me. Does she? Or does she have a message for me?"

"Yeah. Get your butt in front of a camera and tell the world you lied."

She bit her bottom lip so hard he thought she'd drawn blood. "She knows I can't do that." He barely heard the whisper.

Okay. He hadn't expected this to be easy. But he also hadn't expected to stand on her front porch and make a plea. "Are you really that selfish that you don't care about her reputation or her feelings?"

"She's the strongest person I've ever met."

"So that's why you picked her as your fall guy?"

She laughed softly. "That's why she volunteered for the job."

"She what?"

She wrapped herself up again, so small and vulnerable he wondered whatever made her decide to pursue a career that put her in the spotlight. "Guess she didn't tell you everything."

"Guess not." Jocelyn was *in* on this? "Why?"

"To protect me, of course."

"At the expense of her career?"

She shrugged. "It'll blow over and she'll..." She glanced to the side, into the house, then stepped a little farther out of the doorway. "She'll weather this storm much better than I will. It was her idea."

It was? Would she go her whole life sacrificing her own happiness for other people?

Yes, maybe she would. And wasn't that one of the things he loved about her?

He heard a noise from inside the house, and instantly she startled and flinched, throwing a wary look over her shoulder, but no one was there.

"Who was that?" he asked.

"My housekeeper," she said quickly. "And I have security here."

"Then you should feel comfortable letting me in. I'm not armed and I won't hurt you. I just want you to understand what Jocelyn is going through because of you."

"It's not..." She closed her eyes and fought for something—the right word, composure, maybe. Inner strength. She looked like a person who had none, inside or out. There was something helpless about her that reminded him of someone. Not Jocelyn, that was certain. "It's not because of me," she added.

"Miles?"

Her eyes flashed in warning, like a secret message to him.

"He threatened to . . . you know."

No, he didn't know. But he was starting to suspect. "Your husband threatened to hurt you?"

She nodded.

"And Jocelyn suggested you say he was having an affair with her so you could...what?"

She swallowed hard. "Try and leave him."

"Try?" he asked furiously.

"Shhh." Her eyes darted again, fear radiating off her.

"Why? Is he here?"

"No, just the housekeeper."

"Who's your friend, Coco?" The male voice boomed from inside, making her jump as a man appeared behind her.

How long had the son of a bitch been back there?

Unlike Coco, Miles Thayer looked every bit the movie star. Not very tall or broad, but he had the golden good looks and a phony smile that the camera loved. He held out a hand to Will. "I'm Miles. Have we met?"

Will ignored the hand. "I'm not here to talk to you."

"Funny, this is my house. You're on my property. You're talking to my wife. Who the fuck are you?"

"He's a friend of Jocelyn's."

Miles considered that, angling his head and scratching under long blond hair exactly the color of Coco's. They were like a matched set, only Coco was so tiny and defenseless and her husband had nasty all over him.

"And you're just leaving, I take it," Miles said.

"I'm not leaving until one of you calls a press conference and tells everyone the truth."

"The truth's out there, bud. I was boning the life coach."

Coco stared at the ground and Will's fists tightened like a runner just shot off first to steal. Every cell in his body wanted to act. To throw a fist if not a ball. To shut this asshole up.

"You got an issue with that?" Miles asked, using his shoulder to push Coco out of the way. " 'Cause that's our story. And we like it. Right, Co?"

Instantly she looked up at Will, a plea in her blue eyes. "Don't tell her he's here, please. Just go."

"Good advice," Miles said. "Get the hell out of here before I call the LAPD."

"Miles, plea—"

"Get inside." Miles grabbed her arm and practically dragged her into the house. "I'll deal with our—"

Will lunged, ripping the other man's hand away. "Don't you dare touch her."

They both froze and stared at him, Coco shaking her head a little but Miles breaking into a much more real grin. "Did you just *touch* me, dickhead?"

Memories jolted through him with the same force he wanted to use on this bastard.

You touching an officer of the law, young man?

Will took a steadying breath, sizing up the competition.

No gun this time and Will could take him. But to what end? Coco would run into the house and he'd lose any chance of getting her to help Jocelyn.

"Just leave her alone," Will said quietly. "I'd like to talk to her some more."

"Well, she doesn't want to talk to you."

He looked at Coco, tiny, scared, and so powerless. And then he realized who she reminded him of: Mary Jo Bloom. The same expectant look of fear in the eyes of a victim. The same helpless hunch to her shoulders and downward tilt to her chin.

Was that why Jocelyn had gone along with this idea, or even conceived it? Because she, too, wanted to make up for not helping someone in the past?

Coco brushed back her hair, the move shifting her neckline enough for Will to see a deep purple bruise cutting across her flesh.

His stomach lurched as the pictures of Jocelyn's bruises fought for space in his brain, fury firing through his veins.

"You son of a bitch," he murmured to Miles.

"Excuse me?" Miles stepped closer, giving his shoulders a shake. He wasn't six feet tall and sure as hell hadn't spent his life playing sports or swinging a dead-blow hammer. "What did you call me?"

"Please," Coco cried. "Please don't fight. It's my fault for taking him back. Will, just leave."

"Yeah, Will, just fucking leave or..." He lifted his hand but Will got the first swing in, a satisfying right hook that landed on the movie star's jaw and knocked his head back.

Coco screamed and lunged toward them just as Miles recovered from the blow. Miles spun around and shoved her into the house with so much force she fell backwards.

Will shot forward in full attack mode, seizing the man by the shoulder, yanking him around and slamming another fist in his face.

"You fucking—" Miles pushed back, barely getting decent force, but it was enough to knock Will off the step and make him stumble.

Miles leaped out and jumped on Will, getting his own swing into Will's face while the woman shrieked from the doorway. Using all his might, Will whipped Miles onto his back, thrust a knee into his chest, and pinned him down.

With a yell, Miles fought back, but he had nothing on Will. Easily in control of the fight, Will raised his right fist, let the blood surge through his arm—and froze.

Blood dribbled out of Miles's nose, and his eyes squeezed shut as he braced for the impact. When Will didn't swing, the other man whimpered like the coward he was.

Will looked up at Coco, who rocked herself with two arms, also whimpering. For a moment, they held each other's gaze as she, too, waited for his fist to make contact.

But that wouldn't make him any better than this asshole or Deputy Sheriff Guy Bloom or any other man who thought *this* was action.

He narrowed his eyes at Coco. "You want to help him? You want to help yourself?"

Biting her lip, she nodded. "Get in that car and let me get you out of here."

Under him, Miles squirmed. "Don't even think about it, Coco!" Will nailed him with a knee into the chest and jerked his head toward the car.

"Come on, Coco," Will urged. "You can do this."

She took a breath, hanging on the edge, then shook her head. "I can't," she practically mouthed the words. "Jocelyn understands."

"Then do it for you, not her," he insisted. "Get yourself out of jail. You don't have to live like this."

"Fuck you!" Miles shouted, his movie-star looks contorted with anger. "You get in that fucking car and I'll kill you, Coco. I am not kidding!"

"Don't give him the power," Will said quietly. "You

can stand up to him and you can make a difference to a whole lot of women."

She choked softly. "That's exactly what Jocelyn said."

"Then why don't you?"

"I'm scared." She shivered and backed away like a beaten dog.

"Don't be afraid," he said. "Get what you need and get in the car. He can't hurt you anymore."

"And then what?"

Will just smiled at her. "Then you'll be a real star."

"Move and you're dead, Coco," Miles growled.

She stabbed her hair, dragging it back, revealing another bruise by her ear.

"Stay and you're dead, Coco," Will said. "It's just a matter of time."

He held Miles down long enough for her to make her decision.

Chapter 29

Jocelyn fingered the embroidery thread, resting the hoop on her lap, the buzz of activity in the house fading into the background as the weight of loss pressed on her chest.

The whole situation reminded her of the night of her mother's funeral. Except Guy wasn't dead. She hoped.

Please, God, don't let him be dead. I have to tell him—

Zoe came up behind her, putting her hands on Jocelyn's shoulders with a soft squeeze. "Nice gladiolas."

Jocelyn almost smiled and twisted the needle. "I want to finish this for him but I haven't a clue how to do this kind of thing."

"I do." Zoe reached over and took the needle, twirling it like a mini-baton. "I know, who would think I had a crafty bone in my body? But you need to go in the kitchen now, sweetie."

"Why?"

"Deputy Dawg wants to talk to you."

Jocelyn whipped around, the spool of embroidery thread tumbling to the floor. "Slade's here? Did they..." Blood drained from her head instantly.

"No news, I promise. He just wants to tell you what the plan is for the night."

The night. It had been dark for several hours now. After the initial scouring of town, then the streets that led out, the ragtag team of Lacey, Clay, Tessa, and Zoe, later joined by Lacey's daughter, Ashley, had gathered at the house so the professionals could take over.

But no one had seen him. A maid at the Fourway Motel thought she saw a man meeting his description wandering along the walkway behind the hotel, but a thorough search of the building turned up nothing. A tourist at the harbor was certain he saw an older man just like him fishing on the docks, but that lead took them nowhere as well.

And, the worst of all, the UPS guy said he thought he'd seen an old man crossing the causeway. What if he'd fallen off the bridge? What if he was...

Please, God, no.

The ache in her heart as heavy as a lead ball, Jocelyn handed the embroidery hoop to Zoe, refusing to give voice to her dark thoughts. "You can do needlepoint?" At Zoe's nod, Jocelyn just smiled. "You're full of surprises."

"Aren't I, though?" She pointed the needle toward the kitchen. "Go talk to the hot cop."

She started to walk out, but Zoe stopped her. "Speaking of hot, have you reached Will?"

She hadn't tried after that one call to verify that he'd gotten the reporter out of town, since Jocelyn had wondered if someone from the media had actually kidnapped

Guy to get to her. But she hadn't told Will they'd lost him. "He'd just be on the next plane back and miss his interview tomorrow morning. There's nothing he can do."

"He could comfort you," she said.

Not anymore. Jocelyn just shook her head and left Zoe, turning the corner to face a kitchen full of people.

Tessa and Lacey had coffee going and food on the table. Ashley was cleaning up. Clay and some other men were talking to Slade Garrison.

"Do you have any news?" she asked the deputy as he shifted his attention to her.

"We haven't turned up a single person who's seen him, except those I told you about. And, Jocelyn, time is critical. He has to be found in the first twenty-four hours or . . ."

She waved her hand. "I know the statistics."

He stepped closer, his expression softening. Lacey and Tessa also joined the conversation, flanking Jocelyn in support.

"Look, I realize your situation is a bit different than usual," Slade said. "And out of respect for your privacy and the fact that our island location makes it hard to get too far, I've held off on the next step. But I have to issue a Silver Alert, Jocelyn. I have to. I'm sorry."

"What exactly is that?" Tessa asked.

"It's like an Amber Alert for missing teens, but this is for elderly dementia patients."

"Why *wouldn't* you do that?" Lacey asked.

"Because," Jocelyn answered, "it'll have media crawling all over this place by morning."

Slade nodded. "It will, but there's no reason you have to be in the spotlight, Jocelyn. My office will handle media contact."

"But reporters will come here."

"Possibly," he said. "But just as likely someone watching the local TV station will have seen him. That's how it usually works, if we move fast. I normally wouldn't even talk to the family first, but considering the situation and all..."

"Do it," she said without hesitation. "Do whatever you have to do to find him."

He nodded. "I will, Jocelyn. Go get some rest. We'll be working all night."

"Please have your men consider this a base," Lacey said. "We'll keep coffee and food and whatever you need."

Lacey and Tessa's arms tightened around Jocelyn for a quick hug, just as the front door popped open without a knock. Everyone turned expectantly, only to see Charity Grambling march in like she owned the place.

"Did you find the old bastard yet?"

Instantly Lacey stiffened. "Charity, don't make this worse than it already is."

Charity ignored her and slid a gaze to Slade. "My niece told me you were here."

Slade didn't look happy about that. "The best way for you to help is to stay at the Super Min, Charity. You can talk to every single customer and, frankly, that's where he was last seen. We need you there, not here."

"Gloria's there, as you well know. I'm here to help Jocelyn."

Lacey bristled again. "She doesn't need you—"

"Yes, I do," Jocelyn said, stepping forward. Charity had saved her once and no matter what the woman thought of Jocelyn's recent change of heart, she was always welcome. "Thank you for coming, Charity."

Jocelyn could feel Lacey's glare on her, but she guided Charity toward the living room, where Zoe sat on the sofa doing needlepoint. Like bodyguards, Tessa and Lacey followed.

"Can I get you a cup of coffee, Charity?" Jocelyn asked.

The older woman stood in the middle of the room, her strawlike dye job sticking out in a few directions, a pair of khaki pants hanging loose on her hips. She stuffed her hands in her pockets and kept her gaze on Jocelyn. "I know you didn't like what I had to tell you today, but you have to consider the possibility that it's true."

"That what's true?" Zoe asked, either completely oblivious to the strange dynamics in the room or at least pretending to be.

"He's faking Alzheimer's," Charity said.

Tessa and Lacey sucked in a soft breath, but Zoe just pulled a long green strand of embroidery yarn through the pattern. "That's what I thought."

"You did?" Tessa asked.

"What do you think?" Lacey asked Jocelyn. "You know him better than anyone."

"I don't think he's faking it," she said. "He's always been...unstable."

Charity snorted. "He's a fucking criminal!"

The women stared at her, but Jocelyn held up her hands. "That's not true—"

"How can you say that?" Charity practically stomped her sneakered foot. "He damn near killed you."

"What?"

The question came from all three women at once. They stared at her with a mix of horror, shock, and genuine sadness. Jocelyn turned to the kitchen, catching Ashley in the doorway. "Honey, please. Don't."

"Give us a minute, Ash," Lacey said quickly to her daughter, who obeyed by pivoting and disappearing.

"Why didn't you tell us, Joss?" The crack in Tessa's question almost tore Jocelyn's heart out.

"You didn't need to know the details. And, honestly, he didn't…" Yes, he did. "It was a long…" That didn't matter. "I've tried to forget it."

"Well, I haven't." Charity practically spit the words. "And, frankly, if he fell off the causeway it wouldn't be good enough for him."

"Charity, please." Jocelyn reached for her. "I know how you feel. And I know you think that my forgiving him is some kind of personal affront, or not—not showing gratitude for what you did, but—"

"What did she do?" Lacey asked, unable to hide the disbelief in her voice. Of course, Lacey, like every lifetime resident of Mimosa Key, knew Charity as a nasty, mean-spirited gossipmonger. And last year, that mean spirit went to new and personal heights when she tried to stop Casa Blanca from ever getting built.

"I saved her life."

Again, every eye in the living room was on her. Zoe's needlepointing fingers stilled and Lacey just looked positively wretched at this turn of events. And Tessa, the woman who hated secrets the most, was clearly on the verge of tears.

Jocelyn dropped onto the edge of the sofa with a sigh. "I never wanted to tell you guys this."

Zoe put the needlepoint hoop on the table and reached for her. "We kinda knew."

"Not really." Jocelyn looked up at Charity. "Not the extent of it. Not how bad it was."

"I'll show them." Charity reached into her back pocket. "You don't think I was dumb enough to give you the only copies of the pictures, do you?"

"No!" Jocelyn jumped up, but Charity flung the pictures on the table like she was folding her poker cards, an array of bruises, blood, and brutality instantly spread before them.

Oh, God. She couldn't even look—not through the eyes of her friends. Sharp daggers of shame pierced her heart and stung her eyes as she choked on a sob. She had to get out of here. *She had to get out of here.*

"Holy hell," Zoe said. "He *did* almost kill you."

"Why are you doing this?" Jocelyn demanded of Charity. "Why betray me? I trusted you."

"Her?" Lacey almost spit. "Why would you trust her?"

"Because she picked me up off the street when I was running away." Charity had been the right person at the right time. "She helped me."

Charity waved her off. "I'm no Good Samaritan, believe me. I just hate abusers. I hate men who hit." She touched her face as if she could still feel the pain of a fist there. "And I hate Guy Bloom and couldn't care less if he is dead."

Jocelyn closed her eyes. "But I care." She put up her hands in surrender, needing the conversation and the pitiful looks and the hurt for not sharing to stop. As fast as she could without actually running, she left the room, headed down the hall, and darted into Guy's bedroom, fighting the urge to slam the door just to get rid of some of the emotion surging through her.

Dropping on the bed, she let the sobs escape.

Now they knew everything. Just like Will, they'd never look at her the same. They'd never look at Guy the same and, at one time, that wouldn't have mattered, but now it did.

Now she not only didn't hate him, she actually cared for him. She—

"Hey." The door popped open and Lacey's reddish-blonde curls edged in. "Can we come in?"

Everything in her wanted to scream no. *Go away. Leave me alone.*

Alone being her default and most preferred place to be. But alone was so—alone. And now she knew how much it sucked to be alone.

"Yeah."

In a split second, the three of them were in, surrounding her on the bed, cooing, sighing, laying their hands on her back with so much love and support she almost started crying again.

"I'm sorry, you guys," she murmured. "I should have told you."

"It's okay," Lacey said.

"We understand," Tessa added.

"You owe us for life," Zoe teased.

She looked at them, one after another, her heart swelling with love. "Obviously, I'm embarrassed."

"With us?" Tessa tapped her leg. "There's nothing about each other we don't know or haven't seen. We love you."

"And"—she took a deep breath—"I don't want you to hate him. Because when I find him—and I am going to find him—I'm going to forgive him and take care of him for as long as I'm able."

She braced for the onslaught of judgment and opinions, but got none.

"He's a different man now," Zoe finally said.

"He's forgotten," Tessa added. "So it's pretty damn wonderful of you to do the same."

Lacey rubbed her hand up and down Jocelyn's arm. "It's going to be tough, though. Charity's hellbent and might not keep your secret any longer. She's pissed that you're letting him off the hook. You'll need to face that."

"I'd face anything if that'll help find—" Suddenly a thought sparked in the back of her tear-soggy brain, forcing her up. "The media. The tabloids."

They stared at her.

"Forget a Silver Alert. If *I* called a press conference to talk about Coco, just imagine how far the message would go. Network TV, *Entertainment Tonight*, they'd all have to carry the story. And maybe someone saw him, maybe someone knows where he is. Even if"—she cringed at the thought—"even if he is faking it and hiding out or something. I don't know what's going on in his head. All I know is I have to find him. What better bullhorn to use than national media?"

They looked at each other, obviously unsure.

"I think those rags are more interested in your dirt than in your dad," Zoe said.

"There *is* no dirt," she said.

"Then you need to tell them the truth and let them know why you're the fall guy in a marriage you didn't break up."

Would she do that? Would she sell out Coco to find her dad? "Maybe I can just not address that." No, that would never fly.

"Just tell them the truth," Lacey said softly. "What's the worst that could happen?"

"Nothing to me. But Coco." She fell back on the pillow. She couldn't put Coco in that kind of danger. She couldn't hurt poor, sweet, weak Coco who was just so much like another poor, sweet, weak woman that she'd stolen a permanent place in Jocelyn's heart.

But maybe if Jocelyn had forced her mother's hand, she wouldn't have lived in fear.

"I'll decide in the morning," she finally said. "Maybe they'll find Guy overnight."

"Maybe," the others agreed.

But no one sounded very certain.

A nasty mosquito nibbled on his neck, but Guy was too tired and too scared to move and slap it. Where was Henry? Shouldn't he be here to flap his wings and ward off these horrible bugs?

Guy curled deeper into the tiny opening he'd found in the mangrove hammock, the cloying stink of rotten honey from those darn white flowers making him want to puke. The sharp smell of the pepper trees made him sneeze. He sniffed again, then started sniveling like a toddler.

Which he might as well be.

Turning from the stiff tree root that poked his back, he brushed some sand and dirt off the side of his face. Something crawled on his finger and pinched.

Fire ant. Shoot.

He shook it off and tried to get comfortable, back into the place where sometimes, when everything was really quiet, he could clear those cobwebs in his head.

Because some things really did stay in his memory.

They got mixed up, sure, and tangled like that cheap red yarn he'd used when he took up knitting. But the gist of the memory was there, so he could close his eyes and imagine the face on that picture.

Oh, that picture. That was what had gotten him into trouble in the first place. He'd wanted to go back and get it, and he didn't want Missy running after him, telling him to stop and go to some hotel.

If he didn't get that picture, the *Clean House* people would throw it away!

And then he'd die for sure because it was his only picture of the girl who called him "Daddy."

He couldn't remember her name. Maybe it was the same as her mother's. It seemed to him it was. But he could remember her face. Brown eyes and a big space where her front teeth would grow in.

But they never grew in, did they? No. Because she—

Tears stung. Jeez. Hadn't these old eyes dried out yet? Did he have to get all weepy like a woman every time he thought about the child he'd lost?

He didn't actually remember. He just knew there'd been a girl. A sweet little girl who went fishing with him.

And there'd been pain. A deep, aching, numbing, changing pain because he had lost a child. So...

What happened to her?

Another mosquito buzzed by his ear and something splashed in the water just a few feet away. Oh, boy. Hope the gators weren't hungry.

How the heck had he gotten out here? He squeezed his eyes shut and tried to remember what had happened. He'd been so careful not to be seen taking those old back streets.

He'd remembered the way, somehow. But then he got to the house and needed to get in the back door and there was the old boat leaning against the side and—

But now the boat was upside down and covered with water and Guy was all alone.

No William. No Missy. Not even Henry the Heron showed up to keep him company.

His stomach gurgled with hunger and all he could do was swallow some spit to wet his parched throat.

Another splash, only louder this time. Closer.

"Henry? Is that you?"

Maybe it was Missy. Maybe it was William! He sat up and listened, but only cicadas and crickets sang and mosquitoes buzzed.

Guy just covered his face with his hands and let the tears fall until they burned his cheeks. This was it, then. He was going to die tonight, for sure.

And somewhere, way in the back of that clouded up brain of his, he knew the truth. He was just getting what he deserved.

The splash was so loud Guy jumped and called out. "Go away, gator! Go away."

Nothing.

If only someone were here with him. If only Henry would fly over and lay his head next to Guy for his last night. Because surely this was Guy's last night, and after this he'd be headed to another place. He wasn't sure why, but he had a feeling it wasn't the *good* place.

He pulled up his legs and wrapped his arms around them, burying his head in the darkness. What had he done? What in God's name had he done?

He didn't know. All he knew was how he felt right

now. Slowly, he lifted his head and looked at the stars, as deeply into the darkness as he could, to speak to whoever might listen.

"I don't know what I did, but I know it was bad. And I'm sorry."

But he doubted very much that anyone heard his confession except the bugs and the gators and the birds that had flown away like his memories.

Chapter 30

⌒

Jocelyn sat straight up just as the clock radio next to Guy's bed clicked to 6:00 a.m., the light blanket one of the girls had covered her with shoved to the foot of the bed. Outside, the soft drizzle and pre-dawn darkness cloaked the room in a dreary shroud.

Sliding off the bed, she opened the door, but the house was completely quiet and dark. Where was everyone?

Asleep, she discovered after a quick walk through the house. Tessa and Zoe spooned on a twin bed in Jocelyn's old room. The sheriff's men had left. Clay and Lacey had taken Ashley home earlier and must have stayed there.

She went back to Guy's room, circling the bed and standing in front of the dresser that used to be her mother's. It was empty now, no perfume bottles or that pretty pink jewelry box with a big embroidered rose Jocelyn had loved as a little girl.

Was that jewelry box gone, too? She hadn't seen it in any of her cleaning and organizing, but they hadn't finished the closets. She turned to Guy's closet, opening the door. The moment she snapped on the light and looked down, she was rewarded with the very thing she'd been looking for. Not only had the jewelry box not been thrown away, it sat on the floor, wide open.

Kneeling down to examine the contents, she lifted an old not-really-gold chain that had turned black with time, and two tiny rings with blue stones, vaguely recalling that they were her mother's birthstone.

A top shelf lifted out to reveal more space at the bottom, empty but for a picture.

Oh. A piece of her heart cracked and left a jagged edge in her chest as she stared at the snapshot. The edges were worn from handling, the photo almost warm to the touch.

And the memory of the moment so clear in her mind, Jocelyn let out a little cry when she looked at it.

It was her seventh birthday, so January 4, 1986.

January of 1986? That was the same month—

She put her hand to her mouth as pieces fell together. This was the last time they'd gone out in the rowboat. After that, Guy had changed. Life had changed. Everything had changed.

Had Guy been looking at this photo when she'd come to drag him away to Barefoot Bay? Had he realized his "Missy" and this little girl were one and the same? Did he remember that day when they went out on the row—

With a soft gasp she shot to her feet. Had anyone looked for the boat? Had anyone thought to check the islands? She needed to call Slade. They had to search out there right now.

Clutching the photo, she ran down the hall, not bothering to wake the girls. She needed her phone. Turning in circles, she couldn't remember where she'd last seen it, a low-grade panic and certainty making her whole being tremble with the need to know if her hunch was correct.

She pushed open the garage door and looked around for the rowboat, but she and Zoe had left it outside to dry in the sunshine. Barefoot, she darted across the garage to open the door and run to the side of the house to find the—

"Holy shit," she mumbled, staring at the empty spot where they'd left the boat. "Is it possible?"

She squinted into the breaking dawn, wiping raindrops from her face.

Was Guy out there in the canals or on the islands *alone*?

Fueled by that fear, she started to run, slipping in the wet grass and ignoring the chilly breeze that came with the rainy cold front. She didn't bother to look when she ran across the street, but in her peripheral vision, she saw a car pull out of a parking space up the street.

A fine chill raised goose bumps on her arms. The Silver Alert had gone out hours ago, her name most certainly attached as the next of kin. The wolves waited for her with cameras and microphones.

Fine. If her suspicion was wrong—and, God, she prayed it was—then she'd do whatever was necessary to find her father. Even tell the truth if she had to.

She plowed through some shrubbery in the neighbor's yard, not bothering with the access path to the canals. How far could he have gotten? Was he out there rowing? Lost? Or—

She let out a soft cry as she reached the water's edge, the muck squishing through her bare toes. The canal wasn't deep, maybe four feet, and she could wade or even swim it, but not for long. And not safely.

She turned left and right, thinking hard and fast, spying a bright-yellow plastic kayak leaning against a dock two houses away. She took off for it, a million rationalizations spinning through her mind. But no one called out to stop her when she dragged the lightweight craft down a stone path, used the oar to push off, and hopped into the single seat.

Rain bounced off the water and made a popping sound on the plastic kayak, falling just hard enough to make the effort completely uncomfortable and the world wet and blurry.

Or maybe her vision was blurred by tears, because without her realizing it, they were pouring out of her eyes.

Just thinking about Guy lost out here, alone and terrified, ripped her heart to shreds. *Please, God, please let him be okay.*

Dragging the paddle through the water, she squinted at the little mounds of mangroves that made up the islands, a question nagging at her, as incessant as the rain.

When had he started to matter so much to her?

Why did she love a man who had made her life a living hell?

"Because that man is gone," she mumbled into the rain and breeze. And in his place was a new man who deserved a second chance.

Just like Will.

Maybe Will hadn't sacrificed his career for her, or come after her when they were separated, and maybe he'd opened his heart and life to a man Jocelyn thought she hated. Maybe Will needed her forgiveness, too.

Maybe Jocelyn needed to let go and love instead of holding on to hate.

There was no maybe about it. But first, she had to find her father.

A loud splash made her jump and almost drop the oar, but she clung to the slippery stick, her eyes darting as she expected to come face-to-face with an alligator. But it was a mighty blue heron who'd made the noise, a helpless fish hanging from its mouth.

"Henry," she whispered, a sob choking her. "Have you seen my daddy?"

He tipped his head back, devoured breakfast, and stretched his wings to take flight, heading south to disappear in the rain. Without a clue which way to go, she followed, staying close to the shore, her arms already burning from the effort of slicing the kayak through the water.

This was lunacy. He wasn't out here.

But who had taken the rowboat? a voice insisted.

How had he dragged it across the street and into the water all by—

The kayak hit something hard in the water, pulling another gasp from her throat. What the—

A narrow tip of aluminum stuck straight out of the water. The tip of a sunken rowboat. No, no. Not *a* rowboat. Their rowboat!

Shoving wet strands from her eyes and tamping down panic, she looked around, zeroing in on a mangrove hammock about twenty feet away. It was the closest island, the only place a person could swim to from here.

"Guy!" she called out, the words lost in the rain. "Guy!"

With every ounce of strength she had, she plowed the oar through the water, reaching the island in about fifteen burning strokes. He had to be here. He *had* to.

She climbed out of the kayak, stuffing the edge of the oar in the muck for balance, her foot landing on a sharp rock that made her grunt in pain. Dragging the kayak to dry land, she remembered the picture she'd taken from the house and found it pressed to the wet bottom of the kayak seat.

Wanting it with her, she unpeeled it from the plastic and turned to squint into the rain and through the mangroves that lined the island's edge.

"Guy! Are you here?"

Shoving branches out of her way, she headed toward the middle of a hammock that was not more than thirty feet in diameter. In the center there should be some clear space and—

She spotted him rolled up in a ball under a Brazilian pepper tree.

"Guy!" Ignoring the roots and rocks stabbing her bare feet, she ran to him, falling on his body as relief rocked her. "Oh my God, are you okay?"

He moaned, murmured, and turned slightly, his glasses completely bent from the weight of his head, his poor face marked with bug bites, his teeth as yellow as ever as he bared them in a smile.

"That you, Missy?"

He was alive. Relief rocked her. "Yes, Guy. It's me." She folded him in her arms and squeezed her eyes against the sting of fresh tears.

"Are you mad at me?" he asked, as contrite as a kid.

She sat up, tenderly holding his head while she slipped the ruined glasses off his face. "No." Her voice cracked. "Just tell me you're okay."

"I'm fine."

But she could tell by his gruff, hoarse voice that he wasn't. He was scared and suffering, and surely wouldn't have made it out here much longer.

"Did I miss the yard sale?"

She almost laughed, but shook her head, rocking back on the wet dirt and grass with him in her arms.

"We waited for you." She inched him away to search his face, so battered and bitten, so old and tired. He didn't even resemble the man of her childhood anymore. Not inside or out. "What happened, Guy? Why did you leave me?"

His eyes clouded as he shook his head. "I don't remember."

Really? Was he telling the truth? "You really don't remember anything, Guy? Not why you left or what your life used to be like or "

"I wanted this! How did it get here?" He snapped up the wet picture that had fallen to the ground.

"I . . ." She slid the picture from his fingers, the image so water-damaged that it was almost impossible to make out any details. "It's mine," she said.

"You know that little girl?" His voice rose with a mix of fear and hope.

Jocelyn nodded, biting her lip, fighting more tears. Finally, she looked up to meet his gray gaze. "I am that little girl."

Something flickered in his eyes, a flash of recognition, a split second of awareness, then the fog came back.

"Do you know that, Guy?"

He closed his eyes and shook his head, abject misery in the tiny move. "I forget."

She cupped his face with her hand. "Then so will I." She leaned closer so her forehead touched his. "I forget and I forgive."

He heaved a great big sigh.

She lifted her head, pressed her lips to his wet forehead, and gave him a kiss. "Let's get you home, Daddy."

The tailwind that got the flight across country by dawn East Coast time turned out to be a cold front that left all of southwest Florida in a mist of cool rain, snarling up traffic even at this crazy early hour.

Was it Will's imagination or was the causeway just more crowded than usual?

Next to him Coco stirred, finally taking off the baseball cap and sunglasses she'd kept on since before he'd returned his rental car at LAX. Must be the standard L.A. disguise, he mused, thinking of Jocelyn and her designer cap.

Coco had slept almost the whole flight, stayed pretty quiet when she woke, and had been remarkably ignored by almost everyone.

Of course the way Will looked at anyone who came within five feet of her kept any curious celebrity hunters at bay.

"You sure she'll be here?" Coco asked as his truck rumbled over the causeway toward Mimosa Key. "Because I will *not* do this without Jocelyn."

He didn't respond, weaving through way more traffic than he'd have expected at this time of the morning.

"You are sure, aren't you?" she pressed.

"I'm not sure of anything," he said honestly.

"Except that you love her."

He shot a surprised look at her. "That obvious?"

For the first time, she laughed softly. "Maybe you should step back and review your behavior for the past day. Have you even slept? No, you've just flown cross-country—twice—and threw yourself at the mercy of a woman you've never met, sucker-punched a movie star, and kidnapped me to—"

"I didn't kidnap you," he shot back. "You were ready to leave him."

"I thought I had. Then I took him back. I'm done now."

"What finally changed your mind?"

She let out a dramatic sigh. "You."

"Because I beat up your husband?"

"Because you love Jocelyn enough to do what you did. I want that," she said simply. "I saw it in action and it wasn't in a movie script. It was real. I want that for me."

"Then you should go find it."

"This is the first step, big crazy lover boy."

He grinned at her. "You think I'm crazy?"

"I do, which makes you absolutely perfect for Jocelyn, in my opinion."

"Why, because her role in life is to fix crazy people and make them better?"

"No, because she's a nutcase herself."

He took his eyes from the road to glance at her. "Are we talking about the same woman? I've never met a person more sane than Jocelyn."

"With the compulsive list making?"

He laughed softly. "Yeah, she's a list maker, but that

doesn't make her crazy. It makes her organized and gives her a sense of control." And he loved that about her.

"And the neatness?"

"Like I said, control and organization. She's not OCD."

"Borderline. And, sorry, but there is nothing sane about hanging on to your virginity into your thirties."

He slammed on the brakes, getting a deafening horn from the poor guy behind him. "*What*?"

"You didn't know?"

A few white lights popped in the back of his head, blinding him momentarily.

Jocelyn had never slept with anyone?

That wasn't possible. That wasn't *normal*. And that wasn't true anymore, even if this woman had her facts straight, which he sincerely doubted she did. "I don't think she's the kind of woman to talk about that to her friends."

"Oh, we talked about it. She talked about everything with me."

Probably not everything, but he wouldn't be the one to share her secrets.

"I know about her dad."

Okay, maybe everything. He flipped the wipers up a notch as they passed through a band of heavy rain. "He only... only beat her once," he said, hearing the shame in his voice. Did she know Will's role in that spectacular night?

"Once was all it took to freeze her up in the sex department."

He slipped around a slow-moving van, spraying water as the end of the causeway beckoned. And, he hoped, the end of this conversation. "I don't think you know what you're talking about."

He prayed she didn't, anyway. Not that he didn't like the idea of being the only man who'd ever made love to her, but had he played a role in stealing *that* from her, too? Guilt pummeled his chest.

"I know what she said. Her old man damn near killed the guy she was fooling around with. Her dad—he's one for the books, isn't he? Anyway, she told me he caught her with the guy and beat the holy hell out of her. Called her a whore over and over again. With each punch, he said it again—"

"Stop it." He pounded the steering wheel, his eyes stinging. "Just…stop it."

"Oh my God, it was you." She reached over and grabbed his arm. "You were the guy she was with that night. She never told me it was Baseball Boy, just…a guy."

Of course not, because she was *still protecting him*. He shook off her hand, gritting his teeth in silence while new waves of hate rolled over him. Remorse and regret roiled through his stomach, making him sick.

"She never told me his name," Coco continued, on a roll now. "She was just, you know, trying like hell to convince me to leave Miles when the whole story came pouring out of her. And I…I couldn't just walk. I was chicken and so she came up with this fake affair for me. She let me save face and him, too. We hoped that would be enough to…"

"To what?"

"Keep him away from me."

He grunted. "That's what restraining orders are for."

She just shook her head and shifted in her seat. "Jocelyn's one in a million, you know?"

God, he knew. *Fifteen years.* That was a damn long time to be alone. Too long.

As if he could cut some of that time short, he smashed on the accelerator and fishtailed a little as he swerved through more traffic.

"Holy shit!" She dove down like someone had shot through the windshield, fighting to get her seat belt undone.

"What's the matter?" He looked at the car next to them, right into a telephoto lens. "What the hell?"

"Just drive. Fast!" She pushed onto the floor, scrambling for her hat and sunglasses. "How much farther?"

"We're almost there." But the dark van slid right behind them, on their tail, and stayed there until he turned onto Sea Breeze and hit the brakes one more time to stare at the spectacle that made absolutely no sense. Except that it did.

"Um, Coco."

She didn't move from her hiding place below the dashboard. "What?"

"About that press conference."

"What about it?"

"I think it started without you."

Chapter 31

⌣

They were drenched by the time Jocelyn managed to get Guy back to the dock where she'd found the kayak. The whole deal took well over an hour since the kayak was built for one. She managed to squeeze them both in, keeping him calm, getting him in and out of the water, tenderly helping his bug-bitten body make the short journey.

By now she'd have expected the kayak owners to be awake, but all of the houses seemed unnaturally empty. And quiet. Still, someone was making noise. She could hear voices—quite a few, in fact.

Jocelyn put her arm around Guy and guided him across the grass.

"You're going to be okay," she promised, leading him along a thick six-foot hedge of hibiscus trees that blocked the view of the street and his house. "We'll get some ointment on those—"

The voices suddenly grew even louder, almost like a crowd screaming in the stands at a game, making them both slow their step.

"What was that?" Guy asked, clinging tighter to her.

"I don't..." But deep inside, she did know. Deep inside, she knew exactly what they were going to find when they reached the street. Reporters. Cameras. Paparazzi.

"Guy, I have to tell you something."

He didn't answer as he navigated the wet grass and drizzle that smeared his glasses.

"I need you to brace yourself for when we get to the street."

"Why?"

"Because..." She took him a few steps farther, the crowd noise rising up as if they already saw her, the constant clicking of cameras like a serenade of crickets, a few voices shouting, the words impossible to make out. Neighbors she recognized gathered in small groups outside their houses, some still in bathrobes, some with cameras of their own.

"There she is!" someone yelled.

"With that man!"

Jocelyn turned left and right, confused. No one was pointing at her. No reporters came running at them. She took a few more steps and rounded the shrubbery to get a view of Guy's house.

"Oh, my word, Missy, look!" Guy practically stumbled as he pulled her forward and they saw the crowd covering her front lawn and driveway and spilling into the street.

"I know, Guy, I know."

He turned to her and threw his arms around her. "You did it, girl!" He knocked his glasses to the ground but didn't even notice, practically jumping up and down. "You got the crowds here for the yard sale! Look at all the cameras!"

She couldn't help laughing at his exuberance and the pure innocence of his assumption. "Guess we did, Guy." She dipped down to get his glasses, wiping them with the hem of her shirt, which didn't help at all but gave her a second to collect her thoughts as she peered past him at the pack of reporters.

Why were the cameras all pointed toward the street, where a truck slowly—

Not a truck. *Will's* truck. Chills exploded over her skin as she covered her mouth in shock. "Oh my God, he's back."

"William?" Guy greedily grabbed his glasses. "I knew it! I knew he'd come back to me. He always does. Like . . . like . . . like one of the Austrian toys."

"Australian."

"What are they called?"

She just smiled, an inexplicable happiness washing over her like the rain. "Boomerang." Or *Bloom*-erang.

You always come back to me.

"But his interview . . ." *Was today.* Her words were lost in the breeze and crowd noise as the truck slowed in front of the house, unable to get in the driveway.

"Come on." Guy tugged at her, running on pure adrenaline now. "We gotta get over there."

"Wait." The media rushed the truck, surrounding it, shouting questions, pounding on the hood. Did they think she was in there?

Will parked on the street just as the front door of the house opened and about a half dozen sheriff's deputies came marching out of Guy's house. They dispersed the crowd and stationed themselves in a protective pathway to the car.

All for *Will*?

Didn't the media realize the person they wanted was right behind them, standing out in the open? Obviously not, which gave her a chance to change her plan. She had Guy now; there was no reason to make her public plea.

Just then, the crowd roar erupted as Will got out of the truck, rounding to the other side, shouting at the cameramen. A few more deputies surrounded the truck, one opening the passenger door to help someone out.

Oh, not someone. Coco.

For a moment Jocelyn couldn't speak. Shock and disbelief stole her breath and crushed her lungs. Coco Kirkman was here? With Will?

Why?

The press shouted questions, but Will and one of the deputies flanked Coco, who held up her hand in a plea for space. Will shouted at the reporters, but Jocelyn couldn't catch the words over the noise. She'd make a statement? Was that what he said?

Next to her, Guy just shook his head, then patted her back lovingly. "Gotta hand it to you, Missy. I've never seen a yard sale like this one."

Neither had she. "Let's go through the neighbor's yard, Guy. Let's get around the back and into the house through the pool patio. No one will even notice us." Not with a superstar like Coco headed in the front door.

He blinked at her. "Why?"

"So we can..." She rooted around her brain for a reason that would get him to move. "Meet the hostess. That's who they're bringing inside."

"Nicey?"

She urged him across the street, ignoring the strange looks from the neighbors. "Not this time, Guy. Her name is Coco. And I cannot wait to hear what she has to say."

"She's gone. And so is her father."

Will blamed sleep deprivation on his brain's refusal to process what Lacey said when they got Coco inside the house.

Coco processed it, though, and instantly started to whine. "I can't make any statements without her!"

"Wait a minute. Wait." Will held up a hand to silence her, just as he caught Guy's picture in the middle of the TV screen with some reporter talking. What the *hell*?

A bad, bad feeling crept through his gut, but he tamped it down and stayed focused on Lacey and Clay. "Where are they?" he demanded.

"We don't know." Clay said, a protective arm around Lacey, who looked pale and as stressed out as Coco, only she was quieter about it.

"I have to talk to Jocelyn," Coco insisted. "I'm not going out there until I talk to her. I have to—"

Zoe swept in and practically scooped the actress away, and Tessa instantly leaped to Coco's other side.

"Let's get you in the back and calmed down, Ms. Kirkman," Tessa said.

"Yeah," Zoe added, leaning close to Coco. " 'Cause, honey, you could really use a little makeup before you get in front of any cameras."

Will shot them a grateful look and turned back to Lacey, Clay, and Slade. "Someone tell me what the hell is going on."

As they explained, only certain words really took hold. Guy had been missing since yesterday. Woke up and Jocelyn was gone. Silver Alert got the media here.

And they had plenty of questions of their own, but the need to find Jocelyn and Guy shot like liquid mercury through his veins.

"We have to find them," he said simply, marching to the door, ready to take on every damn reporter and an army of deputies to get his woman back. And her father.

Damn it, they all belonged together. They all—

"William!"

He froze at the sound, the punch of relief making his gut drop. He turned toward the patio to see Guy hobbling across the grass with Jocelyn next to him, both of them soaked, bedraggled, filthy, and absolutely the most beautiful sight Will had ever seen.

Ignoring the noisy reaction of the others in the room, Will strode to the sliding glass door and threw it open, running across the patio and practically tearing the screen door off its hinges to wrap these two people he loved so damn much in his arms.

Guy might have sobbed and Jocelyn let out a soft, sweet moan, but for the space of one breath of joy they all held each other and no one said a word. They just stood together in complete union.

Finally Guy pushed away. "Where's Nicey?"

"What the hell happened to your face?" Guy was covered with welts, his glasses damn near collapsed, his clothes filthy and wet.

Jocelyn was just as wet, her face streaked with dirt and tears. "He spent the night on an island in the canal," she said, her voice cracking. "He got...lost." She closed her eyes and dropped her head against Will's chest. "We have to take care of him. Please, Will. Please don't put him in a—"

"Shhh." He quieted her with a kiss on her wet head and a finger to her lips. "We won't. I promise. We won't."

"Where's this hostess?" Guy broke away from them and started toward the house. Will turned to follow, but Jocelyn grabbed him by the shoulders.

"Will, he isn't the same man."

"I know," he admitted. "And neither am I."

She frowned at him. "What do you mean?"

"No more waiting. From now on, I act. And don't be too surprised, but I brought someone back from L.A. with me. She wants to come clean, clear your name, and help other abused women. You don't have to live this lie for her anymore, Joss."

"Oh, Will." She leaned into him for another embrace. "I can't believe you did that. I can't believe..." She pulled away, searched his face, confusion making her frown. "What about the coaching job?"

He snorted. "I turned that down before I left Mimosa Key. I'm not going to L.A., I'm staying right here, building things that last. Like villas and houses and a life with you."

She put her hand on her mouth like she couldn't contain her happiness. "Here?"

"Right here." He pulled her closer, wrapping his arms around her. "Right here where you belong, Bloomerang."

She answered with a salty, sweet, straight-from-the-heart kiss on his lips.

Chapter 32

⌇

Will took over caring for Guy while the five women somehow squeezed into the hallway bathroom Jocelyn had often locked herself in during Guy's episodes, shaking with fear, hating her life, wishing him dead.

Coco was the one shaking with fear now, perched on the toilet seat so Lacey could fix her hair and Zoe could apply makeup. Tessa leaned against the counter, making notes for Coco's speech.

Jocelyn crouched on the floor, holding the actress's tiny hands.

"You don't have to do this, Coco."

Coco looked down. "Yes I do."

"But you do have to look at me," Zoe insisted. "Unless you are willing to settle for less-than-perfect makeup."

Coco complied. "And I want to do this, Joss," she added. "Not just for you, not just for me, but for every woman who's ever been trapped in an awful situation."

"Great opening line," Tessa said, scratching on paper.

"Thanks," Coco said. "I came up with that on the plane."

"You don't need lines." Jocelyn squeezed Coco's hands gently. "You just have to talk from the heart."

"I'm an actress. I need lines."

"You're a woman, just like us," Jocelyn told her. "And if you want to be heard, you will have to look at the camera and speak honestly. And, honey, you have to be prepared for backlash."

"Backlash?" Lacey asked, holding up a strand of Coco's hair as she combed through it. "What kind of backlash could there be for doing something so right?"

"Miles's fans, for one," Coco said. "They're rabid women who would die for him."

Zoe snorted. "Then maybe they should move in with him."

Coco smiled up at her. "I like you. Have you ever thought about acting?"

Surprising all of them, Zoe shook her head. "No limelight for me, doll face. But I wouldn't mind the cash and cars. Close your eyes. I'm going all smoky on the creases."

Coco obliged and gave Jocelyn's fingers a squeeze back. "I'm going to be fine," she said. "As long as you're with me and you field the questions about why we did this."

"Gladly."

"And maybe that'll help you get some clients back," Coco added. "I'm really sorry that your business has crashed and burned."

Jocelyn shrugged. "I'm not. I'm moving on."

Lacey froze mid-comb. "You are?"

"I'm going to be the spa manager at Casa Blanca."

Zoe shrieked.

Tessa gasped.

And Lacey dropped the comb and fell to her knees. "Jocelyn! Thank you!"

"Why are you all surprised?" Coco asked. "She's got the stud ballplayer who'd do anything for her and great friends who rally. And a kind of quirky but very cute little old father."

Jocelyn smiled at her, so eternally grateful that Coco hadn't given her a fight when she'd explained her decision to forgive Guy. "Exactly," Jocelyn agreed. "Why are you all shocked?"

"But I thought . . ." Tessa put down the paper, frowning. "Will was interviewing for a job in L.A."

"He blew it off to stay in Mimosa Key and be the best damn carpenter this island's ever had." And the best damn *man* Jocelyn had ever known.

"The only job he's interviewing for is to be your main squeeze," Coco said. "That man loves your ass."

"Ahem," Tessa said pointedly.

"Amen," Lacey replied.

"I like this girl," Zoe said with a grin.

Jocelyn just beamed. "He might get that job."

"Great." Coco laughed. "It'll be awesome for you to finally let go of that pesky virginity you've been carting around for a lifetime."

That was met with stunned silence and Jocelyn felt heat creep up her neck.

Zoe's hands froze mid-eye-shadow-stroke. "You're a *virgin*?"

Jocelyn swallowed. "Not anymore."

"But...with Will...that was your *first*?"

She nodded, then looked up to Lacey and Tessa for help, but got nothing except open-mouthed, wide-eyed disbelief.

"You know I was never with anyone in college," Jocelyn said.

"But, we assumed...after...no one?" Zoe shook her head as if the thought just would not find a place in her brain. "At your age?"

"Zoe, not everyone is the sexual tigress you are."

"But not *anyone* is a virgin at your age."

"Well I was," Jocelyn said.

Zoe gave Jocelyn a look, then straightened to get back to work on Coco's face, still unable to process the unbelievable news.

"So," Tessa said, tapping her pen on the paper. "You don't tell your three best friends that you're a virgin, but you share that with a client."

"Coco's more than a client," Jocelyn said quickly. "She's my friend, too. And she is a sister in..." She closed her eyes. She'd have to talk about this now, so she might as well practice with the ones who loved her the most. "Abuse."

No one spoke for a few long seconds, but Jocelyn and Coco squeezed each other's hands, the shared experience always there between them.

"All right, Ms. Kirkman," Zoe said, grabbing a hand mirror. "Now you're ready to face your adoring fans."

"Yes, I am." But she didn't even look, standing slowly and pulling Jocelyn up with her. "You guys are all awesome and Jocelyn is lucky to have you."

"We know," Tessa said, reaching out to hug Jocelyn. "We love her even if we don't know her secrets."

"You know them all now," Jocelyn said. "And in a few minutes, so will the rest of the world."

"Except the Oldest Living Virgin part." Zoe grabbed Jocelyn to nudge her onto the toilet seat. "Uh, you need a little makeover, too, Joss. You don't want *the only man you ever slept with* to see you like this."

Ten minutes later, Coco and Jocelyn walked hand in hand to the front patio of 543 Sea Breeze Drive, the place of so many unhappy, violent moments in the past. The sun had finally slipped out from behind the clouds and the crowd of reporters had grown exponentially.

A cheer erupted at the sight of Coco, who walked up to a podium hastily erected by a media outlet after she'd requested one for the press conference.

She glanced nervously at Jocelyn. "Maybe you should, you know, introduce me."

"Maybe you should introduce yourself."

Coco nodded and headed toward the microphone, the papers Tessa had written fluttering on the stand. She tapped the mike, and that just elicited more of a roar and a cringe from Coco. Jocelyn walked up next to her and took her hand.

"C'mon, Coco, you can do this. You can do this for every woman just like us."

"Hello," she said into the mike. When the crowd quieted, she leaned closer and said, "I'm here to speak on behalf of every girl who's ever been hit, every woman who's ever been beaten, and every wife who's ever had to lie to get away from violence."

Complete silence fell over the crowd and a soft gust

of wind picked up one of the papers and floated it away. Coco ignored the loss, looking out to the crowd.

"I have a message to give to you, and I want you to deliver it to every corner of this earth because abuse *has to stop*."

Behind her, the screen door opened and Guy stepped out on the patio, his face the image of confusion. Instantly Jocelyn stepped away, but Coco kept talking.

Jocelyn reached him, turned him around, and guided him inside. Will was in the living room, leaning against the brick wall, dividing his attention between Coco live on TV and Jocelyn.

"He's not quite understanding what's going on," Will said. "I did my best to explain."

"It's just part of the show, Guy," she said, guiding him to his recliner.

"I never saw this part of the show." He slumped into the chair, automatically patting the arm for his remote. "Where's the gifting part? When do you gift me with something special?"

"Right now," she said, kneeling next to him.

Will walked in and handed her the remote. "It was in the—"

"Dishwasher, I know." She smiled up at him. "What do you think we should gift Guy with for all the trouble he's been through these past few weeks?"

Will reached for her. "Let's talk about it." Wrapping her in his arms, he took a few steps away from Guy. "You've forgiven him?"

She nodded. "Completely. I can't let the past ruin the present, Will. And I can't spend whatever time he has left hating him." The announcement felt so good and right on her lips.

"And me?"

"You? I could never hate you. I love—"

"Wait." He cupped her face with both hands. "Me first. Jocelyn, I love you. I want to live every day for you, with you, next to you. I trust you, I need you, and you have always been the only one for me. Always."

A happiness so bone-deep she could feel it down to her toes washed over her. "I love you too, Will."

"Am I on your list of everything now?"

The list that now included family and trust and forever love? "You're right at the top, where I intend to keep you for the rest of our—"

"Excuse me!" Guy called. "My gift, Missy?"

"—lives," Will finished for her, guiding her back to the recliner. "How's this, buddy? We're getting married."

Jocelyn sucked in a soft breath at the announcement, but Guy sat bolt upright. "Really?"

"Yup," Will continued. "We're going to live right next door and keep an eye on you." He threw Jocelyn a questioning glance, and she nodded happily. "And we're having kids."

Guy tried—and failed—to hide his smile. "Kids running around here calling me crazy?"

"No." Jocelyn put one hand on Guy's arm and the other on Will's strong shoulder, gratitude for the gift of forgiveness and love bursting in her chest. "They won't call you crazy. They'll call you . . . *Grandpa*."

Epilogue

～

Seven Months Later

Casa Blanca's parking lot was no longer a gravelly home to a construction trailer, it was a smooth asphalt expanse currently filled with shiny Mercedes, Beamers, and Jaguars. The new surface was so smooth that Jocelyn's high heels made a satisfying tap as Will opened the door of her Lexus and she climbed out.

As her silky skirt slipped way up her thigh, Will let out a low whistle of appreciation.

"Zoe picked this outfit," she said.

"A true believer in form over function." Will loosened the knot around his neck, taking his eyes off her only when the whine of a sports-car engine stole his attention. "What do you call this thing again?"

"A tie?"

Laughing, he took her hand as she stepped out. "I meant this shindig we're all dressed up for."

"A soft opening."

"I like the sound of that." He pulled her closer, inhaling deeply as if he couldn't get enough of her scent. "You know, Artemesia is the only villa not finished yet. I left the back door unlocked. Let's sneak up there and find your soft opening."

She added a little pressure to his embrace, their fit against each other so natural now they didn't even have to think about it. "Later, I promise. But now it's time to entertain the moneyed set from Naples, here for the VIP preview of the resort."

She turned when a candy-apple-red Porsche swung into a space a few feet away.

"Arriving in true style," he noted.

"Don't knock it. These ladies pay top dollar for luxury, and Lacey and I plan to deliver."

"Lacey plans to deliver any minute now, from the looks of her."

She gathered her wrap and bag, tucking her hand into his arm. "As of an hour ago, she was pretty sure she'd be here, but she's been having contractions all day. I have no such excuse and, as the spa manager, I need to make friends and charm potential customers."

A man climbed out of the Porsche looking like he'd been plucked from central casting for the event. Black hair with maybe a whisper of silver threads, jaw-droppingly handsome, dressed in Armani, a phone pressed to his ear.

"If she's not responding to the sandostatin, then we need to closely monitor her kidney function overnight," the man said with gruff authority as he walked around the car to the other side, reaching for the car door. Jocelyn thought there was something vaguely familiar about him. "Administer it with high-dose conditioning protocols for the next three hours and keep the patient sedated. If anything changes, call me."

He opened the passenger-side door and an exquisite brunette dressed in a strapless white dress climbed out, her expression as icy as the diamonds around her neck. "You said your partners were handling the calls tonight."

"This case has extenuating—"

"I don't care. You have to fake this for one more night."

Will put his arm around Jocelyn and guided her past the awkward exchange, keeping her tucked close to his side.

"Promise me we'll never fight," he said.

"Never? I make no such promises. But promise me you'll never drive a screaming-red Porsche."

"Never? I make no such promises."

They laughed, looking at each other and slowing just enough to share a kiss.

"C'mon, Joss," he murmured. "Let's blow this thing off and go hit fungoes at the field." He dragged his hand down her waist and over her backside. "I have a key to the clubhouse now."

"Ah, the powers of a volunteer high school coach," she teased. "Who needs a hundred-thousand-dollar sports car when you can do me against the varsity lockers?"

He grinned. "I love the way you think."

"Behave, Will Palmer," she warned as two uniformed porters welcomed them and opened the doors to Casa Blanca's creamy, dreamy lobby.

Will kept his hand on Jocelyn's back as they scanned

the crowd. There were mainly unfamiliar faces but a few were friendly, like Gloria Vail, who'd agreed to work in the salon against her aunt's wishes. The guests were busy checking out the elegant North African mosaic work along the registration desk and reading informational pamphlets about Casa Blanca's all-organic spa, which Lacey and Jocelyn had decided to call Eucalyptus.

The staff and subcontractors chatted in small groups wearing expressions of pure satisfaction. They'd done it. They'd made the deadline. Lacey's delivery date had become the de facto "end date" for the last six months, and the ever-growing crew of construction, hotel, restaurant, and spa staff had worked nonstop to get the resort ready before its owners brought baby boy Walker into the world.

"Where is everybody?" Jocelyn asked Will.

"And by everybody you mean Lacey, Tessa, and Zoe."

"And Clay." She glanced around, but none of the people she most wanted to see were there.

Suddenly the henna-glass spa doors shot open and Ashley burst out, looking more than a little panicked. When she spotted Jocelyn, Lacey's daughter looked like she'd cry with relief.

"Aunt Jocelyn! We have a problem." She grabbed Jocelyn's arm and pulled her close, her eyes moist with tears. "My mom's in labor. It's happening so fast. Clay took her into the spa and we called nine-one-one and they're headed over the causeway, but, oh my God, I think she's gonna have the baby any second!"

Will and Jocelyn looked at each other, a silent communication instantly exchanged.

"I'll get that doctor," Will said. "Go be with Lacey."

Will rushed off and Jocelyn wrapped an arm around a very shaken Ashley. "Don't worry. She's going to be fine."

"I don't know. She's in so much pain."

"She's having a baby, Ash. There's pain." They hustled through the doors, running as fast as feasible on the heels. Jocelyn barely noticed the Marrakesh silver mirror she'd hung that afternoon or the Moroccan berber rugs they'd just imported for the opening.

Eucalyptus was an exotic, inviting, luxurious spa, but not the ideal place for a baby to be born.

Jocelyn took a deep breath, fighting the old urge to control everything. She sure as heck couldn't control this.

Ashley pushed open the massage-room door, where the lights were as low as they would be for a client but the woman on the table was anything but relaxed. Tessa and Zoe's backs blocked her view of Lacey, but Jocelyn heard the long, low, harrowing cry of her friend's agony.

Ashley froze, then put her hand to her mouth. "Mom!"

"Shhh. Ash. Relax." Jocelyn came around the table to stand next to Clay, who looked as pale as his stepdaughter. He held Lacey's hand, and from the looks of it she was squeezing the living hell out of his fingers. Lacey's beautiful periwinkle silk dress was soaked with sweat, and something else. Her shoes were off, her legs up, her hair a wild coppery gold mess.

"There's a doctor coming," Jocelyn said, taking Clay's other hand. "He'll be in here in one second."

"He better hurry the hell up." Lacey ground out the words and slammed her other hand on the massage table, her distended belly heaving with each gasp. "Because I have to push. I have to push *now*!"

"Don't do that, Lacey," Zoe said.

"Why not?"

"Because in the movies they never want you to do that."

"I can't... help..."

The door shot open and the man from the parking lot barreled into the room, instantly taking over the small space with an aura of calm, commanding control.

"Clear the table," he ordered.

Everyone backed away, except Zoe, who stood stone still, ghost white, and speechless.

The doctor stood at the bottom of the makeshift bed and fired questions at Clay. How long, how many, how often, how bad.

Clay answered as Tessa put an arm around Ashley. "Let's get you out of here, hon."

"No, my mom needs me."

Her mom let out a howl of pain.

"Your mom needs you to leave," Tessa ordered with more force, ushering Ashley to the door.

"Can you deliver a baby?" Jocelyn asked the doctor, who was already getting into position to do just that.

"I went to medical school," he said dismissively. "Get me gloves and a sterilized pair of scissors." He put his hands on Lacey's knees while she endured the next contraction. "And towels."

"Help me get that," Jocelyn said to Zoe, relieved that the doctor seemed so competent.

But Zoe remained rooted in her spot, still staring at the man.

"C'mon, Zoe," Jocelyn urged.

At her name the doctor looked up from his patient, seeing Zoe for the first time. His eyes widened exactly like hers did and, in that second, Jocelyn knew where she'd seen him before.

Oliver. The doctor who'd had Zoe dodging for cover all those months ago. The one whose practice they'd passed in Naples.

"Zoe?" he asked, obviously as stunned as she. "What are you doing here?"

Lacey grunted and annihilated Clay's hand. "For the love of God, I have to push!"

Will appeared with the gloves and scissors, thankfully more focused than Jocelyn was. Jocelyn turned and opened a cabinet, yanking out a stack of fresh towels.

"You can leave now," the doctor said as he pulled on the latex gloves. "I only need the baby's father."

Will gathered both of the women and led them out, having to nudge Zoe a little harder than Jocelyn. In the small vestibule designed for clients to meditate before and after their massages, Tessa stood with both arms around Ashley.

"He's going to deliver the baby," Jocelyn assured them as much as herself. "He seems like a really good doctor."

Zoe snorted.

They all just looked at her, but Will said, "Actually, he's an oncologist. His wife just let me know in no uncertain terms that he wasn't here to work."

Zoe closed her eyes, turned, and walked down the hall away from the group while Tessa continued gentle words of assurance for Ashley.

"C'mere." Will took Jocelyn's hand and tugged her out of the vestibule.

She glanced over her shoulder at the closed massage-room door. "I want to wait here," she said. "It could be any minute."

"We'll be right around the corner. I need something."

At the serious tone in his voice, she followed him into the facial room, completely dark and cool and smelling vaguely of mint and lavender. In the center of the room, a simple bed with clean sheets awaited the first facial ... or ...

She smiled at him. "You're kidding, right?"

"I'm dead serious."

Laughing, she put a hand on his chest. "Let's take it to the villa later."

Will's eyes flashed dark blue as he came closer, wrapping his arms around her. "Don't worry, we will. To celebrate."

"The new baby?"

"Life's curveballs."

"So says the catcher."

"I'm serious." And he was. There was no smile on his face, no humor in his expression. "Shit happens, fast and unexpectedly."

"Yes, it does."

"So, Joss, let me ask you a question. What are you prepared to die for?"

She blinked at him. "Excuse me?"

"That's the question you asked me once, when you were life coaching. You said it told you what was important to someone."

"That was really just a rhetorical question I used to ask clients to get a conversation going."

"I know what I'm prepared to *live* for." He got closer, stealing her air and space and any last shred of sanity as he walked her toward the middle of the room. "You."

She kind of melted, letting him dip her back on the facial bed. "Likewise."

"So why are we waiting for the right time?"

"I know you hate to wait now," she teased, but it was hard to joke in the face of all this certainty. Determination. Focus.

"I don't want to wait another day or night or minute."

She closed her eyes and dropped backwards, the words and the man sweeping her right off her feet. "I've created a monster who refuses to wait for anything."

He laughed a little, kissing her throat. "So, when?"

"Right now, right here?" A shiver of anticipation and desire shot through her, control slipping away as he trailed his tongue along her jaw and settled her deeper onto the bed.

"Maybe next week."

She gave him a little nudge away, to see his face. "Next week?"

"We can't get everything together before then."

"You don't mean for sex."

"No, I mean for marriage." He cupped his hands over her face. "I love you so much, Jocelyn. I want to know we're in this together, forever, as one."

"Oh, Will, I love you, too. You know we're together."

"I don't know anything except I love you." He kissed her, still holding her face, tenderly like she was his prize. "I love your heart."

She put her hand on his chest. "You're the one with the big heart, Will. You're all heart."

He rocked against her. "Not all."

"Okay, and some soul."

He nestled against her, kissing his way to her ear. "Let's make this official then. Jocelyn Mary Bloom, love of my life, girl of my dreams, mother of my future—"

The door popped open and they froze as Zoe stood in stunned silence, taking in the scene. "Seriously, guys? Now?"

Will held Jocelyn firmly on the bed, ignoring the intrusion with an unwavering gaze. "I was just proposing," he said.

"Oh," Zoe whispered. "Well, what'd she say?"

"I don't know yet." Will gathered her a little tighter as more footsteps came toward the room and Tessa's happy laughter floated in.

"We have an audience," Jocelyn whispered.

"I don't care. Where was I?"

"Something about love, girl, dreams, motherhood . . ." She closed her eyes as happiness clutched her heart. "It was all good."

"Say yes, Bloomerang."

"Dying here," Zoe sang from the doorway. "Just say yes."

"Yeah, just say yes, Aunt Jocelyn," Ashley added.

Jocelyn looked into Will's eyes and called, "Tess, what's your vote?"

"Go for it, girl. Break that damn shell around your heart."

She took a deep breath, savoring the word she was about to say, the commitment she was about to make, and the life she was about to live.

At just that moment, Elijah Clayton Walker let out his very first cry and they all yelled out at the same time. "Yes!"

The women in the doorway instantly disappeared, leaving them alone for a better drama.

"You said yes," Will whispered.

"I screamed yes."

"Even better." He gave her that slow, sweet, sexy smile that turned her entire body to mush. "So guess what I finally have?"

"A fiancée?"

He kissed her forehead, her eyes, her cheeks, and put his lips against hers to whisper the answer. "I have... *everything.*"

Zoe Tamarin never stays in one
place for too long, earning her the
nickname "The Tumbleweed"
among her friends.

But when The Tumbleweed rolls
into Barefoot Bay, she finds herself
face-to-face with the one man she
most hoped she'd left behind...

Please turn this page for a
preview of

Barefoot in the Sun.

Whoever invented the expression "the heat of a thousand suns" must have been sitting right here, in a top-down convertible on the black asphalt of Naples, Florida, in the dead of summer. Boiling. Frying. Sizzling like a piece of bacon. Surely no *single* sun could generate the amount of heat blasting down on Zoe Tamarin's head as she closed her eyes and tried to gather the nerve to do what she'd come to do.

She dug deep for inner Zen, came up with nothing, and melted some more against the burning leather seat of her rented 4x4.

Come on, Zoe. Get out of the car and *face him*.

She slid a glance across the wide boulevard that cut a swath through the exclusive business district of the beachside city, studying the two-story Spanish hacienda–style building. Between her and that destination, heat shimmered off the road like burning coals.

I'd walk across fire for you.

Yeah, *right*.

Inhaling some soggy, humid air, Zoe lifted her hair and fanned her face and neck with her other hand. She had to do this. What was a little humiliation, heartbreak, or pathetic desperation between old friends, right? Zoe had been raised on the altar of "signs from the universe," and last night the universe had smacked her over the head with a billboard.

While all her closest friends celebrated the stunning drama of a baby's birth, arriving in breathtaking style during the Casa Blanca Resort & Spa grand-opening party, Zoe merely reeled from the sight of the man who'd *materialized* to deliver Lacey and Clay Walker's baby.

She'd never forget the shock of looking up from Lacey's makeshift delivery table to see the "doctor" who'd swept into the room to help bring a healthy baby into the world.

By the time the paramedics whisked mother, son, and proud papa off to the hospital, the doctor—who'd been a party guest—had disappeared. From the stretcher, holding her little bundle, Lacey had called him "an angel."

Au contraire, my friend. That man was no angel. Quite the opposite. And right now it was time to make a deal with the devil, who happened to owe Zoe, and owe her big. Because if he thought they were "square" when he blew in and delivered Lacey's baby in an emergency, he was sorely mistaken.

They weren't even close to square for what he'd done to her, and it was time to collect.

Fired by that thought, she yanked the keys out of the ignition and jumped out, heat immediately singeing through wafer-thin sandals as she hit the pavement.

Squaring her shoulders, she pinned her gaze on the double mahogany doors and jaywalked to find out her destiny.

Would he or would he not...

He *had* to.

At the door, she took a shallow breath and ran her fingers over the elegant gold lettering that announced exactly what went on in this unassuming building tucked between an art gallery and a frozen-yogurt shop in the ritzy medical district of one of the world's wealthiest cities.

Dr. Oliver Bradbury

Oncology

There was only one way to—

Both doors popped open, shoved from the inside, forcing Zoe out of the way. A woman strode out, stopping to blink into the sun and throw open a giant bag covered with some designer's initials. She whipped out a pair of sunglasses with the very same initials on the side.

But before she got them on, Zoe saw her face.

And her heart fell right onto that sizzling sidewalk and fried.

A phone followed the sunglasses, thrust under silky black hair that brushed her shoulders. "Thank Christ," she said, an amazing amount of sultry in the sarcasm. "It's done."

Zoe stood frozen and mesmerized. As if the woman was suddenly aware that someone was staring, she turned, her eyes hidden by the sunglasses but her glare powerful nonetheless. Zoe still couldn't move as she drank in the stark beauty of the woman's face, the aura of wealth that clung like a spritz of Chanel, and the condescending attitude of dismissal.

She knew that face, of course, thanks to the power of

Google and a few glasses of wine. Small consolation that Oliver's wife didn't look quite as perfect without benefit of photo shop.

"Excuse me," Zoe said, reaching for the door.

"Of course, dear." Adele stepped aside, switching the phone to the other ear. "No," she said into the phone as Zoe went inside. "That was no one. I'm listening."

No one? Zoe spun around, but the door closed, blessedly shutting out the sun and the sight of the woman who'd married the only man Zoe had ever loved.

Inside, cool air settled over Zoe like a perfectly chilled martini as she took in the room's snow-white walls and icy marble floor. She took a moment to let the sensation work its magic, looking around at a reception area that was like no doctor's office she'd ever been in. No mess of magazines on a cheap coffee table for Dr. Bradbury. No impersonal glass panel that slid open and closed like a confessional, either. No worn leather chairs, cheesy art, or canned video presentation.

Nothing but old money and elegant sophistication.

So, *Mrs.* Bradbury must have decorated the offices.

"Can I help you?"

Zoe turned to a striking redhead with a tiny headset in her ear, seated at a glass table with nothing but a tablet computer in front of her. Her smile matched the surroundings, cold and impersonal, just like her Arctic-blue eyes.

"I'm here . . ." Zoe's voice cracked like a teenage boy's. She cleared her throat. "I'd like to see Dr. Bradbury."

The faintest frown pulled. "What time is your appointment?"

"He'll see me." Especially now that his *wife* had just left.

"I'm sorry." The woman angled her head, a practiced mix of pity and power in her expression. "You have to make an appointment, and that requires a referral, and to be perfectly honest, Dr. Bradbury has a one-year waiting list. We can provide you with the names of—"

"He'll see me," she said sharply. "My name is—"

"No." The young woman held up her hand. "Please. If you don't have an appointment, he will *not* see you. There are absolutely no exceptions to that rule."

"I'm the exception. Zoe Tamarin."

The woman didn't move, leveling her icy eyes in a showdown. "Would you like the list of doctors I mentioned?"

"No. I'd like to talk to Oliver. I'm a personal acquaintance."

The woman replied by dropping her gaze over Zoe, lingering on the thin tank top stuck to her sweaty skin. The white cotton skirt that had seemed so whimsical when she'd picked it up at Old Navy suddenly felt like a cheap rag compared to the receptionist's silk and pearls.

Red gave a tight smile and shook her head as she stood, easily six feet tall in four-inch heels. "I'm very sorry for your situation, but you need to leave, now."

Zoe just blinked at her. "My situation?" She didn't even freaking know her situation. "Please call his assistant or whoever and tell him that Zoe Tamarin is waiting to see him."

After a moment the woman touched her earpiece, and Zoe let out a soft sigh of relief. As soon as Oliv—

"Beth, we need security in the lobby."

Zoe croaked out a cough. "Excuse me?"

The other woman completely ignored her. "Immediately,"

she said into the air. Then, to Zoe, "We get a lot of desperate people wanting to see Dr. Bradbury, and—"

"Well, I'm not one of them." Which was a complete lie, but she stepped forward anyway. "Just give him my damn name."

"I'm afraid I can't do that." She looked down at her tablet, like something more important had come up.

Zoe eyed the single door to the back, a nearly invisible slab of polished rosewood that blended right into the wall. But there was a slender silver doorknob that just might not be locked. What the hell did she have to lose? With one more glance at Red, who was pointedly ignoring her now, Zoe lunged at the door.

"Hey!" the woman cried, but Zoe slammed down the handle and pushed.

"Oliver! It's me! Zoe!"

Red got her then, grabbing her arm to yank her back to the lobby. "You will leave the premises, ma'am. Right. This. Minute."

Zoe fought the fingers, wresting her body away with every ounce of strength she had, and suddenly the woman let go and Zoe stumbled forward, tripping to the floor, her hair falling over her face.

"What in God's name is going on out here?"

Velvet. Baritone. Power. *Oliver.* She didn't look up, but closed her eyes and just let the sound of him reach all the way inside and touch her.

"*Zoe?*"

"You know her, Dr. Bradbury?"

The little bit of horror in Red's voice was almost worth the humiliation of looking up to meet his gaze.

But the sight of those bottomless espresso eyes nearly flattened her again.

"Good God," he said, dropping to one knee and reaching out a hand. "What are you...here, get up." His hand enveloped hers, that strong, masculine, capable hand that healed and heated her with one stroke of his fingers. "What are you doing—"

She lifted an eyebrow as she stood to her full height, which was a few hairs shy of five-four, so not as impressive as her adversary and only chest high with Oliver. But, oh, what a chest it was. In a zillion-dollar white shirt so soft and expensive she imagined it was hand-loomed just to fit those incredible shoulders.

"It's easier to get into the Oval Office," she said simply.

He almost smiled, that hint of a smile that sparked the amber in his eyes. "You don't need an appointment to see me."

Zoe was dying to give a dose of "Take that, bitch" to the receptionist, but Oliver still held her hand and inched her a little closer, dizzying her with that clean, smart, crisp smell of authority—and Oliver. "You *do* want to see me?"

The littlest bit of uncertainty almost undid her. "I do."

I do. I do. God, how she'd once longed to say those words to him.

But she said other words, and those had sealed her fate in a completely different way.

But someone said "I do" to him. Someone with dark hair and designer bags and the stink of wealth and family. Big, powerful, undeniable family. The one thing Zoe could never offer him.

She lifted her chin and his expression flickered,

zigzagging somewhere between breathtaking and gorgeous as he studied her.

"Come into my office," he ordered, the words of a man who didn't know the fine art of *suggestion*. She'd noticed that about him last night when he'd cleared the room with one barked order. Authority sat well on those broad shoulders.

So Zoe followed.

"Would you like some coffee? Water?" he asked, pausing before they took a step.

"After what it takes to get in this place? Grey Goose, straight up."

He just nodded to the receptionist. "Tell Mr. Reddick I'll be a few minutes longer."

Zoe blasted Red with a fake smile. "Thank you so much for your help. Attila, was it?"

The other woman looked at Oliver, who bit his lip. "C'mon, Zoe. In here."

He gestured down the hall, staying one step behind her as they rounded a corner wordlessly. She brushed her hands over the wrinkled skirt. Her sandals were silent on plush carpet, but her heart thudded loud enough to reverberate through the hall of Dr. Bradbury's super-plush, mega-exclusive, you-can't-have-an-appointment-for-a-year practice.

His office was large, of course—everything about Oliver was oversized and substantial—but much warmer than the reception area. Cherry, leather, and an aroma of pine and comfort.

She kept her back to him, taking one last inhale and reviewing her game plan.

Which didn't exactly exist for this fairly spontaneous

visit. Should she plead? Demand? Blackmail? Whatever she did, she had to be strong and unyielding. She would not take no for an answer. She would not—

"Turn around."

Melt.

Yeah, she might do that. Because Oliver always melted her. Steeling herself, she vowed not to succumb. For this, Zoe had to be rock solid and ready to fight for what she wanted.

Slowly, she turned, meeting the expression of a man who looked at her like he hadn't eaten in days and she was a human cream puff.

"How is the baby?"

For a minute she couldn't imagine what he was talking about. That was the thing about Oliver. He made Zoe forget her train of thought, her vows of secrecy, her life plans.

"I assume mother and child are thriving?"

Oh, *that* baby. The one he'd delivered last night. "He's...perfect. Just, yeah. You left quickly and Lacey wanted to thank you."

A shadow of disappointment darkened his eyes, gone almost before she could see it. "Is that why you're here?"

She could say yes and be done with this. She had an excuse, and he'd never have to know her real reason.

But then she couldn't have the one thing she wanted most in the world.

Damn it, why did he have to have the power? Why him, of all people?

She blew out a breath, trying to remember a single word of the speech she'd practiced all the way across the causeway. Nothing. The queen of the smart-ass comeback had been rendered wretchedly wordless.

"It was no big deal," he said after a few too many seconds had passed. "I've done a few emergency deliveries in my career." Then he took a step closer, dipping his head almost imperceptibly, searching her face. "Zoe?"

"Oliver, you are one of two people in the world who knows the truth about me."

It was his turn to blink, silent.

"And once you said you'd do anything for me."

He had to work to swallow, no doubt remembering that he'd broken that promise.

"Do you remember saying that, Oliver?" she pressed.

"Of course." He crossed his arms, his power stance. "What do you need, Zoe?"

She took a slow breath, ready to jump. "My great-aunt, Pasha, is sick. Really, really sick. You know that she... she can't exactly sally forth through the health-care system because she... can't."

He just stared at her.

"I need you to treat her. And never report it to anyone, ever."

His eyes narrowed as her demand sank in. "You're asking me to—"

"Do something illegal, yes. I know you are a big, important, successful doctor who shouldn't take any legal risks because that would possibly hurt your amazing, booming practice, but I don't care, Oliver, because after—"

"Stop." He was in front of her in one step, one hand on her shoulder.

"Will you?" she asked, determined to get her yes before... anything else.

He was close enough for her to feel his breath and the beating of his heart. "How could I do that?"

"How? Quietly. Secretly. Under the table, off the books, and away from the prying eyes of your witchy staff." She raised her chin, hating that he could feel her tremble. Let him think it was because she wanted his help, and not because every cell in her was screaming for him. For his mouth. For his body. For what they'd once had.

"That's how you could do it," she finished. "And you will. Because you owe me, Oliver Bradbury."

"I don't know if I can—"

"Oliver!" She pushed his chest, fueled by frustration. "You have to!"

"I'll do what I can," he said vaguely, easing her closer in a move that was intimate and natural and *wrong*. "Within certain parameters."

"So much for the Hippocratic oath." She glanced down at the way his fingers stroked her arm, already taking ownership and pushing boundaries. "Look, even if you weren't married, I'd stick nails in my eyes, cut off my fingers, climb into fire, and hang naked from a tree before I ever—"

"I'm not."

She froze. "You're not asking for sex?"

"I'm not married anymore."

Oh. *Oh*.

THE DISH

Where authors give you the inside scoop!

From the desk of Margaret Mallory

Dear Reader,

I've been startled, as well as delighted, by all the positive comments I've received regarding the deep male friendship—the "bro-mance"—among my four heroes in the Return of the Highlanders series. If my portrayal of male camaraderie rings true at all, I must give some credit to my younger brother, who always had a gang of close friends running in and out of our house. (This does *not*, however, excuse him for not calling me more often.)

Looking back, I admire how accepting and utterly at ease these boys were with each other. On the other hand, I am amazed how they could spend so much time together and not talk—or talk only very briefly—about trouble in their families, divorces, or other important things going on in their lives. They were always either eating or having adventures. To this bookish older sister, they seemed drawn to danger like magnets. And I certainly never guessed that the boys who shot rubber bands at me from behind the furniture and made obnoxious kissy noises from the bushes when I went out on dates had anything *useful* to teach me.

Yet I'm sure that what I learned from them about how male friendships work helped me create the bond among my heroes in the Return of the Highlanders. These four

Highland warriors have been close companions since they were wee bairns, have fought side by side in every battle, and have saved each other's lives many times over. Naturally, they are in each others' books.

Ever since Duncan MacDonald's appearances in *The Guardian* and *The Sinner*, readers have been telling me how anxious they are for Duncan's own book because they want to see him find happiness at last. We all love a tortured hero, don't we? And if any man deserves a Happily Ever After, it's Duncan. In truth, I feel guilty for having made him wait.

Duncan, in THE WARRIOR (available now), is a man of few words, who is honorable, steadfast, and devoted to duty. With no father to claim him, he's worked tirelessly to earn the respect of his clan through his unmatched fighting skills. His only defeat was seven years ago, when he fell hard for his chieftain's beautiful, black-haired daughter, a lass far beyond his reach.

He never expected to keep Moira's love past that magical summer before she wed. Yet he accepts that his feelings for her will never change, and he gets on with his duties. When he and his friends return to the Isle of Skye after years spent fighting in France, every stone of his clan's stronghold still reminds him of her.

Moira's brother, who is Duncan's best friend and now chieftain, is aware that Duncan loves her, though they never speak of it. (Thanks to my brother and his friends, I do know it's possible for them to not talk about this for seven years.) When the chieftain hears that Moira may be in danger, he turns to the man he trusts most.

The intervening years have not made Moira trusting nor forgiving, and the sparks fly when this stubborn pair reunites. After the untimely death of her abusive husband, these star-crossed lovers must survive one dangerous adventure after another. They will find it even more daunting to trust each other and face the hard truths about what happened seven years ago.

I hope you enjoy the romance between this Highland warrior and his long-lost love—and that my affection for the troublesome boys who grow up to be the kind of men we adore shines through in the bro-mance.

I love to hear from readers! You can find me on Facebook, Twitter, and my website, www.MargaretMallory.com.

Margaret Mallory

♥ ♥ ♥ ♥ ♥ ♥ ♥ ♥ ♥ ♥ ♥ ♥ ♥ ♥ ♥ ♥ ♥

From the desk of Jennifer Delamere

Dear Reader,

Have you ever wished you could step into someone else's life? Leave behind your own past with its problems and become someone entirely different?

I'm pretty sure everyone has felt that way at times. When you think about it, the tale of Cinderella is such a story at its essence.

When I was in college, I saw a film called *The Return of Martin Guerre*, starring the great French actor Gérard Depardieu. It was actually based on true events in medieval France. A man has gone off to war but then stays gone for over a decade, essentially abandoning his wife.

One day, though, he does return. The good news is that, whereas the guy had previously been a heartless jerk, now he is caring and kind. The wife takes him back, and they are happy. The bad news is that eventually it is discovered that the man is not who he claims to be. He is an impostor.

Ever since I saw that movie, I have loved stories with this theme. One thing I've noticed is that so often in these tales, the impostor is actually a better human being than the person he or she is pretending to be. In the case of *Martin Guerre*, Gérard's character *wants* the life and the responsibilities the other man has intentionally left behind. The movie was remade in America as *Sommersby*, starring Richard Gere and Jodie Foster. Richard Gere's character grows and *becomes* a better man over the course of the events in the film. He does more for the family and community than the real Sommersby ever would have done.

Please note that a sad ending is not necessarily required! There are lighthearted versions of this tale as well. Remember *While You Were Sleeping*, a romantic comedy starring Sandra Bullock? Once again, she was a better person than the woman she was pretending to be, and she was certainly too good for her fiancé, the shallow man she thought she was in love with. In the end, her decency and kindness won over everyone in the family. They were all better off because she had come into their lives, even though she had initially been untruthful about who she was. And—what's most important for fans of romance!— true love won out. While Sandra had initially been starry eyed over her supposed fiancé, she came to realize that it was actually his brother who was the right man for her.

The idea for AN HEIRESS AT HEART grew out of my love for these stories about someone stepping into another person's shoes. Lizzie Poole decides to take on another person's identity: that of her half-sister, Ria, whom she had no idea existed until they found each other through an extraordinary chain of events.

Lizzie is succeeding in her role as Ria Thornborough Somerville, a woman who has just been widowed—until she falls in love with Geoffrey Somerville, the dead husband's brother. And aside from the fact that it would have been awkward enough to explain how you had suddenly fallen in love with your brother-in-law, in England at that time it was actually illegal: The laws at that time prevented people from marrying their dead spouse's sibling. So Lizzie is left in a quandary: She must either admit the truth of her identity, or forever deny her love for Geoffrey.

In a cute movie called *Monte Carlo*, a poor girl from Texas (played by Selena Gomez) impersonates a rich and snobbish Englishwoman. During her week in that woman's (high-priced, designer) shoes, she actually ends up helping to make the world just a bit better of a place—more so than the selfish rich girl ever would have done. She finds a purpose in life and—bonus!—true love as well.

Maybe I'm so fascinated by these stories because of the lovely irony that, in the end, each character actually discovers their *true* self. They find more noble aspects of themselves than they ever realized existed. They discover that who they *are* is better than anyone they could *pretend* to be. They learn to rise up to their own best natures rather than to simply be an imitation of someone else.

As the popular saying goes, "Be yourself. Everyone else is taken."

Jennifer Delamere

♥ ♥ ♥ ♥ ♥ ♥ ♥ ♥ ♥ ♥ ♥ ♥ ♥ ♥ ♥

From the desk of Roxanne St. Claire

Dear Reader,

I'm often asked if the fictional island of Mimosa Key, home to beautiful Barefoot Bay, is based on a real place. Indeed, it is. Although the barrier island is loosely modeled after Sanibel or Captiva, the setting was really inspired by a serene, desolate, undiscovered gem called Bonita Beach that sits between Naples and Fort Myers on the Gulf of Mexico.

On this wide, white strip of waterfront property, I spent some of the most glorious, relaxing, deliciously happy days of my life. My parents retired to Bonita and lived in a small house directly on the Gulf. On any long weekend when I could get away, I headed to that beach to spend time in paradise with two of my very favorite people.

The days were sunny and sandy, but the best part of the beach life were the early evening chats on the screened-in porch with my dad, watching heartbreakingly beautiful sunsets, sipping cocktails until the blue moon rose to turn the water to diamonds on black velvet. All the while, I soaked up my father's rich memories of a life well lived. And, I'm sorry to say, a life that ended too soon. My last trip to Bonita was little more than a vigil at his hospital bed, joined by all my siblings who flew in from around the country to share the agony of losing the man we called "the Chief."

My mother left the beach house almost immediately to live with us in Miami, and more than twenty years passed before I could bear to make the drive across the state to Bonita. I thought it would hurt too much to see "Daddy's beach."

But just before I started writing the Barefoot Bay series, I had the opportunity to speak to a group of writers in that area of Florida, and I decided a trip to the very setting of my stories would be good research—and quite cathartic.

Imagine my dismay when I arrived at the beach and it was no longer desolate or undiscovered. The rarefied real estate had transformed in two decades, most of the bungalows replaced by mansions. I didn't have the address, but doubted I could find my parents' house anyway; it couldn't have escaped the bulldozers and high-end developers.

So I walked the beach, mourning life's losses, when suddenly I slowed in front of one of the few modest houses left, so small I almost missed it, tucked between two four-story monsters.

The siding had been repainted, the roof reshingled, and the windows replaced after years of exposure to the salt air. But I recognized the screen-covered porch, and I could practically hear the hearty sound of my dad's laughter.

I waited for a punch of pain, the old grief that sometimes twists my heart when I let myself really think about how young I was when I lost such a fantastic father. But, guess what? There was no pain. Only relief that the house where he'd been so happily retired still stood, and gratitude that I'd been blessed to have had him as my dad.

And like he had in life, my father inspired me once again. For one thing, despite the resort story line I had planned for the Barefoot Bay books, I made a promise to keep my fictional beach more pristine and pure than the real one. I also promised myself that at least one of the books that I'd set on "Daddy's beach" would explore the poignant, precious, incomparable love between a father and a daughter.

That book is BAREFOOT IN THE RAIN. The novel is, first and foremost, a reunion romance, telling the story of Jocelyn and Will, two star-crossed teenagers who find their way back to each other after almost fifteen years of separation. But there's another "love" story on the pages of BAREFOOT IN THE RAIN, and that's the one that brought out the tissues a few times while I was writing the book.

The heroine is estranged from her father, and during the course of the story, she has to forge a new relationship with the man she can barely stand to talk to, let alone call "Daddy." Unlike my father, Jocelyn's dad can't share his memories, because Alzheimer's has wiped the slate clean. And in their case, that's both a blessing and a curse. Circumstances give Jocelyn a second chance with her father—something many of us never have once we've shared that last sunset.

I hope readers connect with Jocelyn, a strong heroine who has to conquer a difficult past, and fall in love with the catcher-turned-carpenter hero, Will. I also hope readers appreciate how hard the characters have worked to keep Barefoot Bay natural and unspoiled, unlike the beach that inspired the setting. But most of all, I hope BAREFOOT IN THE RAIN reminds every reader of a special love for her father, no matter where he is.

Roxanne St. Claire

Find out more about Forever Romance!

Visit us at
www.hachettebookgroup.com/publishing_forever.aspx

Find us on Facebook
http://www.facebook.com/ForeverRomance

Follow us on Twitter
http://twitter.com/ForeverRomance

NEW AND UPCOMING TITLES

Each month we feature our new titles
and reader favorites.

CONTESTS AND GIVEAWAYS

We give away galleys, autographed copies,
and all kinds of exclusive items.

AUTHOR INFO

You'll find bios, articles, and links to personal websites
for all your favorite authors—and so much more.

GET SOCIAL

Connect with your favorite authors, editors, and
other Forever fans, and share what's important to you.

THE BUZZ

Sign up for our monthly romance newsletter,
and be the first to read all about it.